Praise for
Léonie Kelsall

'Léonie Kelsall is not afraid to tackle some of the darker sides of human nature in a way that adds depth and emotion to the storyline. With complex and endearing characters who will steal your heart away, these unputdownable books will have you turning the pages long into the night.' **Karly Lane, author of *Time After Time***

'Unafraid to strip characters bare, delving into their psyche and motivations, Léonie Kelsall is my go-to when I want a gutsy rural fiction read.' **Darry Fraser, author of *The Prodigal Sister***

'Léonie Kelsall is a consummate and unique writer of rural romance in that she is not restricted by genre expectations and bravely addresses darker and socially urgent themes in the reality of some of her character relationships.' ***Irish Scene Magazine***

T0349001

Praise for
The Blue Gum Camp

'A great summer read—romance, drama and laughs . . . from one of Australia's best rural romance writers.' **Woman's Day**

'Léonie Kelsall's authentic rural voice shines as she explores some of life's bigger challenges in *The Blue Gum Camp*. The combination of realistic, relatable characters and a stunning South Australian setting will no doubt captivate readers and have them turning the pages long into the night.' **Lisa Ireland**

'The local setting is so vivid and comes alive as familiar towns and landscapes build the imagery brilliantly. This richness combined with characters that have distinct and differing voices enhances the polished story line.' **Happy Valley BooksRead**

'Having characters from different age groups adds diversity to the story. I loved all the sibling banter and light ribbing both with the Farrugia sisters and Lachlan and Hamish. It felt very natural and was filled with humour. The siblings' similarities and differences were perfectly portrayed.' **The Burgeoning Bookshelf**

'The complexities of the two lead characters are also satisfyingly realistic . . . an entertaining book but one with teeth.' **Living Arts Canberra**

'. . . darker and socially important themes are handled with empathy and wisdom. *The Blue Gum Camp* reminds me so much of Nora Robert's novels . . .' **Queensland Reviewers Collective**

Praise for
The Willow Tree Wharf

'Léonie Kelsall has a deft hand when it comes to writing romance. From the moment I started reading *The Willow Tree Wharf*, I was hooked . . . this one was really a standout for me.' **Beauty and Lace**

'Léonie Kelsall really delivers on these rural novels with a slightly darker, grittier edge to them . . . I can't wait for her next one.' **All the Books I Can Read**

'A story of restoration, acceptance, new starts and the healing power of love, *The Willow Tree Wharf* is a rewarding read. It's another more-than-pleasing outing for rural fiction supreme Léonie Kelsall . . .' **Mrs B's Book Reviews**

'A truly entertaining book with a pinch of dark and a handful of romance . . . This book will earn a place on your reading pile and embrace your heart.' **HappyValley Booksread**

Praise for
The River Gum Cottage

'Léonie Kelsall has a way of writing that makes you feel as if you are a part of the town, and that the characters are people you know and care about . . . a delight to read.' **Beauty and Lace**

'Léonie Kelsall has done it again . . . a beautiful and emotional story that dug deep, not to be missed.' **Family Saga Reviews**

'Intriguing and beautifully written . . . an emotional story filled with alarming secrets, betrayal, courage, heartbreak, misunderstandings and romance.' **Ms G's Bookshelf**

Praise for
The Wattle Seed Inn

'Written with warmth, humour and sincerity, offering appealing characters and an engaging story, *The Wattle Seed Inn* is a lovely read, sure to satisfy fans of the genre.' **Book'd Out**

'With a wonderful message about letting go, seizing the day and embracing all experiences on offer, *The Wattle Seed Inn* is an encouraging read I highly recommend.' **Mrs B's Book Reviews**

'[*The Wattle Seed Inn*] is a meditation on the city/country divide, as well as a salutary tale about the importance of finding community. It's also a rollicking good read.' *Australian Country*

Praise for
The Farm at Peppertree Crossing

'Kelsall is a bold and fearless writer who is unafraid of presenting her readership with a plethora of darker-style themes ... authentic, insightful and sensitive in the right places.' **Mrs B's Book Reviews**

'Léonie Kelsall's skilful portrayal of life on the land and the people who live it comes alive. An absolute gem of a book!' **Blue Wolf Reviews**

'... foreboding, funny, breath-holding, sad and sweet. I loved the way Kelsall unwrapped the secrets slowly throughout the story—little teasers that kept me glued to the pages.' **The Burgeoning Bookshelf**

Léonie Kelsall was initially raised in a tiny, no-horse town on South Australia's Fleurieu coast, and then in the slightly more populated wheat and sheep farming land at Pallamana—she's a country girl through and through. Growing up without a television, she developed a love of reading before she reached primary school, swiftly followed by a desire to write.

Léonie entertained a brief fantasy of moving to the big city (well, Adelaide), but within months the lure of the open spaces and big sky country summoned her home. A registered wildlife rescuer and carer, she now divides her time between the lush Adelaide Hills, the location of her professional counselling practice, and the stark, arid beauty of the family farm at Pallamana, which provides both the setting for many of her stories and a refuge for the rescues that can't be released. Follow her social media for an overload of the fluffy, fleecy, furred and feathered inhabitants of her home and heart.

Also by Léonie Kelsall

The Farm at Peppertree Crossing
The Wattle Seed Inn
The River Gum Cottage
The Willow Tree Wharf
The Blue Gum Camp

LÉONIE KELSALL

The Homestead in the Eucalypts

ALLEN&UNWIN

SYDNEY · MELBOURNE · AUCKLAND · LONDON

First published in 2024

Allen & Unwin
Cammeraygal Country
83 Alexander Street
Crows Nest NSW 2065
Australia
Phone: (61 2) 8425 0100
Email: info@allenandunwin.com
Web: www.allenandunwin.com

Allen & Unwin acknowledges the Traditional Owners of the Country on which we live and work. We pay our respects to all Aboriginal and Torres Strait Islander Elders, past and present.

 A catalogue record for this book is available from the National Library of Australia

ISBN 978 1 76106 788 4

Set in 12.5/18 pt Sabon LT Pro by Midland Typesetters, Australia
Printed and bound in Australia by the Opus Group

10 9 8 7 6 5 4 3 2 1

This book may be read by others,
But it was and always will be
For Taylor.

1
Taylor

September 2008

She would probably die today. Road statistics no doubt proved that driving across the country with an emotionally unstable woman at the wheel was not a great idea.

Taylor slid her gaze to her mum. Good, she was holding it together. Michelle usually made an effort when she had an audience, but on more than one occasion, Taylor had come home from uni to find her mother red-eyed, surrounded by a failed attempt at scrapbooking the wreckage of their family life.

Mum generally blamed the mounds of soggy tissues on a Nicholas Sparks' novel that hadn't moved from the coffee table for eight months. When she was really messed up, there'd be chocolate wrappers.

Taylor sighed, making sure to let the sound roll around the air-conditioned interior of their car. She was steadily

1

eating her way through her own chocolate supply as they hurtled—although never above the speed limit—across the featureless plains between Sydney and Adelaide. She needed the sugar. Carbs, too. Pretty much anything that would allow her to stuff her emotions down inside, layered beneath chips and pastries.

There was, though, a degree of almost pleasurable pain—like sneezing or wriggling a limb that had fallen asleep, knowing pins and needles would follow—in being separated early in a new relationship. Angst sharpened desire and heightened yearning. Angst *and* novelty, that was; their recent five-week anniversary had Zac temporarily entrenched in Taylor's 'I can't live without him' territory. It didn't help in the slightest to know that her reaction was endorphin driven. With his inked arms and nipple rings, Zac was high energy, exotic and dangerous, a tantalising contrast to her med school colleagues, most of whom mirrored her own permanent exhaustion.

Gazing glassy-eyed at the brown nothingness of plains untouched by spring-time green, Taylor's mind drifted back to yesterday and Zac's reaction to her plan. 'I can't let Mum go alone,' she'd said. 'She's not in a good place. It's a sixteen-hour drive and she'll crank up some old, sad crap and get lost in memories instead of concentrating on the road.'

What she hadn't said was that it was hard enough to get her mother to concentrate at the best of times. Taylor had inherited ambition and focus from her father, but none of Mum's relentless, thoroughly impractical positivity. The same irrational mindset that now saw them driving across the country for a brief visit to grandparents who lived the best part of two thousand kilometres away. Even with airport delays, two hour flight would have cut three days from the trip—days Taylor could ill-afford to waste. But Mum maintained that flying was for bees, butterflies, bats and birds.

'Uh-huh. And how old is your mum, princess?' Zac's dry sarcasm was sexy as all get-out, except when directed at her. But he'd redeemed himself immediately. 'Nah, that's cool. Honestly, I'm jealous you have that kind of connection with your folks. Mine . . .' He'd trailed off, shrugging expressively, and she'd melted into his arms, wanting to take away his pain. He was wrong, though; over the last few months, Mum had become increasingly distant.

Taylor's sigh lifted her fringe as she reached for a soft drink they'd pulled over to get a couple of hundred kilometres back. Mum wasn't keen on buying from the Golden Arches. Apparently, anything purchased through a window was poison, most likely funded by Big Pharma, because that's where all evil originated.

The soggy bottom fell out of the cup. 'Oh, for—'

'Imagine what it does to your insides if it can do that to a takeaway cup,' Mum said, her bamboo bangles colliding as she handed over a wad of recycled paper napkins from the stash in the console between them.

'Phosphoric acid. I'm well aware of what it does.' Mum should be relieved this was Taylor's only coke addiction. So many of her colleagues used 'medicinal doses' to alleviate the stress of study, confidently assuring—or reassuring—themselves that they were smart enough not to allow cocaine to become a gateway drug.

'All those brains, yet still you indulge.'

Mum never touched soft drink. Or missed the chance for a lecture.

Evidently, if you were an only child, you didn't get to grow up. Pulling out her phone, Taylor pressed her forehead to the window, letting the chill of the air-conditioned glass soothe her turmoil.

Cass. Tell me I'm doing the right thing?

The reply to her text was immediate. Her best friend lived on her phone.

Can't do that, sweets. Zac's hot as, and you've done a runner?? Told you, you're nuts.

Way to be supportive. You know Mum's a bit off the rails at the moment. She says she needs to reconnect with family.

Family? The irony is strong with that one.

Taylor grimaced, but continued reading.

You've seen Zac's groupies. I wouldn't be giving him any alone time.

Yeah, she sure had. Hordes of screaming women—and men—ogling her guy. Research proved that fame enhanced appeal, so it was logical that being on stage added to desirability. The moment she'd seen Zac, though, his shoulder-length jet hair backlit by nightclub stage lights as he powered into a finale, her hypothalamus had gone into overdrive, shutting down her more logical prefrontal cortex. Or, as Cassie maintained, lust trumped lobes.

She huffed another frustrated breath, her fingers sliding over her phone keypad.

Maybe you should keep an eye on him for me?

> I don't have the time or energy for that,
> not even for you. Just sayin', he's
> not the kind of guy I'd leave hanging.

Work, study and Zac's gigs—not to mention the necessary reality of living with her parents in her twenties—meant that, after little more than a month, that's exactly where their relationship was: hanging. Mostly around the uni bar late in the day, when Zac would crawl from his bed and she had an hour's grace between lectures and work. They'd planned to synchronise schedules and grab a hotel room over the semester break. But not this week, thanks to Mum.

Hearing you. But Mum needs me.

Taylor tried not to let her gaze drift toward the stack of textbooks on the back seat. She had to carve out precious minutes to spend with Zac, yet here she was, wasting literally days on Mum.

> M-A-N-I-P-U-L-A-T-I-O-N spells mum.
> Michelle's perfected the art of guilt-tripping you.
> Hats off to Tay's mum.

'The Haylfway mark,' Mum said, pointing at the sign for Hay.

Taylor guiltily set the phone on her lap, screen face down. Cassie was wrong, her mother didn't manipulate. She was just emotionally needy.

'Get it?' Mum continued. '*Hay*-lfway. Did you know this is the flattest landscape in Australia?'

Hopefully her quirked eyebrow would convey her lack of interest in Mum's teachable moment.

Mum flicked her eyes from the ribbon of grey highway. 'So who's the guy? Come on, spill. I know you. You're pining.'

'Zac.' Saying his name set off flutters in Taylor's stomach, though the juvenile weakness irritated her. It wasn't like he was the first guy she'd hooked up with. But he was *different*.

'Zac?' Mum's eyebrows contracted to hide behind her sunglasses. 'I haven't heard that name. Is he one of your usual group?'

'No.' Like Mum had any clue who she hung with. 'But he is in a group.'

'Ooh.' Mum sat up straighter, though she kept both hands locked on the steering wheel, determined to prove how responsible she was. 'Anyone I know?'

'Not unless you're into the Stoned Drifters.'

Mum pursed her lips, the possibility evidently worth her consideration.

'You don't know them, Mum,' Taylor said, reaching for the CD player.

Mum flicked her knee, sticky from the spilled soft drink. 'Hungry?'

'No. Energy in, energy out—we haven't actually moved in like, two hours.' Taylor pressed play, cranking the volume. 'You know, I should have used you for my psych thesis. You're an enabler.'

'I believe in empowerment, not enabling. Eating junk food is self-destructive. If I encouraged that, perhaps I'd be an enabler. But I don't and I'm not. Rice cake or almonds?'

'A force-feeder, then.' Her mother had a thing about clearing plates and eating vegetables so kids overseas didn't starve.

Mum reached across to rummage in the console, then held packets toward Taylor without taking her eyes from the road. As Taylor chose the bribe, her mother cleared her throat. Taylor tensed; she knew what was coming. Mum was desperate to confide in her. And Taylor was equally desperate not to hear a word of it.

'You know, Taylor, Dad and I—'

'Mum, give it a rest. I came along to keep you company. I don't want to be involved.'

Her mother's forefinger tapped the wheel, a metronome measuring her patience, her eyes squinted against the afternoon sun. 'Tay, I'm just concerned—'

She would monologue for the next ten kilometres about selfcare and heart-healing and acceptance of fate, so Taylor jammed her earbuds back in, pretending she couldn't hear. The Stoned Drifters played loud.

Not loud enough to drown out her thoughts, though. Living in a house with cardboard-thin walls, her parents' marital problems weren't something Taylor needed to have confirmed. Nor did she need to be a sounding board for either of them.

The hot vinyl scorched her bare feet as she stuck them on the dash.

'Taylor.'

'Michelle,' she shot back, though she knew what was coming.

'Feet down. They'll get burnt. The glass magnifies the rays. Although the ozone layer is so depleted, we'll all be fried to a crisp soon enough. Fancy some organic corn chips?'

She yanked out her earbuds. 'No.' She stuck her hand in the bag anyway. 'Aren't you sick of driving?'

Mum pushed the sunglasses onto her head and knuckled her eyes. 'A bit.'

'Want me to take over?'

'No. You had wine with lunch.'

'One glass, Mum. Not even a full serve. I'm sure the pub ripped me off.'

'Can't risk it.'

'Trust you to be a stickler for the rules.'

Except those with a 'til death do us part' theme.

౿

They stopped overnight at Hay, the cream, red and brown brick–chequered motel room almost palatial after being cooped up in the car for nine hours.

With only six hundred kilometres remaining, they left late the next morning. 'Roadhouses not responsible for thinning ozone and polar bear extinction, then?' Taylor said as Mum brought steak sandwiches and mugs of coffee over to the tiny chrome-edged table by the window over-looking the highway.

'We're all equally to blame for the problems and responsible for the solutions,' Mum said, chasing a dribble of froth from the side of the cup with her finger. 'It's up to each of us to save the world for tomorrow.'

'There was a lot of weed around in the early eighties, right?'

Five hours later, after her second turn behind the wheel, Taylor settled into the passenger seat, tapping out a message to Zac. He wouldn't be up—probably no one in his house would. She'd been there, just once; a dive shared with a bunch of other musos. Co-tenanting was the only way anyone under thirty could afford a place in Sydney. But Zac didn't plan on hanging around New South Wales much longer. Next year, he'd be on tour. First Australia, then Asia.

She zipped the crucifix along her necklace. Warmed by the sun, the metal was hot on her chest.

Mum glanced across the car. 'I see you wear that a lot.'

'"A lot" being a relative term, given that I've only had it a couple of weeks.' Although it wasn't the type of jewel-lery she normally chose, something about the unexpected gift from her grandparents appealed. 'Do you think it's pure silver? It seems to react with my skin.'

'Gross.'

'Not like that. More a tingle, like it's conducting an electrical current.'

Mum lifted one shoulder. 'Check for the stamp. Should have a 925 if it's silver. And make sure you thank your grandparents for the necklace when we get there.'

'Seriously, Mum?' Her mother vacillated between being a ditzy best friend one moment and parenting as though Taylor was a teen the next.

'Uh-huh. Have a look: 925 for silver; 375 for gold.'

'*So* not what I meant.'

'Off.' Mum tapped Taylor's foot, propped on the dash again.

Taylor squinted out of the window. All the way to the horizon, starry explosions of vivid lemon-yellow flowers crowned paddocks of thigh-high, emerald-green plants. Her eyes watered, sinuses aching in anticipation of hay fever. 'What do you reckon that is?'

'Rape.'

'What?'

'Devil's weed.'

'You just don't like the colour? Or maybe there's something a little more specific you'd care to share?'

'Rapeseed. Brassica. Canola,' Mum expanded. 'But at least the South Australian government has the sense not to allow the genetically modified version here.' She shook her head dolefully. 'Because everywhere else, the bees, those poor bees . . .'

'Speaking of insects, I don't get why you're fixated on camping,' Taylor said, swiftly deflecting the environmental rant. 'I thought the whole point of this odyssey was to catch up with the Grands.' Though Mum made an annual pilgrimage to the farm her parents had moved to as caretakers after a brief flirtation with the grey nomad lifestyle, Taylor hadn't been there since she was thirteen. She could vaguely remember being seduced by patting cute farm animals, but through the intervening years the beaches and friends and malls—and, eventually, nightlife—of Sydney had held far more allure.

'Camping is fun.'

The clipped tone made it sound like Mum was quoting a bumper sticker, and Taylor glanced up to check the car in front of them. Which was about two kilometres away.

'Sounds a bit *Eat, Pray, Love* to me,' she said suspiciously. The book had been keeping Nicholas Sparks company on the coffee table the last few weeks. 'But I'm sure you could *find yourself* in a nice five-star hotel out here.'

Mum snorted with laughter and the lost familiarity of the sound brought a smile to Taylor's lips.

'You really don't remember Settlers Bridge, do you?'

'Why?' Taylor's smile dropped as unease prickled through her.

'There are a couple of pubs, but I doubt you're going to find any five-star accommodation.'

'It has to have changed in the decade since I was there.'

'You think? Gran said it hasn't changed since she was a girl. Anyway, if you remember the town, you must remember that, last time you stayed, we went camping. So I thought we'd do it again now you're an adult. A full-circle kind of thing.'

Taylor bit back her groan. She should have realised. As her marriage floundered, Mum seemed intent on trying to return to a time when things had been happier. Of course, Dad had also been on that camping trip.

'You'll break that if you keep fiddling with it.'

'That's not what the sexual health flyers say.' Taylor dropped the pendant she'd been sliding up and down the chain.

'It was nice of your grandparents to send it,' Mum said in a determined tone.

'It was *odd* of them to send it,' Taylor corrected. 'Given that my entire life, their gifts have been a very predictable twenty dollar bill every single birthday.'

Mum shrugged. 'The face value of money has no relevance to them. It's the thought that counts.'

'Or the calendar entry.' The money arrived exactly two business days before her birthday each year, the note so crisp it must have been ironed.

Mum grimaced and flicked the vent shut as the stench from roadkill filled the car. 'Gramps said they found the necklace, and the owner suggested they give it to someone who would appreciate it.'

Hidden behind sunglasses, Taylor closed her eyes, mentally counting to five. She understood the psychological urge that drove Mum to revert to the familiar behaviour of a period when life had seemed safer, more predictable. And kudos to her; even though she was inappropriately parenting a twenty-two-year-old, she'd managed to stop short of saying, *Don't look a gift horse in the mouth*.

But Taylor would return the necklace to her grandparents. It wasn't worth a sermon about her need to show gratitude.

Her fingers closed around the pendant, holding it tight.

'Look. The Mighty Murray.' Mum nodded at a narrow bridge arching in front of them. 'We could have crossed at the ferry at Tailem Bend, but we'll save that for another day.'

'Yay. Primed for excitement.' Despite her sarcasm, Taylor straightened as they passed the town limits sign. *Welcome to Settlers Bridge.*

The bridge spanned swampy river flats studded with fat brown cows and large white hook-billed birds wading through the marsh on long legs. These ibis looked different—more regal—than the bin chickens of city life. As they crossed the water, a rectangular houseboat contentedly chuntered beneath the bridge, the river parting in a creamy green wake either side of the boat. The upper deck was spread with loungers and beach towels and a woman waved from the prow.

That would have been a better option than camping.

The road surged up a short, steep hill from the bridge, then expanded into four lanes as it entered the town, the pairs bisected by a brick-paved centre strip punctuated with flowering bushes. Taylor took in the short, deserted street at a glance. There were a couple of old two-storey pubs at the bridge end. Faded iron verandahs overhung antiquated shops either side of the road, the drop between the footpath and stone-paved gutter dangerously deep. Further up, she could make out a sandwich board outside a cafe. They wouldn't starve, but that might be the only thing in the tiny town's favour.

Despite the nearness of the river and the great candle-like plumes of orange and pink bougainvillea bushes in the island dividing the roads, the town was dry and dusty, as though summer had already hit.

'I'm sure I hear banjos in the distance,' she muttered. 'Tumbleweed will blow down the street any moment now. Though at least that'll be something moving.'

'Oh, look. How cute!' Mum exclaimed, pulling into a park in front of one of the verandah-shaded shops. 'Ploughs and Pies. Isn't that just gorgeous? I'll pick up a cake to take with us.'

'Spend your money wisely,' Taylor said, jerking a thumb across the road. Almost a mirror image, another cafe sported a similarly painted window, depicting farm machinery and baked goods. 'You might start a turf war.'

'Tractors and Tarts,' Mum read as she took her purse from the console. 'That's awesome. Well, I'm sure we'll end up trying both places. Ploughs and Pies will do for today, though. Come on, we need to pick up some groceries. There's a supermarket sign down there a bit.'

'Like, driving distance.'

'Like, walking distance,' Mum insisted. 'We've eaten enough junk over the last two days. Time to start moving it through our bodies.'

'You are so gross.'

'Thought doctors weren't supposed to be grossed out by bodily functions?'

'I still have a three-year window of getting grossed out before I'm qualified. Anyway, I have to make a call. Leave the air conditioner on.'

Mum gave her a look. 'What we've done to the ozone layer by driving here is crime enough.' Michelle clambered from the car, groaning as she stretched. Then she disappeared, but Taylor knew her mum had flipped forward

14

to touch her toes and would at any second swoop past the window in a flurry of tie-dyed pastels as she arched into a back bend.

It was probably lucky there was no one around to see her middle-aged, harem-panted mother doing yoga in the middle of the street.

As Mum headed into the shop, Taylor wound up her window, privacy more important than the temperature, which shouldn't even be a thing in mid-spring. Obviously, this place was a desert.

'Princess.' Zac's voice was gravelly and she could tell his gig had run late the previous night.

'Hey, Zac.' With nothing particular to say, she was simply greedy to hear his voice. They'd spoken the previous night when she was halfway across Australia and he was halfway to his gig. Mum had been in the shower, so their call had been . . . mutually satisfying.

'Your mum there?' he said.

'No.' She giggled as she realised why he'd asked. 'But she will be in precisely ninety seconds. I'd hate to think you were that quick.'

'Fair call. When will you be able to ditch your guard?'

The comment irked, but she understood his frustration at her mother's chastity-belt presence. 'I'll have a bit of privacy when we get to the farm.'

'Mmm. Come be alone with me then, princess. At least on the phone, okay?'

She was momentarily glad Settlers Bridge was practically a ghost town—there was no one to see her grinning like an idiot. 'Sure. How was the gig?'

'Sweet as. But, hey, princess, I gotta go. I'll give you a call later, okay?'

She knuckled the phone to her ear, trying to bring him closer for a moment. 'Sure. Catch you then.'

Mum smacked a box down on the bonnet. 'The government's banning plastic bags in South Australia from next year,' she crowed. 'And apparently the shops here have already got onboard. How's that for progressive?'

Taylor clambered from the car and hauled the boot open. 'You mean regressive. And you are, literally, the only person in the history of ever to get excited by that news.'

Mum held up both hands. 'People your age are supposed to be all about the environment.'

People her age were supposed to be all about getting on with their lives, not babysitting their parents through their midlife crises.

'Samantha says your grandparents were in town yesterday, telling everyone we were coming over,' Mum said as she slid behind the steering wheel.

'Samantha?'

'She owns Ploughs and Pies.' Mum shook her head in admiration. 'She's probably only about your age, too.'

First-name terms with the locals. Trust Mum. 'Probably hasn't had to spend a quarter of her life at med school amassing a HECS debt.'

'She packed me up a honey Swiss roll. Said it's your gran's favourite.'

'I'm sure whatever stale item she had the most of is Gran's favourite.'

Mum gave a despairing huff. 'I don't understand why you have to be so cynical, Tay. If you give them a chance and get to know them, most people are actually nice.'

Her mother was hopelessly naïve. It would be charming if it wasn't so irritating. 'I'm into science, Mum. Evidence-based fact. And the *fact* is that most people are only out for what they can get. So, you can say people are nice all you like, but if you don't mind, I'll hold out for the proof.'

2
Anna

South Australia, late March, 1877

Even in the earliest hours of the morning, two rooms housing six people were never entirely silent. Father stirred on the far side of the thick curtain, inches from Anna's head, and Mother murmured in response.

Though mice noisly busied themselves in the rushes on the floor, Anna lay unmoving so the crackle of hay in their mattress didn't disturb the rhythm of Emilie's snores. The ceiling she stared at held no more interest than it had each day of the eighteen years she had woken to it. Hessian sacks nailed to wooden beams thicker than her thigh partially hid the iron-sheet roof. Mother had insisted they have a ceiling, rather than naked tin. While most of the tenant farmers in the hundred of Siedlerbrucke—or *Settlers Bridge*, as Father said they must call it—were of German heritage, Mother had actually been born in Deutschland and, as she often lamented while sighing over the girls' grubby hands or knotted hair, she knew what it was to be civilised.

Anna's attention shifted outside. All was quiet, even the white-winged choughs not yet awake. Fingertips pinching her lips to silence her breath, she waited for the rooster to count his hens. If he didn't speak up soon, it might be that a fox had slunk into the coop during the night. Mother didn't need the worry of losing the last of their chickens.

Legs dangling over the edge of the bed, Anna tugged her clothes from the straight-backed chair, exchanging her nightdress for a chemise, flannel drawers, heavy petticoat and a long-sleeved calico day dress.

She twitched aside the curtain that separated her and Emilie's bed from the main room, the velvet soft in her hands. Skirting the scrubbed wooden table and chairs, she made for the door. Despite the latent warmth held in the stone, her toes curled on the flags as she leaned against the knobbly sapling doorframe to tug on her hobnailed boots.

The twins stirred in the cot beneath the single, thick-paned window as the iron hinges on the door protested the weight of the timber, and she quickly slipped outside before her siblings woke and demanded attention. This early in the day, perhaps she could claim a few precious minutes for herself.

The faint light did not bestow a hint of the sun that would, within hours, drive them to seek the sparse shade, but a strong waft of eucalyptus cleared the last of the sleep from her head. The fowl snored and fluffed contentedly in their coop across the yard, and her heartbeat steadied, her pace slowing. Her worry was for naught: they would have eggs enough for another day.

Puffs of dust clouded her boots. After breakfast was cleared, the first of her daily chores would be to take a switch to the beaten-earth square between the house and outbuildings. If more of her brothers had survived, their home and the bakehouse would not be the only buildings constructed of stone the menfolk cleared from the land. Her fingers tracked the dips and hollows of the crumbling pug-and-pine wall of the stable. In a few weeks' time, she and Emilie would help mix fresh mud and grass and pack it between the pine saplings to weatherproof the structures before winter. Mother would pretend to be unaware of their involvement in the task.

A faint scuffle drew Anna's gaze to the scrub beyond the bakehouse. The noise betrayed the presence of a wombat or echidna rooting among dead, crisped leaves for a last mouthful before it tucked itself underground or in a hollow log to escape the heat.

She ducked beneath the lintel of the bakehouse, navigating the three steps to the cellar. Perhaps her brother was not so different from the nocturnal creatures.

'What do you want?' Dieter's deep voice was muffled against the straw mattress.

'It's time you were up.' She tried to emulate Mother's brisk tone. 'I must get the bread on.'

'I have not yet heard the birds,' he grumbled as he thrust aside his thin bedcover.

She tossed him the shirt hanging from a peg on the back of the door and then rummaged beneath the wooden

slab that ran the length of one wall. 'I need the buckets.'
The pails clanged together as she dragged them out.

'Anna,' Dieter groaned. 'Must you make such a din? Is
it not your sister's job to fetch the water?'

'*Our* sister. And yet it seems there is no water in the
house.' Three years younger, Emilie had inherited Mother's
blonde ringlets and blue eyes, where Anna was her
father's grey-eyed and brunette image—thankfully, without
the whiskers. Emilie traded on her beauty, turning on
charm and waterworks in equal measure to avoid chores
and punishment. To be fair, she was good with the four-
year-old twins and spent hours embroidering their clothes
or arranging Frederika's hair. Mother said it was well that
Emilie was pretty and accomplished in the finer skills; being
lazy and forgetful, she would never be of use as a farmer's
wife, so would need to catch a rich man's eye.

Useful and ordinary, Anna was uncertain where this
left her.

Dieter yawned. 'Give me a moment to wake and I will
come with you. The waterhole is full of snakes this summer.'

Although nine years and two dead siblings separated
them, she and Dieter were closer than the twins. He
pulled on boots then stood to adjust his britches, his head
brushing the rafters.

'Perhaps you can dig the floor lower in here so it is less
cramped,' she suggested, though she knew Dieter wouldn't
lower the floor, because he had his eye on Caroline Schenscher. Either that, or he had developed a devout interest
in church, attending weekly for the last three months,
since Caroline had returned from two years in Europe.

Soon he would speak his intention, and then he would look to lease his own land and build a home. Anna didn't like the thought, but that was the way it must be.

At least Caroline would have a life. Anna suspected her own might be spent here, with her parents. Being useful. And ordinary.

As they crossed the paddock below the house, the dead grass beneath their feet powdered to fill the cracks that split the earth. With the gate of wire and posts awkward to open and even more difficult to close, they preferred to scale the stone fence. A chime rang through the air as Dieter rapped on the wall with a ploughshare to scare away the snakes and lizards that populated the caves and crannies. It was a trick many of their neighbours emulated.

The sheep couldn't breach the three-foot high barrier but tufts of soft brown wool decorated where they rubbed against the stonework. The parched land that spread before them was softened by the rosy glow. In a good season, Father's wheat crop paid the rent and allowed a little money to be put aside in the hope of one day purchasing the property. But a bad season—and it seemed those were unfairly predominant—saw him owe yet more money to the government.

Seated on the wall, Dieter flattened his work-scarred hands on the rough stone, his broad shoulders hunched. 'Do you ever dream, Anna?' His gaze was faraway, beyond the paddocks.

She spread her skirts as she settled beside him. 'Of course I dream.'

'No, I mean dream of . . . more. Of a different life.'

Much though she loved Dieter, Anna dared not tell even him of her secret dream; it was too ridiculous to be revealed. Instead, she shared a more acceptable truth. 'I dream that one day I shall marry and have a house of my own. Though it seems the chances of that are negligible and limited even more by our beautiful sister.'

Dieter didn't rise to the invitation to joke about Emilie, but nor did he reassure Anna, so she tried to guess what weighed heavily on his shoulders.

'I know your dream, Dieter Frahn. Your dream is blonde and pretty and attends church each Sunday, nein?'

He grinned, slight colour rising in his tanned cheeks. 'I—'

The scrub at their backs shivered as a kookaburra exploded into mirthless laughter. As always, inexplicable dread tingled down Anna's spine.

Dieter clapped to silence the bird, then pointed. 'Look.' A mob of kangaroos bounded over the wall a short distance from them, two joeys leaning out of their mothers' pouches as though encouraging them to greater speed.

'They play.'

Dieter snorted. 'You're a funny one, Mäuschen. They head for the water.'

Little mouse. He often called her that. Not that she was particularly tiny, although her Sunday corset did nip her waist in to an acceptable proportion.

Glad his melancholy had passed, Anna tossed a piece of shale into the distance. 'You and Father will take the dray to fetch barrels of water tomorrow?' From the corner of her eye, she caught his grimace.

'That we will.'

It would take them six hours to make the journey to Settlers Bridge and return with precious barrels of water pumped from the Murray River. The water would be carefully eked out for household use, filling the animal troughs and sustaining their struggling vegetable garden. Here, water had more value than the gold discovered at Kanmantoo, twenty miles northeast.

'At least you will be afforded the opportunity to swim.' She could not imagine water surrounding her entire body. The weekly luxury of the hip bath, when occasionally it was her turn to use the water first, was as close as she could ever hope to come.

Dieter swung himself off the wall. 'Not much time for that, Mäuschen. Come. Let us finish your sister's task.' Impatient at her clumsiness in long skirts, he lifted her down.

The land dropped gradually from the house to a gorge that seemed to promise the relief of a rushing torrent—but it was a lie. The ravine, worn deep by a flood some time past, was filled with boulders. Between these travelled the slimmest trickle of water, already busy with bees and dragonflies.

Taking an iron pannikin from the well, Dieter slid down the bank to kneel on a raft of bulrushes. He leaned forward and swept away the dull scum on the water. The reeds crackled and he tensed, a dripping finger pressed to his lips to silence Anna.

As clumsy footfalls punctured the hush, Dieter's shoulders eased.

'Lizard.'

A snake would have struck silently.

Droplets showered from the full tin as Dieter clambered back up the slope. He primed the pump with the precious liquid. The cast-iron lever squealed as he heaved it up and down and a grin flashed across his face. 'That will wake everyone.'

'Not before time.'

Pink fringed the eastern horizon. *Red sky at night, shepherd's delight. Red sky in the morning, shepherd take warning.* Hopefully, it would rain today.

Muddy water gushed from the spout, splashing into the pail, and they counted Dieter's pumps in unison. 'One . . . two . . . three . . .' The well wasn't good, a small pool at the bottom of the twenty-foot shaft, and the number of pumps it took to fill a bucket indicated how close it was to running dry. But it was one of few in the district that provided usable water, almost enough to keep them alive. Some of them, anyway. In the nine years since the last drought, Father had restored his flock. But Anna's brothers, who lay in the graveyard beside the church, could not be replaced.

She lugged two pails to Dieter's two heavy buckets as they traipsed back up the paddock. 'You will take lunch with you tomorrow?'

'Have you ever known me to go anywhere hungry?' Her brother's appetite was renowned. 'What treasure would you have me bring you back this time?'

This was her favourite game and she stared into the sun-kissed distance, seeing riches that could only ever exist in her imagination. 'A fan of ostrich feathers should suffice, kind sir.' There was a general store at the river's edge, but Dieter could spare no money. Last winter, the season had been kinder, and when he and Father herded the sheep to the market, Dieter had purchased two lengths of ribbon: red for her and blue for Emilie. Anna's was longer, although Dieter swore he ordered two feet of each. The sisters had tucked the gifts into the hope chests beneath their bed. Mother had started the collections when they were infants and added items as finances permitted, and Anna and Emilie opened the boxes often to review the scant contents, as though they did not have them memorised. Still, they didn't compare to the magnificence of the Aussteuerschrank Mother had brought from Germany. The carved wardrobe protected the embroidered linens and satin, lengths of ribbon and spun lace that Mother had gathered when she was younger than Anna, in preparation for marriage to a man she had yet to meet. The first time she set eyes on Father was at their betrothal, a week after her ship made land in Port Adelaide.

Anna and Dieter carefully skirted the paddock of rye Father grew solely to make their heavy, dark bread and approached the house through the small, struggling orchard and vegetable garden fenced with sticks she and Emilie had gathered from the nearby scrub. Already, the stone cottage offered a haven from the sun, although a wisp of smoke curled from the chimney. The bulk of their cooking was done in the bakehouse, off to one side of the cottage, but a fire was needed in the house to heat water and provide breakfast.

Dieter placed the buckets near the door, wide open now to allow in the light. A dull chime announced their presence as his hip brushed the iron triangle hung low near the door. It was Frederik's favourite job to take the length of forged iron rod and strike the triangle to summon the men in from the paddocks.

Mother straightened from measuring oats into the pot in the hearth, pressing her hand to the small of her back. Guilt pinched Anna's insides, followed by a flash of anger. It was her job to have the breakfast on, but Emilie's fault she was delayed. Eyes on the mound of Mother's stomach, a silent prayer moved Anna's lips. *Please, God, don't let it be twins again.* One more child would add enough to Mother's troubles, let alone two. While Frederik and Frederika seemed hale and hearty, it was only a few years since the older twins had died within a day of each other. Diphtheria claimed Christoph and although Carl had shown no symptoms, when his twin died he had simply lain on their bed and closed his eyes. Forever.

Now, whenever the younger twins fell ill, Anna sensed Mother hold her breath in fear.

'Mother, let me take care of breakfast. You need to ready yourself for church.'

Mother's brow arched. 'You think I become slow? It is well Unser Vater blesses me with your assistance, then.' Mother wasn't particularly religious, but she liked to credit God with anything good in her life. Father, on the other hand, was as likely to curse God—but never within Mother's hearing. 'I do wish this heat would break; it is beyond time. At home, trees clothed in the most beautiful shades herald autumn,' Mother sighed. 'I dream you shall one day see them, Anna.'

It unsettled her when Mother referred to Germany as home. 'Would you return to Deutschland, Mother?'

Mother waved the ladle in her direction. 'Gott in Himmel, never again will I be incarcerated for three months in the bowels of a ship.' Her blue eyes danced to Anna's father as he pushed through the bedroom curtain. 'No, I've made my bed, now it seems I must lie in it. Is that not so, Johann?'

Tugging his short, grey beard into a point, Anna's father pretended to take Mother seriously. 'Ah, Johanna, what am I to do with you? I cannot return you to your own parents—you are named for me. No, we are peas and this is our pod.'

Her skirts brushing the flags, Mother went to him and pressed her hand to his cheek. 'You know I would be nowhere else, husband.' Father took her hand and kissed her palm, then she turned back to Anna. 'Wake your sister. She can ready the twins for church. You must make certain she does her chores while we are gone.'

∽

Her parents, the twins and Dieter had breakfasted quickly and departed early. Mother and the children rode in the buggy but, as Father and Dieter walked, it would take them almost an hour and a half to reach die Kirche.

By the time her family sat for service, Anna had swept the yard, dusted, made the beds with fresh linens and set the dirty ones to soak in the copper tub beneath the silver-trunked gum tree. Emilie, however, seemed to have achieved nothing.

Anna dragged Mother's oak rocking chair aside and rolled the rag rug. One day, the grey and brown history of their outworn clothing would cover the floor. But for now, the rug was small enough that she could take it outside to beat the dust from it.

Her shoulders strained as the two sisters struggled to lift the rug over a rope strung between two trees. 'Emilie, put some effort into it.' They had much to do before the others returned for lunch.

Emilie flapped her thin, elegant hands. 'But it's heavy.'

Anna ducked beneath the rope and tugged the rug from the opposite side. 'No more so than last week. At the very least, stop it from sliding.'

Finally, with the rug balanced, she wedged a forked sapling under the line to lift it from the ground. She dashed a hand across her damp brow. The air was ominously still and thick, like congealed pig's blood, and it was hard to draw breath. Lightning crackled in the distance and she turned to watch the forked flash. She lifted her chin toward the bright illumination. 'I hope rain chases that.'

Emilie followed her gaze. 'I cannot smell any.'

'Nor I. But perhaps a change will blow through. Then Father and Dieter will hunt tonight.'

Emilie's eyes grew huge. 'But it is *Sunday*.'

'Yes, and we shall use the last joint of mutton for lunch. So, unless the rabbit traps come up full, tomorrow you shall be complaining of an empty belly. Anyway, Father says hunting is sport, not work.'

'I would rather go hungry than invite His punishment,' Emilie said.

'I will keep your pious belief in mind if the men bring home a roo.' Anna tried not to allow her lips to pinch together too much, mindful of Mother's admonition that it was an old maid's habit, but sometimes it seemed the twins had more common sense than Emilie. 'As I recall, you enjoy fresh meat as much as any of us.' She wiped her hands on her apron. 'I shall fetch the mutton, if you can see your way clear to stoking the oven?'

Wrapped in calico, the salted meat swung from the coolroom ceiling. Anna unhooked it and sniffed. A little green, but not too offensive. And it was not yet infested by maggots.

The sand-filled root box yielded four potatoes and two carrots. She would make gravy with the scrapings from the vegetables, a little flour and fat rendered from the joint. A jar of Mother's sauerkraut and thick slices of bread would supplement the meal. Far from the worst fare they had eaten. There had been leaner seasons.

The preparations complete, she seized the cloverleaf paddle that leaned against the wall and headed back to the clothesline. Emilie was nowhere in sight. Anna huffed and raised her eyes to the Heavens her sister so respected. Would it be wrong to pretend the rug was Emilie's bottom as she beat the dust from it?

Wrong or not, the pretence helped her find energy in the stifling heat, and she was so invested in her task that the crack as thunder split the heavens caught her by surprise. A willy-willy swirled through on a hot northerly gust, tangling tumbleweed around her feet and throwing grit into her eyes. Skirt billowing, she strained into the wind. Her hands tightened on the wooden paddle and her stomach knotted. She hesitantly licked her lips, wanting to deny the acrid taste that spiked fear through her chest.

The sour tang of burning leaves and green wood filled the air with the smell of death.

3
Taylor

'Come in, loves. The door's open,' a vaguely familiar voice singsonged from the depths of the old farmhouse.

Instead of following the direction, Taylor swivelled, surveying the walled back garden. Parched, like the town she and Mum had left fifteen kilometres back. The only greenery was spindly couch grass thrusting between the pavers that surrounded a weed-choked pond. A small fountain spouted sporadically, as though the effort to pump was too great to be sustained. The sun reflected from the dry ground, the walls trapping the heat so that Taylor stood in an oven that shouldn't exist this early in the spring. Beyond the garden—though it was barely deserving of the title— was farmyard. Kilometres of the stuff. Grass and outcrops of rocks dotted with stands of lanky trees. Dozens of dirty-grey sheep. And millions of flies. Tiny little black things that clustered at her eyes and her lips like she offered an oasis in the desert. God knows what magic she'd imagined in the farm as a thirteen-year-old, but she guessed it had been related to the novelty of petting various barnyard animals, rather than a more adult survey of the surrounds.

Mum dropped the metal bar she'd used to strike an iron triangle hung beside the door. It swung on a piece of frayed black twine as though it had found some breeze in the airless pocket of heat. As the reverberation of the clanging iron died away, Mum took a deep breath. 'Come on, then.' She sounded nervous. Perhaps she anticipated questions about why she'd found it necessary to suddenly flee Sydney. Or worse, maybe she was eager to launch into teary answers? Taylor grimaced. Physical ills could be treated, sutured and medicated, but the heart was an organ, a muscle; there was no point attributing emotions to it, creating issues even the best cardiologist couldn't address. But that fact was one of many she and Mum would never agree on.

The chipped, grey-painted screen door slammed behind them and Mum flinched. A narrow rectangular room stretched to their left and right. Window seats were piled with boxes and empty jars, old newspapers and shopping bags, and one wall was lined with a motley combination of white melamine and towering pine cupboards. Beneath a bank of dusty louvres were a deep stainless-steel sink and a twin-tub washing machine.

'People still use those?' Taylor murmured.

Mum ignored her. 'Hello?' she called.

'In here, Michelle.'

Taylor followed her mother to the end of the room, where Mum squared her shoulders then pushed at another door.

The wood, unlike the hollow doors at home, was carved in four heavy panels. A dimpled glass pane took up the top fifth of the door, well above anyone's head height. Chips in the grey paintwork revealed myriad different colours that would no doubt have thrilled an interior decoration historian.

Taylor's grandparents were seated at a bandy-legged, steel-framed kitchen table. What was visible of the swirly blue Formica beneath alternately placed white and pink placemats was patchy and faded, as though it had been bleached uncountable times over the decades.

'You're just in time,' her grandfather said. After so many years, Taylor wouldn't have recognised him, but there were only two people in the room and she was pretty sure the one sporting a silver-streaked bun would be Gran.

Gramps brushed crumbs from his rounded belly before gripping the edge of the table, swaying forward twice to build momentum, then lurching up from the chair. He collected a black plastic tray from the steel draining board behind him. 'Come on, then.'

Realising the summons was directed at her, Taylor shot Mum a beseeching look. Mum quirked her lips in an 'I've no idea' fashion and gave a little shrug.

Gramps scraped a plate into the tray and shuffled past Taylor, giving her elbow a squeeze with his free hand. 'This way, Peach.'

Peach?

As Taylor followed him, Gran spoke to Mum. 'Pop the kettle on, love. I'll warm the pot.'

It all sounded ridiculously prosaic, as though she and Mum had only visited a day or two ago.

'Don't let the flies in,' Gramps said as he led the way back out of the screen door. He shuffled across the small, walled garden and dragged open a gate. The wood scraped across the pebbled cement path. Then Gramps threw his head back and released a harsh caw, repeating it three times. The noise echoed off the stone sheds that bordered the large paddock around the house.

'What?' Taylor gasped.

'Watch,' Gramps said, grinning in obvious satisfaction at her reaction.

He hobbled toward a small aviary built hard up against a stone wall, the wooden frame splintered and rotting, seemingly held together only by the wire mesh. Stretching up, he tottered so precariously that Taylor hovered close behind, ready to catch him. He placed the tray on the roof of the low building. Then he cawed again.

'Now, count. Quick.'

'Count?' And she thought her conversations with Mum bordered on bizarre.

Gramps nodded. 'It's tea time. See how long it takes them to come.'

As he spoke, a great rustle of wings announced the arrival of two ravens. Midnight blue iridescence sheened feathers as glossy and black as Zac's hair. Clawed feet scrabbling on the tin, they suspiciously assessed Taylor from sapphire eyes before hopping toward the tray.

Gramps chuckled. 'Said you need to count quickly. Some days they're so hungry, the entire coven is out here calling me, instead of the other way round. All righty. Magpie's made pikelets, so we'd better get in there before your mum gets them all.'

'Magpie? Maggie?' Was that Gran's name? It didn't sound quite right.

'Magpie,' Gramps affirmed without further explanation.

Gran—Magpie—proved to be as eccentric as Gramps. Cheerfully pouring cups of tea from a pot on the kitchen table, she passed around a plate of warm pikelets slathered in butter and another piled with generous slices of the sugar-dusted, cream-filled honey Swiss roll Mum had bought. The entire time, Gran kept up an incessant stream of chatter about weather, food and neighbours Taylor and Mum didn't know.

Mum joined in, talking fast. She waxed lyrical about how Taylor had skipped a year of school, completed her Bachelor's degree early, passed the GAMSAT, and was working part-time, despite her crippling postgrad study load. She also managed to get in a humble brag about how many years of sacrifice, guidance and persuasion had gone into getting Taylor to this point.

At cup number two, Gramps insisted Taylor take a tour of the house with him to refresh her memory. He wandered through a warren of rooms she'd never be able to navigate alone, pointing out with all the pride of a homeowner the high cobwebbed ceilings—although he didn't mention the cobwebs—thick walls and tiny windows designed to lock the harsh sun outside.

By cup number three, having apparently avoided any curly questions about the state of her marriage, Mum suggested they head off to set up their tent while they had daylight. Oblivious to Taylor's lack of enthusiasm, she kept up an excited monologue of 'Ooh, do you remember this?' as she eased the car down barely existent tracks where scrawny trees reached out to scratch the paintwork.

Textbooks slipped from the seat and into the footwell as they juddered over an endless series of ruts. 'Great, four hundred bucks down the drain,' Taylor muttered.

'Don't be dramatic,' Mum said as she pulled the car up dead centre of a paddock covered with flat, yellow-flowered plants.

'Is that some kind of canola, too?' Taylor suggested slyly. It would be degrees of hilarious if they camped in the middle of a genetically modified crop.

'I think it's some kind of weed. Bet the bees love it, though.'

Taylor squinted through the window at the acres of scrub bordering the paddock. Why on earth had she thought this place had an Enchanted Woods quality when she was a kid? 'Bet they love being in the world's most boring mandala. Literally everything out here is khaki and yellow.'

'Or, you know, green and gold.'

Taylor clambered out. Within five steps, pollen from the black-centred flowers—which looked like coin-sized sunflowers—had turned her boots bright yellow and she sniffed experimentally. Oddly enough, they hadn't triggered her hayfever. But there was no need to let Mum know that. 'What's with all the holes?' she yelped as she stumbled.

'Wombats,' Mum replied firmly, starting to unload their camping equipment.

'Like *you* can pick their burrows from any other kind.' The ground was pocked with holes and peppered by sparse tufts of short, wiry foliage, like a teenage boy's face.

'Tay, come help.' Mum's lilting pitch meant she was barely hanging on to her temper. 'We need firewood before it gets dark.'

Taylor frowned. Not much threw Mum. At least, it hadn't, until about a year back. Maybe longer, but Taylor had been too busy to notice when it was that Mum had stopped being . . . Mum. When the irritating rose-coloured glasses through which she viewed the world had been smudged and she'd developed deep frown lines.

Taylor jammed her hands into her pockets, her groan shifting a cloud of flies from her face as she stomped back toward the car.

Mum's hair had escaped her ponytail and her pale skin was reddened. Blue nylon puddled at her feet and she waved thin rods at Taylor. 'Wood?' Invested in her pretence that this was a bizarre re-creation of their holiday from years' back, Mum seemed oblivious to the fact that Taylor was giving up precious time. These few days off should have been spent at the club with Cassie watching Zac perform. Or in the hotel room with Zac . . .

She had to remember, though, that she'd chosen to accompany Mum to support her midlife crisis. Had to remember, but didn't have to be particularly happy about it at this moment.

She flung out her arms and let them drop heavily. 'Where am I supposed to get wood from?'

Mum pushed the elastic-jointed rods together, trilling a little laugh as the steel-tipped carbon fibre refused to engage. But Taylor knew the giggle was a pressure gauge release. Mum waved toward the surrounding greyness, the winged sleeves of her boho top drifting in the breeze she created. 'Show a little initiative, love. See the scrub? It's made of—wait for it—wood. Come on, don't be childish.'

Childish? Funny how parents could invoke that accusation with sublime disregard for chronological age. 'Why couldn't we buy a bag from the petrol station on the way here—you know, like *normal* people do?'

Mum's lips pursed into a cat's bum, her tone tightening to match. 'Just get little branches to start with. And watch out for snakes.'

'Jesus, Mum, I'm not thirteen.' Taylor stamped back toward the scrub. Prepared to leap away if something slithered out, she kicked at fallen branches along the fringe of the tangled bushland, then snapped twigs from the closest trees.

A vine covered in tiny white, fluffy stars and hanging from a branch like a ghostly stalactite looked like it would probably be flammable. She tugged the strands. The branch creaked ominously and flowers cascaded, covering her head and shoulders like dandruff.

Returning to the campground, Taylor dropped her bundle of twigs, scowling as she picked minute, itchy blossoms out of her cleavage. 'Impressive. That you got the tent up, I mean, not the Lilliputian dimensions. Where are you sleeping?'

'Don't be silly,' Mum snapped. The assembly had evidently taken the last of her patience. 'It's a standard two-man.'

'Bet a two-man from an actual camping store would be bigger than a Kmart one. You realise that even without a hotel, we could have done this properly? Glamping is a thing. Soft duvet, air mattress . . .'

'We need more wood, Taylor.'

'And a gas barbecue,' she added to her list. 'I collected all the little bits, like you said.'

Mum snapped twigs against her harem-panted knee, exerting rather more force than necessary. She jerked her head at the scrub.

'Where are the keys? I'm going back to the house first,' Taylor said. 'I forgot to go to the loo. By the way, how bizarre was it there? Like we'd never been away. I'll probably need therapy to erase the scars of that weirdness.' Invoking the word 'therapy' was generally a great way to get Mum back on board.

'You can't erase scars. You can only help them fade.' Mum had a knack for sighing without making a sound, a deflation of her entire body and a long-suffering tilt to her chin. 'And it wasn't bizarre. My parents are just easy to be with. If you cut through the scrub and across the paddocks, it's probably only a kilometre or so.'

'What is?'

'The homestead. The toilet.'

'I'll take the car.'

'Can't. The tent's tied to it. Just for tonight, so we can see if it holds up in the wind.'

'You know I wouldn't walk that far even if it was a shopping mall.'

'I'm sure you have to do far more steps in clinical prac.' Mum dusted off her knees and then went to the scant rectangle of shade cast by the tent. She produced a small shovel from behind the esky, unfolding it with a flourish. 'Here you go, then. Toilet paper is in the glovebox. Make sure you bury it.'

'You are joking, right?'

'Not at all. Gramps said the foxes are bad out here. They might dig it up.'

'Not that!' Taylor snapped. 'I mean, you expect me to go . . . out there?'

'People have managed with less.'

'And people died from cholera and dysentery. Generally, humans strive to improve their lot, not voluntarily go back to their roots.' Rivulets of sweat trickled down Taylor's back and, without sniffing too deeply, she knew her deodorant wasn't up to the challenge. Her head itched from the flowers and her hands were filthy. And it had been hours since the grocery store in Settlers Bridge and still Zac hadn't called back—she wasn't sure whether to be more irritated by that or by her need to have him call.

Mum bent from the waist, laying sticks in the sandy pit she had dug. 'Okay. I suggest you take it easy on the food, then.'

Taylor snatched the shovel and strode away, spiky rushes spearing her ankles, the cratered surface seeking to trip her.

Despite appearing sparse, the wood held an air of hushed seclusion as she penetrated beyond the first row of scruffy trees. Jeans around her ankles, she over-balanced, wobbling into a yellow-flowered bush the size of a car. 'Shit!' The plant was covered in thorns hidden by delicate, wattle-puff flowers instead of leaves.

'You all right, love?' Mum called as Taylor stalked back into camp.

'Barely survived.' The shovel blade skidded a curl of dirt from the ground as she flung it toward the tent.

'Make sure it doesn't land in the food,' Mum said. 'Or you'll never want Vegemite again.'

The flash of the mum she remembered slid a reluctant smirk across Taylor's face. 'Gross. Not to mention, infantile. I see you got the fire going. Nice one.' She coughed and waved a hand through the smoke.

'Got to make the most of it before the fire bans kick in next month or whenever. Give me a hand dragging those larger branches over. We need to cook dinner while it's light enough to see the sausages. Traditional camping food, like last time.'

Mum's focus on what had been was a little unnerving. 'Beef?' Taylor asked.

'Tofu.'

'Mum—' Taylor geared up for her regular lecture on the importance of iron for menopausal women. Not that sausages were a great source.

'Should have come shopping with me,' Mum teased. 'That supermarket in Settlers Bridge was perfect. It's tiny, only about three aisles. Absolutely crammed with anything you could want. Loads of local produce, no waste in packaging.'

'And they had tofu?'

'Maybe not.' Mum wasn't the least abashed at being caught out.

The sausages burned as soon as they hit the aluminium pans shoved into the coals, so they disguised the remnants by dipping them into baked beans and fried eggs.

Taylor inspected a charred morsel. 'You'd better not eat this phoenix, what with being a vegetarian and all.'

'Phoenix?'

'Yeah, y'know: risen from the ashes. Though this is more embalmed *in* than risen *from*.'

Mum's blackened teeth showed in a grin, then she waggled fingers coated in grease, bean juice and ash. Wet wipes would never match the convenience of running water and soap. 'S'mores?'

Taylor tossed her sausage carcass into the fire. 'Hard no. Too much American TV for you. Besides, I'm pretty sure they don't contain chia seed or turmeric root, so how are you going to make them?'

'Not much of a challenge for the Royal Easter Show Baking Champion.'

'Jeez, Mum, ancient history. Up yourself much?'

Aluminium sheets flattened across her knee, Mum layered biscuits, dark chocolate and marshmallow. Then she sealed the foil and dropped the package onto the coals. 'Remind me to throw potatoes in early tomorrow. And I brought spelt flour to make damper.'

'How many days have you catered for?' Mum wasn't a great timekeeper, so it was always best to keep her on track. Taylor had her own life timetabled to the last minute. Still, it was nice to have Mum to herself for a bit, and it did feel more . . . relaxed out here. Taylor could pretend for a moment that she didn't have a million things vying for her attention back in Sydney.

'Until we've had enough.'

With deep purple velvet gathered around them, the darkness had an almost tangible density. Something rustled in the scrub fifty metres from their clearing. 'Yup, well, then, I'm calling it: enough. You know this is the first time I can recall being anywhere without streetlights?' Taylor glanced over her shoulder but quickly flicked her eyes back to the comforting glow of the fire. 'I reckon that's enough of a trip down memory lane—we'll go stay at the house now.'

'What, and miss out on telling ghost stories?'

'Start that, and I'm hitch-hiking back to civilisation.'

'In your profession, you'll need to accept death and the afterlife.'

'I'm reasonably confident there's nothing about the afterlife in the med curriculum. And, in an uncomfortable segue, now you've put ghosts in my head there's no way I'm going in there to pee tonight.' She hiked a thumb toward the scrub. It loomed darker and closer each time she looked. 'The front passenger tyre is mine, okay?'

'Done. It is nice out here, though, isn't it?' Mum's casual pose, leaning back in her camp chair to study the stars, seemed contrived.

'*Nice* is stretching it.' Taylor slapped a mosquito on her arm and held up the carcass. 'You know these carry Ross River virus? You've probably signed our death warrant.'

'Death by mozzie. We've all got to go somehow.' Mum used a stick to pull the s'mores from the fire, blowing on her fingers as she juggled the hot packages. Except for being a bit burned, the dessert looked good, chocolate and marshmallow melting across the foil.

'Cheers.' They tapped their biscuits together.

The marshmallow had evaporated, leaving only a sticky memory streaked on the foil. The chocolate had separated into bitter clumps and the biscuits turned to dust in their mouths.

Taylor spat her mouthful into the fire and tossed in the wrapper. 'Did you take out a life insurance policy on me?'

'Perhaps s'mores don't work with organic ingredients,' Mum said around her mouthful of char. 'Make sure you pull the foil out of the ashes in the morning. It won't decompose.'

Taylor stood up to dig in her jeans pocket for her phone. 'Easter Show Champion, huh? You plan to take that recipe to the next one?'

'Maybe not next year.' Mum's smile didn't quite reach her eyes. 'Speaking of Sydney, Dad and I—'

Taylor's heart lurched and she drove the heel of her hand into her eye. 'You have to be joking.'

Mum was instantly on her feet, her arm around Taylor's shoulders. The billowy cotton of her top floated into Taylor's face on a waft of organic mango moisturiser.

'Oh, baby, it's all right. You mustn't get upset. Dad and I both—'

'*Mum*, I'm not talking about *that*.' Ever, if she could avoid it. 'I just realised there's no signal here. Nothing. Not a single bar.' She leaned back, holding her phone high, trying to catch a satellite. 'I can't stay here for days with no service.' Even the thought sent flutters of panic into her chest. She relied on her phone, the internet, the *connection*.

'I'm thinking of staying longer,' Mum said in her typically disjointed fashion, her plans rarely tied to reality.

'No, you're not,' Taylor said firmly. 'I have to be back within the week. And I'll need to find coverage well before that.' Without the phone, work, Zac, her friends, uni— everything disappeared, erased as though she'd been thrust into some peculiar time warp. Which might be novel for an hour or two, but wasn't something she could possibly tolerate any longer.

4

Anna

There was smoke in the wind. Smoke was nothing new; the men burned the scrub to clear the land. But never on a Sunday.

Anna scanned the horizon in the direction of the lightning forks. The sky was dirty, the endless blue smudged with swirling dust.

She hoped it was dust.

Another gust blew in hot from the north. It wasn't dust.

Fear cramped her stomach.

'Emilie.' The word failed to leave her mouth. She swallowed and forced her legs toward the house, her gaze fixed on the horizon, as though to glance away would be to allow the evil to approach. 'Emilie!' Overly loud this time; her panic startled a flock of ravens from the tree overhanging the house.

Emilie appeared in the doorway. The birds cawed harsh laughter as they spread their wings and escaped. Her finger trembling, Anna pointed to the horizon, maybe a half-mile distant, where the plains dipped to an unseen valley. Short yellow stalks of scythed wheat stood stiff sentinel in the paddock, the only fodder for their sheep until the new growth of autumn. Suddenly the straw bent and willowed before an unseen force that boiled across the plain.

Clutching each other, the women staggered as the hot wind erupted against them. The sky to the north—what should be the sky—had turned from blue to black, a malevolent cloud rushing toward them.

'Anna. We must flee,' Emilie shrieked as she reeled against the gusts.

Her panic focused Anna. 'There isn't time. Look how fast the smoke approaches. Run to the stables, set Liesl free. She'll have to fend for herself. Bring me hessian sacks.'

Emilie stared, her lips pouted in a perfect O, her eyes larger than usual.

A low crackle buzzed in Anna's ears and she snapped her attention back to the paddock. The wheat on the far edge was aflame, the fire burning low and fast. A rolling wave of heat wraiths danced before it. 'Emilie, go! Quickly!'

Anna lifted her skirts and dashed to the side of the cottage. Snatching up the heavy buckets Dieter had placed there, she lugged them into the open expanse between the barn and the house. Emilie tottered toward her clutching hessian sacks. Liesl ambled behind, her udder swaying.

Emilie dropped the sacks, her eyes filled with terror. 'Anna, we cannot—'

She would be of no use and concern for her made Anna more scared. She needed her sister out of the way, safe, so she could think. 'Take Liesl into the house.'

'The house? Are you quite mad? Mother will never forgive you.'

Anna could barely hear her sister over the hissing and whining as the earth screamed in agony beneath the flames. 'Better manure on the floor than we lose the cow,' she yelled. 'Go, Emilie!'

Dirt whipped into her eyes as she plunged the sacks into a bucket, willing the coarse fabric to soak up the water. The wind tugged against her skirts, almost unbalancing her.

A six-foot brown snake, sensing danger through the heated ground, slithered past and Emilie whimpered, her fingers digging into Anna's shoulder.

The flames were already halfway across the paddock about a quarter-mile from them, travelling faster than Anna could have imagined. She turned her head to snatch a breath of fresh air but gave a choking gasp. While her attention was on the fire front, embers had blown over them and into the scrub. Tongues of fire licked and flared in the undergrowth close to the rear of the bakehouse.

Something erupted, the wave of noise and air beating against her eardrums. Emilie screamed. Then another explosion, and a ball of flame blossomed in the scrub, forming an impenetrable wall of fire. Without warning, a tall eucalypt flared like a giant candle. Branches exploded into the air, arcing up like arrows in flight then spearing down to stab the parched earth. Far too close to her sister.

Anna dropped the sacks and shoved Emilie toward the house. 'For the love of God, move!'

Emilie dragged on Liesl's halter and Anna slapped the cow's rump. Distended by the calf she carried, Liesl's sides barely cleared the doorframe as she lumbered behind Emilie.

Anna spun back to the yard. A gust tangled her skirt around her calves and she almost fell. Encumbered by the fabric, she could barely move, and if an ember caught her, she would flame like the eucalypt.

'Wait, Emilie.' Hands on the high collar of her dress, Anna looked around to make certain she wasn't observed, although she could see only a few feet through smoke that thickened by the second. She tugged her collar apart and the tiny, painstakingly sewn buttons showered to the ground. She stared at them. She loathed sewing. And, for a moment, that's all she wanted to think about. She wanted the chore of restitching her gown to be the darkest cloud in her life.

Stepping from the yards of fabric, she threw the dress and petticoats toward Emilie, shouting above the crackling inferno, 'Cover the window with this. Block the bottom of the door with blankets. Stay inside until I come and get you.'

Despite their situation, Emilie's fists were on her hips, her disapproval of Anna standing outdoors in her short chemise and knickerbockers patent. Hysterical laughter climbed Anna's throat. But the sting of wind-driven grit against her exposed flesh quelled any humour. She had no time to explain to Emilie that saving the farm surpassed her need for modesty. Besides, there was no one to see but her sister and the cow.

'Now, Emilie. Close it now!'

Emilie slowly obeyed, inching the door shut.

Blinking away smoke tears, Anna scanned the yard. Wind hotter than a breath from the hellfire Pastor threatened the congregation with showered her with tiny embers that singed her skin and hair but disappeared before she could swat them. The fire chasing across the wheat field might burn itself out among the sparse fuel, but the inferno in the scrub had taken hold and threatened their outbuildings.

She heaved the pails toward the straggly vegetation that curved in a crescent around the buildings. With nowhere for them to outrun such a blaze, and the creek too shallow to afford any shelter, she had to defend the house and protect her younger sister. Her parents could not return to find nothing to show for their years of hard work, no compensation for the lives this land had already claimed.

Urgency churned within Anna, yet she could do nothing but watch as the fire approached. Sap screamed as it bled from the burning trees, bubbling and evaporating before it could hit the ground. Eucalypts cracked, popped and exploded. Her eyes smarted and her throat ached as the bitter, vapourised oil gusted toward her. Trees split and fell, acacia bushes burning as fiercely as torches.

Closer still, their precious orchard erupted in a sheet of flame. The smoke was so thick now it formed walls around her and she could not see if the path to the creek remained open or whether the fire in the stubble had burned out. She tightened her grip on the sack.

A sparrow dropped to the ground. It flopped once, twice, beak open, liquid black eyes pleading. Anna dipped in the bucket and splashed a little water over it. Said a prayer for them both. Her underclothes were soaked with sweat, both from fear and the gusting heat that cracked her lips as she licked at them.

Spot fires flared, tussocks of grass spontaneously igniting with no visible cause, and at last she could act. It took all her strength to swing the wet hessian and slap it down on the flames. They smothered and for a second she believed she could control this, that she could single-handedly save her parents' property, but more blazes ignited, growing in number and ferocity as cinders rained like hail, sizzling through the air and scoring pink trails across her skin.

The scrub undulated with the unearthly howls and moans of injured animals and exploding vegetation. Singed creatures crawled from the inferno, less scared of her than of the certain death behind them. A charred lizard appeared as Anna heaved and sweated, dunking the sacks over and again. Lifting them, slamming at the flames that now formed a low wall, creeping toward the house. Toward her sister.

Perhaps Emilie was right. If this lizard could escape the fire, maybe they, too, should have run? The reptile stopped at her feet. 'Keep going, keep going,' she panted at it. Or maybe at herself. She didn't have time to help the beast, but she nudged it with her toe, encouraging it to more speed. It rolled onto its back, charred stumps of legs pointing to the sky. Anna's stomach surged into her throat.

That will be us.

Her back burned, not from the fire, but with grinding pain from hefting the sack. She'd lost both the buckets and her sense of direction as she lunged into thick, swirling smoke, slamming the sack onto the flames over and again, then staggering back to suck in some air. She could only pray that she was retreating toward the cottage; that if she couldn't beat the fire, she'd be able to seek refuge inside with her sister.

A tornado whirled through the smoke, sucking in all the air. Anna clawed at her throat, terrified of suffocation. Robbed of oxygen, the fire guttered, the smoke briefly clearing, and she could orient herself. The house was behind her and the flames threatened the pug-and-pine chicken coop. The hens croaked and clucked desperately, fluttering across the yard in a reek of burned feathers to crowd her feet, seeking shelter she could not provide.

Or perhaps the odour was her hair burning as long strands escaped her chignon to tangle around her arms.

She had to save the coop.

One step, and pain lanced up her legs from her feet, her hoarse scream choked by ash and fear. Bitter smoke tore at her lungs as the ash swirled back in, obscuring the world.

Barely able to stand, Anna could do no more.

The sack fell from her nerveless fingers and tears of futility pricked her eyes. Worried her life would be ordinary, she had failed to appreciate the gift of each breath. And now she would be robbed of both life and hope.

She knew she would die here.

If she died, Emilie would also die.

A branch smashed into her back, knocking her to her knees. The glowing end gouged her forearm, liquefying her flesh.

The pain focused her. If she could not save the farm, she must at least save her sister.

The air was a little clearer near the ground. She filled her lungs before she forced herself up, gagging on the ash. Her boots had melted to the soles of her feet, and tiny burn holes starred her camisole and favourite knickerbockers. She wanted to stare at them, mourn them, let their loss be her largest.

Unable to swing the sack anymore, Anna dragged it through the nearest flames, praying that she was somehow creating a firebreak around their home. Heat forced her to retreat until her back slammed into stone. There was no further escape from the wall of flame that bore down on her, but at least she had found the house and her sister. Yet she didn't dare beg Emilie to open the door; her sister was safer closed inside. Anna slumped to the ground, the rough stone shearing flesh from her naked shoulder. She pressed her cheek against the house, as though she could somehow make Emilie aware that her final thoughts and prayers had been for her.

The earth reverberated beneath her, the pounding of hooves a familiar pulse. Voices loud, commanding and more welcome than a thunderstorm, curled through the smoke.

Relief sapped the last of Anna's strength and her hand splayed like a dead spider, the sack slipping from her grip. Forms smeared past her in the swirling ash cloud. Men, stripped to their shirt sleeves as they dashed toward the flames, snatched her sacks, yelled directions. Their heavy boots crushed the life from the smaller fires she'd battled so hard.

Grit and exhaustion forced Anna's eyes closed.

Arms slid around her and her stomach swooped as she was lifted, held tight against a hard chest. Dieter had returned from the church in time to save them. Still, she could not summon the energy to open her eyes.

As he carried her away from the heat and noise, she sobbed with the effort of drawing breath into her scorched lungs. She should be ashamed that her brother saw her in her underclothes—the women didn't even hang their unmentionables out to dry until the men worked far from the house. Instead, she curled into his chest to hide from the pain as his heavy footfalls crunched through the crisped grass.

The firm tread halted and a disconcerting falling sensation accompanied a breeze as she was lowered to the ground. The grass was longer here; Dieter must have carried her to the creek.

'Let's clean you up a little.'

The voice wasn't Dieter's. Her eyes snapped open. The face that floated above her was too beautiful to be real. A fierce angel.

She flinched at the touch of a wet cloth and the face tightened, all strong planes and hard angles. One arm supporting her, the man ran a hand through hair the gold of harvest wheat. He frowned with a concern that surely shouldn't touch angels, his eyes a deeper shade than the blue summer sky at twilight.

Although she'd not seen him for a year or more—and never closer than across a hall—Anna knew who this was, as she knew all their distant neighbours.

A cleft appeared in his left cheek, the weathered lines around his eyes deepening. 'Luke Hartmann,' he offered. His fingers chased a strand of hair from her face and tucked it behind her ear.

Humiliation surged through the pain and exhaustion that enveloped her. What must he think? Not even thanking him for her rescue, she lay in his arms, permitting him to sponge her skin. But the water was so blissfully cool and he was so very beautiful . . .

Moisture trickled across her flesh, temporarily diminishing the agony. *Across my flesh . . . across my flesh . . .* The words played through her mind like music. Then, with the ferocity of a cymbal crash, the import hit home. *Across my flesh.* She was practically naked. Spluttering on an indrawn breath, she struggled to sit, to escape this man's far too intimate embrace.

'Slow down.' The words rumbled from Luke's chest, his arm firm against her back.

She crossed her hands over her breasts, unable to speak. Didn't dare look at him. She had no idea how to extricate herself from the situation, short of closing her eyes and wishing for the death she had prayed to avoid. Shame brought tears to her eyes and she sniffled, trying to

choke them back. *Dear Lord, don't let me do this now.*
The sobs fought for escape, tightening her chest so recently
assaulted by the smoke, and she dug ragged nails into her
burned palms.

'It seems the house is out of danger now, but I fear you
are injured,' Luke said. 'The womenfolk will not yet be
back from the church, but is there someone at home there
who can render assistance?'

She nodded without daring to look at him again.

He stood and removed his Sunday jacket to drape over
her shoulders. 'Here, let's make you more presentable.'

His words meant she could not pretend he hadn't noticed
her state of undress. Her mortification absolute, Anna
tried to pull the jacket closed across her breasts, but her
fingers were numb, her hands swollen and uncooperative.

Luke did it for her, his jacket large enough to wrap
twice around. 'Are you able to stand?' Ignoring propriety,
his thumb and forefinger tilted her chin up and his eyes
searched her face as a frown creased his forehead.

She'd not spoken a word. He probably thought her
mute or a halfwit. Or worse—rude and ungrateful.

Again, she nodded. An arm around her waist, he drew
her up. The melted leather of her boots adhered to her
feet, tearing the skin away. She whimpered, staggering
against him.

'May I?'

Not waiting for permission, Luke swung her into his
arms and strode up the paddock toward the house.

Cradled against his chest, although her grit-filled eyes
were almost shut she saw Emilie open the door. Her sister

looked perfect. Blonde hair coiled, a beautiful ringlet arranged on each shoulder, blue eyes enormous as she stared at Luke.

Anna wanted to feel jealous. But all she felt was exhaustion.

Luke set Anna in Mother's rocking chair. 'Emilie.' Of course he knew *her* name. 'Assist your sister.' He knelt beside Anna, although she barely let her glance brush him as darkness swirled around them. 'Anna, are you all right?'

He knew her name also? Surprise pierced the dark cloud as her consciousness slid into an ashy abyss.

5
Taylor

Sinister movement along the edge of the tent snapped Taylor from her dream. Her bleary gaze tracked the stealthy progress silhouetted against the fabric and she exhaled in relief. A raven.

'Butcher bird,' Mum corrected, as though she'd spoken.

'Reassuring name. What's it doing, perving on us?'

The sleeping bag bunched in a rustle of nylon around Mum's waist as she sat, rubbing her face with both hands. 'Hunting breakfast, I imagine. How did you sleep? It got perishing, didn't it? Incredible, considering yesterday's weather. That's spring for you. Oh, and we'll have to move the tent. There's a rock on my side.'

'You felt that through your amazing yoga mat? Bit *Princess and the Pea*.' Stick the word 'yoga' in front of anything and Mum thought it must be good. Hence their lack of proper camping mats.

Mum somehow levitated to her feet, then shimmied to drop the sleeping bag from her hips. 'Don't touch the canvas or the dew will seep in.'

Taylor groaned. She wasn't capable of moving to touch *anything*. It would take her five minutes to unclench enough to crawl out of the tent. She closed her eyes instead.

Mum's bed shirt hit her face. 'Come on, Tay. Up and at 'em. I'd forgotten you snore like a train. The blessings of a big house, huh?'

'Deviated septum,' she protested. 'Be nice to have parents who'd pay to get it fixed. And I'd forgotten how irritating you are in the morning.'

Half out of the tent, Mum pulled on her clothes. 'Speaking of princesses, did you notice Gran and Gramps' house is solid stone? Even the internal walls.'

'Seriously, who talks this much in the morning?' No wonder her parents didn't sleep together. She reached for her phone. Still no signal. Zac would think she'd dropped off the end of the world. He wouldn't be far wrong.

Mum tossed her pyjama pants onto the sleeping bag. 'I'll check for embers and get the billy on to boil.'

'Whatever.' Taylor threw her arm across her face to block the light streaming through the unzipped flap. An elusive dream floated like sea mist on the shore of her memory. The privations of camping had filled her sleep with thoughts of what life would have been like here a hundred or more years ago, but frustratingly she couldn't recall the specifics of the dream. An urge to chase the intangible details furrowed her brow, but forcing the memory to crystallise proved as impossible as catching a rainbow.

The harder she tried, the more a sense of wistfulness carved at her heart.

Fatigue from lying awake half the night, longing to hear Zac's corny ''Night, princess,' probably didn't help. She had thought the biggest challenge on this trip would be keeping Mum under control. But, denied Zac's texts and nightly call, Taylor missed him more than should have been possible. Which meant . . . what? She had never missed a guy before. She'd always been too snowed under with study to pay them much attention.

A kookaburra's manic call silenced the bird chorus outside the tent and Taylor's back brushed the nylon as she scrambled to the flap. Cold droplets, which would probably be welcome in a few hours' time when the sun hit its peak, showered her. She cursed beneath her breath.

'Taylor!'

Maybe not so much beneath her breath.

Mum had swapped out her floaty blouse for a flannel-ette shirt and sweats. Hands wrapped around her ankles, her hair swept the ground. Upward cat, or downward dog, or something.

'Join in, love. Great for stress relief.'

'I'm not stressed.'

Mum stretched into a plank, her stomach swaying to the ground, her back hollowing and her neck elongating as she faced the rising sun.

'But I did just have *sun* and *rising* in the same thought. Should never happen on holidays,' Taylor continued.

'Best time of the day. Check the side zip of my bag. There's a spare pair of yoga pants.'

'Of course there is,' Taylor mumbled. Not wanting another cold shower, she sat on the sleeping bag to rummage through Mum's stuff, then crawled outside again to pull on the pants.

Mum had one hand on the ground, the other reaching for the sky like a stranded starfish. 'See? Now you're hippie chic.'

'More like hippie shit.' Rescuing a crumpet from the jaffle iron in the coals, she buttered it and smeared on Vegemite, then spoke with a full mouth. 'So, what exactly are we supposed to do all day? Besides hang with your folks?' Without a signal, she'd have to go old school and rely on her textbooks. She chased a line of melted butter from her chin, but had second thoughts about licking her finger, and wiped it on the borrowed pants instead.

Mum poured tea from the billy, flapping at the steam as she squinted into the enamel mugs. 'Pretty much this. Your grandparents have a whole list of medical appointments in the city today—I guess that's the reality of growing old. But that means we'll have some girl time. Relax, enjoy nature. Oh, and collect more wood. That's the last of it.' Her sneaker nudged a charred branch sticking out of the fire pit. 'How about a walk along the creek? Explore a bit.'

'Explore? Seriously? If I wanted to hike, I'd have hit the Kokoda Trail. At least I could have put that up on Facebook.' Eyes closed, Taylor turned to the orange and pink glow on the horizon. Sydney was half an hour ahead; the sun was already up there. Not that Zac would be. 'Mum—'

'What, love?'

She sighed. 'Nothing.' Slow enough to come around to the idea that, although she lived at home, she was entitled to lead her own life, her parents would be incapable of seeing beyond Zac's tattoos and career choice. They'd never recognise the man she knew: face of a fallen angel, heart of a dreamer.

'Talk to me, Tay.'

'Let's go do that exploring.' It wouldn't hurt to exercise a little before she found somewhere to sit—hopefully out of the sun and away from the flies—to get some reading done. And the phone signal might improve further from the camp.

The creek a few hundred metres away was a non-event. Despite a deep gully carved through startling terracotta-red earth, only a ten-centimetre wide, scum-covered trickle dribbled through straggly rushes. Somehow, the lack of water didn't surprise her. 'Ha. Déjà vu,' she said, the odd sensation raising goosebumps along her arms.

'What do you mean?'

The oily slime released her boots with a reluctant slurp. 'Ugh. I mean I've been to Hell before. These are brand new.'

'Lucky that's what they're for, then.' Mum nudged the mud with a stick. 'That, and the Kokoda Trail.'

Propped against a low stone structure, Taylor scraped the muck from her boots on a rock. A rainbow petro-chemical iridescence shivered on the black sludge. 'What is this stuff? It reeks.'

'Your grandfather said there's an old mine upstream that used arsenic. Or perhaps the arsenic was a by-product of the mining? I don't remember. Anyway, the poison leached into the waterway, making it toxic.'

Taylor stared. Mum was talking about environmental damage, but couldn't recall the facts? On any given day, she could quote the cull numbers for the Japanese whaling fleet or the global warming temperature rise of *exactly* where they stood. Unease prickled through Taylor. Her mind raced through the clinical presentations of Alzheimer's, Parkinson's, Huntington's.

'Toxic? And you're only now telling me?'

'Well, I imagine it's fine if you don't drink the water. Lucky no one's reliant on it anymore.' Mum's bangles clacked as she waved at the wall Taylor leaned against. 'That well will be contaminated, too.'

Jerking her hand from the stonework, Taylor scrutinised her palm. 'I guess we're not yabbying, then. Unless you fancy crayfish with three heads and one eye?'

'No, that's fine,' Mum replied, poking at scrubby plants and hard-baked mud with her stick as she wandered away.

Taylor frowned after her. 'Wait up.'

Mum might be engrossed in the whole midlife crisis, trying-to-find-herself thing, but, even in broad daylight, Taylor wasn't keen on being alone out here.

～

Her mother squinted at the sun like the position meant something to her. 'Lucky I put the potatoes and damper in a while ago.'

Taylor scowled at her useless and almost-dead phone. Nearly six. Somehow the day had sped past, although all she'd done was avoid talking about anything meaningful, prepare meals, stare at a textbook, take a siesta inside the hotbox of a tent and collect wood. Well, they'd collected wood until a couple of hissing, spitting lizards, locked in some kind of courtship ritual or mating dance, scared the heck out of her. Apparently, they didn't appreciate an audience.

'I'll do some sausages, too?'

'Unrefrigerated meat? Gastro is a thing, you know.'

'See, tofu would have been better. In any case, the ice bricks are still frozen. So the sausages will be fine.'

'And I repeat, no thanks.' Instead, Taylor split the damper and potatoes open, smothering them with butter and baked beans. Safe carbs and canned goods.

Mum hoed into her plateful of salmonella like it was lobster, then held up the biscuit packet. 'Do we try s'mores again?'

'Not a chance. How did you screw them up anyway?'

'No idea.'

'If I had internet, I could tell you.'

'You want to be wary of being too reliant on technology,' Mum said.

'Probably not a great thing to say to a doctor.'

'I'm sure medicine allows for an organic approach.'

'I'm sure science doesn't.'

'That reminds me,' Mum said. 'About our discussion last night. You pointed out that you need to get back for uni. And of course, you're right. But after your exams, I'm thinking of coming back here.'

'For Christmas, you mean? I know they don't like leaving the farm, but perhaps the Grands could fly to us, instead?' Although the end-of-year holidays hit close to three months, Taylor didn't have time to come here again. The window before Zac headed off on tour was closing by the day.

Mum rescued a piece of foil from the ground, crumpling it smaller and smaller, ignoring the black ash on her hands. 'Your grandparents are getting older.'

'Beats the alternative.' The gallows humour of med school was rubbing off on her.

'More frail. They think—and I agree—it would be wise if I was closer to them. So I'm thinking of moving.'

'You can't be serious.' Taylor's aluminium pan dropped to the dirt as she flung her arm wide. 'Here? We'll never see you. It's not like this is the most accessible spot in the world.' She was supposed to be the one who eventually moved out of home, her parents the ones who got to miss *her*. Not the other way around.

'Dad and I've discussed it. Tried to work out what is best for you.'

'Wait, what? Why are you bringing *me* into this?' Taylor grabbed her crucifix, zipping it up and down the chain. 'This has nothing to do with me.'

Mum focused on stirring the embers with a stick. 'Tay, we can't keep the house in Sydney. You know Dad's at the mines most of the time; we can't afford to have the house sitting empty.'

'The house won't be empty. I'll be there.' Excitement at the thought of having the house to herself warred with sadness at Mum's desertion. 'And Dad'll use it on his fly-out week each month.'

Sorrow pulled down the corners of her mother's mouth. 'Dad and I need to sell and split the money so we can both get a new start. Somewhere smaller, more affordable.'

'You mean I'm homeless?'

'That's a bit of an overreaction, though finding somewhere to rent is going to be a problem. Dad will bunk with mates, but you . . .?'

Taylor rubbed her temple where a migraine throbbed a dull warning. 'I'll find someone to share with.' She was already mentally running through her friends, although the Sydney rental market meant most lived at home.

'On a part-time income? I don't think that's going to be feasible. And obviously, with your current study load, you can't work more hours.' Her mother sighed. 'Dad and I've gone over the figures so many times, trying to see if there's any way we can support you but, at least initially, we're going to have a lot of extra expenses ourselves.'

'So you expect me to quit med school?' Taylor said, a knot of fear twisting in her stomach. She'd been focused on medicine since junior high school and her parents had greedily claimed bragging rights over every minor achievement.

'Of course not.' Mum's vehement reply was reassuring. 'But I was hoping that, once you saw the farm again, you'd want to move here, too. We could live with Gran and Gramps—'

Taylor uttered an incredulous bark of laughter.

Mum moved into her personal space as though she could crowd out her negativity. 'You could transfer, Tay.

Adelaide Uni has an outstanding reputation in medicine. Or there's Flinders, if you prefer.'

'Outstanding in South Australia, maybe. Not the real world.' Her legs suddenly unsteady, Taylor dropped into a camp chair. 'You can't seriously think I'm going to change universities because you two are having a midlife crisis? What about my job? My plans? My friends?' *What about Zac?* 'I can't simply switch unis, you do realise that? It doesn't work that way.'

'I'm sure the universities must have some kind of reciprocal agreement.' Mum waved her hand, either shooing flies or the problem she didn't want to deal with. 'Dad thinks this would be the best idea, and you know he'll have considered it from every angle.'

That was terrifyingly true. Taylor also recognised her mother was trying to lay the blame for this mess at Dad's doorstep, rather than give him any credit.

Mum picked up Taylor's pan, banging it against hers. She placed one inside the other, then reversed the order. 'I'm sorry about the timing. But the fact is you have no means to support yourself, no rental history, and because of your age, it seems you're probably not eligible for anything useful from the government. If you can come up with a viable alternative, fine. But moving here is *logical*.' The least logical person Taylor had ever known, Mum intoned the word as though it held magical properties. 'And whichever uni, you'll get the same qualification and be able to pursue your dream.'

'*My* dream?' Sudden exhaustion washed over Taylor in a crippling wave. It seemed that for months now she had been striving harder and harder, pursuing focus and drive with increasing intensity. But had she been chasing her dream or attempting to somehow ward off this very moment? Had the ambition to become a doctor ever truly been hers, or had she allowed herself to be shaped by her parents' desires, unwittingly adopting their dream at an early age, believing it would bind her parents, her family, together? The realisation that perhaps she didn't have the autonomy she'd always thought was chilling.

Taylor swallowed the fear. 'This is a terrific way to inform me you're splitting up, by the way. Very caring.' She deliberately disregarded the number of times Mum had tried to bring up the matter over the last few months.

'As you're so fond of pointing out, you're no longer a child. Dad and I've made this decision for our own emotional wellbeing.'

Taylor's camp chair tumbled backward as she thrust to her feet. 'You literally spent years encouraging me to commit to something that will affect the next five decades of my life, but now you're pulling it out from under me, and I'm not even consulted? You know what? That's fine. Do whatever you want.' Appalled at her own childishness, she gulped for breath. 'Move. Divorce. Tear our family apart. I don't care.'

Except, she did. Because no matter how much of an adult she was, her parents' divorce made a lie of every Happy Birthday, every Merry Christmas, every family holiday. She would never be able to look back at photos without trying to discern the truth: At what point had they started pretending? Or had their happy family only ever been a juvenile fantasy?

6

Anna

Mother burst into tears, surveying their charred property as a neighbour helped her from their dray. Anna retreated from the protection of the doorway; Mother had not yet seen the evidence of Liesl's occupation of the house.

Tears running unchecked down her face, Mother waddled across the threshold, toward Anna and Emilie, stretching her arms to embrace them both. The child in her belly kicked in fierce protest. 'I couldn't bear to lose another of you, my Lieblings, not another,' she sobbed.

Anna peered over Mother's neatly coiled hair as Father appeared in the doorway. He'd gruffly talk some sense into her or, true to form, make a jest. To her astonishment, his eyes glistened in a face blackened by soot. He crossed the room swiftly and wrapped his arms around all three of them.

'Well done, Anna, my Engelein. Well done.'

Pain shot through her back and she struggled from the embrace. She was hardly an angel. She had done nothing that anyone else wouldn't have done. Well, anyone except perhaps Emilie. Who now sniffled into Father's shoulder.

His face drawn and severe, Dieter stomped inside, knocking ash from his boots. A glance from Mother, and he stooped to unlace and remove them. Despite the cow, Mother was not about to relax the rules to *that* extent.

He hung his hat and jacket on the pegs near the door, then ran a hand across his face, streaking the soot. 'We've lost the feed paddock to the north, but everything south escaped. However, it seems Mäuschen is in sore need of cooking lessons. This time she's managed to blacken even the outside of the bakehouse walls. The structure remains sound though.'

Foolish tears pricked Anna's eyes and Dieter strode across the crowded room, taking her elbow as she swayed.

'Sit, Anna. I tease. You did well. You know the lime for the walls must be baked anyway. Just think, the fire saved Father and me a job.'

Father grunted. 'Yass, and the burned ground around the house is also goot. Ve vill not have to vatch for the snakes so much,' he said, his accent unusually thick.

Anna barely understood Father's words, exhaustion seeming to dull her brain. Fingers curling around the arms of the rocking chair, she lowered herself gingerly. The gleam from years of polishing by forearms and palms caught her eye and she glanced down. The breath stilled in her throat. She wore Luke Hartmann's jacket—and little else. Grimy fingers splayed, she desperately tried to cover herself. She sat before her father and brother in no more than her underclothes!

Full realisation rushed in, the shame scalding her cheeks. It was not only Father and Dieter who had seen her in this state. Now the tears truly started and she lurched from the chair, hobbling into her sleeping area.

'Anna? Anna, are you all right?' Dieter's voice was close to the curtain, but only Mother or Emilie would venture beyond it.

Father was gruff with concern. 'Vat is wrong with her? She is hurt?'

'Johann, she is in her underclothes. Men saw her.' Mother's appalled tone cemented Anna's humiliation.

'Johanna, even after almost thirty years, you don't understand it is different here?' Father grumbled. 'You expect too much from our girls. Our daughter saved the farm. This is not the country for ladylike behaviour.'

Anna pulled the embroidered comforter over her head, confusion pounding at her temples. She longed to emulate her elegant mother, her mind shying from the words that proved her a disappointment. But she also didn't dare dwell on their near escape. The fear, the stench of incinerated animals, the sounds of death and the terror of the encroaching flames all lurked, waiting to haunt her sleep.

Only one image could chase away the nightmares or impart any beauty to the horrendous day.

Twilight-shaded eyes.

Hands trembling, she pulled the lapel of Luke's jacket across her face. Inhaled deeply.

The only smell was smoke.

And that made her cry even harder.

⁓

It had been a week since the bushfire, yet still her family treated Anna as though she were fragile. The attention was unwarranted. Although an ugly suppurating burn covered eight inches of her forearm and hand, and she hobbled on the tender soles of her feet, the graze on her shoulder had scabbed and now itched satisfyingly. Her back ached only a little—less each time Mother tucked a corked bottle filled with hot water behind her.

She had been excused most duties. Emilie even tried not to sulk too much about picking up her chores. Each evening, Emilie and Mother worked together, poring over some sewing task, but Anna didn't mind that they excluded her. Taking advantage of the unusual leniency, she curled near the oil lamp with a hot water bottle and her Christmas gift. *Great Expectations* by Mr Charles Dickens was one of five books in their house—not including die Bibel—and the first she could call her own.

Mother had taught all of her children to read. Anna was slow, her finger tracing each line as she squinted in the wavering light. After three months of ownership, she was on page one hundred and fourteen. Even if she had not found the practice so laborious, there was usually little opportunity to read during the day and scant light by which to read at night.

Although Emilie never picked up a book herself, she taunted that Anna's lips moved as she sounded out the unfamiliar words—and there were so many. But Father had promised that if she finished the book, he would purchase the next volume when the autumn lambs were sold.

Her heart squeezed at the thought. Father and Dieter tried to downplay it, but they'd lost both their stock and the feed for the surviving sheep in the fire. It would be a frugal year.

Mother and Dieter colluded at the dining table, blonde and dark heads bent close to one another. They shot glances toward her, which was somewhat unsettling. She snapped the book shut.

Pushing her unwieldy bulk from the chair, Mother crooked her finger at Emilie. Then she winced, stooping over the table. One hand resting on the pink-flowered teapot, she pressed the other into the small of her back, her mouth tightening. As she caught Anna's gaze, she forced her lips into a smile, her face softening. 'Anna, it is Emilie's turn to attend church tomorrow, but she is happy for you to take her place.'

Anna glanced to Emilie, expecting her anger. Church was an outing that neither of them liked to miss. Their turns fell only once each month, as someone must remain at home to prepare the luncheon and see to the chores. The service was one of few chances they had to visit with friends from the district, exchanging news and gossip.

Her fair curls jostling, Emilie nodded encouragement, tripping lightly toward Anna in her thin house slippers. Emilie moved with a balletic grace even when she wore the ugly yard boots that forced Anna to wade like a farmhand. 'Yes, Anna, do take my place.'

She shook her head. Whatever Emilie's reason, Anna didn't care to leave the house. She *couldn't* leave the house. The ugly burn on the back of her hand, thickly salved and bandaged, should provide excuse enough to hide.

Because she couldn't go beyond these walls. Ever.

'Come, Mäuschen,' Dieter said. 'I need your company. Besides, I wish to speak with you about something.'

Caroline Schenscher. Anna indicated Mother and then the twins, who were tucked into the single pallet cot against the wall. 'There would be little opportunity for conversation, Dieter.'

He leaned one shoulder against the doorframe, pulling on his boots. 'Only us, Anna.'

She raised her eyebrows at Mother, begging explanation.

Mother patted her stomach. 'I think I shall be permitted one week of non-attendance. The journey becomes uncomfortable. And if I do not attend, wild horses will not drag your father there.'

'I cannot go,' Anna muttered. 'I've nothing to wear.' She referred not to her dress, but to the ruined knickerbockers. Cut into thin strips, they would form another round of the rag rug, which Mother had scrubbed clean of the smoky taint.

'Dieter, please leave us,' Mother said.

Anna flinched. For Dieter to be dismissed, she must be in for a dreadful reprimand. She replayed the last week in her mind, but could think of no transgression beyond the ordinary. There may have been harsh words to Emilie, and she did leave the hairbrush on the kitchen table, but normally she would be disciplined for such misbehaviours in Dieter's presence.

Mother squeezed her shoulder as the door closed behind Dieter. 'Look, Liebling.'

Emilie shadowed Mother, her hands behind her back. With a triumphant flourish, she produced a bundle of material, shaking it loose in front of her dark dress.

Great Expectations slid from Anna's hands. With trembling fingers, she brushed the fine linen her sister held. Between them, Mother and Emilie had produced the most beautiful pair of knickerbockers she'd ever seen. Slightly shorter than her scorched pair and trimmed with festoons of softest lace, they were narrow in the leg and open at the crotch.

'Emilie and I decided not to emulate the new fashion of stitching the centre seam,' Mother said. 'The notion is ludicrous, as your corset would make it impossible to bend to manipulate the undergarment. But, other than that, we've followed the latest templates. This is the height of fashion.'

The fabric was soft under her roughened fingertips and Anna snatched her hand back. 'But the material?' She had recognised it immediately: the bolt stored in Mother's Aussteuerschrank in hope of their eventual marriages. As Emilie had far more likelihood of attaining that happy union, Anna feared she had stolen from her sister.

'Emilie wanted to find a way to thank you. As we all did. There's more.' Mother's eyes glinted mischievously in a flare from the lamp. 'Although I seem to carry a bustle before me at the moment, I think it time you have your own, to affix in the appropriate spot. You are no longer a child, but a young lady. Emilie, would you please?'

Emilie disappeared behind the curtain. She returned, her arms piled high with an extravagance of material. Shaking it free, she displayed a detachable bustle skirt, the panels of sky-blue and white-striped cotton a perfect match for Anna's Sunday dress. Seven tiers of fabric gathered into a cascading waterfall from a waist dotted with tiny buttons, used to attach the skirt to the rear of her bodice.

She had only graduated to full-length skirts a year ago. A bustle was beyond her wildest dreams.

'I trimmed your bonnet to match,' Emilie offered shyly.

Anna pulled back, not wanting to see. There was only one thing with which Emilie could have trimmed her bonnet, and shame flamed her cheeks as all the petty thoughts she'd ever had about her sister crowded her mind.

Emilie produced the hat, the blue ribbon Dieter purchased for her glory box tied around the crown and folded into a soft bow on one side.

Her mother and sister beamed, so happy with themselves it was hard for Anna to find her voice. 'I don't want to go,' she whispered. Yet her fingers strayed to the beautiful fabric. Some wild, unchaste part of her had been unleashed and she longed to parade it.

Emilie dropped the bustle over the new knickerbockers as Dieter leaned around the doorjamb.

'All set, then?'

Anna shook her head, beseeching him with her eyes. 'I can't go. Not out there.' Her voice trembled and her knee jiggled up and down. She pressed her palm against it. Dieter would understand, he always did.

Not pausing to remove his boots, Dieter crossed the room, dropping to his haunches alongside her hard-backed chair. 'Anna, remember when you fell off Arabella and Father told you to get right back up there? You did as he tasked you. And it was nowhere near as bad as you anticipated, correct?'

She tried to nod, but her teeth chattered.

'Mäuschen, this is the same. Once you have faced the brethren, you will find it isn't so terrible. You have no need for fear.'

'But Dieter, they saw . . .' She could not finish the sentence, could not mention what it was a dozen or more men saw.

What one particular man saw.

Her nails bit into her knee.

'They saw a brave young lady fighting off a bushfire. Nothing more.' Dieter compressed his lips into a firm line, then his voice dropped deeper. 'Believe me, sister, no one will dare say any different.'

7

Taylor

Taylor woke coughing. Smoke grated the back of her throat.

Flat on her back, she scowled at the pitched nylon roof. This time she recalled the dream more vividly. Women in long dresses, the hems sweeping the dust of an arid, isolated farm. Men in braces and Sunday hats. Privation and poverty. The dream had been disconcertingly realistic and, even after waking, she wanted to pursue the threads, find out how the story ended. Had Anna gone to church? Had she seen the handsome Luke again? The echo of the dream left a gnawing ache of unfulfilled longing deep inside her and she didn't want to crawl from her sleeping bag and lose the fantasy.

Or perhaps she simply didn't want to face her own reality, one where, despite being an adult, she was still affected by the whims of her parents.

She cleared her throat. Mum must have thrown magic mushrooms or something equally organic into the ashes of their campfire, causing her to dream of a bushfire.

They hadn't spoken after Taylor stormed to bed, although zipping the tent flap shut had lacked the satisfying finality of a slammed door. Particularly as Mum had later needed to unzip the tent and crawl in alongside her while Taylor lay stiff and silent, still burning with resentment. She hadn't wanted to think about Mum moving so far away, so she'd lain awake—Mum's rock somehow having migrated to her side of the tent—wondering whether she really had taken on medicine to make her parents proud. Now, immersed in their own lives, it seemed they didn't care what she did, whether she succeeded. She should feel betrayed, but she just felt . . . exhausted. Somewhere in the almost twenty years of study, she'd lost her way, perhaps lost her passion.

'Coffee's hot,' Mum called, her voice raised over the crackle and snap of burning twigs.

Evidently, they were pretending last night hadn't happened. Mum was likely still under the misconception that changing uni was an option, as simple as switching the logo on her high school jumper.

As Taylor emerged from the tent, a keening filled the air.

Mum stumbled back from the campfire. 'Good lord, what is that?'

'Sap.' Taylor poked a stick into the flames, stirring at the molten drips of gum that let off a high-pitched whistle as they melted.

'How do you know that?'

Taylor squinted at the goo. 'Wonders of hypnopedia, I guess.' She often left the TV on for company as she studied into the small hours.

Mum eyed the coals dubiously. 'Come on, then. I've unhooked the car. We may as well head over to the house and grab a shower rather than cook breakfast on . . . that.' She nudged a smouldering twig with her foot.

Taylor raked her fingers through her hair, trying to catch the flyaways in a ponytail. 'Are the Grands already in on your decision?'

'No, Tay.' Mum's tone was carefully neutral. 'I wanted to discuss it with you first.'

'Discuss!' she snorted as she headed for the car. 'Do you want a dictionary to check that definition?'

$\backsim$

'A scone? Or how about a jelly cake, love?' Gran said as she fussed around the kitchen, setting the scrubbed table with yellow gingham placemats. 'I got a lovely recipe from Tracey over at the CWA. She puts dehydrated strawberries into the sponge and chopped fresh strawberries in the cream. Such a simple trick, but goodness me—'

'—it makes a difference,' Gramps finished approvingly.

A jam jar filled with twigs covered in balls of fluffy wattle sat in the centre of the table. Taylor wondered whether the small mound of pine cones alongside had a purpose, or if her grandparents were into aesthetics. The comfortable but slightly scruffy furniture she had noticed on her tour of the house a couple of days earlier didn't make that seem likely.

Despite the hour, the room smelled deliciously of baking. Her stomach rumbled. She covered the noise by shifting her chair as she leaned forward to fill her teacup from the blue china pot. Odd. She was sure the pot had been white with pink roses a couple of days ago.

'You should have let me know you'd be here for breakfast, Michelle. I'd have done bacon and eggs.' Gran barely paused for breath, her head bobbing like a little grey sparrow as she cast around the room, apparently looking for more food, as though they were in imminent danger of starving.

'Michelle would want that *faking* stuff, not bacon, wouldn't you, love?' Gramps said.

'Facon, Dad.' Mum sounded weary and Taylor wondered if perhaps she hadn't slept well either.

'Sounds like an American politician,' Gramps said.

'Unhealthy, is what it sounds,' Gran reproved, thickly buttering a scone and placing slices of cheese on it. 'Nothing wrong with a nice rasher of—'

'—streaky bacon,' Gramps finished, rubbing his belly.

Taylor chuckled. 'Bacon would be fantastic, but I'm with you, Gran. Can't beat cake for breakfast.'

'Or I have some nice organic muesli made up, Michelle?' Gran suggested.

'Go with that,' Gramps advised from the far end of the table. 'Needs some shredded wheat with it to make it edible, but Magpie's muesli will—'

'—line your stomach,' Gran said, poking hairpins into her bun to secure errant silver strands. 'And I keep telling you, there's no point me making you organic muesli if you add that commercial rubbish to it.'

82

Mum pushed aside her plate. 'I'm going to grab a shower.'

Taylor stabbed a pink, coconut-freckled jelly cake with her fork. 'Gramps, do you get service? I've got nothing.' She tilted her phone to show him the lack of reception, but immediately jerked it back, not ready for questions about the wallpaper of Zac, his wiry torso inked with black Celtic designs. Even without a signal, she'd been able to spend hours looking through their photos and that made her feel a little closer to him.

'Runs off the satellite, Peach, so can be a bit dicky.' Gramps hiked a thumb toward the back door. 'Go sit on the garden wall near the toilet. Sometimes—'

'—you get a flicker out there,' Gran said. 'Or you can use the landline, love.'

Evidently, poor mobile service was one of the perks of country living. Along with an outdoor loo.

Following the short cement path up to the outhouse, Taylor found the brick wall and straddled it. Warmth from the morning sun already radiated from it, cosying the walled garden. Her heart leaped as the phone pinged, missed calls and messages flashing onto the screen.

None were from Zac.

Most were Cassie. Taylor chuckled—she'd have to check her phone plan had unlimited overseas hours before Cassie headed to Europe at the end of the year. Decades back they'd bonded over comparing their Disney Princess knickers on the monkey bars at playgroup. Their friendship survived through primary school and into the silk-and-lace lingerie years. They'd seen less of each other once Taylor had started her post grad, and if she was honest, lately she had pretty much deserted Cassie for Zac. But Cassie, who was never short of male company, knew how it was in that first heady rush of desire.

Taylor swiped back to a photo of Zac, frowning. Was it *more* than desire? Zac's passion and enthusiasm for his career were contagious. He was authentic, raw and extreme, living life to the full. Perhaps that was what she liked: Zac wasn't constrained by the rigid confines that bound her life, and that made him exciting and desirable. In classic 'absence makes the heart grow fonder' fashion, being away from him actually hurt, the pain manifesting as a tightness in her chest. Psychogenic, she knew. Yet, in a non-literal sense, being apart from Zac was breaking her heart.

Which was ridiculous. She didn't have time for that kind of thing.

Teeth worrying at her fingernail, she stared across the surprisingly lush paddocks as she waited for the call to connect. Grassy stems bore heavy seed heads, the crop undulating in an invisible breeze, a green ocean flowing to the horizon.

Zac didn't answer, and the call cut out. He didn't have a message service, maintaining that anyone who really wanted him would call back.

She called back.

After the third try, she dialled a different number.

'Yo. Whaddup, girlfriend?'

'That greeting, for starters. Gangsta made a comeback while I've been gone?'

Cassie snorted. The sound of wind chimes tinkled through the phone and Taylor imagined her friend lounging beside her pool, the comforting hum of traffic in the background, the neighbours' townhouses shading the paved oasis. 'Don't think you've been gone long enough for that particular miracle. How's it going over in the boonies?'

Taylor dragged her fingertips across her forehead. 'Mum's moving out.'

'The divorce finally a thing, huh? Shame you're too old to benefit from double birthday presents and parental manipulation. Will she get a place with a pool?'

'Do they have swimming pools in South Australia?'

'You're shitting me. South Australia? For real?'

'For real.' Taylor turned her head to avoid a bee-sized blowfly that blundered across the struggling lawn to the fishpond Gramps had so proudly shown her on the way back in from feeding the ravens. He'd gone into enthusiastic detail about how he'd dug and lined it, how many fish Gran had in there, and how often they liked to be fed. How Gran insisted the dirt constantly be cleaned from the bottom, although he believed the fish liked a little mud, a bit of entertainment to poke around in. Her grandfather was kind of hilarious.

'You're going to miss her,' Cassie said with a rare flash of empathy.

'According to Mum, I won't. Because supposedly, I'm going with.'

'What? Why would you? Man, I love Michelle to bits, but she's really whack sometimes. Why would anyone in their right mind move to South Australia?'

'Long story. Finances. Elderly parents. Heavy on the et cetera.'

'Okay, so that covers her. But did you miss the bit a couple of years back where we turned twenty-one? I mean, I know it was a wild party and all, but ... Listen, your folks made their bed. What they do in it is their business.'

Taylor laughed mirthlessly. 'I guess they're not doing anything in it, and that's part of the problem.'

'Hard pass. My brain can't handle thinking of Michelle and Mike in that way. Specially not this early in the morning. But however their divorce goes down, your *mum* is not your responsibility, Tay.'

'I know. Yet here I am, stuck in the middle. If I don't go with Mum, she's hurt. I do go, and Dad thinks I'm bailing on him, plus my life is completely screwed.' She rubbed her forehead again. She couldn't move to Settlers Bridge. But the thought of Mum trying to make a life on her own ...

The occasional squirt from the fountain spattered into an old zinc bucket balanced on the pavers, the mottled grey dampness an ever-changing pattern. Taylor tipped her head to one side as something nagged at the recesses of her mind. An elusive thought flitting behind shadows and mist. Fragments of last night's dream? Not really memories, more like *feelings*. Fear and determination. Emotions so raw, they shivered through her.

'Tay? You still there?'

She dragged her attention back. 'Unfortunately. Hey, later on, can you call Zac for me? I can't get through and I'm not sure if it's his phone or because there's basically no service here.'

'Really?'

'Yeah, dead zone.'

'I meant you really want *me* to call the Player?'

'Cass, give it a rest.' Her sleepless night was beginning to tell, her left eye ticcing in time with her pounding head. 'I don't know why you're so down on him. Just let him know to keep trying my number. If he texts, I'll get it at some point.'

'Yeah, sure. But anyway, back to the important bit—moving?'

'Mmm. Not happening, obviously.' She had a life, and every facet of it belonged in Sydney. Cassie was right, Taylor was not her mother's keeper. While she had no idea how she'd work out the finances—and the issue was a whole lot of extra stress she simply didn't need—checking whether she was eligible for any kind of government assistance would be a starting point. Mum's easy dismissal of the likelihood was hardly reliable. 'Can you come up with a list of anyone you know looking for a flatmate? And if you want to rethink your plan of disappearing to Europe . . .' There was no chance of that; Cassie had been hanging out for her dad's new posting. 'Call you later, okay?'

Grass crackled beneath her feet as she approached the pond. The bucket rang hollow under the strike of her boot. Her hand twitched, forming an empty fist. She knew exactly how the cracked wooden handle would feel against her palm. Inexplicable fear butterflied in her stomach as the sour odour of smouldering hessian filled her nose. As if she'd know what that smelled like, she thought with an dismissive toss of her head.

Taylor turned her back to the pond, keying Dad's number into her phone. The call went to his service, so she texted.

Hey, Dad, I missed the game, who won?

Dad always asked her to watch with him, but she'd avoided it since she was about twelve. Wasn't even sure who was playing. Maybe, when they got back, she'd catch a game. There was no hardship in watching hot guys in short shorts.

'Tay-lor.' Gran drew out the two syllables. 'Mum's out of the shower. You need to hurry before the cold water fills up the service.'

Whatever Gran was talking about with such dire inflection was doubtless something nasty that wouldn't happen if her grandparents had opted for a normal retirement near the beach. In Sydney.

Gramps held the back door open. 'C'mon, Peach, in or out, don't dither. The flies sure won't. I'm going down the yard to fetch you some eggs to take back to camp.'

The screen door bit her heels as he let go. Though he was a big guy, broad-shouldered and rotund, somehow Gramps seemed hollow, clutching a walking stick and rolling on the outside edges of his feet as he tottered to the side gate. Taylor's fingers twitched toward the door handle. She could run down to the hen house in the middle of the farmyard and collect the eggs before he made it out of the garden.

But it was his fault that Mum was moving.

8

Taylor

She couldn't call Zac with only fifty centimetres and a packet of organic biscuits separating her from Mum in the car, but she could text. One more text wouldn't look clingy.

Hey Zac.

Her phone beeped in instant response.

Hey princess, where you been?

She rolled her eyes, but caressed his image with her thumb.

Just escaped Settlers Bridge. We're
heading home a few days early because
the weather's coming in.

Not to mention that, having divulged the news that had obviously been eating her up for months, Mum was in a hurry to tie up loose ends in Sydney. It was typical of her to be so disorganised and reactive that they ended up driving the vast distance twice in less than five days.

> Tag-teaming and driving straight
> through. Hanging to see you.

> I want to SEE you more. xox ;-)

She sagged against the window, holding in a smile as anticipation tickled through her chest.

> I promise you will xx

> Can't wait. But right now I gotta go :-(
> Call me when you get back xox

Mum shook a packet of seaweed crackers at her. 'That Zac? What's up?'

Taylor frowned at her phone, then resolutely put it in the glovebox. Zac was always busy and not the kind of guy who devoted time to staring at a screen. 'Nothing.'

She should talk to Mum. Until the past year, they had been close, more like sisters, and this was one of the last times they would do anything together. The thought of not seeing Mum almost every day, of not having her as a sounding board, of not getting irritated at her quirks, yet always running to her with any little problem, was unfathomable.

Her breath caught unevenly in her chest and she coughed to hide the sudden welling of tears. She had to remember that the disconnection, both physical and emotional, was Mum's choice. Not hers.

A tractor beetled across the horizon. The massive machine, looming large on the skyline, would be a vast improvement on working the land with one of the heavy plough horses the men had ridden to Anna's aid in Taylor's dreams. Perhaps the benefits of modern agriculture included less labour for animals and more time for farmers to chase love and dreams?

She clicked her tongue in irritation. LSD was made from fungus—maybe there'd been something similar growing on the wood they'd tossed on the campfire, giving the smoke hallucinogenic qualities. Because, just like the come-down from a trip, the dreams of a time long-gone left Taylor oddly pensive, feeling that something precious had slipped away and might never again be found. She tapped her teeth as she pondered the effect.

'Seven thousand dollars of braces,' Mum reminded her.

Hallucinogen persisting perception disorder was rare but Taylor couldn't drag her mind from the dreams. Did the origin really matter, though? Unlike reality, her dreams couldn't cause pain.

～

It took forever to wind through the outskirts of Sydney, the traffic lights innumerable, daylight fading fast. Gardens drooped beneath the weight of burgeoning spring greenery, the verges overgrown with spongy lawn. Taylor rolled up her window to close out the air, thick with rubber and petrol.

Illuminated by the glow of streetlights, home looked the same as it always had. It shouldn't. It could never be the same. It was an empty shell, temporarily holding their possessions. Forever holding the lies.

'Dad's home.' Mum lifted her chin toward the light in the upstairs study window. Her voice held a false note like she was trying too hard to sound happy.

'Yep.' Taylor wished he wasn't. How could she face him, knowing they weren't truly a family anymore? Would Dad assume her trip with Mum meant she'd chosen sides?

Mum turned off the ignition and smiled unseeingly in Taylor's direction. 'Leave the bags, love. We'll sort them tomorrow. I'm too beat to do anything but crash tonight.'

As usual they ignored the front door, perched above a crooked dog leg of nine stairs. Instead, Mum pushed open the wooden gate that led up a steeply sloped, dusk-shadowed side passage, the tangled clematis scenting the air with almond.

She unlocked the back door and peered around it as though she expected the interior of the house to have changed. 'Looks like Dad's busy. I'm going to have a shower and head for bed.'

Taylor's shoulders slumped. She'd nursed a brief fantasy that her parents might be glad to see one another. If Dad opened his study door, greeted them like he used to when she and Mum had been shopping all day, then maybe things could stay the same. Not only for her, not only because she wanted to keep her home, but because she wanted to keep her family. Even though she was old enough that her parents' divorce shouldn't hurt.

''Night, love.'

'Yeah, 'night, Mum. Hey, how about we look up how to do those s'mores right tomorrow?' She cringed. Why had she suggested that? As though she clung to the good bits of their holiday. The happy memories.

'Sure, baby.' Mum's door clicked shut.

Taylor walked to her bedroom and dropped onto her bed, staring at the pale blue walls. Nothing new to see. Her room was neat and tidy, as she'd left it. A few clothes on the back of a hard chair. Piles of textbooks and reams of notes scrawled on odd pieces of paper littered the desk. A long dressing table took up most of the third wall, the surface cluttered with cosmetics, a hairdryer and two straighteners. Photos, pinned, taped or framed, covered the wall above it: friends, senior formal, graduation of both school and uni; her and Cassie at so many different ages. Collages of family snaps, interspersed with calligraphy inspirationals. *Peace. Love. Hope. Family.*

Taylor clenched her fists. Such trite, ridiculous words. As if pinning them to the wall could magically invoke togetherness.

She plugged her charger in. Before she called Zac, she'd catch up with Cassie.

'Hey, Tay, back in the twenty-first century?'

'Ha. Funny you'd say that. I had the weirdest dreams the last couple of nights; remind me to tell you about them.' She slumped on the bed, shucking off her shoes. 'Want to hang tomorrow?'

'Sure thing. It's going to crack thirty. Got to love a spring like this. Bring your bikini, we'll swim.'

Swim was a euphemism for float around in the tepid water. They hadn't done anything more energetic since they were about thirteen. 'Sure.'

'Zac got a gig? I thought you'd be rushing to meet up with him tonight.'

'He has, but I'm kind of wrecked. Not in the mood for hitting the club.'

'Hmm.' Cassie sounded dubious. 'In the mood for hitting on him, though, right? I mean, he's a douche, but there's no denying he's a hot douche. A hot douche who's been left alone for a week.'

'I'm aware.' Cassie never bothered with a filter, but her constant bagging-out of Zac was getting irritating.

'Have you called him? I tried, but he didn't pick up.'

'Yeah, he's pretty shit with the phone.'

'Makes a long-distance relationship out of the question then, doesn't it? Not that there's any, ah, *tangible benefit* in long distance.' Cassie dropped her voice lewdly.

'Long distance is definitely not on the cards.'

'Ah, so if the douche boy means my best girl will be staying here, maybe I can almost bring myself to like him.'

'Big of you. Except you're running out on me anyway, remember? Paris and all that jazz?'

'That's only for a few months, though. So we just need to arrange for Mr Hot Douche to keep you busy for a while and I'll be back before you know it. Maybe we can get a place together at Bondi? You know how good I look on the beach.'

'Clearly you're planning for me to win the lotto while you're away.' Taylor tapped her chest. 'Struggling student. Poor as the proverbial, remember?'

'Problem for another day,' Cassie said breezily. 'Step one, sort your man, so I know you're *taken care of* while I'm away.' She giggled, clearly enjoying her innuendo.

Having Cassie so flippantly dismiss her problems—even though she didn't offer any viable solutions—did make them seem more surmountable. 'I'm glad you at least stopped short of actually saying "wink wink",' Taylor said dryly. 'But if I go see him tomorrow, I'll have to blow you off. You won't be mad?'

'Course I will. But I'll forgive you. Only if you stop playing with that bloody necklace, though. The noise is like a dentist's drill in my brain.'

'Not like you were using that particular organ,' she teased. 'I'll let you know when we can catch up, okay?'

~

A couple of hours later, after she'd showered and unpacked, Zac picked up on the third ring.

'Yeah.' His voice slurred wearily.

'Hey.' Taylor cradled the phone closer. 'I didn't think I'd catch you.'

'Princess, you back?' He instantly sounded awake, his voice embracing her.

Comforter tucked under her chin, Taylor curled onto the bed. 'I missed you.'

'When do I get to see you?'

'I've got to catch up on uni; I didn't get anything done while I was away. But I guess that can wait another day, so how about tomorrow?'

'Ah, I might be busy.'

'A daytime gig? That's different. I could come along.'

Bedding rustled, Zac's voice becoming momentarily distant. 'It's kind of a closed-room, private sesh.'

'Oh.' Disappointment threatened her bubble. 'Well, I guess that's cool.'

'Sure. Hey, princess, I did something today.'

'Tell me more.'

'I finished that song I promised I'd write for you. The guys and I played it through. Came out sweet as.'

'You're kidding?' Zac carried a pen in a special pocket sewn inside his trademark slashed-leather waistcoat. Though she'd initially thought the habit pretentious, he said it was because he liked to commit his inspiration to paper, so the words would last forever. 'Zac, that's . . .'

He chuckled as she trailed off. 'You know there'll be a price, right?'

She grinned. The first time they'd met, Zac had bought her a drink at the club. As she had reached for it, he'd held the glass over his head and tapped a finger on his lips, clearly intimating that the drink came at a price. One she'd been more than happy to pay. She closed her eyes, remembering that first kiss, the electricity, the promise of the moment.

Down the hall, a door slammed. Then another. Hushed voices from her parents' room—Mum's room, really. Dad's bed was in the study, and they all stuck to the lie about him snoring.

At least they wouldn't have to do that anymore.

The voices down the hall grew louder. Now she strained not to hear them. There was something awkward, almost obscene, in being able to hear her parents' intimate arguments when she was an adult.

'Princess, you listening?' Zac said.

'Sorry. Crap line,' she lied. Her stomach clenched. In public, her parents pretended a cold civility. Behind closed doors, they hated each other. Considering the years they'd spent reprimanding her for playing music too loud, they should know the plasterboard walls did nothing to block raised voices.

'You told her? You had no right.'

'. . . seemed like the moment . . . not a child . . .' Mum's low voice was harder to pick out than her father's bark, but the meaning was clear.

'No. We never agreed to that, Michelle.'

'Are you still there?' Zac's voice startled Taylor.

She stared at the phone in her white-knuckled grip. Cleared her throat. Loudly, hoping Mum and Dad would hear, realise that she could hear them. 'Sorry. Listen, this line is really bad. I have to go. I'll call you tomorrow.'

Not waiting for the ''Night, princess' she'd longed for all week, she disconnected. Pulled up the covers to muffle the voices. Just like she had when she was a kid, and hadn't realised where the arguments could lead, hadn't recognised the slow, poisonous finality of harsh words thrown in anger.

9
Anna

Early April 1877

Dieter concentrated on the rutted road, apparently lost in his thoughts. Arabella's steady pace meant the journey to church would take more than an hour, and Anna wished her brother would talk as he had promised. Distract her from the dread that cramped her stomach. For the first time in her life, the reason for her fear was not something she dare raise with her brother.

Spindly trees cast a lacework shadow over them. Dry leaves crushed beneath the iron wheels of the buggy, adding to the strong scent of eucalyptus in the morning air. Arabella's rhythmic clopping lulled Anna and her eyelids drooped.

She jerked her chin up. If she slept, she would dream. Either of flames or of eyes that shaded to the blue-purple of—

Her breath caught and she spluttered, 'Dieter, the jacket?' The jacket that had covered her nakedness. Remembrance shuddered through her, despite the unseasonal warmth.

Dieter kept his eyes forward. 'Returned it when I picked up the trap.' The men had unharnessed the carts and ridden bareback from the church to fight the fire, leaving behind the slower vehicles.

Held rigid by the corset, Anna couldn't reach to curl her fingers around the edge of the leather seat. Instead, she linked her gloved hands, squeezing so hard it hurt.

One hand holding the reins, Dieter covered her fists with his other. 'Anna, I promised you it would be all right, did I not? Have I ever lied to you?' He removed his hand, swatting at the bushflies that clouded them in the growing heat.

Her chin wobbled and she bit the side of her cheek. Why had she allowed him to persuade her to do this?

The small chapel came into view, a crowd of traps and buggies pulled up in the dust, horses hitched to posts set firmly in the ground beneath the shade of the eucalypts. Anna's tongue cleaved to the roof of her mouth. Sympathetic though he might be, Dieter was nonetheless a man; he could have no concept of what she faced. No matter how well-meaning their neighbours, her immodesty would have been the subject of all conversations for the last week.

Dieter dropped to the hard-packed earth. He hitched Arabella to a post, then came to Anna's side of the buggy.

Parishioners stared in their direction. Heads jerked and bobbed with curiosity as they alerted others. More faces turned.

Anna shook her head, her lips silently forming the words she couldn't speak. Nausea roiled in her stomach and tears pricked at her eyes. She stared at her lap so no one would see.

Dieter squeezed her hand. 'Anna, you look beautiful. Walk in with your chin held high. These are our cousins and our friends. I promise you, nothing will happen.'

This was the one promise she knew he couldn't keep. But the longer she sat in the buggy, the more people would stare. At least inside, they must pretend to focus on Pastor.

Dieter swung her from the seat. She flinched as her burned feet met the ground.

'Mäuschen?'

'It is nothing.' There was no point hoping to hide in the slight shadow of the buggy.

'Come, then. Walk tall, Little Mouse.' Her hand in the crook of his elbow, Dieter guided her through the circle of horse-drawn vehicles, avoiding the parishioners who milled in the shade of the tall gums. No one said anything untoward, only made the usual courteous greetings. Dieter nodded to each but didn't stop to speak.

Anna loosened her grip but kept her eyes downcast, instead of greeting those of her friends who had also taken their turn at this week's service. Many of the men present had seen that which should have been saved only for her husband. If she ever found one. Because she met so few people and was cursed with a beautiful sister, her expectation of attaining such a union had always been low. But now she had a reputation, and though Father would not cast her out, there was little joy to be found in the thought of a life spent caring for her younger siblings.

Dieter paced slowly. She clutched his arm, trying not to wince as they mounted the six broad steps. The heavily panelled double doors stood wide, offering sanctuary. Even to the fallen.

The familiarity of the interior of the church calmed her. The smell of Sunday-best clothes, infused with the scent of cedar from the chests in which they were stored, and the beeswax-polished woodwork evoked soothing memories from childhood, hours spent drowsing against Father's arm as Pastor droned.

Dieter indicated a pew and followed her in. Buttressed by a stone wall and hemmed in by his broad shoulders, Anna could relax for an hour. Well, relax as far as her clothing allowed; she perched on the edge of the pew, the bustle taking up far more space than her person. A smile tweaked her lips as an absurd image formed, and she leaned closer to her brother.

'Imagine if all the women were to present in the height of fashion; you and the other menfolk would be forced to stand at the rear of the church.'

Dieter snorted. 'My collar is starched so stiff, standing could well be a relief.'

Despite the steepled roof of die Kirche, the temperature climbed quickly. Heads nodded along with Pastor's soporific tone. A blowfly battered the stained-glass window high in the lime-washed wall above the pulpit. Cicadas buzzed soothingly in the gums outside.

Eventually, a stirring among the congregation signified the end of the sermon. Prayer books were folded, bibles placed back in reticules, fans energetically deployed.

The doors swung open to admit harsh sunlight and, blinking like wombats dug from their burrows, the parishioners exhibited great liveliness as they made for the church hall, fifty feet across the yard.

As they waited for the chapel to empty, Dieter leaned close. 'That wasn't so bad, was it? I don't know about you, but I enjoy the opportunity to catch up on a little sleep.'

Anna's smile wavered. Sitting through the sermon had been easy enough, but the thought of morning tea, normally the best part of the Sunday outing, terrified her. In the hall, she would be separated from her brother.

'Dieter, could we—' She bit her tongue, remembering Dieter's real reason for attending the service, although he'd not mentioned Caroline on the ride here. She could not drag him away now.

'Anna? What is it?'

She stood, pausing to adjust to the pain in her feet. 'Nothing. Let's go. The sooner tackled, the sooner finished, Mother would say.'

'I'll keep an eye upon you, Mäuschen. You've only to nod in my direction and I will be by your side.'

His offer was kind, yet they must abide by an unspoken rule. The congregation socialised in three distinct groups before morning tea: men, young men, and women.

Dieter smile apologetically as he deposited her on the fringe of the women's group. Grateful for the dove-grey gloves hiding her sweating palms, Anna wished Emilie had accompanied her.

Her friend Marta Krueger, her eyes wide with feigned shock, swooped on her like a hawk. 'Anna, dearest, is it true? Did you really fight a bushfire . . . in your unmentionables?'

Anna longed to reply that they could hardly be considered unmentionable if Marta insisted on mentioning them, but she was interrupted by Wilhelmina Ernst. Although Mrs Ernst's husband had died more years ago than anyone could remember, Anna had yet to see her in anything but widow's weeds.

The stern slash of Mrs Ernst's mouth failed to twist into anything approaching a smile, but she nodded apparent approval. 'Well done, Miss Frahn. I'm informed you saved your father's property, as well as your sister's life.'

Startled, Anna's words caught in her throat. She didn't want to claim unwarranted glory, but she was certainly not going to argue with the matriarch.

A flutter of interest surrounded them, whispered conversations teasing her ears. Someone tittered. She clenched her fist, studying the floor. She should have carried a fan, so she could hide her burning face. As the whispers grew, it was evident the tale was extending to those pious farmers whose properties lay beyond the weekday reach of the rumour mill.

Aware of her rudeness, Anna forced her gaze back to Mrs Ernst, but no words would come. The women's group converged upon them, a spiralling carousel of colour.

Her corset was far too tight. Her bosom heaved as she hunted for air.

Mrs Ernst's beady black eyes, reminiscent of the intelligent gaze of a magpie, regarded her unblinkingly. 'Miss Frahn, take my arm. Come promenade with me.'

The hall was small. There was nothing to see other than the occasional icon hung on the whitewashed walls and the thrill of the repast laid out upon the tea table, but strolling with Mrs Ernst would remove Anna from the group who hung on their every word.

She laid her palm on Mrs Ernst's bombazine-covered forearm but recoiled as the older woman placed a hand over hers.

Mrs Ernst frowned at the bulkiness of Anna's gloved hand. 'You are injured, Miss Frahn?'

'A small burn.'

Skirts rustling, Mrs Ernst swept in front of her. 'Let me see.'

Although she had no wish to further expose herself, no one refused Mrs Ernst. Anna tugged each fingertip, trying not to wince as the glove peeled off.

Mrs Ernst unwrapped the rag covering the suppurating wound, clicking her tongue as Anna's tightly buttoned sleeve hampered her ministrations. Shock hissed through the group of women as the extent of the burn was revealed.

Although the sight of the blistered flesh made Anna cringe, Mrs Ernst lifted her arm. She sniffed, seeking the taint of rotting flesh. 'This will become infected if you are not cautious. Have your mother visit. I have a suitable balm which will relieve the pain and aid healing.' She peered more closely. 'Though it cannot prevent the scar you shall bear. Your mother should know better than to cover a burn. It must breathe.'

Anna moved to draw the glove back on, but Mrs Ernst snapped, 'No! *Uncovered*, child.' With a firm but surprisingly gentle grasp, she replaced her hand on Anna's arm. 'Come, standing still for too long does my back no good.'

Apparently, the male–female boundaries of the room did not apply to Mrs Ernst, and she sailed regally forth, drawing Anna with her.

'How old are you, Miss Frahn?'

'E-eighteen.' Old enough not to stutter, but the attention of the dowager and the glances from the group of men they approached disconcerted her.

'And no young man has your eye? I am surprised. You are a presentable young woman and evidently more resourceful than many here.' Mrs Ernst pitched her voice as deliberate admonishment to the cluster of women trailing them.

Anna stared at the polished floor, wishing for the boards to split apart and swallow her.

A group of men stepped from their path, bowing slightly toward Mrs Ernst. Anna pretended not to see, praying Mrs Ernst would hold her tongue until they were beyond the men's hearing.

She did not.

'Some young man will be fortunate to find you, Miss Frahn. A useful woman is more valuable than a fine horse. Unlike those flibbertigibbets more interested in fashion than farming.' Her eye strayed to the fashionable bustle following Anna and her lips tightened.

Anna was eager to avoid having the sin of vanity added to her list. 'It is my younger sister who bears the looks.'

Mrs Ernst tapped a bony forefinger upon Anna's arm. 'Unwarranted modesty is no modesty, child. Accept a compliment. I think it time we indulge in a cup of tea.'

As though scheduled to her whim, a small bell tinkled, summoning the three groups to join at the table for morning tea.

As Mrs Ernst moved away, Dieter handed Anna a plate holding a scone piled with clotted cream and strawberry jam. This was one of the best things about church—they rarely had flour to spare for such treats at home.

'You are all right? Has it been every bit as bad as you feared?' His voice was low.

The only way to avert his concern was to joke. 'Brother, you were correct, as always.' Eager to prevent him questioning her further, Anna lifted her chin to where he had stood with the other soberly dressed young men. 'I cannot believe you attend every week. What can you possibly find to discuss?'

Dieter shrugged. 'Stock, crops, weather.' He grinned. 'And maybe a little about which girls we like.'

Anna expelled air through her pursed lips, imitating Mother's disparaging sound. 'Well, that's nothing new, is it? You're always talking about girls.' She inclined her head to the left, where Caroline, striped pink seersucker matching the becoming flush in her cheeks, was discreetly working her way toward them. Or, more specifically, toward her brother.

Dieter took Anna's elbow so he could speak close to her ear. 'Ah, you assume it was me doing the talking. Miss Schenscher is not the only young lady who has admirers.'

Anna stepped back from him so she could read his face. His grey eyes, so like her own, flicked to the far side of the room, then back to her.

She swivelled, enjoying the reminder of the slight tug of the bustle. 'Oh!' Heat rushed to the tips of her ears as the crowd briefly parted to reveal Luke Hartmann standing against the far wall. She must turn back to her brother, though surely Luke would not notice her observation?

Luke grasped the crown of his hat and tipped it in her direction, dipping his chin in acknowledgement.

Like a child, she spun her back to Dieter, feeling the colour drain from her face.

'Anna,' Dieter chided, 'why so afraid?'

'Dieter, he saw . . .' *So much.* Her lip trembled as she tried to compose herself.

Dieter took her elbow, gripping it tightly. 'Anna, enough now. What women label an indiscretion, we view differently. I assure you, the only conversation among the men centres around the highest regard for your actions. Now, pinch your cheeks. I've promised Luke an introduction.' He took her plate with its uneaten scone and slid it onto the table, then raised a hand toward Luke.

Anna closed her eyes. *Unser Vater, please do not let me make a fool of myself again.*

When she opened her eyes, Luke was striding across the room, his route direct and certain. She stood tall, determined to show her brother this mouse was not as timid as he believed. But her bravery was bolstered by the knowledge that Dieter would allow no unpleasantness to transpire.

For a week, she had insisted to herself that Luke's beauty was only in her imagination, the vision a combination of nerves, smoke, fear and exhaustion.

The closer he came, the more apparent her lie.

'Luke Hartmann, please allow me to present my favourite sister, Miss Anna Frahn.' Dieter's voice was deep with laughter, though his palm remained firm in the small of her back, transferring his strength and support.

Luke's eyes were violet in the unlit hall. Anna could not break her gaze, even though her perusal could be considered audacious.

He bowed slightly from the waist. 'Miss Frahn, the pleasure is all mine.'

She thought he stressed the penultimate word, but it was hard to tell as her heartbeat deafened her. Willing her voice to calm, she offered her hand. 'Mr Hartmann, it is a delight to *formally* make the acquaintance of one of my more distant neighbours.' She and Dieter often played word games and she prided herself on turning a conversation using intonation. If her tongue were clever enough now, she could pretend a composure she was far from feeling.

Except she had forgotten the deplorable state of her ungloved hand. As Luke enfolded her hand in his grasp, shock rippled through her at the intimacy of their flesh meeting.

The lines of good humour disappeared from Luke's face. 'You are sorely injured.' His thumb stroked the back of her hand, careful not to touch the burn. 'That looks terrible. Well, the burn does. The hand, however . . .' He pressed his lips to her knuckles.

The power of speech deserted her. So much for her witty repartee.

Mrs Ernst joined their small group and Luke lowered Anna's hand carefully, as though he considered it fragile. A crease ran vertically up his cheek as one side of his mouth again curved into a smile. His courteous nod to Mrs Ernst was brief, his eyes leaving Anna's for only a moment.

Mrs Ernst snapped her fan closed and tapped it against Anna's uninjured forearm. 'It is indeed a nasty injury, Mr Hartmann. Miss Frahn's mother will call on Wednesday to collect some unguent to assist the healing. Which brings to mind, Mr Hartmann, it has been some time since your own mother has paid me a visit. Perhaps you would be so kind as to extend her an invitation for afternoon tea on the same day?'

Luke bowed his head in acknowledgement. 'As you wish, Mrs Ernst.' His eyes danced as they returned to Anna's—perhaps the arrangement hadn't escaped his notice?

Mrs Ernst took Anna's arm. 'Come, Miss Frahn, I don't believe we completed our perambulation.'

No. She wanted to scream the word, to resist the pressure of the elderly woman's hand. Anna had thought

Mrs Ernst understood the undercurrents—or had Anna herself grievously misinterpreted them? Was Luke's interest merely amusement?

'Miss Frahn.' Luke's deep voice shivered through her. 'I do hope to see you at the service next week.' Inclining his head, he took a polite step back, making room for the women's sweeping skirts as they turned.

Mrs Ernst paced silently toward where Anna's friend, Marta, stared in almost open-mouthed amazement. A few years ago, Anna and Marta had childishly giggled behind their fans about how handsome Luke Hartmann was. Now Marta would want every detail of their interaction. Their curtailed interaction. Anna resented every step Mrs Ernst forced her to take, just as she resented the woman's interference. She pressed her lips together, biting the inside of her cheek. This might have been the only time a man would speak to her. It was most certainly the only time a man would kiss her hand. Could she construe Luke's farewell to be anything more than standard politeness? Unable to restrain herself, she glanced over her shoulder.

'Come, child, it is not seemly to throw yourself at him. Allow the man to make the chase.' Mrs Ernst's words were so low she almost missed them.

But it didn't matter what Mrs Ernst said, for Luke stood with Dieter, making no pretence of not watching her. An unusual sensation throbbed deep within Anna and she lifted her chin, defying the whispers of her neighbours.

Then she gasped, for Luke was not the only man whose eyes were upon her. At least half-a-dozen of these men had seen her, calves bare, breasts unfettered.

Why should they now pretend she did not deserve their judgement?

10

Taylor

Taylor woke with crusty eyes and a clear mind, the room dark except for the permanent glow that came with living in Sydney.

She couldn't go back to South Australia. Couldn't stay here. Couldn't stay with Cassie, at least not until much later next year.

But although she didn't have a permanent solution, she certainly had a perfectly practical temporary one. And maybe that's what life should be: a sequence of little steps, one foot following the other, rather than making momentous choices and binding decisions. Perhaps she tried too hard to achieve, to please, to succeed. There was no gain in sitting around here listening to her parents unravel their lives, destroy their memories. While Zac's place wasn't ideal, and his plan to hit the road next year complicated things, for now it would be a safe haven. And all she

112

needed was a 'for now' plan—it was a bonus that it was with the man she couldn't get out of her head.

It took only minutes to pack up her life. She bundled her laptop, toiletries, wallet and chargers into her backpack. The large duffel bag, stuffed with what she could carry of her clothes, pulled her down, anchoring her in the room that had been hers forever. Next time she stood here, it would be as a visitor.

Her fingers twitched over the pad on her desk. She generally let her parents know where she was; Dad always said Sydney was a dangerous place, and it paid to adopt safe practices. Not leaving a note would be childish, a juvenile *fuck you* to her parents. But perhaps they deserved to suffer. Besides, given their expectations, knowing the choice she'd made would probably be worse for them than not knowing. She'd had expectations of them, too. She had believed she had a right to happiness, security, support. But apparently all those things had an expiration date when it came to family. Zac would be different, though. She *chose* him.

Taylor crept down the stairs, her fingers trailing the gyprock. Mum hated when she did that, it discoloured the paint. At the end of the passage, where it expanded into the open-plan lounge and kitchen, her fingers slid with easy familiarity into a rough-edged gouge. When she was about four, playing chasey with Dad, her trike had sped across the shiny white tiles. She had misjudged the corner, careening into the wall. Rushing to pick her up, Dad had slipped. He broke a crystal vase on the side table and the little finger on his right hand. He'd always said he would fix the chipped wall, but the raw scar remained a permanent memory.

In the kitchen, she took a glass from the cupboard above the sink, then changed her mind. The pump on the water filter would create a racket in the sleeping house. Silently, she placed the glass upside down on the counter where Mum used to sit her while she baked. Although Taylor had no recollection, there were so many photos from her childhood of her covered in flour or sticky with cake batter, her fat little legs crossed on the granite bench, that it seemed like a memory. She did recall the hours spent perched on a bar stool, Dad standing on the opposite side of the counter as he handed her orange segments, explaining the mystery of algebra.

Her earliest true memory, though, was of Mum, her face glowing behind a floating island of candles as she moved through the darkness to the dining table. Cakes that looked like caterpillars, butterflies, rainbows, teddy bears and Barbie eventually gave way to Black Forest gateau. But two things remained constant: the birthday cakes were always lost in a forest of sparklers, and the three of them were always together.

Her throat aching, Taylor went to the side door. She flicked the lock, making certain it latched behind her. Keeping Mum and Dad safe. She had the oddest sense she was deserting the house. Stupid—she would have to leave in a few months, anyway. And the eviction would be worse knowing new people were moving in.

In any case, home had been gone for a long time.

By the time she reached the end of the familiar, tree-lined street, Taylor realised she should have taken a wheeled suitcase from the hall cupboard. The station was a couple of blocks away and despite the pre-dawn gloom, the cement and bitumen surrounds held the previous day's warmth.

Starlings twittered in the trees she carefully skirted, their song the only melodic note in the never-sleeping city. Sudden nostalgia for the full-throated joy of the morning chorus at her grandparents' farm shot through her. The cacophony of wild birds challenged by the rooster crowing in the distance, guiding the sun. Ruffled from their sleep, the chickens would join in, waking the sheep and cow.

For a bizarre, confused moment, it seemed that the barnyard noises were her norm, rather than this drab, inert world of concrete and steel, and it took Taylor a few seconds to realise that the animal chorus actually belonged to her recurring dreams, rather than to her recent visit. She shook the odd thought away as she entered the station and leaned against the mosaic-tiled pillar of the platform to surreptitiously adjust her underwear. The cute panties had plans to choke her. She'd hit the duty-free Victoria's Secret store when they went to Hawaii on a family holiday to celebrate her acceptance into medical school. Fulfilling her parents' dreams, like a good daughter. Her mouth twisted bitterly.

When had *family* become a synonym for *betrayal*?

The train buffeted through the inkiness of a tunnel and she clutched at the swing strap. Excitement warred with sorrow at the memory of what she left behind, the impossibility of returning to life as it had been. She should have emancipated herself long ago, before she was forced to.

The crucifix burned against her chest, the irritation—which had disappeared in South Australia—heightened by the humidity. She should take it off before the reaction worsened. Instead, she flipped it over her shoulder. Dragged in a steadying breath of air that had already passed through thousands of lungs.

A heavily accented voice crackled over the PA system, announcing the next stop.

Home. Well, home-to-be.

～

It was a bit of a hike to Zac's from the station—last time he'd driven her here, cautioning that the train wasn't safe. She settled her backpack and hefted her bag.

Twenty minutes later—and she'd be willing to swear every one of them was uphill—empty bottles rolled from the porch of Zac's house as she lowered her bag with a groan. Dropping back down the two steps, she found a tap hidden in a patch of green grass. She splashed her face, then glanced around before wiping her hands under her armpits.

The rickety door finally creaked open the fifth time she knocked, just as desperation was setting in. She didn't have a Plan B, and hadn't called ahead. Zac didn't rise before noon, and wouldn't answer his phone before then, either.

Confronted by saggy Y-fronts and greasy hair cork-screwed into a matted man-bun, Taylor stepped back. The Stoned Drifters' drummer, Erik, gusted foul morning-breath into her face.

'Yeah?'

'Zac?'

Erik squinted at her, then nodded. 'Oh. Yeah. You're that chick.' He snorted in the back of his throat and hawked phlegm onto the path, then turned back into the house, scratching his backside.

Rather than stare at the rear of Erik's discoloured jocks, Taylor concentrated on navigating the hall littered with bottles, fast-food containers and discarded clothes. Surely it hadn't been this bad before?

'Y'know where his room is, right?' Erik called over his shoulder.

'No.'

'Thought you all knew. Down the end. The one with a track worn in the carpet.'

'Yeah, hilarious.'

Erik flopped a hand toward the end of the hall, slouched to the left and shut a grime-covered door in her face. A drawing pin popped from the top corner of an Anthrax poster, the tattered edge bowing gracefully to cover the door handle and wafting the rank odour of weed.

Taylor dropped her duffel, followed by her backpack. No one would notice a couple more things to trip over. Excitement darted through her. This was the start of their forever, even if realistically that only lasted a few months.

She'd had plenty of thinking time on the train. Maybe medicine wasn't for her. If she quit now, got an unskilled job that paid low, she'd never have to pay back her HECS debt. And she'd be free to hit the road with Zac. No stress, no tears. Just love.

She snorted at the irony. Perhaps she was a genetic hippie? She should have kept Mum's yoga pants.

The door handle sticky under her fingers, she slipped quietly into Zac's room—*their* room.

A tattered blanket hung across the window, daylight casting murky spotlights through the holes. She blinked rapidly, adjusting to the gloom in the squalid room. The sooner they were on tour, the better.

An involuntary gasp raked her throat.

Zac was in the tumbled bed. Awake.

And not alone.

A girl faced the door, propped on her hands and knees. Eyes closed, mouth open. Zac knelt behind her. His undulating torso glistened, dappled black and white by the oily light of a lava lamp. The room reeked, sweet and hot, incense used to cover the smell of sex and sweat.

Shit.

Without turning, Taylor fumbled for the door handle behind her.

'That's it, princess. Hold it right there.' Zac spoke through clenched teeth, and she froze.

But his eyes were closed. He was speaking to *her*.

Cassie had called it: Zac was a player.

Taylor scrabbled desperately for the handle. It couldn't possibly be that hard to find, it was there a second ago. But she couldn't tear her eyes from Zac, and now he was looking at her.

His sensuous lips curved and he slapped the naked bottom before him. The girl uttered a squeak of protest and he placed a hand on her butt, pushing himself from the bed. Naked, he stalked toward Taylor.

'What a pleasant surprise, princess. Was I expecting you?'

She had to escape before she humiliated herself with tears he didn't deserve. 'No, I'm—' She wouldn't apologise, because she had a right to anger, but she had to get out of that damn room. She found the door handle, jerked it open.

Zac's hand smacked the door above her head, slamming it shut. His body pressed against her, slippery and hard. 'You must have come here for *something*, princess.' His pupils were huge and his breath stank like dank vegetation. She didn't need clinical indications to realise he was stoned.

'Open the door.' She willed her voice firm, refused to give in to her impulse to swear at him, to accuse him of betraying her, even though they'd never made a commitment. She just needed to get the hell away from this embarrassment she'd caused herself.

Zac grabbed behind her thigh, jerking her leg up and aside, and sudden fear shot through her. His hips ground against hers, his words hot and wet on her neck. 'Come on, a chick only turns up in a guy's bedroom for one thing.'

She twisted to avoid his mouth, trying to squirm from beneath the crush of his body.

His pelvis pinned her against the door and his hand snaked under her shirt, inside her bra. 'This is what you came for, isn't it?'

'No!' Loud and firm. He had to hear her. Had to listen. Because if he didn't . . .

'Let her go, Zac.' The blonde girl on the bed had dropped her arse down, elbows on the mattress, her chin propped in her hands as she watched. 'She's clearly not into it.'

'Shut up,' Zac snarled, his breath bouncing off Taylor's face. 'Come and join us on the bed, princess.'

'I'm not bloody joining you anywhere!' she spat furiously. 'Let me go.' Voice unsteady, her nostrils flared, hunting for oxygen.

Zac's twin nipple rings pressed into her palms as he crushed her against the door. 'You know you want it, princess,' he murmured against her cheek.

Her fingers curled through the hoops she'd loved playing with. 'Please, Zac,' she gasped.

'I knew you'd beg for it, princess. And that's before you've even heard your song.'

'No! I-I don't want—'

'See, I'm one of the nice guys, princess. But now it's time to pay for the play.'

She seized both of his nipple rings. Tugged down, hard.

11

Taylor

'You bitch!' Zac staggered backward, hands on his chest covered with blood. The girl splayed across the bed behind him clambered to her knees, her mouth wide in horror.

Not daring to turn away from Zac, Taylor reached for the handle behind her. She yanked the door open and then raced down the hallway. Her foot caught on rubbish. She tripped, snatching at the wall for balance. Ragged breaths ripped at her throat, deafening her to sounds of pursuit. The front door shuddered on its hinges as she slammed it open, bursting from the house into the early morning emptiness of the street.

Free.

But not covering ground fast enough. Fingers hooked into a wire mesh fence, she clawed the strappy wedges from her heels. Dropped them.

Ran.

Gravel scraped and bit her feet. Air exploded from her mouth with each stride. Her lungs hammered her rib cage. A corner loomed and she slid around it. Another. Turned again. Never a straight line. An elderly man stared as she pounded toward him, his garden hose a limp question mark over straggling rose bushes, thick-rimmed glasses magnifying his concern.

'You okay, love?'

She couldn't answer. Couldn't stop. Couldn't think.

She had to outrun her stupidity.

The soles of her feet burning, she raced over bindi-strewn verges, broken beer bottles, dog shit and cracked bitumen. The rise of the kerb sent her sprawling and she twisted awkwardly, shearing skin from the back of her hand and arm as she slid.

Get up. Keep going. He's coming.

She ran until she couldn't, then doubled over, hands on her knees. Retched. So dry nothing came up. The dilapidated weatherboard houses that wavered in her tear-soaked gaze were unfamiliar, the occasional well-maintained garden jarring with the old lounge suites or blocked-up cars decorating other front yards. A couple of snot-nosed kids sat on a doorstep, staring at her over a breakfast box of Cheezels.

Intent only on putting distance between her and Zac, Taylor had lost all sense of direction.

The heel of her hand dug into her chest did little to ease the pain, her breathing still ragged. She needed to find the train station but had no idea where to head. A cab would be safer. She reached for her backpack. Froze. The sweat

122

sheeting her face turned cold. Her bag, her credit card, her purse, her laptop—everything was at Zac's.

A signpost hard against her back, she slid to the ground, sobs of defeat and hysteria heaving her lungs. She had to go back to retrieve her things. But she couldn't. Couldn't face him. Couldn't risk it.

Slowly the traffic increased. Cars occasionally honked. A couple of guys paused on the opposite side of the street, watching her, their heads close as they conferred.

She wasn't safe. She had to move on.

As she levered herself up, her hand brushed her back pocket, then clenched over the bulge. She still had her phone. *Please, please don't let it be broken.*

Zac's shirtless image smiled at her.

Oh god, oh god, oh god. Who could she call? Not her parents.

Cassie.

'Cass?' she sobbed the second the call clicked through. 'Cass.'

'Tay? Is that you?' Cassie's voice was sleep-muddled.

'Cass.' She needed to do better than that, but clutching the phone to her ear brought Cassie closer. Made her safer.

'Taylor, are you okay? What's wrong? Tay, where are you?' Taylor could hear the wooden slats beneath Cassie's bed creak as she sat. She closed her eyes, imagining the safety of Cassie's room, where she had spent so much of her life. 'Tay, you're scaring me.'

'Sorry.' If she said more than one word at a time, she'd lose control. She bit out staccato syllables. 'Lost my bag. I need a . . . ride.'

'Can't you get the train? The bus? Where are you?'

'Near Zac's place.'

Cassie sucked in a breath, putting the story—a story, some story, because whatever she imagined couldn't be the truth—together. 'What's the problem? Do you want me to come get you?'

Taylor squinted at the sign above. It flared and blurred, reflecting the sun. 'Forsyth. Street.' The phone trembled. She fumbled and dropped it. *Pick it up. Pick it up. Pick it up.*

'Forsyth? You mean that's where you are? Tay, stay on the phone. I'm waking Peter up. We'll come and get you, okay?'

Afraid the phone would snap, Taylor tried to loosen her grip. Couldn't. 'Cass, don't you come. You'll lose the signal in the tunnel. Don't hang up on me.' Now the words gushed forth. 'Cass? Promise you won't hang up?'

'Okay, Tay, just hold on. I'll stay on the phone.' Feet slapped on tiles. Doors slammed open. Murmured, urgent demands as Cassie spoke to her brother. 'Peter is on his way. What's going on, Tay? What happened?'

Taylor shook her head, though Cassie couldn't see. 'You talk, Cass.' Eyes closed, she sagged against the post. She didn't care anymore what passers-by thought:

She already knew how their judgement felt. She could remember . . .

People stared, judging her, although she'd done nothing wrong . . . *but Dieter was there, he'd protect her.*

The squeal of tyres rubbing the gutter intruded on Taylor's thoughts. Were they thoughts, though? It seemed she'd again slipped into her dreams, but her pain now mirrored Anna's, her bare feet burned, her arm raw and stinging.

A car door slammed, footsteps slapped against the bitumen.

Peter thumped to his knees alongside her. 'Christ, Taylor, what happened?'

She shook away the last thread of the dream and tried to stand. But Peter slid an arm beneath her legs, the other around her back, grunting as he straightened.

Mad laughter rippled through her throat. In her dreams, Luke picked Anna up effortlessly. Yet the first time a guy picked *her* up, he grunted.

Peter lowered her onto the car seat and buckled the belt. Squatting in the doorway, he peered at her face. 'Taylor, are you hurt? Do you want me to take you to hospital? Jesus, did some bastard touch you?' His knuckles shone white like shark's teeth where he gripped the doorframe.

She had to speak or he'd take her to Bankstown Hospital. There was no need to clog up the overtaxed emergency system for this . . . nothingness. 'Just a stupid fight. Then I ran off. Dumb.'

His eyebrow lifted disbelievingly, Peter slid behind the wheel, pulling the car onto the road in a squeal of rubber.

Cassie's tinny voice, more frantic by the second, screeched from Taylor's fist and Peter reached across, prying the mobile from her grasp to set it on the console. 'Cass, I've got her.'

'Is she okay?' Cassie sounded close to tears.

Peter blew out a heavy breath, the warmth enveloping Taylor as he turned her way. 'Says so. I don't know. Where am I taking her? She seems . . . shocked, or something.'

Taylor made an effort to sound normal. 'I'm fine.'

'Bring her here.'

The burns on her feet and hand hurt, and she wished the salve pot wasn't empty.

Eyes still closed, Taylor frowned. There was something wrong with the thought, but she couldn't work out what.

Someone moved beside her, a rustle of clothing. Or straw. *Emilie?*

No, that was wrong, too.

Reluctantly, she forced her eyes open.

'Tay? You okay?'

Cassie. Of course.

The mattress squished beneath her as she pushed herself up, the comforting familiarity of Cassie's room surrounding her. Pain shot through her hand, drawing her gaze.

Bandaged.

And she remembered. Perfectly.

'Tay?' Cassie said cautiously.

'Fine.' Her voice was a croak and Taylor licked at her dry lips.

Cassie snatched up the water bottle, always alongside her bed. 'Here. You feel better now you've slept?'

'No.' Stupid was what she felt. She'd thought she and Zac had something special. 'Christ, I'm an idiot.'

126

Cassie slammed the bottle back onto her side table, a fountain of tiny drops cooling Taylor's skin. 'You reckon? Just because you were out wandering the streets in Scumsville by yourself, when it's barely daylight?' Now that she knew Taylor was okay, Cassie was angry. 'For a smart chick, you make some dumb calls.'

'I wasn't sightseeing—I took off from Zac's.'

'Why would you do that?'

'Because he was screwing someone else.'

Cassie wrinkled her nose. 'You know I'd be the last person to defend him, but are you sure you're not jumping to conclusions? He seems pretty into you.'

She snorted mirthlessly. 'I promise, I am not who he is *into*. Screwing, as in I caught them together. In bed. In the act. What is it called, *flagrante delicto*?' She tried to inject humour that she didn't feel, alleviating what had clearly been an overreaction on her part. Surely she'd never really been in danger?

Cassie clicked her tongue and huffed. 'Aw, shit, Tay, that blows—'

'And he tried to force me to join them.' Her voice hitched, a ghost of the fear snatching at her. 'So I cleared out. Left my bag there. Laptop. Wallet. Everything.'

Hell, she'd thought she had herself under control, but now the sobs clawed up from her chest, wrenching free in ugly hiccups at the memory of the fear, the powerlessness she had felt. It would be impossible to hide the loss of her stuff and that meant everyone would know what had happened.

The mattress dipped as Cassie sat, throwing an arm around her shoulders. 'Hey, don't sweat it. I'll text Pete.

He'll go get your things in his lunchbreak. I know he'll appreciate the chance to sort that dickhead ex of yours.' She picked up Taylor's phone from the bedside table. 'Your mum called. Twice.'

'You didn't answer?'

'I texted on your phone to say you're staying here. She sent back yada yada yada, put your washing out and it's kind of weird you got up so early to leave, but maybe you picked up good habits camping.' She cocked an incredulous eyebrow at the last and held up the phone as evidence.

The display read 10.36 a.m.

That couldn't be right. Taylor knew hours, maybe even days, had passed. Knew, because she had spent the time with Anna.

Cassie's face loomed into view, then retreated swiftly. 'You still look white as a sheet. Why don't you lie down a bit longer? Everyone else is at work and I'm just going to grab a shower.'

'Can I go first?' She needed to scrub the sweat and filth from her body. His touch.

The bed creaked as Cassie stood. 'Sure. I'll do some avo and eggs for brunch in the meantime.'

Coffee-coloured towels and chocolate-coloured face washers decorated Cassie's opulent ensuite. Taylor reached for the tap and realised her unbandaged hand was clenched so tight it had cramped. She took deep, calming breaths, in through her nose, out through her mouth. Nothing had actually happened. She needed to get a grip, control her reactions.

Slowly, she uncurled her fingers. A gold hoop lay in her

palm. She gagged. Flung it to the floor, shaking so hard her teeth chattered uncontrollably.

Nothing had happened? She had maimed him.

And he'd deserved it.

She whirled into the shower, doubling over as she vomited until nothing more would come up.

First do no harm. The classic ethical standard of medicine, which formed part of the Hippocratic Oath doctors had sworn for so many years.

Yet she'd harmed Zac.

And she wasn't even sorry.

⌒

Though he adopted a nonchalant pose against the doorframe, a frown clouded Peter's face. His hand rasped against blond stubble as he rubbed at his jaw.

Trying to pretend he wasn't there, to forget the humiliation of how he'd rescued her, Taylor scrabbled through her backpack.

'Got everything?' He sounded almost like he hoped something would be missing.

'Yeah. All good.' She'd always been comfortable around Peter, had known him most of her life. But now everything was awkward. 'Thanks for picking up this lot. Crap way to spend your lunchbreak.'

The rasping stopped and Peter's hand fisted. 'Not a problem. I'm surprised your stuff's all there, though. Shit area, and the tosser threw your gear out into the front yard. Too gutless to answer the door.'

'He's pissed. I kind of hurt him.' She swallowed the bile as she remembered the bloodied nipple ring, which she'd used toilet paper to pick up and hide in the bathroom wastebasket.

'Good. But if he did anything to you, tell me. I'll sort the bastard.'

She stared down at her bandaged hand, trying to ignore his inference. 'No. Nothing like that. Just an argument. It doesn't matter, I'm done with him.' Avoiding Peter's gaze, she pawed through the contents of her duffle bag.

Peter cleared his throat. 'I've got to get back to work but call me if anything crops up. Or if he tries to reach you, okay? Guys like him need to be taught a lesson.'

Curled in a chair in the corner, Cassie barely waited until Peter had left before sitting forward. 'I've hatched a plan that you and Peter are going to love,' she said glee-fully. 'I was waiting for you to come back from the sticks to tell you, so you can appreciate my brilliance in person.'

'Shoot.'

'We're heading to Europe early.'

Taylor's heart sank. How was this the start of any kind of brilliant plan?

'At the end of this month, instead of January. I mean, *Noël à Paris*—how can a girl refuse?'

'Christmas in Paris? A girl cannot.'

Cassie was deserting her. The realisation sat like coal in the pit of Taylor's stomach. She hadn't comprehended that, until this moment, she'd been clinging to a faint hope that the trip to Europe would be like many of Cassie's plans: hastily conceived and rapidly forgotten.

'This way we can get set up before winter closes in, do some sightseeing,' Cassie gushed. 'And Dad can travel with us instead of going ahead to take up his new job. I hate trying to work out airports and so does Mum. But it's second nature to Dad, so heaps easier if we go with. You know, just kick back with some bubbles in the business class lounge and let him handle all the messy bits.'

'Uh-huh.' She knew she had to do better, fake enthusiasm to match Cassie's. But now she would be entirely alone.

'But wait!' Cassie threw up her hands theatrically, and Taylor flashed back to the years of dance classes they'd taken together. 'I told you, I have a plan.' She pushed up from her chair to pace the room. 'I can't think of anyone who's looking for a roomie—at least, not anyone you won't pick up the plague or something worse from— but why not stay here while we're away? Five bedrooms.' She flung her hand wide, a game show hostess displaying the prize. 'And Dad won't want any rent. In fact, he'd be stoked, because you'll stop Peter from trashing the place. And I knooooow,' she drew the word out, making her blue eyes huge, 'that Peter would be stoked. Who's to say that maybe my bestie and my brother won't discover they have more than just *moi* in common . . .'

Yesterday, she would have seized the lifeline, such an easy solution to her predicament. But now Taylor was resolute. 'No offence to Peter—you know I love him like, well, like a brother—but I am done with guys.' At least, the kind that actually existed. The dangerous kind. The kind that could break her heart. 'I don't need a knight in shining armour—or, in this case, a guy with a house—to sort my life.'

'Well, actually, *I* was doing the rescuing,' Cassie huffed. 'And you can't write off a whole breed just because of super douche, you know.'

Cassie sounded genuinely appalled at the prospect and Taylor chuckled, her friend's focus reminding her momentarily of Anna's sister. For a second she was tempted to feign a need for more sleep, so she could escape back to the comfort of her fantasy world. 'I think you mean gender, not breed. And you know what? I think super douche has actually helped me sort out my head.' She used the slur casually, pretending to herself that she didn't need to mentally unpack what had happened, fathom how, despite being an intelligent woman, she'd allowed herself to be seduced by Zac's attention, blinded by his apparent interest.

How? Because that's precisely what love was—momentary blindness. Her parents had discovered that. Just more slowly than she had.

Cassie blew out a dismissive breath. 'I don't think that helping anyone with their mental function was high on super douche's to-do list.'

'True enough. But he was part of the reason I shot down Mum's suggestion. Well, that and shock, because I sure didn't see it coming. Bit of a theme there, I reckon,' she added dryly.

'Wait, back it up sister: not saying I don't agree with that last bit, but you don't mean you're onboard with your Mum's whack plan?'

Taylor screwed up her face uncertainly. 'Except maybe it's not so whack. Gran and Gramps are never going to leave the farm, but Mum's right, they are a bit doddery. They probably do need someone nearby to keep an eye on them. I just didn't want that to be Mum, because I didn't want to lose her. And I didn't want to lose Zac.' She winced. It was going to be a long time before saying his name stopped hurting. Right now, she wanted to replay their time together to see if there had been red flags or if it had truly been as wonderful as she'd built up in her mind.

'Er?' Cassie tapped her chest.

'Or you,' Taylor agreed. 'But you're leaving now for, what, six months?'

'More like twelve.' Cassie looked guilty as she disclosed the extension. 'But like I said, stay here . . .'

Taylor shook her head. 'I wanted to be here for you guys and uni, but really that's about it. Not like I can't pick up a checkout job somewhere else, is it? Well, perhaps not in Settlers Bridge—you wouldn't believe the size of that place, Cass.'

'You're not considering moving there,' Cassie said flatly.

'I don't really have a valid reason not to, do I? No house here. No you. Dad's working away and bunking with a mate when he's back. Really, uni is the only tie.'

'I can't believe you're ditching uni like that. All those years of study.'

She wasn't ditching uni, she was putting it in the 'too hard' basket for right now. There was so much going on, too many speed humps in her life, and for the first time, she couldn't deal with them all at once. 'If I couldn't even let Mum go on a holiday to South Australia, how can I let her move there alone? Especially when she's so messed up.' They were both messed up. But perhaps that was actually part of being an adult? Maybe not everything went to plan, despite her best efforts.

'She's not your problem,' Cassie reminded her, slowly sinking back into the chair.

'But she is, Cass. She's my family.' Mum had been there for her through all the meltdowns and exam nerves and late-night assignments. Literally sitting alongside her every time. What right did Taylor have to desert her mother now?

Cassie shook her head. 'Seriously, you're not thinking what I think you're thinking, are you?'

Taylor chewed on her bottom lip. 'I think I am.'

Better to be isolated in the middle of nowhere with Mum than alone in a city of millions.

~

Harnessing her anger at Zac, as soon as Taylor got home she grabbed garbage bags from the kitchen drawer. Headed to her room and bundled up everything she had ever worn with Zac. It could all go to charity. She tried not to think of the occasion tied to each piece of clothing. Tried not to recall Zac's approval of the revealing tops, the shorter shorts; his favourite dress, high on the leg, low on the chest. *You look so hot in that, princess. I like seeing more of you.* Yeah, there had been red flags. She was an idiot.

By the time she'd finished sorting, bagging and vacuuming, sweat soaked her shirt, She headed for the bathroom. With the shower turned to full pressure, she lifted her face to the torrent. She refused to cry, denying the tears of humiliation at her own stupidity, of anger at Zac's expectation and demand, of fear at the thought of how easily the situation could have escalated into something far worse, of relief at escape. Above all, of sorrow at the realisation that love was a lie.

She snuggled into her old dressing-gown, the well-worn, well-washed fabric wrapping her like a hug. The newly cleared surface of her desk beckoned. If she was serious about going with Mum—*hell, yes, I'm serious*—then she should start researching what was involved in changing her degree to another university. She could guarantee it was a lot more complex than Mum seemed to think, but maybe that was good. It would keep her mind busy.

As she opened a bunch of tabs and scrolled screens on her laptop, an ad for genealogy.com appeared in the sidebar, a relic of a long-forgotten assignment that proved the age of her system. A stern, monochromatic woman glared at her. As no one would wish to claim the severe matriarch as even a distant relative, it wasn't the best marketing.

Taylor squinted and the image softened, taking on an odd familiarity. Perhaps the woman wasn't as forbidding as she initially appeared. A smile twitched Taylor's mouth: had she been real, Mrs Ernst probably would have looked like this. A heart of gold hidden behind a steel façade.

Her hand hovered over the keyboard. She held down CTRL and tapped the P then sat back, looking at the sepia-toned image the printer spewed out.

Taylor's smile grew. What the hell. It was her dream, so she would control the narrative. Wilhelmina Ernst would be a fairy godmother and Anna would get the guy. The *nice* guy. The only kind of guy who was worth the effort and came with a happily ever after.

A fantasy.

12
Anna

April 1877

Only words of polite praise would dare be spoken in Mrs Ernst's presence and Marta was not known for her tact, so Anna avoided her friend and shadowed the older woman around the church hall. However, Marta made no move to approach; perhaps she was actually shunning Anna, not wishing to be tainted by her reputation?

Focused on her misery, Anna trod upon the hem of Mrs Ernst's bombazine.

Mrs Ernst snapped around so quickly, Anna flinched. 'Child, what ails you?'

It seemed she had worn out her welcome. Her skirts lifted, Anna hastily stepped back as Mrs Ernst moved into another group, regally dominating their conversation. Anna's bustle brushed the tea table and she jerked around, the great lump of fabric sweeping along the edge of the bench.

Caroline Schenscher glided forward, saving her from disgrace by steadying the teetering contents. 'Horrible things to become accustomed to, are they not?' Her smile was open and friendly and though Anna searched, she could not find the condemnation that should lurk. Caroline was a little older, closer to Dieter's age, and Anna didn't know her well—unlike the boys, girls didn't attend school, so their acquaintanceships were formed through church, occasional weddings and funerals.

Caroline offered her hand, continuing smoothly, 'I find it helps if you always move forward. Avoid backing up and limit turning. Have you mastered sitting? Or are you, like me, doomed to forever stand?'

Anna's lips twitched. 'I did manage to sit upon a straight-backed chair. Well, once, anyway.' Caroline's smile encouraged her to complete honesty. 'And not the first time I attempted it, either.'

Caroline's laugh light and melodic, humour sparked in her eyes. The reason for Dieter's attraction was clear. She linked their arms, drawing Anna to walk beside her. 'Isn't it ridiculous we must practise such things? Oh, to be able to wear trousers.'

Anna stifled her gasp, her sudden halt pulling her arm free. 'Caroline, you cannot—'

'Cannot what?' Caroline's look of innocence was contrived. 'Cannot speak as I think? Or cannot do as I wish? Both would seem to be our fate, but I tell you—' she leaned closer, shielding their faces with her fan '—when I am married, I fully intend to purloin a pair of my husband's trousers and adjust them to fit.'

A part of Anna thrilled to believe her. 'You cannot be serious.'

'Entirely serious. It is only clothing. An intelligent woman will realise style should come secondary to practicality. I'll tell you one more thing.' Caroline's face became sombre and she dropped the fan, inviting an audience from those who tried to eavesdrop. 'I do wish I had half your courage.'

Two women drifted elegantly toward them. Caroline flipped open her fan to include them in the conversation. 'Mrs Dorothea Schultz, Mrs Henrietta Schultz, I'm sure you are acquainted with my firm friend, Miss Anna Frahn?'

Both women dipped their heads, and Anna curtseyed slightly, acknowledging their seniority.

'Johanna Frahn's eldest girl, are you not?' one of them asked.

'Yes, Mrs Schultz.'

'Oh, you're the young lady about whom everyone speaks?' the smaller, darker woman interrupted eagerly.

Anna took a step backward as Mrs Schultz confirmed her worst fears: she was the subject of gossip. Caroline's arm snaked around her waist and Anna hoped the woman could not feel the tremble that coursed up from her toes.

Still, she must reply, and could only find the pluck to do so by pretending it was her irritating sister to whom she spoke. 'If I am being spoken *about*, then I am not being spoken to, so I'm afraid I cannot confirm the fact.'

Caroline snorted softly, and Anna was almost certain she laughed.

The darker Mrs Schultz waved the words away with her fan. 'Oh, I did not intend any offence, Miss Frahn.

Quite the opposite. I only wanted to ascertain that I tender my admiration to the correct person.'

'Wilhelmina Ernst has spoken with Dorothea and me,' the other Mrs Schultz said. 'She is quite taken with your bravery. Both in fighting the fire and—' she glanced around and leaned into their little circle, lowering her voice in a conspiratorial fashion '—and in presenting yourself here today. We all understand how difficult that must be for you.'

The trembling shifted to Anna's jaw and she clenched her teeth, lest it give her away.

'Oh no, do not take on so,' Dorothea exclaimed, reaching into her reticule and retrieving a small linen square. She pressed it into Anna's hand. 'Miss Frahn, if it alleviates your distress at all, my husband, Walther, attended the fire. He claims the smoke was so thick, the heat so intense and the danger so evident, he passed you right by, never noticing your ... *déshabillé*.'

'Yet obviously someone did, for the fact to have reached your ears.' Anna's words were jerky.

Henrietta nodded, her tone practical. 'Most certainly, some noticed. And it has occasioned comment—I believe Pastor may owe you a debt of gratitude as, save Easter and Christmas, rarely is the service so well attended. It seems you have quickly gained a degree of notoriety. However, your exemplary appearance now will go a long way toward quashing any idle gossip.'

'Oh, tosh,' Dorothea disagreed. 'Henrietta, we are all the same beneath our dresses, as you know. Why should this merit such interest? The majority of the men who attended the fire are married and quite familiar with a woman's undergarments.'

Anna glanced around, expecting Pastor to appear, breathing fire and brimstone at such language used in his church hall.

'Oh, well said, Mrs Schultz,' Caroline agreed. She tugged upon Anna's waist. 'Come, Anna, don't we long for the day when a man becomes familiar with our unmentionables?'

Torn between scandalised laughter and tears, Anna dared not reply. The Mrs Schultzes smiled at Caroline's audacious words, though discreetly, behind their fans, as they took their leave.

'Oh no, your brother comes to claim you.' Caroline sounded positively woebegone.

'Am I to believe your disappointment is based solely upon losing *my* company?'

Caroline's cupid-bow lips lifted. 'Am I so very transparent? Promise you shall *both* attend service next week?'

'As yours is the second request I've received, I may have to entertain the notion.'

'The second? Do tell, who else wishes to steal my new friend?' Although she spoke to Anna, Caroline's focus was on Dieter, her body canted toward him.

'L-Luke Hartmann asked if I shall attend.' Anna stumbled over his name, although she'd rehearsed it a thousand times in her head during the week. She wasn't sure whether she should mention him, but she was desperate to share the thrill. Only the thought of telling Emilie about Luke kissing her hand made her disappointment at leaving anywhere near bearable.

Caroline's attention snapped to her. 'Luke? Oh, but he is lovely. Such a handsome man. He is very close friends with my brother. So that is settled. I shall see you next Sunday?'

Anna nodded, although Emilie had already forsaken her turn this week and should, in all fairness, attend the church the next. Anna would have to find a way to persuade Mother to allow her to go.

⁓

Anna was silent as the buggy jolted and creaked over the dry, ridged road. The thick velour curtain swayed behind her, occasionally billowing in a hot gust to catch at her hair. Though she was desperate to attend church the following week, she did not see how it could be managed. If she told Emilie there was a chance of Luke taking an interest, her sister would most certainly not trade her turn again. In all honesty, she would feel the same were the situation reversed. Yet, if Emilie attended in her stead, who was to say Luke wouldn't kiss her sister's hand as he had hers?

She tried to tear her mind from the conundrum, shifting her bustle so she could skew sideways on the seat to face Dieter. She longed to press him for information on Luke Hartmann, to ask exactly what words were spoken about her, but Dieter's farewell to Caroline had been protracted, and now he looked utterly miserable. Whereas before she would tease him, now she ached with empathy.

'Caroline seems very nice.'

Dieter shifted his hat forward, hiding his eyes. 'She is more than nice, Mäuschen.' He flicked the reins, a cloud of dust and bushflies rising from Arabella's broad back at the slap of leather. The horse's ears twitched, eavesdropping. Dieter cleared his throat. 'I . . . With harvest complete, I intend to court her. I shall speak to her father next week.' He ended in a rush as he committed.

'That's wonderful, Dieter.' Although she'd known the truth, hearing the statement aloud stole her breath. Her brother would no longer be all hers. She forced enthusiasm into her voice. 'Does Caroline know you intend this?'

'She's . . . very encouraging. You must get to know her, Anna. She's a thoroughly modern woman. Unlike anyone I've ever known.'

The tone of wonder in his words did little to mitigate her jealousy, but she forced her mind to how kind Caroline had been. 'I am happy for you but envious of her, Dieter. I shall be sad to lose you.'

'No need for your envy, Mäuschen.' Dieter's body vibrated against hers on the small seat and she could tell he restrained laughter.

A flock of galahs screeched from the cool shade of the gum trees, startling her as they swooped close to the buggy, playing a game of dare. She concentrated on Dieter, unable to fathom what now so amused him.

'Dieter? What do you mean?'

'I mean, Little Mouse, you will be far too busy to be envious of Caroline and me.'

The burn on her hand pulsed in the harsh sunlight and she flipped her hand on her knee, pulling a fold of her dress across to shade it. She was unbearably hot now, and sweat trickled between her breasts in a most unladylike fashion.

'You think I must pick up your chores?' Dieter did the heavy work around the farm. Although she was considered capable, she was certain Father wouldn't expect her to assist with clearing and sowing and reaping.

Dieter laughed aloud, unable to control his mirth. 'Promise you will not be angry with me, Anna? I cannot control Arabella if you start slapping at me, you know.'

He jested. She had not laid a hand on him since she was eight when, with the superiority of an additional nine years, he caught her fist and admonished, 'Anna, that is no way to treat a man you care for.'

'Promise,' she snapped, her temper fraying in the heat. If she was suddenly unable to understand the innermost workings of Dieter's mind, had she already lost him?

'Luke Hartmann asked my permission to call on you after church next week.'

Her heart clenched, ears no longer responding to the sounds around them. All her hopes had been pinned simply on seeing Luke at church again, tantalising herself with the foolish dream that perhaps he could consider her more than an amusing novelty. But if Luke had asked to call on her, his interest was real.

'Anna? Are you all right?' Dieter's voice reflected his alarm and he slowed Arabella's already far-from-swift gait. 'You are pale.'

She swallowed, her tongue clicking against dryness as she attempted to sound normal. 'I'm fine. My dress is a little tight. Just—' Her gloves lay across her lap and she used them to mop at her sweating palms. 'I would not know what to say to him, nor how to act. You and Father are the only men I ever speak with.' And she was afraid her tongue would get the better of her. She had found it hard enough to moderate her replies in church; driven by embarrassment, who knew what would come from her mouth?

'Hmm.' Dieter tilted his head. 'I see your problem. Perhaps it is fortunate, then, that the onus is on Luke to impress my little sister, rather than the other way around.'

'But what if . . . what if . . .' She could not articulate the 'what ifs'. Luke already impressed her, though she would not share that with Dieter. But what if she was so much less than he expected? And what *did* he expect? He had met her twice: once inarticulate and near-naked, the next time near-inarticulate and disfigured. Neither occasion had displayed her talents—not that she had any a man would seek out.

She didn't, but Emilie—the air left her lungs in a rush. 'Dieter, are you certain Luke didn't mean Emilie? Did he ask for permission to visit *your sister*?' That made far more sense. Emilie was accomplished and beautiful, but her laziness was a family secret. Spared knowledge of this flaw, any man would be attracted to her. And Luke had already met her, at her stunningly tragic best. Enough to stir any man's protective instinct.

Dieter's groan challenged the rumble of the iron wheels, the buggy lurching as they turned between the whitewashed fence posts that signified the start of Father's holding. 'For goodness' sake, stop doubting yourself. When I returned his jacket last week, Luke asked after your wellbeing and whether you would attend church today. You. By name.

Clearly, the man has yet to hear of your appalling inadequacy with a sewing needle, as it seems he is quite smitten. You'd not reached the far side of the hall with Mrs Ernst this morning before he had asked my permission to call on you.'

'Your permission.' She bridled, trying to buy time to order her thoughts. Turning from Dieter, she studied the sparse, straw-like stubble of the scythed wheat field, hiding her flaming face. Hawks, their finger-tipped wings fluttering minutely to adjust height and direction, hovered above the short stalks, hunting the sunbathing snakes and lizards. 'Why would he ask your permission?'

'In Father's absence, it is my right to deny your suitors.'

She turned back, the blood draining to her toes in a rush that left her chilled and lightheaded. 'You would not.'

Dieter's smile dropped, his eyes suddenly hard. 'I would, Anna. In a heartbeat, if I had any reservations about the man's suitability. Fortunately, although he is a little older than me, I know Luke well and hold him in high regard. But if he ever does anything to hurt you . . .' Dieter's hand clenched on his knee, his mouth tight.

⌒

'But it is not fair.' Although she knew the words were childish, Anna was unable to contain them. All her hopes and half-formed dreams crumbled around her. For almost three days, she had dreamed of Luke, vacillating between hope and the fear that, despite Dieter's assurances, Luke

146

had her confused with her sister. Even if it was not so, when Emilie attended church in her stead, Luke could not but help his eye falling upon her.

'Anna,' Mother chided, 'I understand your disappointment, but it is Emilie's turn to attend church. I shall attend with her—I am certain it is the last time I shall be able to make the journey for a period.' She patted the bump that sailed before her. 'Mr Hartmann will be prepared to wait another week. I shall invite him to dine the following Sunday. Perhaps you may travel from church with him if your brother will escort you.'

Mother knew how to temper the blow.

'I do so wish ...' Her voice whined like an angry mosquito, but as her mother wiped the back of her hand across her sweating brow, Anna bit her tongue.

Mother plodded toward her chair. 'I thought you would enquire about my visit to Mrs Ernst?'

'Of course, Mother.' She strove to make her tone dutiful, rather than sullen.

'In an interesting coincidence, Mrs Hartmann happened to be visiting Mrs Ernst at the precise time I had arranged to call.'

Breathless with sudden interest, Anna tried to maintain an air of indifference, returning to flicking her dust cloth over the furniture. Yet her pounding heart wanted to tumble the questions free: What is Mrs Hartmann like? Did she mention me? Has Luke said anything about me?

Mother waved her closer, the chair creaking beneath her weight. She looked tired, the heat wearing her down. The ride to Mrs Ernst's had not done her any favours.

'Mrs Hartmann is lovely. I have, of course, met her on numerous occasions. It seems we have a little in common.'

Anna dropped to her knees, folding her skirts into her lap to keep them clean. 'In common, Mother?'

Mother loved to tease, and would normally draw such information out for hours, but her breath was short. She puffed her cheeks, blowing the air out as though that would help her take more in, and patted the hand Anna rested on her knee. 'It seems we both have children who are quite lovelorn.'

Anna's nerveless hand fell from Mother's knee. How could her mother speak in such a straightforward fashion? Unless Anna misunderstood? Could Mother be speaking of Dieter—although, as far as Anna knew, only she was aware of his intentions toward Caroline Schenscher?

Despite her desperation, she could not question Mother directly. She would embarrass herself by leaping to conclusions and seeming overeager. 'Children, Mother? How many does Mrs Hartmann have?' Perhaps she was mistaken in believing there was only Luke.

Mother patted her bulge absentmindedly. 'Sadly, she has only been able to carry one child to birth.' Despite the gravity of the sentiment, her eyes were laughing. There was no way to misconstrue her words.

Anna dropped her gaze to the flagstones, her own breath as short as Mother's.

'Anna,' Mother's gentle voice drew her closer, 'you must not be afraid of your feelings.'

'But, Mother, to speak openly—'

Mother clicked her tongue, dismissing Anna's protest. 'Child, it is almost eighteen eighty. We must learn to adapt and change with the times. Is that not what your father is so fond of telling me? That this is a whole new world, with a new set of rules?'

It was fortunate that tar paper strips dangled from the ceiling to catch the flies, for Anna's mouth hung so far open, it could have housed two dozen. To hear her genteel mother, so fond of her European customs, speak of progress, left her speechless.

'That is not to say all the old rules are to be set aside.' Mother waggled a cautionary finger at her. 'And one of the rules is that you and Emilie take turns attending church. Next week is your turn to prepare the family luncheon, and that is what will happen. Believe me, it will do the young man no harm to wait a little longer.' As she patted her daughter's arm, Anna tried to hide the disappointment that etched her face. 'Now, pray fetch my basket from the trap. Mrs Ernst has provided an unguent that she advises you apply liberally to your wound. An extra week should be adequate time for it to heal and become somewhat more attractive.'

Uncovered, as Mrs Ernst directed, the burn was a mess of dead skin and pus, slewing off on the sleeve of her blouse. Mother was correct, of course. Anna had been worrying about how best to disguise her hand for church as she would very much like Luke to kiss it again. Properly.

Or improperly. The forbidden thought thrilled through her and she hastened to her feet.

Emilie sat outside the back door on an upturned churn, braiding Frederika's blonde hair as Frederik splashed in the zinc washtub at her feet.

'Emilie, would you like to borrow my burgundy dress for church? It is far more becoming on you than me.'

A mixture of charity and guilt prompted Anna's offer. And, with Emilie substantially taller, the gown would fall only to her calves; reinforcing that, at only fifteen, *she* was not yet entitled to full-length skirts.

13
Taylor

November 2008

The skeletons of the distant city stalked the skyline like giant, predatory insects in the rear-view mirror of the car.

It was about five hundred kilometres and two bathroom stops before Mum hit her stride, launching into an exceptionally off-key impersonation of Willy Nelson. Eventually, Taylor joined in. Windows down as their car barrelled along the highway, they belted out 'On the Road Again' at the top of their lungs as they fled from what they had each thought was love.

A startled mob of emus spread their useless wings and briefly ran alongside, peering into the car. Cranking up the window, Taylor frowned at the dashboard. 'Looks like well over a hundred to me.'

Mum dropped her sunglasses to the end of her nose, hiking an eyebrow. 'No speed limit on the plains.'

'Yeah, right.' There was no way Mum would break the law. Dad, though; he'd plant his foot to get this stretch of nothingness over and done with.

Which was why it was odd that he'd suggested they take a long settlement on the house when it had sold within two days of hitting the market. He was—predictably—not keen on Taylor going to South Australia. But, as he'd missed the newsflash that Cassie was headed to Europe, most of his solutions were a version of her house-sharing with her best friend. Despite his concern, Taylor could sense a lightness about him, as though, like Mum, he was relieved to be finally moving forward.

Somehow finding time that didn't exist in a gruelling life of study, exams and work, Taylor had gone to a football game with him, helped move some gear over to the mates he'd be bunking with, and reassured him that it was her choice to get out of the city, even as she mentally pleaded for him and Mum to come to their senses, and get their lives back together so she could get on with hers.

Though Mum had been willing to stay in Sydney for Christmas, Taylor couldn't face another round of pretend happy-family cheer. With Cassie gone, Mum unusually resolute, the house sold and life determined to change around Taylor no matter how hard she dug her heels in, the longer they delayed what was now inevitable, the more daunting her spontaneous commitment to her mother seemed.

After the stress of final exams, coupled with the emotional gutting of what felt like a three-way divorce, by the time they hit the road in mid-November, the farm at Settlers Bridge offered a refuge. Somewhere her dreams could be of another life, rather than the nightmare of her present.

Mum jerked her head at Taylor's pendant. 'You know you're driving me crazy with that?'

She slid the crucifix faster. 'Can't believe there'll be no Bondi this summer.'

'South Australian beaches are cleaner.'

'Beaches? Maybe you missed it, but the Grands' place is in the middle of a desert.'

'It's only ninety minutes or so from the beach. And Gran said she always used to swim in the river as a kid.'

'I'd look like an idiot tanning on the banks of the river.'

'You'd look like an idiot tanning full stop.'

Taylor closed her eyes, turning to her fantasies. She'd discovered that she couldn't force Anna and Luke's story to move forward—she was stuck in a loop, as though unable to turn to the next page of a book. But at least the nightly dreams brought Anna's world vividly to life: the coarse, hay-stuffed fabric of her bed replaced Taylor's soft mattress and smooth linen, and the sweet scent of stable manure overlaid the smells of suburbia on the evening breeze, as the sounds of the untamed bushland dulled the thrum of traffic.

Even awake, Anna's emotions echoed within Taylor. She rubbed absently at the back of her hand. The graze from her fall had healed quickly, leaving only a small scar. Yet the pain was still there. And, oddly, in her heart. She woke each day filled with wistfulness, like she had been touched by the fleeting promise of a love so beautiful it hurt too much to allow herself to remember. She knew that love hadn't been with Zac. What she'd felt for him had never been that intense. But Luke . . . Luke was safe and perfect and imaginary.

'What are you smiling about?'

Mum's words jerked her eyes open. 'Nothing.'

'Uh-huh.' Mum put on her conspiratorial 'we're all girls together let's share' voice. 'Well, that's good. You've been moping around for weeks. I guess the singer—Zac, was it?—got kicked to the kerb?'

Nice that Mum assumed she'd done the dumping. 'Sure.'

'And does this new "nothing" have a name?'

'No.' She wasn't sharing Luke with Mum. She barely wanted to share him with Anna.

Mum waved a packet of rice cakes toward her. 'Tell you what, how about we take a look around Settlers Bridge on the way through? It seemed such a cute little town. Maybe we can find something to rent there. And I'll see what the go is with leasing consulting rooms.'

Taylor licked the seasoning from a rice cake, wound down her window and tossed the base. 'I thought the idea was to be there for the Grands?'

Mum turned the music down. 'It is. But they're not incapacitated. They won't need me twenty-four-seven. Not yet, anyway.' Mum seemed unaware she had just proved her reason for moving was not entirely selfless. 'And I don't want it to be *too* miserable for you.'

Miserable. Was that what she was? Purposeless, irres-olute, loveless. Transferring uni was proving as difficult as she'd suspected, and right now, literally everything in Taylor's life seemed pointless and exhausting. She crumbled another rice cake in her lap. She had considered quitting or deferring to go overseas with Zac next year; perhaps she should take the year off, anyway. Regroup. Reassess.

Because Zac may not have been the only wrong path she'd chosen.

⌒

'What exactly do you do out here?' Taylor asked.

The afternoon sun streamed through the window over the kitchen sink, spotlighting dust mote fairies dancing above the bunch of lavender that matched the purple-striped placemats Gran had out today.

Two o'clock and the fourth cup of tea. Her fourth day at the farm, at an average of six cups a day, meant she was awash with a grand total of twenty-two cups of tea. All accompanied by scones, lamingtons or jam drops, depend-ing on the hour.

The maths pretty much answered her question: With no phone coverage and internet connection speeds that would make a caveman cry, *this* was what they did out here. The enforced social media cleanse, cut off from communication with the outside world, should have had a positive effect on her stress levels. Yet she felt . . . lost. Disconnected.

Gramps looked at Gran, seated beside him. He lifted thick white eyebrows over faded blue eyes, repeating Taylor's question with a note of surprise. 'What do we do? Well, we're custodians of the scrub.'

Taylor snorted, trying to bury her mirth in her cup. 'I'm not sure whether that makes you environmental warriors or pixies.'

Mum glared at her.

Gramps nodded sagely, his grey hair sticking up in tufts, more from his nose and ears than his head. 'You could say either, I guess. The Germans who settled here getting on for two hundred years ago set great stock in their folklore. Anyway, this property has the only remnant of pre-European-settlement woodland in the district. It's protected by a heritage agreement. That's why Magpie and I keep the weeds out of the scrub—'

'—and make sure the sheep don't get in,' Gran added.

Great. Mum's tree-hugging tendencies were inherited. No doubt her grandparents were up at sunrise each day, blessing Gaia. Well, not her. The solid stone walls of her new bedroom made for a womblike, soundless sleep. With the wood-framed double-sash window shut tight and the curtains drawn, time had no meaning. And her dreams were different each night now, encouraging her to linger. Anna's life offered a purity and simplicity that Taylor had never experienced, and she revelled in the escape.

'And there's the CWA meeting on Thursday,' Gran offered.

'I'm not much for baking, Gran. That's more Mum's thing.' Taylor didn't dare meet her mother's gaze. If one of them had to volunteer, she'd drop the Royal Easter Show champion in it quicker than blink.

'It's not only baking. We've got a nice craft area set up, too.' Gran wrinkled her nose 'Though, as you're young, you might be more—'

'—into the politics,' Gramps said.

Taylor had neither need nor desire to get involved in the small-town machinations behind the local old chooks group. 'I think the Settlers Bridge Progress Association or whatever can manage without me.'

'No, it's the CWA,' Gran said.

'They're very political,' Gramps added.

Taylor hid her incredulity in her cup. When did judging scone baking become politics?

The screen door at the rear of the farmhouse banged and she jumped, glancing around the table. Neither of her grandparents paid any attention, though Mum cocked an eyebrow.

'That was your back door,' Taylor said. 'Did you want me to get it?'

'That'll be Bert,' Gran said comfortably.

'You might get to meet her sometime,' Gramps said, creaking as he leaned across the table, reaching for another cake. 'Later this week we'll take the bikes out, and I'll run you round the boundaries. There are a couple of sandy spots where the wombats keep digging under the fence. The holes need to be filled in or the lambs get into the heritage scrub.'

'Bikes? I'm not sure I even remember how to ride.' First month of summer and it already had to be thirty-five degrees outside, the dry heat scorching like a blast from an open oven.

'Ag bikes. I picked up an extra one when your mum said you wanted to move over here.'

Wanted? That was a bit of a stretch. Taylor stuck her feet up on a vacant chair beneath the table.

Mum narrowed her eyes. Maybe her legs weren't that well-hidden. 'Motorbikes, Taylor.'

Her feet hit the linoleum. 'I don't have a licence.'

'Licence?' Gramps sprayed coconut from his lamington like a snow machine. 'You don't need a licence out here.'

Gran leaned over and dusted at Gramps' beard then daintily licked her fingers clean.

The plates crashed as Mum slammed them together and stood to take them to the sink. Behind her parents, she mimed gagging.

Taylor was delighted to see the flash of the mother she knew so well.

'Oh, here's Bert,' Gran said as the door to the lounge room creaked open.

Her grandparents had no common sense, no idea about home security. Taylor had locked the back door herself the last couple of nights after finding it wide open to let the breeze through the screen.

Gran leaned forward in her seat, making a high-pitched noise through vibrating lips. A shaggy black cat jumped onto the table, accompanied by a shower of dirt. The cat smooched Gran's face, imitating the rolling 'brrt' noise she made.

'Ah. Brrt, not Bert?' Taylor said.

'That's it,' Gramps said cheerfully. 'She's always made that noise. Sounds like she's calling kittens, but she uses it to round us up. Generally means she's brought a mouse or a rabbit in to feed us. It'll be running around in the lounge room, I suppose. Brrt seems to think she needs to look after us.' He creaked to his feet, looking more ancient than a man of seventy-four should. Older than he had only a few months ago, anyway. Chills rippled through Taylor. Anna was right: Everyone's time was limited. Had she and Mum moved here just to watch her grandparents die?

Gramps straightened, his back cracking. 'Anyway, we'll do the boundaries later. Right now, the wind is flat, and I'm—'

'—going flying,' Gran said, feeding a piece of cheese to Brrt.

Taylor's teeth clicked as her mouth snapped closed.

Swiping a faded tea towel over the cake plates, Mum barely glanced up. 'You renewed your pilot's licence then, Dad? Still flying old Smurf?'

'Got myself a nice new two-seater Jabby.' Gramps perched sunglasses on the grizzled tumble of what was left of his hair. 'Magpie and I figure when our time's up, we'll fly out of here together. Y'know, in a blaze of glory, or something similar. No going gently into the night for us.'

'Good plan.' Mum flicked the towel at a fly. 'But we only just moved here, so let us settle in first.'

'What kind of *weeds* do you have in that scrub?' Taylor blurted. Despite her habit of retreating into a fantasy world of psychedelic dreams, she was the most normal person in the room.

14
Anna

Anna rose before dawn so she could sneak up on the largest rooster. With a whispered apology, she had taken an axe to him, his duties now usurped by one of his sons. Seated in the warmth of the barn, she'd drawn the giblets, dropping them into a bowl to be made into a thin gravy. Her fingers ran over the bristly yellow skin of the carcass, meticulously checking every inch she'd plucked. There could not be any pin feathers left on the bird. He must look perfect. The down stuck to her hands and she scraped the feathers into the bucket at her feet. They would be used to stuff a cushion. Or perhaps a pillow for her glory box.

But now that the time to depart drew near, she felt ill. She clutched one hand to her stomach as she carefully set the plates on the breakfast table.

'Mother, I believe I may be coming down with something.'

Mother shuffled around the scrubbed wooden table and pressed her palm to Anna's forehead. 'I think you will be just fine. I shall give you a bromide powder before you go, but hurry up now. Take the leg of mutton from the cold store to the bakehouse before you go. We shall have both meats. The chicken will not be enough for all these men.' Mother sounded breathless with excitement. The inclusion of two cuts of meat, other than at Christmas and Easter, was unheard of. 'Make sure you put an apron over your dress.'

Anna would wear the blue pinstripe and the bustle again, of course. Not solely because it was beautiful, but because it was her only Sunday dress.

Dieter entered the house, kicking off his work boots as Mother started to chide him. Setting down the pail of milk, he grinned at the interrupted reprimand and gestured at the table. 'Flowers for breakfast, is it?'

Anna blushed furiously. She'd hoped no one would notice the sad bunch of wilting grasses and few wild-flowers. Well, not *no one*, but no one in her family.

Mother flicked a washrag at Dieter. 'If you want to eat, son, I suggest you keep a civil tongue in your head. I have both ears and eyes, and am aware you have news of your own that has the congregation gossiping.'

Dieter had the grace to look abashed and dropped into a chair, shovelling salted porridge into his mouth.

Anna could not eat. 'Are you certain the meat won't be dry? Don't let Emilie over-stoke the fire. You know what she's like. It's all or nothing. And the twins will be neat and tidy?' There was a list of other things she'd like to check on, but Mother's expression warned that the interference would not be welcome.

'I think I am quite capable, Anna. Now, get yourself into the trap, or you will be late. Unless, of course, you wish to stay here and allow Emilie to go in your stead?'

Although Dieter assured her Luke did not attend church with any degree of regularity—and indeed, informed of her unavailability, had not been present last week—she was not about to tempt fate.

Thirty minutes later, the buggy lurched across the uneven ground. Despite the horrid black flies trying to dart into her mouth, Anna hoped conversation would divert her from the unprecedented tingle bubbling from her chest through to her fingertips.

'Have you spoken with Caroline's father?' Unable to get past the fingers covering her mouth, the flies attacked her eyes instead.

Dieter grunted, a guttural sound from his stomach. 'No.' He twisted his lips and squinted into the harsh light. 'This business is rather more complex than it appears, is it not?' He kept his gaze on the horse's withers. 'If I ask and Caroline's father rejects my suit, what will I do then? I think . . . I think I cannot live without her.'

She had not realised her brother's voice could hold such agony. 'Why should he refuse you, Dieter? And Caroline, will she not make her own feelings known? It seems to me she is an intelligent woman and unafraid to speak her mind. I imagine she is entirely able to create and adapt to a new set of rules, as Mother advises.'

The reins fell slack in Dieter's hands. '*Mother* said that? Are you certain?'

She laughed, retying the bow on her bonnet, made loose by the hot wind. 'Indeed. Along with some other intriguing advice.'

Dieter lifted an eyebrow. 'Do tell me more, Mäuschen. Does this new insight mean you will not toy with Luke's affections, as some girls would?'

Still trying to process Mother's words herself, she was not prepared to share more, but she certainly did not intend to squander a precious minute on coy games.

A shiver of premonition chilled through her and melancholy settled heavy within her chest. Was it possible that she hoped for love so hard that she hurt? Could it be that sadness was inextricably linked to joy?

She did not know the answers. And, while she was scared to find out, she was more scared not to.

～

It was unfair but, despite Mother's words, the world had not changed and the old rules apparently still applied. After the service, women eddied to one side of the hall, men gathered on the other. Mrs Ernst came to check on Anna's scar. Not wanting to occasion her displeasure, Anna had the wound uncovered. But she had another, more important reason for obeying the edict: if Luke chose to kiss her hand again, she did not intend for the embrace to fall upon her glove.

Her heart seemed to stop as she spied him across the room, head and shoulders above all men. Unabashed, he stared at her, his indigo eyes drawing her like a hapless moth toward the sole light on a dark night.

Mrs Ernst's fan rapped on Anna's arm. 'Keep walking, child. There will be time enough to speak later.'

Time enough? Maybe not.

'I understand Mr Hartmann will pay a visit to your parents this afternoon?'

Manners forced her gaze back to Mrs Ernst. 'That is so.' Excitement coloured her words.

Mrs Ernst's mouth tightened, but Anna was uncertain whether it was disapproval or if the older woman hid a smile. 'Ahead of us, in the navy twill, you will recognise Mrs Augustine Hartmann. Perhaps I should introduce you?'

Sweat puddled inside Anna's glove and she removed her injured hand from Mrs Ernst's arm, scared of staining her sleeve.

Mrs Ernst laughed, a surprisingly melodic sound, given her stern countenance. Her lips folded in upon each other until they were invisible, though her eyes creased at the corners, betraying the stifled mirth. 'Come, Anna, do not look so terrified. Augustine is a dear friend of mine, and almost as eager to renew your acquaintance as her son.'

Her eyes lowered, Anna could see the deplorable rush of blood sweep her chest, exposed by her square-cut bodice.

Mrs Ernst's skirts whispered across the floorboards. 'Augustine, allow me to present Miss Anna Frahn. Miss Frahn, Mrs Augustine Hartmann.'

Luke must have his father's eyes, as Mrs Hartmann's were a far lighter blue, almost transparent.

Anna dropped a curtsey and Mrs Hartmann moved a hand to stay her. 'Miss Frahn, Anna—may I be so forward as to call you that? Anna, it is such a pleasure.' Her gaze rested on Anna's injured hand and her mouth puckered. 'Oh, this is the grievous injury that has my son so concerned? It certainly appears painful.'

Luke was *so concerned*?

'It is far better now,' Mrs Ernst said. 'Almost completely healed. As the outcome of the day could have been far worse, I would rule this an inconsequential price. Do you not agree, Anna?'

Mrs Ernst's black eyes were lively and amused, and Anna understood: the shame and pain of the bushfire were a small price for Luke's interest.

Mrs Hartmann glanced over Anna's shoulder as the morning tea bell rang. An infectious smile quickly lifted one corner of her mouth, a grin so like her son's, Anna could barely tear her gaze away. Mrs Hartmann lowered her voice. 'Truth to tell, the morning tea is my favourite part of Sunday service.' She linked her arm through Anna's and drew her toward the table.

Toward Luke.

Anna was suddenly oddly reluctant to approach—this moment was a test of her dreams. What if Luke was not all she remembered from their two brief encounters? What if she had been blinded by the fact he was the first man to pay her any interest? Worse still, what if she disappointed him? She wished she'd had the forethought to pop a vial of smelling salts in her reticule. It seemed she would need them at any moment.

'Miss Frahn.' Luke brought her hand to his lips and kissed her knuckles in quite chaste fashion. As he bent over her hand, she allowed her gaze to travel his features.

Catching her perusal from beneath the blond forelock that fell across his tanned forehead, the lines around his eyes deepened.

'Mr Hartmann.' His name was perfect. Like everything about him.

Luke straightened but did not release her hand. 'It is most kind of your parents to invite me to dine with your family. I very much look forward to it.' Now his eyes positively danced, acknowledging that he had manipulated the invitation.

'Father is indeed eager to hear your views on preventing flystrike in the sheep, Luke,' Dieter said, the chuckle in his voice perhaps obvious only to Anna.

'Miss Frahn.' Mrs Hartmann lifted her chin toward a group of women at the far end of the tea table. 'It seems we are missing quite a lively discussion about Russia's declaration of war on the Ottoman Empire. Shall we join them?'

Mindful of her bustle, Anna turned. As her hand left his, Luke's fingers stretched toward her, then quickly retracted into a fist. He doffed his hat.

'Lunch cannot come quickly enough, Miss Frahn.'

~

Hands clenched in her lap, Anna tried not to be too obvious in her study of Luke astride his fine chestnut gelding.

Dieter had made it clear he would love the opportunity to trade places, lumbered as they were with the grey-speckled back of the plodding Arabella, an odd companion to the sleek black buggy that was a reminder of more prosperous years. But she had beseeched him to stay; she was not ready to be alone with Luke in the confined space of the buggy. And she could not afford any more gossip attached to her name.

Caroline had also pleaded her case. 'Don't rush them, Dieter. There's plenty of time.'

But her words had swept a chill through Anna.

Now Luke rode close enough that he and Dieter might make conversation over her head—the crops, the weather, Father's well and the preponderance of snakes—all the things Dieter promised her were normal manly topics. Her participation unnecessary, she was content to allow the deep bass of Luke's voice to thrill through her and entertain nerves at the thought of how she was to manage the next few hours. Luke's frequent glances left her certain she would be unable to stand when they arrived home, much less walk to the door.

Moving ahead to open a gate, Luke stood in the stirrups to lean forward and release the chain. How would his impossibly broad shoulders look without the disguise of the stiff-collared shirt, tight waistcoat and dark frock coat?

Circling back to the buggy, he caught Anna watching him. 'Do you ride, Miss Frahn?'

'Not as often as I would like, Mr Hartmann. As you may have noticed, Arabella's girth is a little broad to cinch.'

He grinned at the ludicrous notion of saddling a draught horse. 'Your brother tells me you handle the reins with great skill.'

'My brother is eager to make me appear more accomplished than I am.' Dieter could have mentioned their discussion of her. 'Do you ride often yourself, Mr Hartmann?' One glance at the confident manner in which he handled the eighteen-hand beast beneath him made her question plainly unnecessary. She dropped her gaze, employing her fan to create a much-needed breeze on her face.

'I do, Miss Frahn. Although lately I find myself lacking a pleasurable destination. Perhaps you can suggest some-where I should ride?'

She suspected he was being flirtatious. Or was he genuinely interested in recommendations? 'I am not well travelled. In fact, I rarely leave the confines of our farm. You would do far better to ask Dieter for suggestions.' She twitched her hand, hidden by her skirt, against Dieter's leg, silently imploring him to rescue her from her stuttering foolishness.

A smirk lifted her brother's lips. 'I doubt there is necessity to travel far to find the entertainment you seek, Luke. My own experience is that the most pleasant distractions are to be found within our district. Indeed, our holding provides a number of attractive . . . vistas.'

As the buggy rolled through the gate, Anna noted the deep cleft appearing in Luke's cheek. 'I suspect that may be exactly what I desire. Miss Frahn, do you think your father would object to me trespassing upon your property?'

Anna was sure they joked about her. Or did she want so badly for it to be about her that she imagined it?

She took as deep a breath as her corset allowed. 'I believe, Mr Hartmann, were you to request permission, such a venture would not be considered trespass.'

His horse snorted and shied sideways, instantly controlled by a press of his knees.

Emboldened by her own wit, Anna turned to face him, dropping her fan to her lap. 'Your animal appears spirited, Mr Hartmann. Is that your preference?'

His eyes met hers. 'Indeed, Miss Frahn. I have little interest in timidity.'

Perhaps it was fortunate, then, that Mother often chided her for a forthright tongue—though she would not have him think her a fishwife.

Luke dropped back to close the gate and then returned. 'So, as I have shared my desire, what is it you dream of, Miss Frahn?'

He rode so near the buggy she could touch his leg—if she dared. Blushing and grasping for something to say that would not reveal that he was the subject of many of her dreams, she blurted her secret. The one she had been unable to share with Dieter at the well; the one Emilie would tease mercilessly about, should she discover it.

'I would like to attend university.'

Luke quirked an eyebrow. 'An interesting notion. You have given consideration as to how you would achieve this?'

She shook her head. Although women had been permitted to attend university for the last four years, her lack of schooling made her aspiration ridiculous. 'I think perhaps

I should settle for obtaining another book to read, instead. 'Tis nothing but an idle dream.'

'I live in the hope that dreams may come true,' Luke said. He cantered toward the final gate.

Although normally he would drive straight to the barn and unharness, leaving Anna to walk across the yard, Dieter drew the buggy up in front of the house. He flipped the reins over the dash rail and dropped to the ground, but Luke was already alongside, waiting to assist her down the low step she was quite capable of navigating.

As she stood, Luke grasped her waist and then swung her free of the buggy. His light touch was entirely appropriate, barely felt through her layers of clothes, and she had yet another reason to wish corsets were not a necessary fact of life. Hidden from view by the closed sides of the vehicle, Luke's hands spanned her waist, his thumbs touching in front. He did not release her instantly, as decorum demanded. Instead, he looked deep into her eyes. Fearing he would hear the pounding of her heart, Anna held her breath to try to still the frantic beat. But she did not flinch from his gaze.

On the far side of the buggy, Dieter cleared his throat meaningfully and Luke slid his hands from her waist. He cocked his head toward the house as he offered his elbow.

The men hung their hats on the peg inside the door as they entered. Luke ran a hand through hair the gold of summer wheat, forcing it off his face and into order. Anna would have liked to do that for him. Instead, she went to assist Mother, hiding her urge in necessary busyness.

The twins had been scrubbed and their faces shone. Obviously well drilled, they sat at the table in unnatural silence, their identical blue eyes growing larger as they took in Luke's frame dominating the room.

Mother had taken the best china from the bow-fronted leadlight cabinet. The polished, although slightly tarnished, silver lay alongside the embossed crockery. The table crowded with tureens and platters, the spread was reminiscent of their Easter feast. Anna's wilted arrangement looked sad by comparison. Could she slide the vase from the table without being noticed? Although the flowers did add a sweet fragrance to air heavy with the rich smells of roasted meat.

Father extended his hand. 'Mr Hartmann, good to see you.' The men of the district knew each other well, often exchanging labour on their properties. 'You are most welcome in my home.'

Evidently, Anna did not need to share the fears Dieter had about Caroline's father not accepting his presence.

Emilie simpered and straightened a fork, managing to convey the notion that the beautiful presentation of the table was hers. It likely was. She hurried to seat Luke alongside Dieter, fussing to pour them cider from the stoneware crock, making herself indispensable. Anna's fingers itched to slap her, but she realised that probably would not impart the impression for which she aimed.

Anna barely ate. In part, because she had no appetite, but also because, upon her request, Emilie had drawn her corset extra tight that morning. Whenever she glanced up, Luke's eyes were upon her. Swallowing the merest morsel was unthinkable. She only prayed Father didn't comment on her unusual behaviour. Fortunately, it seemed he was too busy, the men discussing farming as they ate heartily.

The meat and vegetables finished, Mother stacked empty plates. 'Emilie, assist me please.' A nod of her chin directed Anna to remain seated.

Luke's eyes found her across the table. 'You said you have travelled little, Miss Frahn?'

Her family's interest turned to her, intrigued as to how she would reply. No more so than she. 'Little? I don't believe I exaggerated to such an extent, Mr Hartmann. I have not set foot outside the district.' She tried to meet his gaze, but her eyes refused to leave the curve of his lips.

Those lips quirked. 'You have no interest in moving from here?'

She was reading hints into every word the man spoke. It was her parents' fault. Given the opportunity to socialise more, surely she would not find him so fascinating? 'Much as I love my parents, Mr Hartmann, I certainly do not intend to stay under their roof forever.' Dreams of university aside, she would be entirely content with husband and hearth. But it seemed not the moment for such an admission.

Father snorted. 'Much as we love our daughters, we certainly do not intend them to stay under our roof forever.'

Mother banged the ladle as she piled dishes in the sink. 'Johann. You must not speak so.'

'Is it not true, Johanna? Do you not long for a few less children in the house?'

Mother laid a hand on her distended belly, pursing her lips, although her eyes laughed. 'You would ask me such a thing now, husband? Shame on you.'

Emilie turned quite pink. Even the tips of her ears blushed. Of course, it was an attractive flush, adding to her charm. Fortunately, Luke had not looked her way.

'I'm certain Emilie shall leave soon enough,' Father teased. 'But it may be in my best interest to keep Anna here. Who else will protect my property as she does?'

Shock quivered through Anna. She could not believe Father would mention such a matter in company.

'But Father, you would not wish for your daughters to have reputations?' Emilie chimed in, calculatedly ingenuous. 'Would you not be humiliated to have them considered manly in their abilities?'

Dieter cut across her. 'Would you not be humiliated to have no roof over your head, Emilie? The clothes you love so much reduced to ashes?' He turned to Luke. 'Despite Anna's brave efforts, we shall be short on fodder this year. Are you leasing paddocks?'

The talk returned to farming.

As mortified as she felt, Anna could not allow Emilie's input into the conversation to be more memorable than her own. Masking her discomfort, she forced herself to speak.

'Mr Hartmann expressed interest in specific features of your holding, Father.'

Luke leaned back in his chair, toying with his fruit knife. He appeared not the least discommoded by her garrulous family. His gaze fixed to hers, a slow smile lifted his mouth. 'Indeed. I am prepared to invest considerable time and effort in pursuit of what I seek.'

Her heart skipped. 'That should not be necessary, Mr Hartmann. You will find Father's well not at all difficult to locate. I am certain he will be happy to provide you with precise information regarding the drawing capacity.'

Luke inclined his head, acknowledging a score to her.

Mother signalled Emilie to remove the rose-patterned comport, which held thin slices of the remnants of the Easter Königskuchen, rich with raisins and currants and spread with blackberry jam. 'Dieter, perhaps you and Anna would care to show Mr Hartmann around the property?'

As the men retrieved their hats, Mother crooked her finger, beckoning Anna beyond her bedroom curtain. 'Anna, come take my parasol. You don't want to ruin your complexion.'

Anna hid her laughter. Expected to take the bulk of the yard chores while the men worked further away on the property, it was a constant source of vexation to Mother that she rarely remembered to don a hat.

They could not speak freely with the men only feet away, but Mother pressed her cheek against Anna's. Her lips close to Anna's ear, she risked a whisper. 'He is incredibly handsome, Liebling. And his manners are almost European.'

Anna stifled a gasp, certain this was the highest accolade she would ever hear Mother give.

As they exited the house, Luke held open the door for her. Careful to look only straight ahead, she was aware of him ducking to clear the lintel behind her. Father and

Dieter were tall, but never had she seen anyone need to stoop through their doorway.

They blinked to adjust their eyes to the harsh sunlight of the yard, the house kept dim to enhance the illusion of coolness.

Dieter shuffled a few feet away. 'I must stable Arabella,' he lied. He had only to unharness Arabella and give the single word command and, like any plough horse, she would take herself to the stable.

Luke nodded at him, the gesture appearing curiously like thanks. 'Then, with your permission, Dieter, perhaps your sister could accompany me as far as the creek. As our properties share the same watercourse, I should very much like to see your father's successful well, which I would like to emulate on my own property. But I am concerned I shall run short of time.'

'Of course, of course.' Dieter waved them away. 'I'll give Arabella some oats. And maybe a rub down.' The words floated over his shoulder as he led the horse across the yard.

Luke laughed openly now, offering his arm. 'Shall we?'

They crossed the stubble-filled paddock to the creek, the smell of the scorched earth harsh in Anna's throat. Broad trails crisscrossed the ground, created by the passage of millions of tiny feet as bull ants scurried back and forth along the same track over hundreds of years. She wondered if the paths would remain when both the ants and her own family were long gone. It was something of a sad thought, an acknowledgement of the transitory nature of life, and she pushed it away.

'Tread carefully,' Luke cautioned, as though she'd not walked this way countless times.

Despite the farmyard noise around them—the strident call of ewes summoning their lambs, birds carolling, the bees buzzing as they searched the red flowering gums for nectar—her world was a vacuum. All her awareness was focused on Luke's proximity. She knew each time he drew breath, could see the pulse in his throat from the corner of her eye, felt his corded forearm beneath her modestly light grip.

She gestured at the well as they neared, but Luke drew her toward the privacy of a pepper tree, the leaves willowing to the ground on soft lime fronds.

He held aside the branches, revealing a green cave, the air redolent with the spicy scent of the pink pepper berries. 'It will be cooler under here,' he murmured. 'Miss Frahn. May I call you Anna?'

She nodded. Her mouth dry, a nervous beat fluttered high in her chest.

Luke took her parasol and set it against the gnarled trunk of the tree. Turning her hand to expose the palm, he traced a finger across it. Tiny jolts thrilled through her and she bit at her lip, determined not to tremble. Scared to look elsewhere, she focused directly ahead, on his chest rising and falling.

'Anna, I do not wish to alarm you, but I intend to be honest with you. You intrigue me. You are quite the most beautiful young lady in the district, and it seems you are also spirited.' He took a deep breath, closing his hand around hers. 'I mean to pursue you. If you should wish me not to do so, it would save me much heartache if you spoke up now.'

For once, she had her tendency to blush under control—perhaps because she was not embarrassed. All she felt was a rush of intense longing. And disbelief. But, should this be some aberrant dream, she intended to enjoy it. 'Mr Hartmann, I fear I am not a terribly fast runner. And, as I have a tendency toward clumsiness, perhaps it would be better for all concerned if I make no attempt to flee your pursuit?'

His breath escaped on a low chuckle. 'I shall be eternally grateful to whichever parent bequeathed you such ineptitude toward athletic pursuits.' His forefinger and thumb tilted her chin, so she must meet his eyes.

She tried not to swallow, knowing it would be audible in their enclosed proximity. Luke leaned close, his breath warm and sweet against her cheek. She thought—she hoped—he would kiss her.

'I shall very much enjoy courting you, sweet Anna.' He lifted her palm to his mouth, pressing his lips firmly against it.

She swayed toward him, her knees weak, her fingers curled, keeping the kiss. She might never wash her hand.

A slight frown creased Luke's forehead, a shade of regret constricting the indigo eyes. 'Your brother summons us.'

'Truly?' Her utterance was embarrassingly breathless. She could not hear anything beyond her own heartbeat and Luke's words.

'Truly. And, if I am to go now and ask your father's permission to court you, it is probably best we are not caught alone here.'

15

Taylor

'What you up to there, Peach?'

Taylor held up her phone as Gramps stumped into the kitchen. 'Farm Barn.'

Gramps squinted. 'What's that, now?'

'Virtual farm kind of thing. I have to move sheep and cows and chickens and stuff into sequence to have them disappear from the screen.' A horrifying thought nagged: was this what taking a year off would be like? She felt uncentred, unanchored, pointless.

Gramps stared at the screen for a long moment, then at Taylor for an even longer one. 'Guess it's time we got to those bikes, huh?'

She'd hoped she had escaped that threat–promise, as each day Gramps had either declared the flying weather too good to resist or had already checked the fences by the time she got up.

'C'mon, shift your legs,' he ordered, heading back outside.

He plodded down the rocky slope to one of the large stone sheds that bordered what she had learned was called the house yard. Gran and Gramps were very particular about the designation of each area, though Taylor could see little difference. Immediately around the house was the garden, with the pond and a few struggling plants. Then the house yard, a vast paddock populated with chickens, geese and ducks, separated from the acres beyond by stone sheds and tumbledown fences. Next was the home paddock, where pet sheep, a cow and a pair of buck-toothed alpaca roamed, the last apparently existing only to spit at unwary visitors. Beyond all that were the paddocks, either sown with crops or home to wandering mobs of sheep.

'Gramps, how is looking after all of this any kind of retirement?'

'How is it not?' He glanced sideways at her and Taylor immediately wished he'd focus on the uneven ground. Given his age and instability, he was a falls risk.

'Well, it's not like you get to sit around and relax. Gran's got that huge house to look after and you always seem to be out in the yard.'

'Retirement just means that you do what you've always longed to do, Peach. Not that you curl up and die.'

She flinched. Her grandparents were far too comfortable with that word.

'Now, if you're smart,' Gramps continued, 'you make sure you find your passion when you're young. But it doesn't always work out that way. Magpie followed me around for years while I chased my career. But when I quit, she finally put her foot down, said she wanted to come back to Settlers Bridge. She spent her childhood near here and said it's always felt like home. So, after forty years, it was her turn to call the shots. And I'm darn glad she did. Would never have discovered flying if she hadn't dragged me out of the rat race.'

'You didn't fly when you were younger?'

'Expensive hobby, Peach. If you're young enough to climb into the cockpit without psyching yourself up and spending ten minutes trying to work out how to get your damn legs in, you can't afford it. Young enough to do it or old enough to afford it; life's always a balancing act. Nothing works out perfectly.'

Two motorbikes rested on stands near a row of battered jerry cans and an assortment of funnels, rags and buckets in the large stone shed. 'You drive, don't you, Peach?'

'Of course.'

Gramps gestured at the dusty blue bike. 'Kick start. Toe down through the gears.' His knobbly hand moved to the handgrip. 'Accelerator, clutch, brake. When you speed up, go up a gear. Slow down, you kick back.'

She gazed at him, slack-jawed. Seriously, those were supposed to be instructions?

Gramps chuckled. 'Easy to remember, right? Because kicking back *is* slowing down.'

'Yeah, I got that. Not much else, though.'

'You'll manage just fine, Peach. It's as easy as . . . riding a bike.'

Obviously, Gramps thought he was hilarious. He slowly straddled his faded red bike, the vinyl seat noisily expelling air. At least, she hoped it was the seat.

'Helmets, Gramps?'

He gave her another of those long looks. 'Just follow me, Peach.'

Evidently, helmets were as overrated as licences.

'Don't run over any snakes, they'll still get you after you've squashed them.'

'Awesome.' Gramps would putter along so slowly she'd end up *parked* on a snake.

Except, with a heady waft of petrol, he'd already gone. The roar of the engine echoed around the blue smoke-filled shed. Tucking the crucifix safely into the neck of her shirt, Taylor wheeled the bike out of the shed. She climbed on, encouraged by how easily the motor started. It rumbled throatily, the seat vibrating beneath her. She kicked the bike into gear and released the clutch.

And stalled.

Not as easy as the total lack of instruction had implied it should be.

Toeing her way back to neutral, she tried again, releasing the clutch more cautiously.

The bike lurched and stalled.

And again.

Her grandfather had disappeared by the time Taylor finally got moving, though his dust trail hung like a sheer curtain in the boundless, achingly blue sky.

Hands wrapped around the grips, trying to balance her fear of speed with the need to stay upright, Taylor wobbled along the dirt track that sliced between paddocks waving with golden crop. Opaque, baby-pink rocks lined the edge of the road, the quartz glinting and glittering as it caught the sun. As she cautiously accelerated, the breeze whipped hair across her face and her eyes watered. Dust filled her nose, somehow clean and earthy, nothing like the dankness of rotting vegetation she was accustomed to.

A curl of the throttle and the engine surged between her knees, her hair streaming back, wild and free. As she dragged in great breaths of the dry heat, the tension that had cinched her chest for weeks eased and her heart swelled. Surrounded by open paddocks, far-reaching views and endless sky, the freedom she hadn't realised she was seeking arrived in a startling rush.

Free. No job, no uni, no career, no clubs, no beach, no friends, no partner.

The last two plunged a stab of loss through her chest, but she gritted her teeth and pursued the thought. Was the move here the one opportunity she would have to reinvent herself? To choose her own path? For the first time in her life, nothing was preordained. A completely blank page, waiting for her to write upon it. Her future lay in her hands.

Well, not totally in her hands, she decided, as she spotted Gramps waiting further up the fence line.

Remembering to slow and kick down a gear before she executed a wobbly turn, Taylor headed cross-country, the bike jouncing over ploughed ridges and ruts on the edge of the wheat field.

She followed Gramps along a narrow strip of red dirt as he patrolled a fence separating the field of dry yellow crop from the dappled shades of green in the scrub.

When his bike rolled to a stop, Gramps put one foot on the ground and pointed to where the bottom wire of the fence was bent into an arch like the Sydney Harbour Bridge. Beneath it, a patch of dirt was rubbed into a smooth bald spot.

'Here you go, Peach. See the long scrape marks on the far side? This one was a roo, not a wombat.'

'A kangaroo? Wouldn't they jump over?'

'They do. That's why we leave the top rail loose on the wooden fence next to the cattle grid: it's their favourite crossing. That way, if the roos hit it, the plank falls and they don't get hurt. But there's a mob lives in this scrub and when the adults go over, the joeys often go under. Funniest thing you'll ever see, a kangaroo with its arse in the air, crawling under the fence. Shovel is on the back of your bike.'

Taylor peered at her hands. She should have brought gloves. But what the heck, it wasn't like they were surgeon's hands. And, unlike Anna, she had no dashing farmers queuing to kiss them.

She grabbed the shovel and scooped soil into the hole, fountains of dirt cascading over her boots as she stomped it down. It felt both unusual and satisfying to do something physical, something with a readily identifiable purpose and assessable impact.

Gramps had walked up the fence line a bit and now waved her over. 'Look through there, Peach.'

She peered in the direction his wavering finger indicated. Predictably, nothing but scrub.

'Where?'

'Those rocks. Under the spiny acacias. See them?'

'Yeah. They're rocks, all right.' And those were the same huge bushes that had attacked her on their camping trip a few months earlier, the thorns no longer disguised by pretty yellow flowers.

'There's a load of termite mounds over there. Might be an echidna burrow under the rocks. Go take a closer look.' Gramps stretched the top strand of wire up, placing his hand between the sharp barbs twisted into it every few centimetres. In a fluid move she couldn't have predicted, he lifted his foot, forcing the second wire down with this boot. 'Off you go. Scoot between. Tell me what you find.'

Snakes, most likely. She wouldn't know an echidna burrow if she fell down it.

Taylor tramped across the few metres of open ground patched with straggling, dead vegetation. Then she threaded between the trees, cautiously approaching the acacia bush as though there was a chance it would attack. Rather than push through it to reach the rocks Gramps wanted her to investigate, she circled a clump of gum trees. Multiple slender white trunks sprang from a single dead stump. The twittering of fledglings echoed loudly from within the hollow wood.

The outcrop Gramps directed her to wasn't just a couple of rocks. Hidden behind clusters of dead tumbleweed and festooned with the creeping vine she had used for the campfire, the rocks formed a partially tumbled wall.

Gooseflesh shivered across Taylor's arms. *A stone fence.* Her knees thumped into the dirt. She brushed her palm across the rocks. Patterned with dry, crumbly moss, they'd probably been hidden for a hundred years. Untouched. Unremembered. A marker of a long-gone world, a forgotten history. But a past that seemed so close, she could almost recall it . . .

Yearning flared within her, as though a secret waited for discovery, if she only knew where to look. What to look for.

Driven by a bizarre compulsion, she wormed her fingers into a crack between the stones, scrabbling to reach deep inside the heart of the wall. She didn't care about the snakes or the spiders or the dirt. Because this rock hadn't been touched since Anna and Luke's time. If she could drive her fingers deep enough, perhaps she could reach them.

Her heart ached with longing.

Eyes closed, she willed a connection. Sunlight flickered red and orange across her eyelids.

The buzz of bees filled her ears. Her blood pounded as Luke leaned closer. The fragrance of crushed pepper berries tickled her nose, his warmth wrapped her like silk. His lips caressed her palm.

A gasp exploded from her lips and Taylor jerked her hand back. Stared at it, appalled.

What was she doing? Luke and Anna weren't real.

She shoved to her feet and backed away from the wall. Then she turned and stumbled toward Gramps.

'So, echidna burrows?'

She lifted one shoulder. 'Looks like a stone wall.'

'Just a fence?' Gramps sounded disappointed.

What was she supposed to say to that? That the touch of the rocks had left her inexplicably sad, like something beyond precious had been stolen from her? 'Yep. Saw some stonework where Mum and I camped, too. That's a few kilometres from here, isn't it?' She pointed into the scrub.

Gramps chuckled and took her hand, swivelling her one hundred and eighty degrees to point across the paddocks. 'Thataway, Peach, though the creek winds through most of the properties hereabouts. Kept them all connected, I guess. Lot of history in these parts.' He chewed on a stalk of dry grass. 'Used to be more farms, but they've merged into bigger properties over the years. Guess it takes more land to make a living, nowadays.' He offered her a piece of straw like it was gum. She stuck it between her teeth and he nodded. Considering Mum had said that he was city born and bred, her grandfather was probably taking the whole farmer thing a bit far. Yet he was kind of cool.

Warmed by the sun, the pendant on her necklace eased the ache in Taylor's chest. 'Hey, thanks for the necklace, Gramps. Forgot to say it when we came over last time.'

Her grandfather looked confused for a moment, then focused on the chain she twisted around her fingers. 'Ah, that thing. Not really me you need to thank.'

'Mum said there was some story about it?'

'Bit of a funny one.' Gramps tipped his head back, watching a small plane circle far above, as though it would round up his memory. 'Your gran found it hanging in the spare bedroom—your room. Thing is, it was on that nail above the fireplace, plain as day, but we'd never noticed it.

187

Guess, when you get old, you look back more than you look up.' He gazed across the scrub. 'Landlord suggested we might know someone who would like it.'

'Landlord? You don't own this place?' she said, surprised.

'No, Peach, forty years working for the government doesn't see you walk out with enough super to afford an acreage this size. Well, speak of the devil.' Gramps lifted his chin and she peered in the direction he indicated.

'What?'

'That flicker of movement, yonder? It'll be the owner or his cousin Matt riding through.'

'I can't even hear a bike.'

'Horse.'

'You're kidding? I thought mustering was done by heli-copter.' Settlers Bridge had a certain old-world charm, but surely the farming practices had moved with the times?

Gramps snorted. 'No helis round here, wrong kind of land. Lad has more bikes, cars and trucks than you could poke a stick at, though. Family's been out this way forever, from what I hear, and they do okay. But Luke's got a rare way with horses. Rides the biggest chestnut gelding you'll ever see. Likes to take him out on the trails along the creek.'

Taylor's blood turned to ice, the tiny crystals filling her lungs. She couldn't miss the approaching horse now, the rider sitting easy in the saddle, rolling with the beast's unhurried gait that managed to eat the distance between them with merciless speed.

Luke.

It was a common name. She had to pull herself together.

Gramps shifted the stem of grass to the other side of his mouth. 'G'day there, Luke. I was just telling my grand-daughter about your horse. Peach, Luke.'

She shook her head. 'Taylor.' Her voice came out rusty as she squinted up at the rider's silhouette, trying to make out his features.

'G'day.' The guy didn't dismount, merely flicked a finger to the Akubra that shaded his face so completely she wondered whether his Aviators were necessary. 'Your grandparents mentioned you were coming to hang out for a while.'

Perhaps she was overly sensitive, but it seemed he inferred she had nowhere better to be. No career, no aspira-tions. 'They also mentioned this necklace belongs to you,' she said, to prove he, too, had been the topic of discussion.

'I was telling Peach that when you insisted I hand it over to someone who'd appreciate it, my favourite grand-daughter came to mind,' Gramps said.

'Only granddaughter,' she corrected. Somehow, the fact didn't detract from the title.

'Seems perhaps it's where it's supposed to be, then,' Luke said.

'The crop is looking good.' Gramps waved an expan-sive arm at the paddock.

Luke nodded. 'Not bad considering the lack of rain. Not that we want any now.'

Taylor kicked at the baked earth with the toe of her boot. 'Why not? Seems like the ground is thirsty.'

'It is,' Luke agreed. 'But a decent fall now makes it harder to get the machinery through the paddocks. Then there's the risk the grain will go mouldy. Plus yield loss: too much rain literally washes the seed so that it gets smaller. Smaller seed means less weight, means less tonnage, means less money.'

His horse tossed its head, sidestepping, and Taylor moved further back. The huge animal was the reason for her heart pounding. Totally. 'I guess that explains why farmers are so focused on the weather. Well, reputedly,' she added, her knowledge on the subject coming only from news reports.

Luke grunted. 'Yeah, stock, crops, weather. That's pretty much the sum of our conversational skills.'

Taylor stared at Luke. Did he have any idea what he'd said? Of course, his words were prosaic, entirely logical.

Yet totally unnerving in their similarity to those uttered by Dieter . . . in her dream.

'Righto.' Gramps filled the silence. 'Be seeing you, then.'

Luke nodded and lightly tapped the horse's flank with his booted heels. 'Hope so,' he said as the gelding whickered, then moved off.

Her pulse still inexplicably racing, Taylor refused to stare after him.

16
Anna

Anna had seen Luke only once during the week, a few hours under her mother's chaperonage when he came to take tea with them. Winter approached and, like all farmers, he ploughed the land ready to seed with the first, long-overdue, rains of the season. Sunday was the only day he wouldn't work from dawn until after dusk. Much to Emilie's disgust, Mother ruled that Anna might again attend church.

Luke entered as the service commenced, sliding in to share the Frahns' pew. Anna's heart skipped several beats, then rushed to catch up. Separated from him only by her brother, she prayed for the sermon to be lengthy, to extend the rare few minutes of their proximity. Her gaze fixed on the large, work-hardened hands braced on Luke's knees. Hands that had held hers and briefly stroked her face.

191

Her thoughts were most definitely sinful.

As the service ended, Dieter offered her his arm. Luke stepped forward at the same moment and Dieter looked to Anna for permission, then placed her hand on Luke's arm.

Sparks flared through her as she closed her fingers on the muscularity beneath layers of clothing. She longed to draw closer, to greedily inhale his fragrance of sunshine and earth, as though she must store the memory.

Sadly, it took only seconds to stroll to the hall under the beady eyes of the entire congregation. Wary of the quivering interest of their neighbours, their conversation was carefully limited.

'Miss Frahn.' Luke tipped his head, eyes dancing. She knew that, in his mind, he was calling her Anna. 'I found much to enjoy in Pastor's sermon today.'

'I only wish it had been longer.' She was certain neither of them had heard the sermon. 'Perhaps we could walk a little more slowly? It is difficult to match my stride to yours.' She hid her smile; Luke already strolled at such a leisurely pace, elderly parishioners had moved around them in their eagerness to reach the burdened tea tables in the hall.

'My apologies, I have no wish to rush you . . . at least, not in this.'

The hidden meaning stole her breath and she dared not speak again as Luke delivered her to Caroline's side with a finger to the brim of his hat, a slight tilt of his head.

Caroline narrowed her eyes at his broad back as he left them. 'Rather delicious.'

Panic fluttered in Anna's chest. Caroline was quite beautiful, and so much more worldly than her. If she chose to set her cap at Luke, there was no hope for Anna. Nor for Dieter.

Caroline pursed her lips and glanced at Anna. 'I confess, I am quite jealous.'

'Jealous?' Anna squeaked. Clearing her throat, she tried to sound less terrified. 'Jealous?'

'Indeed.' Caroline drew her into the promenade. 'I rather liked the idea of introducing you to my own brother.'

Relief rushed through Anna. 'I'm sure my sister, Emilie, would be most happy to make your brother's acquaintance.'

'Ah, an interesting plan. I shall see what I can arrange.'

They walked the hall for several minutes, making polite conversation with the other women until the tea bell melodically tinkled.

Detaching from the group of men, Luke strode toward them.

Caroline tapped her fan against his forearm. 'It is an unusual pleasure to see you at church again, Mr Hartmann.'

'It seems my life is replete with unusual pleasures at the moment, Miss Schenscher.' He offered Anna his arm. 'If you will excuse us, I would steal Miss Frahn to greet some of my friends.'

'Of course.' Caroline waved her fan in dismissal. 'Just don't monopolise her for too long. I rather enjoy her company.'

As they crossed the room, Luke brought his elbow close to his side, trapping her hand to draw her in tight. 'It gives me pleasure to be in a position to introduce you, Anna.' His quiet words burned the side of her neck. 'But rather less pleasure to know that my friends long to meet you.

Please excuse my boorishness if I manage to find nothing complimentary to say about any of them.'

⁓

Luke rode alongside them for part of the journey home, and she tried to persuade herself that she was content to watch him from the corner of her eye, listening as he conversed with Dieter.

Dieter held Arabella back, allowing parishioners headed in the same direction to outdistance them. He reined the buggy to a halt beneath the drooping gums and leaned across Anna to look up at Luke.

'Luke, could I beg a favour of you?'

'It is yours for the asking.'

'It's far too long since I've ridden anything but the broad back of this old mare.' Dieter flicked his crop disparagingly at Arabella. 'I'd very much like to feel an active beast under me again. If I could prevail upon you to drive my sister, perhaps I could take your fine horse until your turnoff?'

Dismounted before Dieter had finished speaking, Luke draped his reins loosely across the pommel of his saddle. The far side of the buggy lifted beneath Anna as Dieter left, then dipped as Luke climbed aboard. The narrow leather seat made it hard for him to avoid touching her—yet she made no effort to move closer to her low door.

'Go on ahead of me,' Dieter called. 'It will take me a little time to become accustomed to handling a horse again.'

Releasing the brake, Luke clicked his tongue and shook the reins. Arabella snorted her judgement at the interruption to routine and pulled forward.

Luke turned to Anna, his knees grazing hers. 'I was becoming afraid I'd have no time alone with you this week.'

'I doubt you were any more worried than I.'

Luke gave a lopsided grin. 'I am grateful for your lack of artifice.'

'I have given the matter much thought.' She shot him a glance, making certain he understood her innuendo. There had been little but him in her thoughts. The cleft in his cheek deepened, so she took a breath and plunged on. 'We may live eighty years, if we are fortunate. Therefore, I am already near a quarter the way through my allotted time. It would seem wasteful not to enjoy every moment that remains.'

Luke looked at her and she glanced away, fanning the flush that climbed her neck.

'I could not have articulated the matter better myself, Anna.' He took her hand and she wished she had extended Mrs Ernst's direction to leave the burn uncovered by one more week.

He read her mind. 'Would you mind removing your glove? The reins are not particularly clean and I would not wish to ruin your best gloves by transferring dirt to them.'

The rhythmic creak of the buggy springs disguised her loud swallow. Pinching the fingertips of her glove, it seemed she undressed before him—the thought excited rather than appalled her.

Luke recaptured her hand and, so gently she was not certain whether his lips made contact or only his breath caressed her, he kissed her injury. 'I believe I may love this scar.'

The hours she had spent rehearsing effortless, witty repartee had been a waste: she could barely think of a response. Anna moistened her lips, hoping Luke couldn't feel the pulse that beat frantically in her wrist. She could not believe he dared use such a word. 'Then perhaps you love too easily, Mr Hartmann.'

Luke returned his eyes to the track, as though sensing she would dissolve beneath his gaze. He placed her hand on the seat, but linked his fingers through hers. 'On the contrary, it is not an emotion to which I have ever previously laid claim.'

Surely there was no way she misconstrued his words or intent? 'I think our timing lacks.'

'Why?' The word was sharp.

'Only that you are so busy at the moment.' Anna gestured toward the paddocks, the loam ripped by horse-drawn plough.

'Oh.' The syllable sounded like relief and the hard set of Luke's shoulders eased. 'But winter approaches and there is less to keep me outdoors. I shall soon be seeking amusement inside.'

'Then I shall brush up on my parlour games.' Her stomach jumped all over the place at their banter. Every word he uttered seemed a promise—and she was quite sure he intended her to read it that way. She was more than happy to play this game.

Despite Luke slowing Arabella's pace, they reached the branching of their paths far too quickly.

Reining in, Luke turned to her. 'Anna. I would present you with a token of my affection.' He stretched his legs, feet hard against the buckboard to provide the necessary room, and reached into the inside breast pocket of his suit.

As if by magic, a small blue velvet box appeared in her hand.

'Open it,' he urged.

Her hand trembling, Anna fumbled open the lid. Inside lay a fine silver chain, a tiny crucifix sparkling upon it.

Luke's breath stirred her hair. 'I pray it will keep you safe when I cannot be with you.'

She tried to speak, to say that she did not want there to be a moment when he was not with her, but her throat was thick with tears, her eyes misted.

As he vaulted from the buggy, cold emptiness filled the space alongside her. Yet her heart remained warm and full.

17

Taylor

Riding the boundary of the heritage scrub with Gramps had become a regular thing for Taylor over the past few weeks. As the days got hotter, they headed out earlier, particularly as Gramps' age seemed to catch up with him later in the day.

The paddocks had been harvested, the tall golden stalks lying in neat furrows to dry before being baled. The evidence that Luke had been there, close enough to see and yet invisible, made him frustratingly similar to the Luke of her dreams. Of course, that was because she was a normal red-blooded young woman and he was the only guy she'd spoken with in weeks. Which was exactly how she wanted it, Taylor reminded herself. Even though she hadn't decided what to focus on next year, she knew what *not* to focus on.

Gramps held up a hand as Taylor reached toward the door of the homestead. 'Hang on there, Peach.' He shook the strips of bright orange plastic that hung over the opening. Clouds of fat blowflies droned their annoyance at the disturbance and he pulled off his cap, using it to wave them away. Taylor barely noticed the insects anymore.

Gran called from the kitchen 'Don't let the flies—'

'—in,' Gramps finished, the screen door slamming behind them.

Mum and Gran were at the table, ubiquitous cups of tea in front of them.

'I was just telling Michelle that we attend the Christmas Eve service now.' Gran's hooded eyes seemed to beseech Gramps for backup.

Mum's lips were a thin line. 'And I was saying I can't understand why you would go to a Lutheran service.'

Gramps moved slowly, old again. 'Why wouldn't we go to a Lutheran service?'

'Oh, I don't know. Maybe because we're Catholic. Maybe because we've always gone to the Christmas Day service, not Christmas *Eve*.' Mum spat the last word as though it was poisonous.

It wasn't like her to get worked up. Taylor scooted her chair closer, pressing her thigh against Mum's in a show of silent support. As they only attended church once a year—twice, tops—she didn't understand the big deal.

Neither did Gramps. 'This is a Lutheran district, Michelle. What difference does it make?'

'I just can't see why you would need to change something that's a family tradition.' It was typical of Mum to ignore the fact that she'd not attended a service with her parents for decades.

Gramps creaked into a chair. 'Sometimes change is warranted. And sometimes you have to adapt. It doesn't necessarily mean it's wrong.'

'Come on, Mum,' Taylor cajoled. 'You're always going on about inclusivity and growth.' Anna's mother's words flashed into her mind. 'This is a whole new world with a new set of rules, right?'

Yeah, there was nothing odd about quoting an imaginary person. Or about the fact that she'd worked the gifted necklace into her dreams. She'd skimmed a couple of psych sites on the net—waiting in an agony of nerves for the pages to load—and been both reassured and terrified to discover biocentrism, the belief that space and time don't physically exist but are merely concepts; therefore dreams are as much reality as anything in the physical realm. She'd swiftly closed the tab. The only takeaway she cared to acknowledge was that it was entirely normal to carry parts of daily life into dreams. Everyone did it. She'd added the necklace into her dreams of Anna and Luke purely because she hadn't allowed herself to process the coincidence of meeting a real Luke.

Gramps slid a Tupperware bowl of salad toward Taylor as Gran topped up the teapot from the kettle. Here, meals both started and ended with tea. 'Anyway,' he said with a wink, 'it's a midnight service, and I'm interested to see if Peach can stay awake that late.'

She did spend a lot of time in the cool solitude of her room, both in preparation for the increasingly early starts and because it seemed that only when her mind went to sleep could her heart be wide open. Asleep, she could allow and envy the love Luke and Anna had for one another, although she knew that reality was vastly different.

'Well, whatever, I'm heading into Settlers Bridge after lunch,' Mum said, changing the subject with unusual firmness. 'I've arranged to look at some consulting space.'

'I'll come with,' Taylor said. Perhaps worrying about work was what had Mum riled. Though the Sydney house had sold, settlement had a sixty-day term, so they were currently living off savings. It didn't help that Taylor had nothing to contribute to their income pool, either. So much for coming over here to support Mum.

'I wouldn't think you'd find much in the way of professional offices in Settlers,' Gran said, checking the grill beneath the electric stovetop. Taylor could smell fish fingers. While they weren't something she would have considered eating previously, she'd been persuaded by Gramps' enthusiasm for the questionable mashed and crumbed fish product, which he spread liberally with mayonnaise and topped with canned beetroot and baked beans. He swore that, if you put salad on the side, all the important food groups were covered.

Mum twisted her lips disapprovingly. 'I'm not at all sure these are professional, as such, but we'll see.'

'Do you think there'll be much call for counselling services?' Taylor said, encouraging Mum to open up about what was bothering her. 'You know, with the relaxed lifestyle and all this fresh country air. Besides, aren't farmers notoriously tight-lipped?' Except about stock, crops and the weather, apparently.

'Oh, it'll take a good while before you're accepted,' Gramps said unhelpfully. 'But there's not only farmers—'

'—around here. And there's always plenty of gossip to be unearthed.' Gran chortled.

'I don't work with gossip,' Mum reproved. 'I help clients progress their lives to attain greater fulfillment by increasing self-awareness.'

'Of course, love,' Gran said, not batting an eyelid at the rhetoric.

Taylor barely held in her groan. She'd heard it all before, but it was hard to buy into Mum's promise of self-actualisation when she was on the verge of divorce *and* the brink of a breakdown, judging by her tantrum earlier.

'In any case,' Gran continued, plopping a plate piled with golden fish fingers in the centre of the table, 'you have perfect timing. I'm heading in for the CWA meeting this afternoon. This time you'll have to come along and meet the girls.'

Taylor passed the bowl of mixed green leaves, high-lighted with a few wedges of tomato and, for some obscure reason, chopped gherkins, back to Gramps.

'You're in for a treat,' he teased. 'Those girls at the CWA really know—' He frowned and brushed the top of his head, two sharp movements from the crown to the front.

A small creature, about ten centimetres long, dangled for a moment from Gramps' straggly grey forelock, then dropped into the salad bowl.

'What on earth?' Mum squealed, lurching from her seat. 'A lizard!'

'No, a gecko,' Gran corrected, leaning over for a better view. 'See the pads on its feet? Skinks have claws, geckos have pads. Don't often see these little guys around, just occasionally on the flyscreens, chasing moths at night.'

Gramps dug around in the salad bowl, trying to trap the reptile, which cannoned from one side of the plastic dish to the other in panic.

'Put it outside before Brrt cottons on, love,' Gran said. 'She'll have her paws in your lunch, otherwise.'

'Will do.' Gramps started to push to his feet, but then held his closed fist toward Taylor. 'Actually, you do it, Peach. You can get up and out quicker than me. Lucky that salad's not dressed. I don't imagine the poor little bugger would take too kindly to being covered in mayo or oil.'

As Taylor warily took the animal, Gramps passed the salad bowl to Mum. 'There you are, love, dig in.'

'We're not going to eat that, now!' Mum gasped.

'Course we are,' Gramps said. 'You should see all the bugs and bits Magpie has to clean off when she picks the leaves from the veggie garden. And our eyes aren't what they used to be. There's probably as much still in as goes out.'

Taylor darted from the room, smothering her laughter at her mum's horrified expression. She'd be sure to give her own plate the once-over for caterpillar pieces before she ate, though.

The real estate agent, Claire, showed them through two rental options. One was a shed on a back street that ran parallel to the main strip. The other was a vacant butcher's shop, complete with steel sinks, a cool room and an old-fashioned timber butcher's block that took up an entire wall.

As the four of them walked out of the shop on the main street, Gran paused to chat with a couple of women hugging the shade of the footpath. The scalloped edges of the bullnosed verandahs were strung with twinkling fairy lights, although it was hard to tell whether they were turned on or simply reflecting the sunlight. Strings of larger, coloured bulbs, interspersed with shiny baubles, linked the fountains of bougainvillea that decorated the paved centre of the road. Each of the four-metre-tall wrought-iron cages containing the leafy vines was topped by a large star wrapped in gold tinsel garlands. The bases of the plants, bedded in half wine barrels, were surrounded by the brightest red and purest white petunias. With the lime green foliage, the tubs looked like Christmas packages.

The windows of the shops they'd passed in their stroll from the agent's office—also only a short block away, like everything in this town—had themed displays. Gingerbread houses in Ploughs and Pies, the candy gardens oozing sugary stickiness, chocolate buttons melting to form rainbow rivers. Crayoned posters decorated the window of the IGA, and a nativity balanced on hay bales— heavy on farmyard animals in a mindboggling mix of different sizes—filled the front of Tractors and Tarts so completely that it was impossible to see into the shop. Even the vacant butcher's shop window was framed by garlands of thick, sparkly, green streamers. The riot of colour and over-zealous decoration made it obvious that Christmas was a big deal in the sleepy little town.

Perhaps most surprising, though, was the music. High on the verandah posts were bullhorn speakers and a seemingly endless playlist of carols filled the street with virtual snow, dashing reindeers and figgy pudding.

Mum shook her head. 'I really don't know, Claire. I don't think either of these are quite what I'm after. Though the shed would be a good size for yoga classes, it's too hot in there at the moment. And I don't doubt winter would be freezing.'

'You could put in a portable AC,' Claire suggested. 'And in winter, get one of those gas patio heaters; that'd work fine. The hardware shop sells them,' she added, as though procuring the item was the only possible hiccup.

'Hmm,' Mum said, and Taylor knew she was searching for a polite way to refuse. Not only because the offered spaces were inappropriate, but because she'd take issue with the environmental impact of running gas heaters and electric coolers in an uninsulated space.

'We need something that offers more privacy,' Taylor suggested quickly before Mum enlightened Claire on the egregious nature of her suggestion. If they were going to hang around Settlers Bridge, they didn't need a town crier to announce their oddities. 'You know, like professional medical rooms. Is there a general practice? Perhaps you could rent a room from them, Mum?'

'A doctor's clinic, you mean?' Claire snorted. 'Well, nice as that would be, there's nothing between Mannum and Murray Bridge.'

Gran had finished chatting with her friends and waved them off as she rejoined the conversation. 'Rooms, Taylor? That does give me an idea. Well, only if you could use a whole house, Michelle.'

'I can't afford a whole house,' Mum said, stepping back like she was ready to run from the rapidly escalating responsibility.

'We'll see,' Gran said. 'Bye now, Claire. You'll be coming past the trading table next week? Last one before Christmas, if you've been too busy to get your own baking done.'

Taylor tried not to laugh at the idea of anyone here being 'too busy'. Everything, from the caressing breeze to the dog slinking along the far side of the street, seemed to move at a treacly, drowsy pace. Even the occasional vehicle on the generously wide road meandered, as though the driver wasn't intent on getting to any particular place at any particular time.

Having neatly dismissed the real estate agent, Gran turned back to them. 'Lynn over at the IGA and her husband, Michael, own a couple of older houses in Settlers Bridge. I imagine they're vacant, as there's no work here. Which means the rent should be low.' She glanced at her watch. 'Lynn's probably headed over to the meeting at the clubrooms already. We'll catch her there.' Gran ushered them through a walkway between a couple of the shops to where she'd parked in the shade of a tree on the street behind.

'I can't commit to a house,' Mum muttered. 'I've no idea what kind of a practice I can build here. It's not like I have any contacts. I'd have to work out a marketing plan.' She enunciated the last two words with such animosity it was clear the concept was unfamiliar. And unwelcome. 'And advertise.'

Tied down by administration and hampered by logistics, the spark of excitement that had fuelled her mother's plans would be snuffed out. Over the last few weeks, with the tear-jerkers and tissues packed away along with everything else from their former lives, Mum had seemed happier and Taylor wasn't ready to lose her again.

'Come on, Mum,' she chided. 'Thinking outside the square's your thing, isn't it? You were talking about looking for somewhere to live after Christmas. Maybe you can rent a house and use one room for your counselling practice and another for yoga?'

'I told you,' Gran said, 'you don't need to worry about clients. There're plenty of people around here looking for someone new to hear their troubles. You won't need any of that marketing or advertising stuff.' Her airy wave, dispensing with things she didn't understand, was redolent of Mum's usual attitude. 'Word of mouth is what works. And I promise that's one thing this town is *very* good at.'

It was barely worth them getting in Gran's old sedan as the clubrooms, fronting onto a football oval, turned out to be a handful of streets away. Gran pulled in beneath a flowering jacaranda.

Taylor pointed at the carpet of fallen blue blooms. 'Christmas time is near.' Evidently, the unusual amount of vitamin D she was getting lately—thanks to roaming the property with a thinly veiled interest in the possibility of running into the enigmatic Luke—had lifted both her serotonin level and her mood.

'And speaking of,' Gran said, reaching into the glovebox. 'Christmas earrings are compulsory at this meeting.' She handed Taylor a pair of tiny crystal Christmas trees. 'Yours are sustainably sourced, Michelle.' She passed Mum wooden hoops encircling an intricately braided rattan snowflake.

'Oh, they're perfect! Did you know rattan is one of the most environmentally friendly renewable resources?' Mum sounded happy to be back in familiar territory.

'Of course, love.'

Unable to tell rattan from bamboo from pine, Taylor was clearly the odd one out.

Gran tapped her own large snowflake earrings. 'Mine are recycled glass, although I'm never certain the processing makes them truly eco-friendly.'

Mum smiled. 'I'm sure we're allowed some leeway for Christmas.'

Gran ferreted in her tatty old Glomesh purse, some of the green-tinged gold links hanging by a literal thread, and handed them each a couple of two-dollar coins. 'Donation to the club for wearing the earrings. I can't recall what charity the money is going to this time, but Marian will know.'

Whoever had come up with the Christmas earring fundraiser obviously had some clout—no matter where Taylor looked, holiday-themed jewellery flashed, twinkled, tinkled or actually played Christmas music, although the last was hard to catch over the loud greetings and Mariah Carey's serenade filling the football clubroom. It was evident that, although Gran had left Settlers Bridge years ago, she had been accepted back into the community when she and Gramps retired here.

'How often do they meet?' she murmured to Mum as the fifth woman hugged Gran and turned to be introduced to them. Around the hall were groups of tables, several pushed together to form a large work area, each station spread with dauntingly crafty-looking ventures. At the back of the room, the roller door above a long bench was retracted. The room beyond was a kitchen, with two stoves and a fridge clearly visible. The countertop of the tinsel-festooned servery hatch was loaded with plastic-wrapped plates—an issue Taylor hoped Mum wouldn't find it necessary to address—and Tupperware-protected food.

'I think Gran said fortnightly? Maybe monthly. I'm not sure, but oh, what a lovely community, isn't it?'

Taylor checked her reply as an austere woman approached. A delicate-featured woman almost skipped to keep up with her.

Gran embraced the smaller of the two women. 'Tracey, Marian, this is my daughter, Michelle, and my grand-daughter, Taylor. Tracey, I love your hairband.'

'Indeed, why stop at earrings?' the taller woman said, although her smile was of tolerant amusement at the plaited, glittery tinsel halo that rested on her companion's fluffy blonde hair. Her gaze settled on Taylor. 'Your grandmother has been very excited at the prospect of you moving here. I can't quite recall, how old are you?'

The question was odd, perhaps even more so because it struck a chord; Mrs Ernst had asked much the same of Anna.

In my dream, Taylor reminded herself firmly. 'Almost twenty-three.'

Marian exchanged a glance with Tracey, as though the information had some hidden significance. 'And your gran tells me you're studying. Medicine, isn't it? That's something of a commitment. I admire a woman who knows what she wants from life and is willing to make the necessary sacrifices.'

Still toying with the idea of quitting medicine, or at least deferring for a year, Taylor flinched like an accusation of fraud had been levelled at her. Without the pressure of upcoming exams, the laidback lifestyle of the farm had insinuated itself over the last month and she was finding it increasingly easy to fit into the natural ebb and flow of the days. A breakfast cup of tea, then feeding the chickens and house cow. Another cup of tea, then perhaps she'd check the fence line—although she refused to venture back into the scrub. The wistfulness the touch of the ancient wall had evoked was somehow beyond sad, so instead she focused on making sure the rambunctious lambs from the paddock above the scrub hadn't strayed into the heritage-protected area. She kept one ear always cocked in case Luke was working somewhere nearby. Only because she didn't want to get caught out in the dirty T-shirt and ripped jeans, which had become increasingly comfortable with wear. Then there'd be more tea, sitting on the front verandah as the bees foraged noisily in the purple agapanthus. She'd allow her mind to wander, enjoying the respite from years of *focus*. Her gaze lingering on the sheds, she'd wonder at their history, imagining the lives of the men who had built them stone by stone, fleshing out their history with the details her dreams provided. But none of that was conducive to actually making a decision about her future.

'What woman would be foolish enough to make sacrifices for a job?' From the corner of her eye, Taylor had noticed the woman striding across the hall as though on a mission. Now she interrupted like she was owed an answer.

'One who is passionate about a career, I guess,' Taylor replied reluctantly, when it seemed no one else wished to take up the slapped down gauntlet.

'Christine, this is Taylor and Michelle.' Gran had taken an instinctive step back, distancing herself from potential argument.

'You're the one who is studying medicine?' Christine demanded. 'Where do you plan to go with that?'

'Initially, into general practice. Eventually into specialist practice.' Somehow, reiterating the plan that was the result of so many years work seemed like an affirmation. Taylor felt a shift inside her. It was as though some of the stress of the last year lifted and the tiniest tingle of passion darted through her.

'Where *geographically*.' Christine's tone made it clear the misinterpretation of her question was Taylor's fault. 'We've no use for a specialist.'

Taylor lifted one shoulder, trying to blink away her confusion. 'I wasn't applying for a job here.'

'We need a GP,' Christine snapped. She fixed Marian with a glare. 'Correct?'

'We do,' Marian said, seeming slightly amused by the conversation.

Christine held up a hand, stopping potential disagreement from the other silent women. 'But I'm quite sure none of us cares to pay good money to fund a search for a husband.'

'A husband?' Taylor blurted.

'For a woman, a *career* is a means to an end: husband, home and heirs.' A glint of satisfaction, probably at her alliteration, lit Christine's countenance. Her dead straight bob, streaked with grey, barely dared move as she nodded sharply, underscoring her point. 'So this *sacrifice* that Marian likes to tout is pointless. No employer is going to put on someone who will be forever taking time off to have babies or care for their own children.'

Taylor tried to politely temper her response. 'I'm not certain employers can make those assumptions—'

'Of course they can. And do,' Christine snapped. 'Perhaps not in so many words, because we live in a world where we have to pretend this ridiculous political correctness, even though it flies in the face of all logic and practicality.'

Taylor doubted that cultivating diplomacy or sensitivity had taken up much of Christine's time.

'But the thought will certainly be there. You'll have your work cut out to talk your way into a job here.'

The imaginary position in a mythical practice, that was.

'Wouldn't it be nice to have a female doctor, though?' Tracey sighed wistfully.

212

'It'd be nice to have *any* doctor. Are we finally getting a practice?' Marian and Tracey moved apart to allow a woman, whose metallic scarlet hair competed with the Christmas streamers, to join their group.

'Lynn,' Gran breathed with something that sounded very close to relief, 'I was telling the girls that you may have a house to rent that would be suitable for a business.'

'A general practice?' Lynn said eagerly. 'I heard we had a young doctor moving to town. What a wonderful idea. Although you'll be lumped with an awful lot of smear tests,' she added, pulling a wryly apologetic face at Taylor.

'Lynn!' Tracey clapped her hands to her cheeks. 'You'll scare her off!'

'No, you won't, but I'm not ... I don't ...' Taylor stammered, looking desperately to Mum and Gran. How had this snowballed from a conversation about her studies to the assumption that she'd be the new Settlers Bridge doctor?

Mum looked amused. Gran looked ... away. Taylor squinted at her suspiciously. Perhaps the conversation wasn't as random as it seemed.

'I'm years from being qualified and I've no idea either what or where I'll practice,' she said firmly.

Was that disappointment that crossed Gran's face?

Marian's gaze narrowed and Taylor wasn't sure whether her outspokenness was being silently applauded or her decision decried. 'Anyway,' the older woman said smoothly, 'I'm thrilled to see you've all worn your Christmas earrings. The donation tin is alongside the afternoon tea. This year the funds will go toward four-ply for the beanies for the premmies spending Christmas in the Women's and Children's.'

'*You're* knitting, Marian?' Christine demanded.

'Of course not. But I shall see that the knitters are reimbursed. And I'll have Jim deliver the hats, along with some teddy bears that Sarah's group have made.' Marian drew her shoulders back and clapped her hands together, just once. 'Anyway, Christine, I will speak with you about the rosters for the final trading table for the year a little later. Lynn, you were going to look into a house for Michelle and Taylor? And Tracey, I think it's time for afternoon tea.'

With her companion trailing cheerfully in her wake, the formidable woman strode across the room, bestowing regal nods to those who moved from her path.

18

Anna

May 1877

Wilhelmina Ernst had become something of an angel in Anna's mind. Mother had left the farm early to visit with her on the pretext of returning the unguent bottle from Anna's healed burn, although Anna suspected the trip represented Mother's first opportunity to discuss her *news* with someone.

Pleasantly distracted by thoughts of Luke, Anna was slow at her work, rhythmically wielding the small wooden paddles to shape and smooth the freshly churned butter into even pats. When it was squared to her satisfaction, she left the cool dimness of the storeroom. The sun had already passed the midpoint in the sky, the unbroken drought rendering it unseasonably warm. Her sister, who had been drawing in the earth with a pointed stick to amuse the twins, had retreated indoors. The twins napped in their iron-framed cot.

'Mother is late returning.'

Seated in Mother's chair, Emilie looked up from her embroidery. 'Perhaps she is waiting until the temperature drops. I have fed the twins.'

Anna cleaned the refuse Emilie had left on the table, transferred the crockery to the sink and tipped hot water from the kettle over it. The small fire, kept only to boil the kettle and heat the stew, was nearly out—of course— and the timber bucket empty. She sighed, picked up the pail and headed outside. Her boot poised to warn off snakes by kicking the wood stacked against the eastern wall, she jerked around at the rattle of the trap on the long, rutted track.

Eager to hear her mother's recount of her visit, she crossed the yard and took Arabella's halter. The horse's velvet nose snuffled into her shoulder.

'How was—' Anna bit off her question on an indrawn breath. Beneath a sheen of sweat, Mother sported a sickly pallor so deep it mimicked the pale green of wheat sprouts breaking the hard earth. She was barely able to tumble from the seat of the buggy.

'Mother, you've stayed too long in the sun. You should have remained with Mrs Ernst until it became cooler.' Anna wrapped her arm around her mother's thickened waist, almost carrying her inside. 'Emilie, fetch me wash-cloths. Mother has heatstroke.'

Emilie jumped up as Anna helped Mother to the chair.

'Unbutton her dress, loosen everything, quickly,' Anna said, laying the cloths Emilie had plunged into the water bucket across the back of Mother's neck. Going to the kitchen table, she tossed aside the beaded lace doily that kept insects out of the jug. Water slopped onto the scrubbed table as she poured it into a cup.

Mother's teeth chattered against the pottery, but her pallor gradually receded.

The twins had woken. Hands entwined, they stared at Mother in solemn concern.

'Frederik, take your sister out to play,' Anna directed, keeping her voice calm, though her chest was tight with fear. Sunstroke wasn't anything new; they'd dealt with it many times. But death was a close companion to any ill. 'Don't stray from the shady side of the house, though. Go on, Mother just had a little too much sun.'

Removing the rest of her mother's sweat-soaked clothes, Anna sponged her and dropped a clean nightdress over her head, averting her eyes as she did so. Mother's swollen stomach scared her. By Mother's calculation, it was another month until this babe was due to make an entry to the world, yet her belly looked painfully tight and hard, as though the infant would burst through the skin.

Emilie brushed Mother's long blonde hair until it was smooth, then braided it, pinning the lengths in a neat coil on each side of her head.

Mother didn't protest the attention, but nor did she speak. Slumped in her chair, limp and wasted, only the mound of her belly moved, the odd angles of tiny feet and hands visible through the thin fabric of her nightdress.

The men's voices and the high-pitched greetings of the twins penetrated the thick walls. Finally, Mother stirred, gesturing for her wrap to cover her nightclothes. A smile moved her lips, although her eyes didn't light in their normal manner. Still, relief washed over Anna; with Father home, the responsibility for Mother was no longer hers.

As though nothing untoward had occurred, Mother found her voice. 'Emilie, stir the stew, please. I smell it burning. Call the twins to set the dinner table. Anna, did you get the butter churned today?' Her blue eyes slid across Anna. 'Oh, and girls, don't tell your father of my foolish turn. He frets so and has enough to concern him.'

There was nothing untoward in her request; they seldom spoke of their ailments in front of the menfolk. Yet, unaccustomed to the sight of Mother sitting while there was a trace of daylight, Father was instantly attentive.

He went to the rocking chair and squatted alongside, the back of his hand pressed against Mother's cheek. 'Johanna, mein Schatzi, you are ill?'

Mother smiled, covering Father's hand with her own. 'It is nothing, Johann. Simply the heat exhausts me. I feel a storm brewing. When it breaks, I shall be better.'

Father's knees cracked as he adjusted his position. 'Dieter, you will take the sheep to the saleyard tomorrow. I shall stay here.' He was decisive, as though his authority had the power to stave off illness.

Though Dieter nodded, Mother clicked her tongue against her teeth, her favourite expression of exasperation, and one Anna often emulated. 'Johann, can you bring me the rain? Nein? Then there is nothing you can do here for me. Twenty miles is too far for Dieter to drove the sheep by himself. You must accompany him. And I have a list of items I should like you to get in the town. I will have neither time nor inclination to go there before this next child of yours is born.'

It was unusual to drove sheep now: they were breeding stock, and the market provided more favourable prices for the fat spring lambs than for the ewes. But feed was sparse because of the drought and Father must offset the loss of the fodder in the burned paddock. To do so he had to venture to Edwards Crossing, more distant than the seasonal saleyard at Settlers Bridge.

Refusing dinner, Mother watched as the men and the littlies dined. Neither Emilie nor Anna were able to eat, a creeping sense of portent stealing their appetites. Mother's intense gaze ranged the room, resting often on the foursome at the dinner table, as though she memorised everything. Yet she seemed to avoid Anna's scrutiny.

As Father finished bolting his food, Mother pushed herself to the edge of the rocking chair, using the momentum to assist her to her feet. 'Come, Johann, help me to bed. I am tired and you must be off early in the morning, before the full heat hits.'

Despite Mother's declaration, Anna could hear her toss and turn for the few hours they lay abed. Anna focused on the whine of mosquitoes. The barking cough of foxes in the scrub temporarily silenced the night-time rustling of echidnas and wombats rooting in the undergrowth. The air grew thicker by the second, until breathing became like inhaling treacle.

The bed coils creaked as Father rose and Anna no longer needed to feign sleep. She pulled a shawl across her nightdress before dragging open the front door, hoping for the merest breath of air to break the ominous stillness. Instead, suffocating heat stole the breath from her lungs. The moon-painted paddocks were an ethereal mockery of daylight, and she created her own winter, imagining snow covering the colourless world.

Moving as quietly through the house as men were able, Father and Dieter prepared to leave. Father kissed her forehead as she passed them muslin-wrapped bread and Blutwurst, the near-black blood sausage. 'I trust the care of my house and my family to you, my Anna.'

The formal farewell was Father's tradition and she should not read into it. Yet she pulled the light shawl closer, fighting a chill that came from within.

With hours to wait until daylight, she sat in Mother's chair. A peculiar mood haunted her, urging her to recall every moment with Luke, even the mundane or embarrassing; store away every memory for a time when there would be no more. Although butterflies of excitement fluttered in her chest, she was hollowed by a presentiment of yearning and loss. It was almost as though she was afraid to allow her love for Luke, knowing she would then spend a lifetime afraid of losing him.

As light crept beneath the door and melted through the curtains, Anna shook off her gloom, which was no doubt due to the lowering weather, the incipient storm Mother had forecast. She woke Emilie, a cautionary finger to her lips. 'You must listen for Mother while I stoke the bakehouse fire and put the bread on. Don't let the twins disturb her.'

Although she pulled on boots, she didn't dress before making her way to the bakehouse. Mother's advice—and Caroline's encouragement—had given her a new right to defy the rules of the world. Of course, with the nearest neighbour miles distant, her brave flouting of authority would go safely unchallenged.

Perfected by practice, Anna completed the chores quickly, the dough proving on the deep window recess, the fire stoked and oats put to soak. The creak of the barn door under her touch sent rats scuttling for shadowy corners. Liesl eyed her reproachfully. Although her udders must ache now they had sold her calf, Anna had come too early for her pleasure. The cow lowed testily as Anna pushed her head into the bail, dropping chaff into the trough to entice her. Stamping her indignation, the cow clanged a hoof against the metal pail as Anna squatted on the three-legged stool Dieter had carved, her head resting against the cow's sweet-smelling belly.

Splashing water across Liesl's udder, Anna gripped the cow's distended teats and closed her fingers progressively, from udder to tip. 'Come on, Liesl, let it down for me.' The cow shook herself, the movement rippling from shoulders to haunches, showering Anna in dust. She slapped the cow's side lightly and returned to the milking.

The strong, white jets splashing into the bucket soothed her, the familiar rhythmic motion soporific. Too soon, Liesl was stripped, the pail more than half full.

Anna poured the milk through a clean muslin screen into the crockery pot in the storage room and covered it with a ceramic disc to keep rodents and vermin out. Later, when it had settled, she would skim the cream and churn more butter.

The house loomed oppressive, a sense of foreboding urging her to stay away. Her excuses to remain outside were exhausted, but perhaps she'd take a basket into the scrub to collect the white, starry festoons of Old Man's Beard that hung from the trees, perfect for encouraging the tiniest flame—

'Anna! Come quick!'

Emilie's fear-laden shout had her running toward the house before she could think.

At the door, Emilie blocked her entry. 'Anna, Mother— I think she's started . . .'

'Get out of my way.' Anna pushed past her sister.

Mother lay on the bed, one hand pressed against the mound of her stomach. Her lips curved, but fear narrowed the pupils of her pale blue eyes. 'Anna, Liebchen, it seems your little brother or sister is eager to join us.'

'What would you have me do?'

'Nothing, child. It may pass. The pains are far apart.'

Anna dressed and busied herself in the house, removing items from the Aussteuerschrank and dusting the shelves. She returned each item to the exact spot Mother kept it. Polished the single window with a rag. Swept the floor. Avoided eye contact with Emilie; if she read her sister's fear, her own would feed from it.

She was relieved when the twins woke. 'Wash and feed the little ones, Emilie. Keep them quiet.' Directing Emilie calmed Anna's own nerves and she felt a little more in control as she moved to the window, shifting the thick curtain to squint at the sun. Still low in the eastern sky, she estimated the hours until Father's return. Too many. He would not yet have reached the saleyard and, as he had taken Arabella, Anna could not go in pursuit.

Washed, the twins took advantage of the unaccustomed luxury of having Mother lie abed. Despite the oppressive heat, Frederik lay along one side of her on the brass-framed bed, Frederika cosied up on the other. As always, they mirrored one another, Frederik's left thumb in mouth and right index finger twirling flaxen curls, Frederika the opposite. Mother read to them in a desultory fashion, pausing frequently as the contractions squeezed her body.

When the book fell from Mother's hand, Anna scooted the little ones out. 'Emilie, take them to the bakehouse to play. Give them a little of the bread dough to shape. When they grow bored, have them help you churn the butter.'

Mother only slept for a few minutes, waking with a cry of agony. The pains came closer now.

Anna's hand trembled as she mopped Mother's forehead, glistening in the muted light of the closed house. She had been fifteen when the twins were born, had witnessed her mother give birth, but never before had she been in charge.

'Mother, I shall send for the midwife.'

Mother panted, snatching at her hand. 'No, Liebchen. After seven healthy babies, I know better than any how to do this.'

Mother avoided spending money they could scarce afford, but Anna couldn't help but think that two of those babies had died within hours of birth.

'Then allow me to send Emilie for someone else. Mrs Ernst, perhaps?' To find help of any kind, Emilie must walk five miles. Hampered by her skirts, it would take two hours. Already, the calling of birds in the scrub had stilled as they plumped their feathers to insulate themselves against the cruel heat. The remaining sheep moved away from the house, their plaintive bleats becoming distant as they sought whatever shade they could find. The world held its breath as the climbing temperature sucked life and will from the land.

Mother patted limply at Anna's hand. 'No need, child. It will be quick this time.'

She was wrong.

⌒

By the time the sun was high in the sky, Mother no longer looked like Mother. Her soft, pale skin was reddened and blotchy, the whites of her eyes suffused with blood. Weals scarred her palms where her hands twisted in the linen strips she'd had Anna tie to the bedposts. As she strained against the fabric, trying to push the child from within her, the bones of her skeletal face protruded.

She released the binding, dropping her hand to Anna's. 'Liebchen.' Mother's voice was little more than a breath of wind. Anna bent close to hear her. 'Child, I did not realise I would be robbed of the time to tell you all I needed.'

Anna shrank back. 'No.' If she refused to listen, Mother could not say the words. And if she could not say goodbye, she would not leave.

With surprising strength, Mother's hands clawed into Anna's, broken nails digging into her flesh. 'Child, listen to me. Take what you can from this life. Do not be afraid to chase what you want. Our allotted time is so brief, and true joy even more transient.' She broke off with a moan, her body arching under the loose sheet.

'Hush, Mutti.' Anna fell back into the vernacular of her childhood. 'Father will be home soon. He will ride for help.'

'Your father.' A gentle smile softened Mother's ravaged face. 'This much I can tell you. Life is full of sadness and surprises. But amidst it all, you will find joy. No matter how brief, love is worth the cost. Tell your father—' Mother's teeth cracked together and tears slid from the corners of her closed eyes as she fought the pain.

The contraction lasted too long—minutes—but then Mother continued like the agony could not interrupt her train of thought. 'Tell your father it is as well it ends now, as one hundred years—even one thousand years—would not be enough to assuage my greed for him. Tell him I go to care for our lost ones.'

Anna clenched her fists. She could not cry.

She must not cry.

She must bake bread. Father would be home soon. The men would be hungry.

Mother recognised her need to escape. 'Liebling, send Emilie to me.'

Anna kissed Mother's forehead. 'I will be back in a moment, Mutti.' They both knew she would not.

Covered in flour, sneaking sticky dough into their mouths, the twins played quietly in the bakehouse, as though aware of the import of the moment.

'Mother wants you.' Anna twisted the pendant on her necklace, unable to meet Emilie's eyes. 'Call me from the door when you are finished. Do not leave her alone. It will not be much longer.'

She didn't mean until the baby came, but she would not say the words.

Unable to hide in the bakehouse in peace as her conscience kept her close company, Anna returned to the ominous silence of the house within minutes. Bidding the twins to stay in the kitchen, she slid behind the curtain closing off the bedroom.

Although Mother's eyes were closed, Anna had seen death too many times not to recognise it now. Emilie sat alongside the bed, holding Mother's hand. As though she did not know. Did not understand.

'Emilie, go to the little ones.'

Her sister nodded, her eyes too bright.

Anna lowered herself into the chair Emilie had vacated. Mother was peaceful now, but Anna wanted her to hurt. She wanted her to cry and writhe.

Because then she would be alive.

She bent, resting her head on Mother's breast. 'Breathe, Mutti, please breathe.' Warm and soft beneath her, Mother could not be dead. 'Mutti, I need you.'

Her chest moved and Anna gasped, lifting her head. 'Mother!'

But it was not Mother stirring, it was the child in her belly, feebly kicking. The child who killed her.

Anna stared at the trembling mound, loathing it.

Murderer.

Her sibling.

Her father's child.

Mother's last baby.

She knew what she had to do. When she was younger, she had accompanied Father to the paddocks and watched him.

Her lips brushed Mother's forehead, then she pushed herself from the bed. Trudged to the kitchen bench, not speaking to Emilie or the littlies.

She set aside the unwashed porridge pot and rummaged around, making her careful selection. Only the finest would do.

A blast of hot air scalded her lungs as she opened the door.

She crossed the yard. One step after another, the distance vast, yet covered too quickly. Unlatched the barn door. Chickens squawked from her path.

A scooped pannikin of water dousing the huge whetstone, she cranked the iron handle on the side. Her arm aching, the burn scar tore open as she turned the heavy, whirling disc, spinning faster and faster, as though she could rewind time.

The knife blade bucked and jerked against the stone, trying to fight free of her hand.

She returned to the house. *Bitte Gott, let it have stopped moving.*

Mother's belly heaved beneath the sheet, swaying ponderously from one side of the bed to the other.

Anna ran her tongue across her lips. Tried to swallow.

She had seen Father do it to the sheep.

But this was not a sheep.

She bared Mother's belly and carefully dug the tip of the honed knife below her distended navel. Blood beaded and Anna looked to Mother's face, hoping for a reaction.

Nothing.

Mother's skin split easily, like an over-ripe paddymelon.

The sac encasing the baby was tougher, and Anna gritted her teeth as she struggled with the slippery, viscous mass. Slicing, then tugging it open with her hands.

Blood. So much blood. For a moment, she both feared and hoped Mother was alive—for how could Death contain so much blood?

She severed the cord, upended the child, slapped its back. It drew breath and she moved numbly to the door.

'Emilie. Take it.'

Not brother. Not sister. She refused to look.

It.

Murderer.

She returned to Mother, lifting the sheet to cover her.

Stopped. She could not leave Mother like this, disembowelled for Father to find. She must look unbroken, peaceful.

'Emilie. Bring me the sewing box.'

Tears pricked her eyes. She had only black cotton. Black cotton against Mother's fair beauty. The needle pierced Mother's soft skin, the thread snagging as it drew unevenly through flesh. Brief anger flared; Emilie should do this. Her needlework was finer.

Finished, Anna bit the strand short with her teeth, her cheek in the congealing blood on Mother's stomach. It was still distended, and that seemed unfair. But her face was serene now, the blotchiness receded, the agony erased.

She must complete her job before Father returned. Pouring water from the pitcher, she bathed Mother, the water turning pink. Blood crusted in jewelled crescent moons beneath Anna's nails. If she never washed, she could keep something of Mother.

She awkwardly slid a clean nightdress onto Mother's unmoving form and smoothed the embroidered counterpane over her lifeless body. Then she crawled onto the bed and laid her head on the pillow, her dark hair mingling with Mother's blonde. Her fingers twined desperately through Mother's unresponsive grip, clinging, holding to the last of the warmth.

'Goodnight, Mutti,' she whispered brokenly.

19
Anna

May 1877

Luke's deep baritone was easily discernible in the whirl of sympathy and shock eddying through the curtain that separated Anna's bedroom from the front room. The rattle of wheels as more neighbours arrived to pay their respects drowned out most voices. She was certain the visitors had not removed their shoes and Mother's flagstones would be filthy. She hoped—and doubted—Emilie had the sense to lift the rag rug.

She tried to close her ears to Luke's voice, focus instead on the squeal of chair legs drawn across the floor, the chink of china, the occasional burst of louder noise, as sorrow was forgotten in a moment of remembrance. The smell of donated food nauseated her. When her brothers died, the generosity of their neighbours had seen them eat better than she could ever recall.

Still she could hear Luke, or perhaps it was more that she could feel him. But she could not go to him.

She had her mother's blood beneath her nails.

Emilie slid around the bedroom curtain. 'Anna, please, you must come out.'

Anna shook her head, hugging her knees to her chest under the bed cover, shivering beneath the thin fabric of her chemise. She could not recall when she'd last left the bed. Nor could she remember changing out of her blood-soaked clothes, scouring her arms with borax to remove the red stains, throwing her dress into the fire, despite the stench of burning, bloodied fabric. She could not remember Father coming home, or his wail of grief, the sorrow in his eyes as he clutched Mother's lifeless body against him.

She could not remember anything.

Because she dared not.

If she allowed herself to start remembering, she'd recall Mother's pain and fear. Her own cowardice, leaving the room as Mother died. The knife. She would recall what she did to her mother and the angry squawk of the baby who stole Mother from her. The boy child who had died that same night, anyway.

It was easier to stay in the bedroom. If she didn't talk, she didn't have to remember.

Emilie knelt upon the bed in front of her. 'Anna, please.' Perfect tears appeared easily in her eyes. 'I can't manage without you. There are so many people here. I need help with the twins. I don't know what I'm supposed to do.'

Annoyance flashed through Anna. She'd done her share. She had carved up their mother. And she'd tried to put her back together again.

'Anna? Anna, please, may I come in?' The heavy brocade curtain moved as Luke pressed close.

Why wouldn't they leave her alone? Panic jolted through her, heart crashing against her ribs. Was a sense of propriety and a piece of fabric enough to keep him out?

She snatched at her sister's wrist. 'Emilie, you must not let him in here.' Her voice scratched her throat. She hadn't spoken since . . . since she said goodbye to Mother.

Emilie covered Anna's hand, holding onto her wrist as though she needed the contact. 'Anna, I'll keep him out, but only if you promise to get up. Please—you're scaring me.'

Guilt stirred among the emotions Anna tried to keep buried. She was not the only one to lose a parent. In fact, she had more years with Mother than did Emilie or the twins. She was being selfish. But she feared if she was not selfish, it would hurt too much.

Now she understood why she had been besieged by such a premonition of loss.

'Anna? You will get up?'

Anna's nod was enough to galvanise her sister. Feet slapping the floor, Emilie thrust her head through the curtain, holding it around her neck. Luke must be close, as she spoke so quietly, Anna could barely hear.

'Mr Hartmann, my sister is indisposed at the moment. But she promises she will speak with you at the funeral tomorrow.'

'Miss Frahn . . . please . . .' Luke's voice broke and Anna winced. How was it she hurt everyone when all she wanted was to hide?

His heavy footfalls moved away with obvious reluctance, and Emilie scooted back to the bed.

'He is terribly upset. I have never seen a man look more miserable.'

'Even Father?' Anna snapped, deliberately rubbing salt in her own wound.

Emilie lifted a hand, trying to fix Anna's hair. 'It's different for Father. He and Mother had a long time together.'

Anna slapped her hand away. 'And you think that makes it better? You think there's a point where it's enough time? Mother told me it wasn't, that it could never be enough. And I'm supposed to tell Father that. How can I tell him, Emilie? How can I tell him that without destroying him?'

Emilie traced the patchwork quilt with one finger, biting at her full bottom lip. 'Mother wanted you to tell Father that?'

Anna nodded, winding her loose hair around her hand, pulling it tight until the tips of her fingers bleached white. Black rainbows of Mother's blood lined her nails.

'I can tell him.' Emilie's voice was near a whisper.

'What?' The word bounced from the walls.

Emilie was almost shy. 'I said, I can tell Father. If it makes you feel better. Tell me exactly what Mother said and I shall relay it to Father. It'll be all right, Anna, I promise it will. Mother wanted Father to know—but the carrier of the message is unimportant, as long as he receives it.'

'I think . . . I think I should.' Anna wanted Emilie to talk her out of her decision. Because if she faced Father, she would not be able to maintain her brittle facade of control. She would blame him for not being there, for allowing Mother to have so many children, for putting yet another baby inside her, for fathering the murderer. All things that she knew were none of her business—yet she was not sure she could forgive him for killing her mother.

And she was terrified he would not forgive her for not saving his wife.

'Anna.' Emilie slid her arms around her sister's neck, trying to hug her.

Anna stiffened. Emilie looked like Mother, all blonde, pink and blue, like a porcelain doll. But she wasn't.

'Anna, you've done enough. You don't always have to do everything. Let me do this for you.'

Ungraciously, Anna nodded. 'You'd better get back to the guests. Make sure they have tea. Use Mother's good china from the buffet.' She choked on the words. 'But be careful with it.'

Emilie started to rise from the bed. 'I've made our mourning clothes.'

Of course she had. Yet Anna had no right to be uncharitable. She'd done nothing for two days and Emilie had taken control. She had to pull herself together. Mother trusted her.

'How did you manage that?'

Emilie dropped her chin guiltily. 'Mother has—had—an entire wardrobe of black, from the boys' funerals. I have reworked some of them. I had to remove a ruffle from the bottom of yours to shorten it, but I think it looks quite pretty.'

Only Emilie would consider appearance at their mother's funeral. 'And yours?' Anna asked, feigning interest but intending to ignore the long dissertation she knew would follow. She listened for Luke's voice, wondering if he had left.

Just because she would not see him, did not mean she didn't want him there.

♄

Anna came close to breaking her word to Emilie, procrastinating until morning about leaving the bedroom. It seemed too hard to face the naked grief of the remainder of her family, not yet masked in terms of polite acceptance. But Mother would have clicked her tongue and shaken a dishrag in irritation at her sloth.

Rigid as Father hugged her and dropped a kiss on top of her head, Anna could not bring herself to look at him.

'Engelein.'

She didn't know what he meant. Of course, she knew the translation—angel—but she had no idea why he used it.

Dieter also hugged her, but everything felt false.

They all knew what she'd done, and they all knew how she'd failed.

Pretending normality, she focused on the trivialities. Performed her chores, got breakfast on the table, made certain the twins were scrubbed. Tossing commands at Emilie, she knew she was being unfair; having managed for three days without help, Emilie didn't need her directions now. But being in control of her sister was the only way to remain in control of herself.

The twins were subdued, but it was more a reflection of the sombre tone in their usually lively home, than because they missed Mother. The loss was too new, too raw, for them to realise the permanence.

A neighbour—she didn't know which and cared even less—lent Father a trap and horse. Both that carriage and their own were hung with black mourning curtains. She and Dieter took Arabella and their trap. Father, Emilie and the twins travelled in the larger borrowed contraption. The undertaker had moved the coffin to the church the previous day, though she'd not seen it go. Nor had she viewed the body or enquired what Mother had been dressed in. Anna had seen Mother for the last time when she had lain beside her.

'Anna,' Dieter said as the trap rattled out of the yard.

Her eyes were fixed on the house. She didn't want to return, not ever. Mother wouldn't be there, slamming pans on the range, singing German folk tunes in her pleasant contralto, shaking her head as Dieter tried to sneak in without removing his boots and chastising the twins as she tended to a dozen other things at the same time. Without Mother, the house would be empty of love.

'You should have told Mother about Caroline,' Anna said accusingly, wanting someone else to have made mistakes. 'She would have been happy to know you wished to be settled.'

Dieter didn't strike back, though she longed for him to do so. 'Mother knew. Mrs Ernst is Caroline's godmother.

As Caroline's mother passed several years ago, Mother visited Wilhelmina to discuss my suit with her.'

She did not know how to process that. She had thought Mother fell ill visiting Mrs Ernst on her behalf. 'But . . . but Caroline has a mother.' She seized on the inconsequential, trying to ignore the fact that Dieter had kept a secret from her. Her world was falling apart.

'Stepmother,' Dieter said heavily.

How dare she believe herself special? Caroline had already been where she was.

Though Caroline would not have cut her mother open.

'Anna, are you all right? You seem . . . different.'

She heard the frown in Dieter's voice and turned from him to stare across the bare paddocks. Mother said a storm was coming. They needed the rain desperately.

'Mäuschen, you need to talk.'

She shook her head, lips pressed together. He should understand that she could not speak. She could not filter what she shared, so she dare not open the floodgates.

'If not with me, then with whom would you share?' He sighed heavily, but he had no more enthusiasm for the conversation than she.

A crowd filled the small graveyard, mourners flocking like ravens. Mother would be laid, the babe in her arms, between the four small graves she had visited each Christmas and Easter. Of the nineteen plots behind the wrought-iron fence, now more than a quarter of the scars on the earth belonged to Anna's family. Devoid of greenery, the mounds were well-tended, bordered by pink quartz rocks, the crystals throwing stars into her eyes.

The memorials, whether simple wooden crosses or beautifully wrought and engraved granite headstones, where sorrow warred with privilege to erect the most ornate monument, were clean and fresh. There was love in this graveyard. But not enough for her mother.

The soaring blue sky endless, the first hint of autumn crispness freshened the breeze. And that was so wrong. It should be black with thunder, thick with rain, the ground a slippery quagmire. Instead, magpies carolled their relief at the cool change and tiny fluff-tailed rabbits appeared from where they burrowed beneath the fence to stare curiously at the intruders.

The crowd and the unusual opportunity to mingle energised the twins. They broke free of Emilie's grip and rushed to find other children, bounding without care across the mounds like puppies escaped from their yard. Emilie reached for them, but Father stopped her.

'It does not matter, Emilie. Let them be happy. It is no disrespect.'

Dieter took Anna's arm. 'Father speaks to you as well, you know.'

She didn't want him to try to make it better, just to let her get through it. She counted the steps to the grave. The steps until she said goodbye.

No, that wasn't true. She'd already said goodbye.

Crying prettily, Emilie was surrounded by sympathy and offers of handkerchiefs. But Anna had no right to tears.

Caroline glided toward them, pressing her cheek against Anna's. 'I know there is nothing that will make

this any less painful, but I am here when you wish to talk.'
She took Dieter's arm, the sweetness of her smile belying
the directness of the action. He bent his elbow, folding her
hand close to his heart.

Anna's ragged intake of breath was so loud her brother
glanced at her.

Caroline's evident concern for him, their unconscious
mirroring of one another's movements, the way they
leaned close, hammered home a truth: love did not die
with Mother. The world did not end. But Anna's universe
had become a little colder.

The parting words said as others cried their tears, the
coffin entered the summoning grave. Shovelfuls of dirt
thumped on the polished wooden lid with the finality of
a hangman's drum beat.

Covering Mother.

Burying the last possible chance that Anna was
mistaken, that Mother wasn't dead.

Anna clenched her fists, shaking her head as Pastor
gestured her forward. She could smell the fresh earth, the
eucalyptus leaves beneath their feet, the distant sweet waft
of wild honey in a scrub. Things Mother would never
again experience.

She would not drop dirt into the open grave. Would
not help create that final barrier.

She bit the inside of her cheek and the iron tang of salt
stung her throat. Blood.

Like Mother's.

Her breath was short, as though the dirt pressed on her
own lungs. The crowd closed around her, their billowing

darkness suffocating. Panic pounded at her chest. She couldn't allow them to do this to Mother, who adored light and sunshine and fresh air. Who loved to watch the sun rise, predicting the weather from the colour of the dawn clouds. Her blue eyes were made to reflect the sky, her pink cheeks to be touched by sunlight.

Mother abhorred dirt.

They couldn't cover her with it.

She must stop them.

No.

She must allow it. But she couldn't watch.

She whirled away, heedless of the murmurs of surprise, ignoring the snatching hands that sought to restrain her. She had to escape.

Tall eucalypts, their smooth trunks stripped bare and glowing white, formed a grove surrounding the church and the graveyard. Anna stumbled toward them. A kookaburra whooped with cruel laughter. She needed to be alone, yet the trees offered no privacy.

Her arms folded across her stomach, Anna hunched, hampered by her corset even in grief. The tears she refused to allow cramped her insides and ripped at her chest. She couldn't breathe for wanting to cry.

Strong arms encircled her from behind. She gasped, struggling against the imprisonment.

'Anna.' Luke's deep voice was so close it was as though he was inside her heart.

Protection, not imprisonment. 'Luke—' She didn't know what she wanted to say. She only knew she didn't want him to let her go. She didn't want to be alone.

'Shh. It's all right, my love.' Gently he turned her, pulling her against his chest. His arms wrapped her tightly, burying her face against his waistcoat. 'It's all right, Anna. No one can see you now.'

He understood. He understood so perfectly. His broad shoulders sheltered her from the curiosity of the other mourners and the ugly tears came hot, fast and hard, racking her body until she was unable to stand unaided.

'I didn't save her, Luke, I didn't save her. I saved Emilie, but I couldn't save Mutti or the baby.' She didn't know if he could make sense of her words as they tumbled, the hysteria rising.

A heavy sigh swelled Luke's chest against her cheek. 'Anna, they weren't yours to save. All death is preordained. It is not your fault. Let it go now.'

'But I don't want to be alone!'

Luke allowed her incoherent sobs until the tears gave way to shuddering gasps of pain and sorrow that tore at her throat. Then he gripped her upper arms, pushing her slightly away. 'Take a deep breath.'

She spluttered and hiccoughed, struggling to obey, turning her swollen face from him.

'Good. And another. That's better.' Pulling her close again, Luke's hands traced up her back, his lips moved in her hair. 'Ah, Anna, my heart breaks for you. But it will be all right. I promise you it will get better.'

His heartbeat was strong, even over her jerky breaths. She wanted to close her eyes and stay like this, listening to life pulse within him. But she must move away.

'Luke, we cannot see one another—' Despite the pretence of her weak struggles, she longed to remain in his arms.

Luke's arms tightened. 'Stay, Anna.' He refused to release her from their illicit embrace.

Her fingers grasped at the fabric of his waistcoat; his jacket wrapped her in a cocoon of safety. Melting into him, she inhaled his musky, salty odour. Luke was so tall and broad, surely no one could see her indiscretion. And, if she pressed herself hard enough against him, perhaps the warmth of his body could still the ache in her heart.

As she lifted her head from his chest, his eyes darkened, his thumb brushing across her bottom lip. 'It *will* be all right, Anna. I swear you will never be alone.'

20

Taylor

Heart crushed against her ribs, Taylor could barely breathe as sorrow swelled her throat.

She had welcomed the new dreams since they returned to the farm, immersing herself in fantasy.

But now she didn't want them anymore.

Hidden in the night-time shadows watching Anna and Luke fall in love, she had replaced her own broken family with an imaginary one that was both whole and wholesome. Yet now the nightmare had torn them apart in a way her family would never be.

Her heart lurched. How could she know that? Luke said death was preordained, and even if he wasn't right, death was inevitable. What if her dreams were precognition? Abraham Lincoln had famously dreamed of his own funeral just days before his assassination. She hadn't spoken with Dad for a week, hadn't heard Mum this morning. And Gramps was both aged and frail.

The floorboards were cool on her feet as she surged from the bed and crossed to the door, left open in hope of catching a breeze to stir the summer stillness.

Mum whistled tunelessly in the kitchen, the kettle clanging in the steel sink as water hissed into it.

The outside toilet flushed, eventually followed by the shivering bang of the screen door.

'Don't let the flies—'

'—in,' Gramps finished Gran's singsong warning.

Taylor's pulse slowed and the pounding in her ears diminished as she forced deep breaths. It was only a dream. Still, sadness sat like a weight on her chest.

Even after three weeks of searing temperatures, the thick stone walls cooled her trailing fingertips as she padded along the hallway, trying to soothe herself with the house's aura of permanence. Grey eyes tinged with red greeted her in the tiny bathroom mirror. Her necklace glinted in a shaft of sunlight streaming through the louvre window. She fingered the clasp. Perhaps removing the silver chain might help curb her rampant imagination?

Instead, she turned from the mirror.

The high side of the claw-footed bath made for an awkward scramble and she showered quickly under a trickle of water. Mum hadn't missed the opportunity for an environmentally friendly lecture on the way over: South Australia was the driest state on the driest continent.

Lack of water would have been just one more hardship for the settlers who sought to tame this ancient land. *Like Anna's family.*

An exasperated snort burst from her lips. Taylor twisted the taps closed, caught the last few drips and sluiced her face, trying to scrub away the memory of the dream. Her chest shuddered as a sob snuck up on her. God, what was wrong with her? She took measured breaths, forcing herself to search for reality, for logic. It was the let-down effect: after a tumultuous, stressful year, she was now emotionally crumbling, evidenced by her visceral reaction to something as silly as a dream.

But the grief couldn't have hit her any harder if it had been her own mother who had died.

Taylor groaned, leaning her head against the tiles. What was she thinking? *Nobody* had died. There was no Anna, no dead mother, no reason for sorrow. She'd allowed herself to become immersed in a fantasy world, much like she used to as a kid. The difference was, this was impacting her behaviour in the real world. The adult world.

She dragged on shorts and a tee, then tousled her damp hair as she headed for the kitchen. Mum leaned her thighs against the duck-egg blue cupboards, scraping a black piece of toast into the sink, apparently oblivious to the last fading chirps of the struggling smoke detector.

Taylor wrapped her arms around her mother from behind, resting her chin on Mum's shoulder.

Mum stiffened and half-turned. 'Oh, you startled me. What's up?'

'Nothing.' She muffled her voice in Mum's kaftan. 'Have you had any more thoughts about coming to the service next week, Mutti?'

Shit. How did that word slip out? She shivered, the ghosts of her sanity trailing icy fingers along her spine.

Mum gave up on the toast, tossing it into the chook bucket. 'Of course I'm going, love. You know me. Anything Christmassy, I'm up for it.'

Not exactly what she'd said only days ago, but whatever. The backflip was classic Mum, and one of the things that Taylor loved about her.

'There's a price, though. Gran's put us on the roster for the CWA trading table today. It'll be fun. Help us get in the mood,' she added hurriedly, anticipating Taylor's argument.

An argument she had no interest in making. 'Sure.' She let go of Mum's waist, skirted the table and went to the fridge. 'Can I help with breakfast? What do you need out? Marmalade? Jam?'

'Help?' Mum's voice was incredulous. 'Good Lord, call the police. My child's been abducted and replaced with a changeling who both functions and speaks before coffee.'

'Yeah, you think you're funny . . .'

Mum rattled the drawer under the sink, locating a butter knife. The fridge held open with her knee, Taylor slid jars onto the table. She reached around the huge defrosting turkey to find the old-fashioned china butter dish Gran had picked up at an op shop. Though larger and brighter yellow than the pats Anna had formed with her wooden paddles, the square of butter almost looked fresh churned.

Taylor's hand fell from the dish.

No, no, no.

Mum never allowed margarine and apparently Gran was the same, so the spread had no significance. Yet it felt like fragments of her dreams were invading her life, creating links to her fantasy.

Prickles of anxiety choked her throat and she cast around the room. She needed fresh air, to do something physical that would sweep away the memory of the dream.

She snatched up the scrap bucket. 'I'll take these to the chickens before Gramps gets to it.'

Mum set a plate of slightly less cremated toast in the centre of the table, waving a hand to dissipate the smell. 'You'd have to be a lot earlier to beat him today. He's already fed them and been flying. Wait until after breakfast and add the toast scraps, save yourself a trip.' She dragged a chair across the floor and slid into it with a sigh, as though the toast had been as arduous as her championship Easter baking. 'Gran's taken a book out to the front verandah. Put the kettle back on, love. She must be due for a cuppa.'

Taylor stared numbly at the kettle as she waited for it to fill. Tomorrow, she would get up even earlier. Danger lurked in sleeping longer than necessary.

Yet, challenging her fear of the nightmares, luring her like a drug, was the temptation that lived in her dreams. *Luke.*

Gramps banged in the back door, his hair sticking straight up, his face sunburned. 'Morning, Michelle. Morning, Peach. Where's Magpie?'

Mum chased a dribble of jam from the side of the jar. 'Rocking chair, front verandah. Tay's about to take her a cuppa. Do you want one?'

'Is the Pope a Catholic?' Gramps dropped onto one of the orange vinyl-covered chairs. 'Any of that toast going begging?'

Taylor pushed her plate toward him. 'You've already been flying?'

'Sure have, Peach. But I'll go up again if you want to come?'

'I, uh . . .' She looked to Mum, signalling for rescue. She wasn't keen on getting in a car with Gramps, never mind an aeroplane.

Her mother didn't skip a beat. 'Tay's scared of heights, remember?' she said smoothly. 'That's why we drove here.'

Gran wandered in as Mum spoke. She dropped her reading glasses to swing from a lime-coloured plastic chain around her neck. 'In any case, we've too much to do today, with the trading table. In fact, the whole week is busy. I was about to suggest we all attend the shorter Christmas Eve service, instead of the midnight one. This year's turkey is so much larger than usual, I'll need to get up at four to put it on.'

'You do know it's forecast to be over forty degrees?' Taylor had to rush to say something, to point out the ridiculousness of a roast meal in the middle of a summer heatwave. Because the truth was, the idea of a traditional European dinner fluttered excitement in her stomach.

Anna and Luke would spend Christmas like this, surrounded by family.

∽

It seemed impossible, but the Christmas cheer in Settlers Bridge had ramped up from the previous week. Although it was school holidays, the local primary school students were grouped beneath one of the loudspeakers, competing with the carols cranked to be heard over the festive joy of the locals.

'Perhaps Marian decreed the attire for everyone today.' Taylor leaned in to her mother to murmur the comment, but then had to repeat herself more loudly. Dressed in the traditional red, green and white Christmas colours, including the odd elf hat and lairy T-shirts sporting cartoon reindeer and polar bears, people spilled across the road in the afternoon sunshine. Instead of honking and berating the pedestrian traffic, the occasional vehicle progressed slowly, windows down, the driver waving as though in a pageant, or randomly braking to chat with friends. Apparently, road rules were optional in Settlers Bridge at Christmas time.

The trading table backed onto the empty butcher's shop window with enough room behind it for a wall of eskys. Taylor, Mum and Gran had been assigned to help Marian and Tracey serve, while Christine Albright and Samantha from Ploughs and Pies were kept busy topping up the table from the eskys. At the far end of the trio of trestles, three women whose names Taylor couldn't recall were replenishing the supply of oven mitts, aprons, tea cosies, jams, relishes, pickles, crochet-fringed tea towels and flannels, and knitted stuffed toys from cardboard boxes.

'No wonder they don't have many shops here,' Mum said incredulously. 'What you can't buy on the CWA trading table, you don't want.'

Tracey chuckled. 'Other than the food, I think most of the sales are destined to be Christmas gifts. Where in the city could you buy an egg-collecting apron? Or a hand-knitted baby's beanie?'

'Well, I'm definitely here for the food, not the tea towels.'

Taylor glanced up.

Tall. Akubra. Sunglasses. Far from the only guy in the street dressed that way—although probably the only one with a flashing green and red tartan tie hanging casually loose around his neck. Something about him stirred a sense of familiarity.

'Luke,' Marian said. 'How's the family? Girls excited for Christmas?'

Luke. Instinctively, she'd known it was him. Taylor could kick herself for the ridiculous way her heart leaped at his name. And for the time she'd spent thinking about him over the last few days. He had a family.

'The girls are pinging off the walls, I reckon the chocolate component of their advent calendars is a bit generous.'

'And how are the renovations coming along? I imagine renovating is harder than a new build?'

'You'd be right there, Marian. Renos are slow, but I guess there'll be a bit of downtime after Christmas to get stuck into them. Is Matt closing the practice over the break? I'll hit him up for a hand. Need a couple of guys to help with some cementing.'

Practice? The women had definitely said there was no GP in Settlers Bridge—and if there had been, she would have spotted it by now. Taylor made a show of rearranging the jewel-bright fruit cakes so she could stay near and eavesdrop.

Marian shook her head, deftly serving someone else while continuing the conversation. 'Technically shut, but he'll be on call, of course.'

'No worries. I'll try some of the others.' Luke started to move along the trestles, checking out the baked goods. He paused as he came level with Taylor. 'You're finding enough in Settlers to keep you busy, then?'

Flustered, she fumbled a tray of jelly cakes. Predictably, they landed cake-side down. She winced, hoping Marian didn't notice the roadkill of pink sponge and fresh cream held together only by plastic wrap. The woman had the air of someone who didn't suffer fools or tolerate mistakes.

Luke dug in his pocket and held out a ten-dollar note. 'I'll take those.'

'No, they're—' She waved the packet of crumbled cake. She'd buy them herself as soon as she had the chance and hide them in Mum's bag.

'I noticed,' Luke said, reaching across the table to take them. His left cheek creased, a laugh deepening his voice. 'So, busy?'

'Ah, yeah, I guess,' she gabbled. Why would he take the broken cakes—and turn the tray so that it was hidden against his chest? 'I really only came here to support Mum.'

'No great calling of your own?'

'Well, uni's on break.' She wasn't about to admit to the hours she spent playing on her phone. Or riding the fences on the off-chance she might run into him.

This *married* man. With a family. Who was busy with his home renos. And had just purchased jelly cakes for his wife. Although, he could have at least bought her the uncrushed ones.

'Uni?' He tipped his head to one side and she imagined he cocked the brow hidden behind sunglasses.

'Mmm. Going into third year post-grad med.' Although that sounded more impressive than sharing that she had levelled up on Farm Barn, it didn't escape her that it was the second time in the past week she'd felt the urge to use the defence. Was that simply because people seemed impressed? At least, unlike Anna, she had options, could study and be whatever she chose. Except—what if that was no longer the case? What if Adelaide Uni didn't accept her transfer application? For the first time, the thought that her future might not be her choice chilled through her.

'I see.' For some reason, Luke's tone was thoughtful, as though the information was more interesting than it could possibly be. 'Well, if you're on a break from that, do you ride?'

'Horses?' Her heart pounded. The other Luke had asked Anna that.

Of course, he was just making polite conversation; they'd already established that he rode through the property regularly.

He nodded. 'I've a couple you can choose from.'

'I haven't . . . ridden for years.' Being led around the petting zoo on a Shetland guided by a rope counted, didn't it?

'Give me a call some time. Your grandparents have my number.' Luke dipped his head to her, then strode down the street.

She tried not to stare after him. Tried not to acknowledge her breathlessness, the weird fluttering of her heart, her too-fast pulse. But, even hidden beneath sunglasses and hat, with that height and breadth of shoulders, Luke was definitely stareable.

And a family man. She had to remember that. The good ones were always taken—and that was one hundred per cent fine, because she totally wasn't interested.

In him or anyone else.

21
Anna

June 1877

Dieter was the only one who spoke of Mother. Anna both resented and envied him the ability. Yet if she didn't speak of Mother, would her memories disappear? After only four weeks, the tune Mother hummed as she kneaded dough escaped Anna. Each morning, Anna thumped at the floury mixture, her anxiety increasing. If she couldn't get the melody right, her bread would be heavy. As heavy as her heart. But if she followed Dieter's example and spoke of Mother, she would be unable to hold back the tears.

She was relieved Mother had not fallen ill visiting Mrs Ernst on her behalf, but she did not blame Dieter for his part in the tragedy. Like her, removal from the one he loved above all others was his punishment. Still, their punishment was temporary, while they observed deep mourning; Father's sentence was forever.

She brought her crucifix to her lips. Her heart ached with longing for Luke. Only he could fill the emptiness within her, assure her that life would go on. Because, right now, she and her family only existed; too scared to allow grief, too hurt to admit pain, too guilty to take blame—because to do these things would mean they must accept the finality of Mother's loss.

It was all Anna could do to continue with the basic functions of life: rise; milk Liesl; cook; feed the chickens; eat; clean. Remember to breathe. And then lie in bed at night, pretending to sleep, both desiring and terrified of the ghosts that haunted her dreams.

♈

'But Father, you must come to the memorial service.' They were all dressed in black, Emilie's blonde curls shining against the dark fabric. All, that is, except Father.

He leaned against the door to pull on his muddy work boots. 'Engelein, do you think I need a service to remember your mother? She will be with me as I work.'

Each day he worked longer and later. When Mother was alive, he would try to be home for dinner, disappointed when droving kept him away overnight. He would return, sweep Mother into a bear hug and smack his lips against her cheek. Laughingly complaining about the 'uncivilised muck and mud' on her floor and her clothes, Mother would return the embrace, then fend Father off, ordering him to the bucket outside to wash as she served his food, his plate piled high at the head of the table. Father believed every meal should be a celebration, the opportunity to enjoy the blessing of family and food. It was as close to acknowledging and thanking God as he ever came. Flouting custom, Mother wouldn't sit in silence at the opposite end of the table but set her place alongside Father's, the dinner table loud as they all ate, sharing the events of the day.

Now, the seat next to Father's remained empty—and his heavy carved chair was also often vacant. Instead, he took his hard bread and cold meat to the fields. Early each morning, the winter rain gusting through the door signalled his departure while it was dark. Shivering alongside Emilie, Anna knew he wouldn't return to their empty-feeling house until night had fallen. Sometimes he didn't return at all, the bed on the far side of the curtain remaining cold and unused.

Dieter told her Father was building more fences, longer and higher, walling in their property as though he could protect them all.

But she knew he was trying to wall out the pain.

'But Father—' She put out a hand to stay him as she swivelled to her brother. 'Dieter?'

Dieter shrugged, his eyes fixed on hers. She understood: *Let Father deal with it in his own manner.* But she could not. The sanctity of Sunday was one of Mother's firmest rules.

'Father, even if you won't come, you cannot work. It is Sunday.'

Her father's face was hollow, his hair and beard now completely grey. Wrapped in trying to contain her own misery, she hadn't looked at him in the month since Mother died. The hand he dropped to her shoulder shook as though palsied. 'For nearly thirty years, I honoured that rule. What good did it do me?'

'Then I shall stay and make you lunch.' Fingers crossed behind her back, she prayed he would refuse. They were invited to dine with Caroline's parents after the service. She had no particular wish to partake of lunch with them but she did not want to return here. Mother had always been home when she returned from Sunday service, the house aromatic with roast meat, regardless of the weather. Her family would sit to lunch together and recount the blessings of the week.

It would never again be so.

'I don't need food.'

The door shut firmly behind Father. The twins paused in their teasing to stare at the vibrating wood.

Anna clapped her hands, forcing gaiety into her voice. 'Okay, littlies, put your wet weather clothes on. It is filthy outside.'

Mother had warned of the approaching storm. With the onset of winter, the drought had broken in spectacular fashion and now it seemed the rain would never stop. Wind moaned under the door, a mournful dirge washing mud across the flagstones. The floor had not looked clean since Mother left. Anna stared at the window as if assessing the chance of a break in the weather. In truth, she could not see through the glass. Instead, she counted the tears running down it.

'Come on, then.' Dieter swung Frederika onto his hip, pulling her black bonnet forward. 'I have pulled the trap up close.'

Emilie and the twins would ride. Anna could have squeezed in with them, a child crammed on each of their laps, but she preferred to walk with Dieter. The misery of the weather suited her mood.

Vague concern stirred her apathy. Luke would be at the church. No matter how clever Emilie's needlework, six miles through wind and rain would leave Anna looking like a bedraggled orphan.

She was not an orphan. Her father still lived.

Just.

The wind stole her gasp of shock as she stepped outside, chin tucked to her chest, and tugged the door closed behind them. The rain slid under her bonnet to sting and blind her. As she dashed in the direction of the trap, her sister halted in front of her.

'Emilie, for goodness' sake, get the twins out of the weather.'

Without turning, Emilie reached backward, her fingers scrabbling at Anna's wrist. 'Look.'

Frederika was already in an unfamiliar black buggy. Not their trap.

Barely visible through the rain streaming from his great-coat and hat, Luke lifted Frederik into the high vehicle, then turned to the women, beckoning Emilie from where she hesitated in the scant shelter of the house. She dashed into the rain, accepting his help to clamber in. As Emile settled her skirts, Dieter leaned across her from the driver's seat, tipping his hat to Anna, who was still standing in the rain. He shook out the reins and the vehicle rolled forward, the mud sucking at the wheels like wallpaper paste.

They were leaving her.

Luke strode toward her, splashing mud as he squelched to a halt. 'Anna, go inside and dry yourself a little before we leave. We shall take Arabella and the small trap.'

Rain plastered her hair to her face and ran down the inside of her collar. She stared up at Luke, not daring to look away in case he became another of the apparitions that now haunted her life. Frozen fingers fumbling behind her for the handle, she fell through the doorway. Luke followed, jamming his shoulder against the door to shut the wind out.

The noise of the storm was abruptly amputated, though rain poured from the iron roof sheets, creating a waterfall beyond the window. Luke sluiced water from his face. He removed his hat and raked a hand through saturated hair. His presence woke a pain in her chest.

The ice was thawing—and she did not know if she was ready for that to happen. The only way she'd been able to cope with Mother's loss was to act as though she had never existed. Not allow herself to feel anything, not a single emotion.

'I could not wait until church to see you.' Luke reached one hand toward her.

She stared at his feet. Mud puddled around his boots. On Mother's floor.

'Anna?'

Arms wrapped around her waist, she shivered. Or trembled. She did not know which. Luke stood in her house. Unchaperoned.

And she could not respond.

He had come for her—and if he moved toward her now, she might never let him go.

Luke lowered his hand. 'Do you have a cloth I may use?' His was voice gentle. 'I would dry off a little before we go. We had best hurry or Dieter will wonder where we are.'

Her boots slid on the stone floor. Rags hung over a wooden rail near the range and she ran her hands over them, searching for the driest.

Luke hooked his hat on a peg, running a finger around the inside of his high collar.

Clumsy with his eyes upon her, she returned to him across the suddenly vast room. As his hand closed around the fabric, his fingers brushed hers. She jerked away, a sob rising in her throat.

Luke seized her arms to steady her. Certain she had regained her balance, he stepped back with his hands raised, as though calming a skittish horse. Or perhaps proving he would not touch her unless she wanted him to.

She wanted him to. His hand felt warm and real. A tear slid down her cheek. 'I do not want to be crying every time you see me.'

Luke gestured at his dark suit. 'I would embrace you, but it appears I am even wetter than you.'

'It seems I work on matching you.' She sniffled, dashing her eyes with the back of her hand in a far from lady-like manner. Mother would click her tongue against her teeth, sigh in long-suffering reproach and pass her a delicate handkerchief.

Mutti.

A harsh gasp shuddered through Anna, as though she had been unable to properly draw breath for a month. The dam holding back her emotions breached, the tears fell unrestrained, releasing the farewell she had been unable to make.

Luke tugged her in tight, held her without speaking as she closed her eyes and finally allowed the memories of Mother to return to her heart, where they belonged.

Eventually, when she stepped from his embrace, he gently pressed the cloth to her cheeks.

'Better, my love?'

She nodded, his breath warm against her skin as he chased a rivulet of water running from her sodden hair down her neck and across her chest.

He snatched his hand back. 'Ah. It would be better if you dry yourself. And better yet if I wait outside.' His sheepish grin took any sting from the words.

She turned away, allowing him a moment of privacy to compose himself, and patted at her damp hair and bodice. She turned back. 'Presentable?' It seemed ridiculous that in the midst of her aching remembrance, she must still be woman enough to worry about her appearance. Yet Mother would have been the first to chide her on being unkempt or untidy.

'So very much more than presentable, Miss Frahn. Shall we?' Reaching for his hat, Luke offered his arm. 'No, wait a moment.' His eyes raked the room, coming to rest on the curtain to her bedroom. 'May I?'

Her heart beat fit to leave her chest, but she nodded. Panic fluttered in her breast. Where was Father? In the yard?

Surely he would not have gone to work on the fences in this weather? But was she worried because she wanted Father to appear or because she wished to be assured of his absence?

Luke pulled aside the curtain, disappeared for a moment, then returned with the quilted blanket from her bed. He bundled it under his coat, held up one finger, then dashed out into the rain, returning within seconds. 'Now I think we are ready to proceed.'

The interior of the trap was damp as Luke lifted her in. He strode around to his side, removing the blanket from his seat before climbing aboard. Leaning across the bench, he tucked the fabric securely around her, his handsome face inches from hers.

'Is that better?'

She shook her head and swallowed laughter as droplets sprayed him.

The springs of the trap creaked as he drew back. 'Why not?'

'Because I cannot hold your hand.'

As Luke stared at the hand she wriggled free of the quilted cocoon, Anna feared she had been too forward.

His tongue ran across his lips and he blew out a low breath. Eyes locked to hers, he took her hand. Then he kissed her palm, his lips hot and unhurried.

Sparks flew within her as though a log had been tossed onto a fire.

Luke scowled with mock severity. 'Now, Miss Frahn, I really think we should be on our way. There are a number of sins, of the mind if not of the flesh, to which

I should probably devote some time discussing with my God.'

The torrential rain pounded the roof and thin sides of the trap, making conversation impossible once the vehicle was rolling. In any case, it seemed they had little to say— or perhaps little necessity to say anything. The silence was not uncomfortable, it was warm and safe and complete. Hands linked, breath frosting the air of the tiny world created by the trap's panelling, they were insulated from all else by a thick grey blanket of cloud and rain. For this moment in time, only the two of them existed.

And that was perfect.

∽

Through the downpour, Anna could make out the larger buggy at the fork of the road. Dieter waited for them a half-mile short of the church. Her shoulders slumped as tension drained from her body. She had been vaguely concerned about arriving at the service with Luke, unchaperoned— but not concerned enough to withdraw her hand or to protest his scheming with her brother.

Luke relinquished her hand with one last caress of his thumb. 'I thought you would prefer if we did not set tongues wagging. Can you handle the four-seater from here? Rein in centre of the church courtyard and I will hitch it up after you have all dismounted. Dieter will ride with me.'

Surrendering the warmth of both the blanket and the company, she pulled her damp cape tight. Luke swung her free and they splashed across the muddy track to her siblings in his buggy.

Emilie sulked, not even speaking to her as they covered the last half-mile to church. But that was fine, as Anna needed to concentrate on handling the unfamiliar buggy, the reins tugging at her hands. Fortunately, the horse seemed quite capable of navigating the road herself, settling the carriage into the deep ruts.

Dieter assisted them to alight, then shepherded them like a flock of damp ducklings into the vestibule to add their capes to the soggy black mountain. The church was unheated and dank. Anna would have been warmer near Luke, but what remained of her family was required to take the front pew.

She did not want to hear the heavy words of condolence and pity. She did not want to pretend not to notice the glances as neighbours wondered at Father's absence. She did not want to talk or listen, explain or apologise. She wanted only the reassurance of Luke's hand clasping hers, to recreate those brief minutes when all was once again right with her world.

The service was mercifully quick. Perhaps Pastor was also cold and longed to get home for his midday meal. He ushered them from the church, capes held over their heads as they dashed for the hall. As a nod of respect to the gravity of the occasion, there was no separation between men and women, the congregation milling around the tea table.

Although Anna tried to concentrate on the well-intentioned words of comfort from the parishioners, she was aware of Luke, only feet away. Welcome heat flooded her as, hat pushed to the back of his head, his eyes never left her.

The twins gravitated toward Mrs Ernst, who folded them against her capacious bosom. Anna closed her mouth with a snap. She had rarely attended a service with the twins and had no idea of their clearly reciprocated affection for the stern-seeming woman. Clutching her hands with their sticky fingers, Frederik and Frederika circled the tea table, Mrs Ernst encouraging them to eat, evidencing all the fondness of a doting grandmother.

Caroline moved to her side, pressing her cheek to Anna's. 'I have missed you. It seems forever since I have seen . . . any of you. How are you?' Despite her question, she emanated a certain excitement.

Anna lifted one eyebrow. 'Caroline? Is something amiss?'

Caroline toyed with the tiny buttons on her cuff. 'No. Well, yes. In a fashion. I made a decision.' She squeezed Anna's waist and whispered, 'I shall tell you later. Your father is not here?'

'No. He is . . . indisposed.' She would not explain his absence. Could not.

Caroline pouted prettily. 'Then we are an odd number for lunch. Let me see, who should I invite?' She put a finger to her lips, narrowing her eyes. 'Mrs Ernst? Oh no, that is right, she has already accepted.'

She laughed, but Anna would not take her bait.

Caroline turned, assessing the room. 'We shall be a little female heavy, so perhaps a man?'

There were around thirty men present whom she could invite. Surely she meant to settle on Luke, but what if . . .?

'Please, Caroline. I have so little opportunity to see him now.'

Caroline patted Anna's arm. 'Believe me, I know. It is so very hard, is it not? For the life of me, I don't know why we allow ourselves to be ruled by such strictures. In fact—' Her eyes danced and she darted a gloved hand over her mouth. 'No, this is not the place for it. But I cannot wait to tell you, Anna dearest. I must go to talk with someone else, lest I give myself away.'

With so much cryptic conversation, Anna's head whirled. But it was good. If she concentrated on deciphering Caroline's clues, she could not think about the reason for today's service.

'Miss Frahn.'

The deep voice thrilled through her, tempting her to close her eyes so as to better absorb it.

'Unfortunately, it seems this roof is quite sound.' Luke stood close, making certain they were not overheard.

'Unfortunately?'

'Were it to leak, I have only a kerchief to serve as a towel.'

She was torn between the tears that threatened and laughter as a warm blush crept to her cheeks. It was surely improper to display such levity at a remembrance service—at her mother's service—yet she had a need to lighten the misery of the last month. 'Mr Hartmann. How inexcusably short-sighted of you.'

'Indeed, Miss Frahn, I am humbled by my oversight. I can only hope you will permit me the opportunity to make amends.'

'One handkerchief and so many women to protect from the elements?' The sweep of her hand encompassed the room. 'How shall you manage?'

Luke's tone was suddenly serious. 'Have I not made myself clear, Miss Frahn? My protection extends to only one woman.'

Caroline glided toward them. 'Mr Hartmann, I was searching for you. I was beginning to fear perhaps you had not attended the service.' She employed her fan to hide her smirk. 'I discover myself in somewhat of a quandary and should be forever grateful if you could find it in your heart to assist me.'

Luke lifted his hat, bowing slightly at the waist. 'The pleasure would be mine, Miss Schenscher.' He sounded wary, and Anna was glad he did not leap to do Caroline's bidding.

'With Anna's father unable to attend the luncheon, I find myself a guest short. I would be appreciative if you would save us from the awkwardness of odd numbers at the table.'

Luke's swift grin was a flash of white. 'Indeed. I repeat, Miss Schenscher, the pleasure will be *all* mine.'

It was inappropriate for Anna to reach for Luke's hand, so she did the next best thing, seizing Caroline's and squeezing it in a silent display of gratitude.

She would be with Luke for hours. And, almost even better, she would not have to return to the farm just yet.

22
Taylor

Taylor grabbed at the handle above the door as the sedan swung from the main road into a gravelled parking lot surrounded by tall, white-trunked gum trees. Gramps had insisted they all travel to the church service together. Something about 'getting in the spirit'.

Catching her instinctive self-preservation in the rear-view mirror, Gramps chortled. 'That's why it's called a Jesus handle, Peach.'

'Fitting,' Gran agreed. 'Considering where we are.'

Gramps pulled in terrifyingly close to a ute with an unusual dove-grey paint job. The colour snagged a thread in Taylor's memory, but before she could unravel it, her gaze was drawn across the car park. The whitewashed walls of the church were shaded shell-pink by the sinking sun and the solid wooden doors had been flung open to invite the community.

It was Luke and Anna's church. Exactly as she had dreamed it.

Her knuckles ached as she clenched her fists, desperately trying to rationalise. Country churches were likely all much the same, built to a simple, long-held plan. Or she'd seen something similar in a movie, probably one she was half-watching while studying, and subconsciously planted the image in her dream. That was basic neuroscience, nothing odd about it at all.

She peered between the vehicles. Disappointment coursed through her as she realised the hitching rails were long gone and the stone water trough against the boundary fence had disappeared.

No! What was she thinking?

She pressed trembling fingertips to her forehead. The items weren't missing—they had never been there. Never been anywhere but her imagination.

'What's the matter, Peach, someone walk over your grave?' Gran said, and Taylor realised gooseflesh covered the arms she had instinctively crossed over her chest.

'Yeah, I guess. Something like that.' She needed to get a grip, confine her overactive imagination to when she slept. She grabbed the handle and popped the door. 'Okay, people, let's get our Christmas on.'

Her foot hit the ground, the latent warmth from the day billowing up. Taylor froze: she knew exactly how the interior of the church would look. A row of wooden slabs fixed to the wall on the right of the entry, each studded with iron pegs to hold hats and coats. If she followed the aisle of polished floorboards toward the altar, counting four pews on the right, then slid to the end of a hard bench barely deep enough for a bustle, she could lean against the cool stone wall where Anna sat, protected by Dieter's broad shoulders.

No. She was projecting. There was no reason to assume the inside of the church looked anything like the one of her imagination.

She tumbled out of the car, slamming the door behind her. A second building to her left was about the same size as the church, but lacked the peaked roof and lancet windows. Her pulse pounded so hard she felt ill.

'Gran, is that the church hall?'

Gran had to say no, tell her it was a giant storeroom, or an indoor swimming pool, or a basketball stadium. Tell her anything—except what she already knew.

'Yes, love. Supper is in there after the service.'

Gramps shepherded them up the steps, and ushers guided them toward the back row.

The congregation wore jeans and tees, not floor-sweeping skirts and dark suits. They carried phones instead of lacy fans and the ends of the pews were decorated with glittery baubles and tinsel instead of gum leaves and flowers.

Yet Taylor could see beneath the disguise.

She swallowed hard, fighting the black spots dancing before her eyes.

The pastor stood near the altar—how did she know his title was pastor? She had no ecumenical knowledge and Catholic services had priests—his robe billowing as he spread his arms wide, welcoming new visitors to the parish.

The congregation swivelled to smile at them, and Taylor averted her gaze, staring at the ruby-red stained-glass window high above the altar.

Exposed. Looking at me. Talking about me.

As the service began, she clutched her pendant, zipping it up and down the chain. Concentrating on the tiny noise it made, she closed her eyes, trying to slow the pounding of her heart by taking measured breaths. Focusing on a waft of sunshine and hay that came from somewhere in front of her, rather than the open door behind, she tried to not hear the voices that crowded her head, demanding she remember.

It was déjà vu. Nothing more.

Except déjà vu should be a blinding flash, a quick chill, easily laughed off. Not this inundation of imagined memories that clamoured for recognition.

An hour later, the hall was no better.

A laden supper table dominated, the men ebbing to one side, the women flowing to another. The boundaries were fluid, with more mingling permitted than before.

Taylor's hands clenched. *No! There was no* before.

Standing alongside Gramps, she forced her gaze around the room, assessing it. A square, featureless space. Scuffed wooden floor, cream-painted walls smudged by decades of bored children. Nothing notable, nothing unusual, nothing memorable. Nothing to terrify her.

No different from thousands of other square white rooms.

But if she didn't demonstrate some control, she would find herself locked in a square white room. One with padded walls.

Somehow, she had to stop these dreams.

'Giving the old place a pretty hard going over, there,' a lazily amused voice said from slightly behind her.

She spun around. 'Luke.'

He nodded, the cleft in his left cheek deepening. 'Taylor.'

How could he know her name? How could he be *here*?

'Ah, there you are, lad,' Gramps said. 'I've been trying to talk Taylor into taking you up on that riding business. She's got the hang of the bikes, but it wouldn't hurt to have a few more interests.'

Of course. Luke. The *local* Luke. Her heart rate settled a little as she placed him. God, she'd seen him only days ago—although he'd been hidden by hat and glasses. Why was she letting her imagination take over logical thought?

Yet, those eyes? Such an unusual shade of blue, they were close to purple in the dim room. How could he have the same eyes, the same features, as the Luke of her dreams?

She took a shaky breath, forcing herself to be rational. Obviously, she must have seen Luke on the street when they first came to Settlers Bridge three months ago and subconsciously filed his appearance away, even though she'd been focused only on thoughts of Zac.

She glanced behind him, looking for the family he'd mentioned the previous week.

Luke shifted, blocking her view. 'Perhaps I can suggest somewhere you could ride?'

Her heart stopped. His words were far too close to Anna's, too close to the imaginary conversation she had memorised.

Across the room, Gran stood alongside a table, the white tablecloth barely visible beneath the plates, trays, bowls and plasticware laden with supper. She held up a tea plate loaded with pavlova and stained-glass biscuits.

'No such thing as diabetes on Christmas Eve,' Gramps chortled gleefully, promptly deserting Taylor.

She couldn't just stand and stare at Luke, familiar though he seemed. 'I, uh—' she stammered. But the disconcerting sensation of déjà vu, the cloying feeling that she'd lived this moment before, stared deep into this man's eyes and been privy to his innermost thoughts, made words almost impossible to find. She dug deep. 'The truth is, I haven't ridden in years.'

'It's like falling off a bike.'

'I was hoping to avoid that.'

'Fair call. Though, if you're trying to keep up with your grandfather, you'll be in trouble. He's a bit of a speed demon.' He stopped speaking, seeming to assess her. Evidently in no hurry to get back to his family.

'Luke,' a guy hailed, crossing the hall toward them, 'you got time to help cut out some lambs this week?'

Luke turned his head, though he was still planted solidly in front of her. 'Can make time. Swap you for a hand with that cementing I mentioned to Marian. Don't know if she passed on the message?'

The guy, probably close to Taylor's age, levelled a questioning smile at her and Luke made an irritated noise in his throat. 'Taylor, my cousin, Matt Krueger. Not that you'll need to remember his name, as you won't see him around—he's always got his nose in a book. Or hand up a cow's backside.'

'Way to make me sound kinky,' Matt chuckled. 'I studied vet science,' he clarified to Taylor.

'For like half your life,' Luke grumbled.

'Like a quarter. Seems like half,' Matt said. 'What brings you to these parts?' He shared his cousin's build and wheat blond hair, but his eyes were summer sky, not Luke's almost twilight shade.

Taylor took a shaky breath, relieved at the prosaic question that allowed her time to calm her ridiculous reaction. 'Mum and I've relocated from the east coast. Vet science? Where did you study?'

'Adelaide Uni, down on North Terrace. In the city,' Matt added, clearly realising she might not be familiar with the capital.

She nodded. 'I've applied to transfer there. Third-year post grad med.'

Matt winced. 'That's got to be a crippling workload.'

'Probably on par with yours, from what I've heard.' She'd missed this, she realised with surprise; grumbling with peers about study loads and university pressures, yet knowing she was working toward a goal. The last few weeks—relaxing, sleeping in, hanging around the farm—had been fun, a much-needed pause. But perhaps returning to focus and discipline would stop her brain's distracted meandering.

'I was just trying to persuade Taylor to come out on one of the trails,' Luke said. 'You up for it?'

'Hell, yeah,' Matt said eagerly. Then he glanced around guiltily. Rolled his eyes. '*Heck*, yeah. If I can find time. Simon's got a load of jobs he wants a hand with, plus emergency hours at the clinic, of course. And I've got work on for Marian, too.'

As he lifted his chin, Taylor followed his line of sight. A few metres away, dressed in white jeans, polished but worn brown RM Williams boots and an elegant linen shirt with the collar starched to stand tall and the cuffs turned back, the doyenne of the CWA managed to look both expensive and as though she wasn't afraid of getting her hands dirty.

Marian glanced toward them at the mention of her name, and Taylor was surprised by the fond smile on her face. 'My tasks can fit in around your other obligations, Matthew,' she said as she closed the gap between them, shadowed again by her friend, Tracey. 'And recreation is an important commitment. Balance in all things, remember.'

Taylor frowned, wondering what their relationship was if Matt not only worked for her, but took direction about his leisure time.

'Candles and ends,' Luke agreed.

'Luke.' Marian nodded. 'Never rains but it pours, correct? I don't see you for months on end, then twice in a week.'

'Guess it's a given we'll all turn out for the Christmas service.' Luke didn't appear chastened by what sounded almost like a reprimand.

Matt chuckled. 'First time for everything.' He glanced from Luke to Taylor, like that explained his amusement.

'It's nice to see you here, Taylor,' Tracey said cheerfully.

'I was worried we might be muscling in.' Taylor flicked a hand toward the church, although it was out of sight. 'But it looks like half of Settlers Bridge must be here.'

Marian glanced around the room as though tallying up the numbers, but Luke shook his head. 'Not Settlers. This lot is all from the farms roundabout here.'

'With the exception of Tracey.' Marian smiled benevolently at the petite woman. 'She's our token Settlers Bridgeian.'

'I'm a token *something*, all right,' Tracey said with a mischievous glint in her eye.

Marian's lips curved, but she cleared her throat, as if reining in her humour. 'Indeed.'

'In that case, I'm even more surprised at the number of people,' Taylor said. 'Because there don't seem to be that many farms around here. In fact, at night it's flipping terrifying. I've never known anywhere so dark and secluded.'

Luke gave a soft huff of laughter and she frowned, wondering if he was mocking her city inexperience. She didn't look directly at him, though. Couldn't risk making contact with those disconcerting eyes.

'You'll find there's actually a small church every ten kilometres or thereabouts.'

She hiked an eyebrow. 'Why so many?'

'They date back a hundred and fifty or so years, to when the area was settled. The holdings were smaller and travel was slower. So more population meant more churches, and necessity meant those churches had to be close to home. Most of them are abandoned now, though you'll find the odd one converted to a house as part of a lifestyle farm.'

'Lifestyle?' She had to keep her mind busy, not dwell on the fact that she already knew so much of what he was telling her.

'Hobby farm. Too small to be a primary source of income.' He paused, as though waiting to see if she had more questions.

She didn't. It was impossible to look at him and operate her brain at the same time.

'A few of the churches still have a service maybe once a month. But for major events—like Christmas and Easter—many of the congregations head over here. Come on any regular Sunday and you won't see these numbers.'

'Like you'd know what a regular Sunday looks like,' Matt scoffed.

'And you only know because you bring your mum,' Luke shot back.

'Speaking of, we must catch up with Adele,' Tracey said. She laid a hand on Marian's wrist, drawing her from the group.

Matt nodded farewell to the two women, then turned back to Luke. 'True enough. But what's your story? Can't remember the last time I saw you here.'

Luke lifted one shoulder, his gaze roaming the merry crowd. 'I guess sometimes a guy just feels a calling. No better time than right now.' His eyes brushed Taylor. 'Being Christmas and all.'

Taylor's heart seized. The 'and all' had an inflection. Didn't it?

No, she was imagining it. Because Luke had a family *and all*. Just because he featured in her fantasies didn't mean the fascination was reciprocal. Nor should it be. Besides, she was done with men, done with longing and done with allowing her imagination to run rampant.

What she was going to do was appreciate this warm community, enjoy the experience of a country Christmas and get her life back on track.

'So, mate, you coming for that ride?' Luke said.

Matt gave a slow grin, then lifted his chin toward Taylor. 'Would, but I'm pretty sure you wouldn't want a chaperone.'

Taylor felt suddenly sick, the room tilting as though she had vertigo.

~

They had fallen into the habit of going to bed early, probably because they rose with the sun—although Taylor still had no intention of being induced into a multi-generational yoga session.

A couple of hours after they returned from church, Mum wandered into Taylor's room, brushing out her hair. The crackling static billowed it into a shoulder-length cloud. '*Jaws*? Really?'

'Sure. Pretty much a classic, and makes a change from textbooks. In any case, the internet's too crappy to get anything.' Taylor dropped the book onto her legs, which were covered by a thin sheet. She hadn't looked at the title, simply grabbed the fattest book from the lounge-room shelf. It had to last her all night. Brrt looked up at her and yawned massively, stretching in the cream-coloured patch of bed she'd claimed as her own.

Mum winced as her brush tangled. 'Well, I don't know about classic. How are you feeling now, baby?'

'Fine.' She'd stammered a promise to go riding with Luke, then fled the hall. Pleaded a headache when her family came looking.

But it wasn't only her head. The arrhythmia that had suddenly hit her with Matt's talk of chaperones left her nauseous and sweating. In the privacy of the eucalypts surrounding the church car park, she'd pinched her nose closed and exhaled forcibly, using the Valsalva manoeuvre to force her heartbeat back to a normal rhythm.

Mum patted her leg. 'Listen, I know tomorrow's going to be kind of hard.'

'Mmm. Hot roast for lunch. That's definitely out there.' She wasn't in the mood for deep and meaningful.

Apparently, that didn't matter, because Mum was. 'Dad's taken an extra shift over Christmas, so you don't need to worry about him being alone. But I've asked him if he'd like to fly over for your birthday next month. He can stay at one of the pubs in Settlers Bridge for a couple of days.'

'But you guys hate each other.'

'Hate?' Mum sat on the edge of the bed. 'Don't be ridiculous.'

'You're getting divorced, remember? Kind of comes with certain prerequisites.'

'Hate is a very strong word.' Mum switched to her counsellor's voice. 'Of course, I feel some disappointment about the breakdown of our relationship. But I choose not to put negative energy into the world.'

Taylor's fingertips turned white as she wound the sheet around her hands. 'Oh my God, can you just *not*?' Her months of control snapped. 'You know what I hate? And I use the word advisedly—I do mean *hate*. I hate that I could hear you arguing for years. And I hate that you're getting divorced. Most of all, I hate that you say you don't hate each other, but you're tearing our lives apart.' Because maybe, if she hadn't come back here, her brain wouldn't be splitting in half.

'Tay, don't be like that.' Mum stroked Taylor's leg through the sheet, her eyes glistening. 'Divorce can be about realising you simply don't fit together anymore. That wild passion that seizes you when you're young, the feeling that you could never want anything as much as you do right in that moment? It is never enough. Love grows tired and fades. And then you have to search for something new, something to fill that hole, something that makes you feel like you did when you first fell in love. No one loves forever.'

Mum was wrong. She had to be. What was the point in suffering so much pain falling in love, being in love, losing love, if you weren't supposed to try to find a love to hold on to forever?

'How do you explain Gran and Gramps then? Are you telling me *they* don't love each other?'

Mum did her infamous silent sigh and stood. 'Maybe when you get older it's easier to stay together than it is to be alone. But that's not really love. It's friendship and companionship, and a whole lot of good things. Yet it's not the love you start out with: that kind burns so hot, so fierce, it consumes itself. It can't last.'

Mum was wrong.

She had to be.

Taylor *needed* to believe that the love she imagined for Anna and Luke would last through eternity. As would Gran and Gramps'. Because if love that pure and fierce and sweet could just dwindle away . . . then perhaps she wasn't *choosing* not to waste her time on love.

Perhaps the entire concept of love was nothing but a lie.

23
Anna

As propriety dictated she could not ride alone with Luke from the church nor arrive at the Schenscher homestead with him, the menfolk decided that Anna should handle Luke's four-seater buggy, with the staid and steadfast Arabella harnessed to it. Luke and Dieter would take the smaller vehicle with Luke's spirited gelding.

Emilie barely waited for the trap to wheel from the yard before she whined, 'This is supposed to be a memorial service. You and Dieter look so happy. And I cannot believe Dieter allowed you to ride alone with Mr Hartmann.'

Jealousy prompted her sister's words, so Anna held her tongue.

'It is not right. Mother would have a fit. You know she would.'

That stung. 'Mother is not here, in case you had not noticed.'

Emilie whipped around, her face white, cheeks high-lighted by two pink spots. 'Oh, I have noticed.' Her eyes glittered, her voice a sibilant hiss. 'But it does not seem like you and Dieter are particularly bothered.'

The leather of the reins bit through Anna's gloves. Did Emilie speak the truth? Had she chosen to forget Mother in the intoxicating rush of Luke's desire?

No. Her certainty was a relief. It did not matter what Emilie said, Mother would have wanted this—she wanted nothing more than for her children to be happy.

But she would not approve of Anna's behaviour toward her sister.

Anna cast around for a verbal olive branch. 'Emilie, I know how hard it must be for you to fill Mother's shoes.' Her lips only trembled a little on Mother's name. 'But you are doing a wonderful job with the twins. She would be proud of you.'

Emilie's pious righteousness deflated and she sagged into her seat. 'I like looking after them. It makes me feel closer to Mother. I imagine what she would ask me to do.' She stared down at her hands, twisting a black satin ribbon from her cape. 'And I . . . I pretend she is here, that I am doing as I am directed. Sometimes I even pretend she is angry with me for some minor misdemeanour. Anna, I miss her so much, I would be happy to hear her scold me again.'

Guilt draped Anna like a wet horsehair blanket. She swapped the reins to her right hand, wrapping her left arm around her sister. 'I know, Emilie.'

Emilie sucked in an uneven breath, speaking in a rush as though she had held the words in for a long time. 'Anna,

I am happy for you and Dieter, really I am. But our family is ... disappearing. Mother is gone. And you know Father may as well be gone. Now you and Dieter would rather be somewhere else, with someone else.'

Anna could not argue, for Emilie spoke the truth.

As they wheeled into their hosts' home paddock, she understood Dieter's hesitance to ask permission to court Caroline: the Schenschers were clearly affluent. Their stone home sprawled across the land, a multitude of windows shining wetly, glowing with a promise of internal warmth. The yard was neatly bordered by sheds, each of the lesser structures large enough to contain Anna's entire house.

Caroline's stepmother waited at the open door, bidding them to hang up their capes and cloaks, then warm themselves before a fire, which appeared to serve no other function: no cooking pots hung over it; no clothes dried before it.

Upon discovering Caroline's older brother more than presentable, Emilie abandoned her sadness. Anna sighed with relief; her guilt was an uncomfortable burden. Dieter disguised his move toward Caroline under the pretext of greeting their hostess. His gaze was alight with a hunger that Anna did not believe was related to the presence of a polished rosewood table, groaning beneath crystal and porcelain, in an area Caroline referred to as the *dining room*.

Seated male then female around the oval table as was customary, at least four people separated Anna from Luke. But that put him opposite her and she was content to do no more than look.

As Caroline and her stepmother placed laden platters of kraut and bacon before them, Anna surveyed the array of cutlery alongside her plate with bewilderment. Caroline slid an arm over her shoulder and discreetly tapped the outside flatware.

Anna had not finished the food in her mouth before the blue-and-white porcelain plates were cleared. A huge shoulder of roast pork, the salt-crusted skin sparkling like diamonds, took centre place on the table as the women carried out steaming tureens of roast potatoes and carrots, and a platter of bratwurst sausages. The aroma of fresh-baked bread sweetened the air.

Caroline's father, almost as wide as he was tall, stood over the joint of meat. 'My friends, I invite you to lift your mugs of ale and toast this fine beast, and to the bonds of friendship.' His gaze paused on each of his children. 'And I think, perhaps, to Liebe.'

'Hans!' his wife gasped.

'What, Schatzi, we should not speak of such things?'

Mrs Schenscher folded her hands over her apron. 'Not in company, surely, my husband.'

'Then when?' Hans Schenscher lifted his stein. 'To love, and to being in love.' Throwing his head back, he downed his beer in a single draught.

Across the table, Luke's eyes met Anna's. She didn't need to drink the ale. She was dizzy enough.

Caroline's bell-like tone interrupted the laughter and toasting around the table. 'Then, Father, I have an announcement to make.'

'Ah, prepare yourself,' Caroline's brother, Otto, muttered to Emilie, who twisted a ringlet around one finger as she gazed at him. 'This will doubtless be memorable.'

Skirts in hand to free them from her chair, Caroline stood. 'I wish to announce that Dieter Frahn and I intend to court.'

Her huff of surprise hidden in the general commotion around the table, Anna lifted an eyebrow at Dieter. But he did not look to her. He stared at Caroline, his face stricken.

He'd had no inkling of her plan.

Caroline's stepmother also stood, agitatedly brushing flat the front panel of her skirt. 'Caroline, you cannot announce. Hans, tell her she cannot.'

'It would appear that she has.' Caroline's father was clearly more amused than her stepmother. 'This is what you want, daughter?'

'Absolutely.' Caroline's voice was firm and her eyes twinkled. Evidently, she was not averse to being the centre of attention.

His girth making it necessary for him to step back from the table, Mr Schenscher turned to Anna's brother. 'And you, Dieter. It is what you wish?'

Dieter's gaze had not left Caroline. As she bestowed the full force of her smile upon him, his lips curved in response and his eyes softened, though his deep voice was strong. 'Yes, sir, indeed it is.'

'Then it is so.' Hans thumped his tankard down on the table. 'More beer, woman. And let us eat before we must declare this beast has died in vain.'

Aware that Mother would have loved this moment, loss mingled with Anna's joy for her brother.

~

Caroline handed her a delicate teacup. 'How will you travel home?'

Beyond replete, Anna sat before the roaring fire with Emilie and Caroline. The menfolk had moved to another room—there were so many rooms in this house. Mrs Ernst and Mrs Schenscher had taken the twins to a window seat to play with a nest of kittens.

Suspecting a trap, Anna replied to Caroline's question carefully. 'As we came here, I assume.'

'Nonsense. Dieter told me of Luke's little ruse on the way to church. You must travel with him again.'

'But, Caroline, surely that is improper?' Emilie piped up piously.

Caroline cocked a brow. 'And if my brother were to ask you to do the same?'

Cheeks scarlet, Emilie pressed her lips together and shrank into the burgundy velour of her seat.

Caroline placed her cup on the spindly-legged side table. 'Men work hard enough, do you not agree, ladies? Sometimes, we must make our own decisions and relieve them of the pressure.'

She was so very brave—and perhaps she was correct.

Two hours later, the rain had eased and they headed for home, seated as Caroline had decreed. The day faded into the velvet blue of early evening and the wet expanse of the countryside took on a lake-like calm. A little drunk on both food and ale, Anna nestled against Luke, the rolling motion of the buggy tempting her to sleep. The blanket tucked around her created a delicate barrier between them and Luke placed an arm around her waist to draw her into the crook of his shoulder.

See-sawing emotions from a day that contained both endings and beginnings combined to engender such a weariness she could barely speak. But she needed to know his thoughts.

'Do you believe Caroline's move ill-considered?'

Luke remained silent for so long she thought he had not heard. As she opened her mouth to repeat the question, he replied slowly, 'I admire her courage in making such a decision.'

Despite her admiration for Caroline, jealousy flared in Anna.

'However,' Luke continued, 'I do think the allure of the chase is somewhat removed by her actions. And perhaps your brother is a little emasculated.'

She hid her hands in a fold of the rug. 'Although you could never suffer such a fate,'—she blushed at her own audacity in paying a man such a compliment—'perhaps it is well, then, that you did not allow me the opportunity to make such a move?'

Luke turned toward her, his face unusually serious. 'Would you have, Anna? Would you have asked me?'

She swallowed. It was twilight and she was partially hidden. The perfect time for such confessions. 'I should like to say yes. I would certainly have wanted to, but I fear I lack Caroline's bravery.'

Luke's cheek creased and she longed to trace her finger down the deep cleft from the corner of his eye to the edge of his mouth. 'It is enough to know that you would want to take such a step. But I shall be forever glad that I did not wait for you to decide whether you could.'

The intimation thrilled through her. Luke spoke of forever.

Courting did not last forever.

24
Anna

September 1877

Each day, black mould crept further along the steamy windowsill as the fire strove to drive the chill from their stone walls. At least the endless rain prevented frost from settling.

Dieter braved the weather, attending church regularly and often dining with Caroline's family afterward. His initial reserve at being considered a poor suitor had been vastly diminished by Hans Schenscher's unfailing friendliness.

The twins were bored, tired of the confines of the house, a unanimous but undiscussed decision ruling it too difficult to take them to church. On occasion, Mrs Ernst called for them—although, bless her, she never chastised Anna for permitting their religious lapse. Several times now, Frederik and Frederika had remained in Mrs Ernst's care overnight, as she claimed to delight in their company. With no husband and no children, perhaps she was lonely.

Caroline's brother, Otto, had also developed an interest in religion since meeting Emilie, and Anna had gladly relinquished her church-attending rights to her sister. Unlike Father, Anna did not blame God for what happened to Mother. And, as Luke called on her twice a week now, she had everything she wanted. Without the need to pray for more, worship seemed irrelevant.

Father remained withdrawn. Anna suspected he liked her at home so he was not alone—although she could do nothing to lift the loneliness that ate away at him, leaving behind a hollow shell of the man she loved. As far as anyone outside the family was aware, Luke and she were properly chaperoned. In truth, Father rarely lingered within earshot.

One ear cocked to the yard for the familiar splash of hooves above the downpour, Anna made a half-hearted attempt at introducing some decorum back into their lives as she cleared Father's untouched lunch plate.

'Father, you should not disappear and leave us alone.'

A tiny smile tugged at the grey skin of Father's face. 'Why is that, Engelein? What is it I must be afraid of?'

She blushed, giving herself away. 'P-people may talk.'

'People may talk all they want, Anna. My experience is that no words will change a single thing that happens in this world.' Father took his hat from the hook but paused with his hand on the door handle. He lifted his face to the portrait that hung in the centre of the wall. Taken on their wedding day twenty-eight years ago, Mother was younger than Anna was now. Seated, her hair was drawn into a severe bun. Father stood beside her, his beard already dappled with grey. Both appeared stern and unsmiling in the flash of the photographer's bulb—yet nothing could be further from the truth.

Intent on the photograph, Father's shoulders slumped, his head cocked unnaturally for a long time. He seemed lost in memories. Eventually he nodded, as though ending a silent conversation, and turned to Anna. He dropped his hat on the table and placed his hands on her shoulders. 'It makes me happy to know you have found someone. You and Dieter, both. Know that you have my blessing, whatever you wish to do. About Emilie, I have no concerns. She will have her choice of young men. She carries her mother's beauty, although you have her spirit. The little ones . . .' Father sighed, a frown creasing his face. 'The little ones I can do no more for. I am grateful Mrs Ernst has taken them under her wing.'

Fear fluttered within Anna's chest. 'Father, what are you saying?'

He pressed a kiss on her head. 'Nothing of any importance, my angel. Only that I am at peace, seeing my beloved children happy. You need to know that I love you, Liebling. But I must find my way past this pain.' He planted his hat and shuffled to the door. Old man steps, where only months ago he strode.

Luke arrived within minutes of Father's departure and, as usual, Anna had the door open ready for him. As rain showered from his long coat, she took it, stretching to hang it with his hat on the hook near the door.

His arms snaked around her waist, his lips against her ear. 'Three days is too long to go without seeing you. Where is your father?'

Desire trembled through her. She leaned against Luke, resting the back of her head on his broad chest. His heart pounded, hands pressed against her flat stomach, holding her close. His lips brushed the rim of her ear, startling a gasp from her. Anna had never known anything like this sensation—so close, so intimate—and she wasn't sure she could tolerate it.

She wriggled, trying to turn to face him, but for a moment he held her tight, as though afraid she would try to escape. Realising her intention, Luke slid his hands to her hips and she turned.

She was so tempted . . . But if she allowed him to kiss her, Anna feared she'd not be able to breathe. She would make a fool of herself, struggling for air.

But maybe that would not matter.

She slid her hand up the broad column of his neck, her palm tingling at the unfamiliar feel of this forbidden part of him.

Luke tensed, not giving as she tried to tug him closer. 'No, Anna. We must not.'

'Why not?' She would stamp her foot, but her knees were trembling like a newborn calf's and she relied on him for balance.

'Because if I allow myself to kiss you just once, I shall always want you.'

'Good. Because I shall always want you.' Her unplanned admission shocked her, but Mother's words burned in

293

her mind. There was not enough time in their lives. They must take what they wanted now.

Luke's intake of breath was quick and hard. He dropped his lips to her forehead, murmuring hotly against her skin, 'Are you sure, Anna? Are you certain this is what you want?'

On tip toes, she pressed herself against him.

'Ah, Anna,' he groaned. 'Sweet Anna.' His lips moved, softer than a dragonfly's wings, across her face, kissing her eyelids and cheeks, drawing closer to her mouth.

She had never dreamed it could be like this.

He pulled away a little, staring deep into her eyes. 'I love you so much.'

She should answer. She knew she loved him. But she could not speak, could only focus on the full, sensuous bow of his lips. And the hunger building inside her. A hunger food would never assuage.

Slowly, so slowly, Luke dipped his head and pressed his lips to hers.

It was nothing like she had imagined. Nothing like the experimental touch of her lips against the side of her own hand. Luke's kiss was sure and firm, his blond stubble prickling her skin. And warm! His mouth was so warm. But his lips didn't remain still in an almost-chaste press of skin. And nor did hers. As Luke feathered kisses across her mouth, Anna responded, desperately trying to return the pleasure he provided. He tugged at her waist, drawing her against his hard body. Then the tip of his tongue brushed swiftly across her parted lips.

She jerked back.

Luke flushed, loosening his grasp. 'I'm sorry, Anna, I did not mean to scare you.'

'No. Not scared.' She struggled to breathe. She should act demure, should blush and put the large wooden table between them. But she wanted . . . 'More.'

Luke exhaled sharply and then his mouth was hard on hers, his tongue flickering across her lips, demanding entry.

She had never imagined this as part of lovemaking, but it felt so right. His tongue chased hers as one of his hands in the small of her back kept her close, the other working her carefully coiled hair loose. She could no longer understand his words, but whether that was some odd effect of what he was doing or because of the blood pounding in her ears, she did not know. And nor did she care.

Luke staggered, moving his hands back to her waist. His eyes were darker than she had ever seen them, the pupils huge. 'Anna, you do not know what you do to me. We must stop.' A rueful grin drew up one corner of his mouth. 'We *must*. Your father may walk in at any moment.' He tried to stroke her hair into place, abandoning the attempt with a shrug. 'You are so beautiful. I could stare into your eyes forever and not tire of discerning the shades of grey within. They are the rainclouds gathering after a drought, all promise and potential. But your lips, ah, your sweet lips are bruised.' He kissed them gently now. 'Anna, I wish I never had to leave you.'

His words chilled her and she stepped from the protective circle of his arms to challenge him. 'Then don't. Don't ever leave me, Luke.' Hardly ladylike, but then neither was her behaviour.

He drew her back against his chest. 'I do not plan on ever doing so. But, Anna, promise me one thing?'

'Anything.'

Luke's hands easily spanned her waist. 'Promise me you will lose these corsets,' he murmured in her ear, the low growl shimmering through her. 'When I embrace you, it is not whalebone and metal that I wish to feel.'

⁓

The weather finally broke, although Anna would have been content to be screened by the privacy of rain forever.

'Anna, won't you come to church with us tomorrow?' Emilie was far more tolerable now she had an apparent suitor. 'The weather is so pleasant. Dieter can ride with the twins, and you and I shall walk. We can chat.'

Anna longed to compare notes on their beaux, and Emilie was right, the weather sparkled, scudding white clouds across a cool blue sky. It would do her good to move beyond the confines of the farm for the first time in months. Two things gave her pause: she would be forced into the loathed corset—although she should at least be able to wear her bustle once more—and she didn't like to leave Father.

'I don't know. Someone should be here to make lunch for Father.'

'Oh, fiddle, you know he'll eat dry bread and Blutwurst, and only then if he is starving.'

Anna nodded slowly. His hair and beard unkempt, and his once-sharp eyes bleary and unfocused, Father no longer ate regularly, seeming surprised when she reminded him of the necessity. He completed his work with an apathy and disinterest that relied on the rote nature of the tasks. Tomorrow he would be in the fields, bringing the pregnant ewes closer to the house to afford them a little protection from the marauding foxes and the harsh-voiced ravens who would peck the lambs' eyes out. He would not notice her absence.

Sudden excitement found her. 'Do you think Dieter can make the time to ride to Luke's and tell him I shall be there?' It would be nice to dress up for Luke—and even nicer to be seen out with him.

⌒

Despite behaving with careful good manners in the hall after service, Luke waited at the fork in the road. Emilie and the twins boarded the large trap with their brother and Luke took the reins for Arabella.

Though they no longer had need of a blanket to cover them for warmth, Anna snuggled close to Luke. He smelled of sunshine and the fresh green growth of spring. All about them was life. Nestling galahs, the elegance of their dove-grey tailcoats and soft-pink waistcoats at odds with their raucous screeches, created a deafening cacophony as they passed. Bees, golden-trousered with the fuzz of yellow wattle, droned past in the pollen-thickened air. Long-tailed early lambs bounced with a stiff-legged gait across the dark, still-damp loam, calling stridently for their mothers. Promise was everywhere, quickening Anna's blood.

The two buggies rolled into the deserted farmyard. Luke lifted her down, clicking his tongue in pretend disgust at the contact with her corset. As he took her arm, she stayed his hand.

'I will fetch Father for lunch. You go in with Dieter and the others.' It was the first time she had returned directly to the farm after service since Mother died. Despite her joy, her heart was a heavy with remembrance.

Luke dropped a kiss on her forehead and nodded, understanding her need to speak with Father.

Skirts in one hand, Anna picked her way across the rutted yard, listening for a clue. Father might be in the fields, but he was equally likely to be in one of the outbuildings. He had remarked that the cracked pug needed replacing, so he could be packing the wet mud between the wattle saplings of the walls, ready to dry over the long, hot summer.

A kookaburra crackled into feigned mirth in the burned-out remains of the scrub and Anna shivered. As she passed the dim recesses of the coop, she noted the eggs had yet to be collected. Unsurprising, as it was Frederika's morning task. At nearly five, their little sister showed signs of taking after Emilie, which Anna must be sure to nip in the bud. Fortunately, Mrs Ernst had again taken the twins for a few days, and they always returned displaying a temporary improvement in manners and demeanour.

Liesl lowed. Anna had milked her in the morning, so it was not discomfort that caused her plaintive noise. She pressed her hands up against the cow's warm side as she entered the barn. 'Liesl, what ails you? Why are you inside, not out in your yard on such a fine day?'

Liesl swung her huge head toward Anna, dark eyes liquid as she gusted sweet hay breath into her face. A long strand of saliva drooled from her soft chin.

Snatching up her skirts, Anna remembered to step backward before turning, so her bustle didn't brush the cow's hide.

Her breath caught and then she chuckled. 'Father, you startled me. I did not realise you were—'

In the gloom on the far side of the barn, Father did not respond. Anna stepped a little closer. Something was wrong.

He should not be that tall.

His eyes should not bulge so.

A breeze slithered through the doorway, wrapping icy fingers around her heart.

Father's lifeless body swung back and forth from the rafter.

25

Taylor

The rhythmic creak of the gallows rope woke Taylor. Her bedclothes shivered. But not with cold.

Nightmares. That's all they were. Anna's pain, her guilt at being with Luke instead of saving her father, weren't real. This time, Taylor knew what stress had driven her to the imaginary world: she'd promised Luke she would ride with him today. Her throat constricted with the need to cry, and she massaged the sorrow that gouged her chest.

Challenged by the rooster, the morning chorus of the birds in the peppertrees around the house stilled momentarily. The serenade beyond her open window meant it wasn't yet five am. She could hide beneath the covers, return to Anna's world.

But did she dare? Could she face the pain to find the pleasure? Even in her dreams, it seemed that grief was the price of love. And she wasn't sure she wanted to pay.

'Peach?' Gramps didn't believe in dialling the volume down simply because it was early. If he was awake, the whole world should be up.

Dragging on jeans and a tee, Taylor shook off her mood, raked her fingers through her hair and headed toward his voice. 'Hey, Gramps. What's up?'

He stood in the enclosed porch that served as a store-room, laundry, entryway and anything else that took her grandparents' fancy. 'Want to do an early round of the fences? It's going to be a stinker, so best to get it out of the way.'

She laughed. 'You know, if we go much earlier, we'll end up doing it yesterday.' Early worked better for her, as she'd need to shower and change to look at least halfway decent before failing abysmally at the riding. She dropped to the white-painted wooden chair and retrieved yesterday's sweaty socks from where she had scrunched them into the toes of her dusty boots to keep the spiders out.

Gran banged in through the back door and Gramps chortled. 'You let a fly in.'

'Pfft,' Gran snorted. 'You know they don't dare try to sneak past me. They're waiting for you to amble in, old man. You give them plenty of time.'

'I only move slow because I don't want to rush through my life with you, Magpie.' Gramps smacked his lips against Gran's cheek and she batted him away.

'Get off it. You're not even on the sauce yet, and you're all frisky.'

Taylor's mouth twitched.

Gramps handed her the cap she had taken to wearing around the yard. 'Peach will keep me on the straight and narrow today. Right, Peach?'

'Huh? I thought we were checking fences.'

'Spot on. But there's a New Year's do at the flying club later. I thought you might like to come along. You've not been off the property for a week.'

There had been neither need nor point. Sleepy at the best of times, no doubt Settlers Bridge had gone into hibernation after Christmas.

'Love to.' Taylor yawned, feigning a nonchalance she was far from feeling. 'But I've promised to go for a ride with Luke.' She managed to slip it in casually, like the thought didn't terrify her. At least this fear was of something physical, tangible. The pumping adrenaline lent normality to her life and she embraced the feeling greedily.

'Ah, that's right. I'd forgotten that one. Bet you hadn't, though.' Gramps gave her a slow wink, which got confused in the execution and ended up a long blink. 'But it's fine, the lad will no doubt want to be back before it gets too hot for his horses. My thing, on the other hand, is better enjoyed when it's darn good and warm. Drinking weather.'

'Oh, for goodness' sake,' Gran huffed, leaning against the old twin-tub. 'Why on earth would Taylor want to spend an afternoon listening to you old farts boozing and burping? Michelle and I are making apricot jam after lunch, ready for the January trading tables. Taylor—'

'—can help you,' Gramps finished.

She'd seen Mum and Gran in the kitchen together. They squabbled over how to peel a carrot: whether it should be sliced into rings or sticks was likely to be the catalyst for World War Three. 'The airfield sounds cool. I've been wanting to check it out.'

Gramps lowered creakily onto the second laundry chair, pulling on his own socks. 'I bet you have. Afraid the party is at the hangars, though.'

She didn't know what he was talking about, but as long as it rescued her from the kitchen, she would follow him anywhere. 'No worries, Gramps. Wherever.'

Gramps jerked his chin, as though the direction would mean something to her. 'The hangars are over on Darren's property. Off Frahn Road.'

Tiny icicles in her blood scraped through her veins. 'Frahn Road?'

'Sure.' Gramps concentrated on tugging fat burrs from his socks. 'Y'know, on the way out to the church.'

'I never noticed it.' Her voice was reedy. 'I, uh, I'll make a drink before we do the fences. Anyone want coffee for a change?'

She'd seen the signpost and slipped the name into her dream.

That was the only explanation.

The only *rational* explanation.

~

She almost breathed a sigh of relief when she saw the horse Luke brought over for her. Almost.

Though he rode his huge chestnut gelding, he led a far smaller, golden-brown horse on a braided rope. The three of them waited for her in the shade of a drooping pepper tree halfway down the yard.

'She's a gentle mare,' Luke said as Taylor nervously patted the horse's nose. 'The girls ride her, no problem. Here, put your hand out like this. Palm up. The trick is to let her get to know you before you mount her.' He cupped his hand beneath hers and guided it to the horse's chin. 'Bit like foreplay,' he said with a straight face. Only the deep crease in his cheek gave away that he intended the humour.

The horse's nose was surprisingly velvety, her whiskers tickling Taylor's palm.

'That's it,' he said. 'Now you can move to her nose. Stroke, don't pat. A lot of horses prefer that you stroke their chest, but Goldie is fine with having her face touched.'

'Goldie for the colour?' She tried to make conversation, tried to be prosaic, but there was no ignoring the fact that Luke stood behind her, so close his chest brushed her back as he leaned to guide her hand. He smelled like sunshine and hay. God, she'd even invented his smell in her fantasies.

'Goldie Hawn,' he said with a chuckle. 'I was crazy in love with her when I was a teenager. Took me a decade to work out that *Private Benjamin* was made only a couple of years after I was born.'

The movie had to be very early eighties. So that would make Luke around thirty now. Not that it mattered. At all.

'Can't say I blame you. I had a thing for Kurt Russell circa the same period.' There was that whole hot celebrity thing again, she thought with a grimace of distaste.

'Fair. I put the kids' Western saddle on Goldie, seeing as you said you're out of practice.'

'Western saddle?'

Luke walked to the side of the horse, running his hand over the burnished shoulder. 'It has a high pommel and a horn.' He tapped what looked like a vertical grip at the front of the saddle. 'That bit's actually for roping cattle, but you can hang onto it if you don't feel secure. And the cantle—the backrest—comes far higher. It's more like you're sitting in an armchair than a traditional saddle.'

'Yours is different?'

'I use an English. They're lighter for the horse, but also let the rider get closer, more in tune with the animal.'

She nodded. Whatever he was saying, she liked it. Not only for his calm, confident tone, but because it made this thing seem more doable.

He patted his horse's flank. 'Though I reckon Pferd prefers me to ride bareback.'

'Perfeeat?'

'Almost. It's *pfee-ard*.'

'Unusual name to . . . *saddle* a horse with.'

He chuckled. 'It's German for horse.'

'Ah.' She wasn't going to ask. Not a damn thing. She knew the area had a strong German heritage, but she didn't need any details on Luke's connection to it. 'At least, even with a big saddle, I'll be able to get my legs around her.'

Luke looked confused. 'Your legs don't actually go around the horse.'

Of course he had no idea what she was talking about. That conversation had been Anna's. In her imagination.

'I know.' She dubiously squared up to Goldie's side. This might be a smaller horse, but the saddle was still level with her forehead.

'Put your left foot in the stirrup.' Luke tapped the metal hoop. 'Then use that to lift yourself.'

The stirrup was about hip height. She should have taken Mum up on the frequent yoga offers—there was no way she had either the strength or flexibility to get her leg into position. She eyed off the saddle, wondering whether she could brace both hands on top and kind of vault up. Knowing she couldn't.

'Or you could just do this,' Luke said, appallingly close to her ear. His hands closed around her waist and he lifted her, apparently effortlessly. 'Throw your right leg over the saddle,' he grunted.

Okay, not entirely effortlessly, then. Taylor's face burned as she realised the very unflattering view Luke was copping as she clutched the hard leather, lying across the saddle on her stomach as she struggled to swing her leg over. Should have worn looser jeans. Not that she owned any, thanks to Gran's baking.

'Okay. There we go.'

It sounded like Luke was laughing, but damned if she was going to look at him.

'Hold the reins like this.' He threaded the leather through her hands. 'And then, if you don't feel secure, you can also hold the pommel. Like this.' He closed her hands around the horn with the reins in her grip.

Damn right she didn't feel secure. Not with his hands all over hers—and her mind all over the place.

Turning away, Luke laid an arm across his saddle and somehow vaulted onto Pferd in a single, almost balletic movement. 'The trick is to let yourself roll with the horse's gait.' He clicked his tongue and Goldie fell into stride alongside his horse. Luke tilted his hat back so he could see her. Or maybe so she could see him. 'I told you, like riding a bike.'

'It's a heck of a lot further to fall,' she said, holding on for dear life.

'You won't,' he assured her. He brought Pferd in closer. 'I won't let anything happen to you.'

She risked a glance, but only at his legs. 'You're not holding your reins,' she protested, as she noticed the leather lying slack on Pferd's glossy chocolate neck.

'Pferd's intuitive. He can read the pressure of my knees, knows where I'm heading.' To prove his point, his horse veered away from her, back, away and back, executing a neat zigzag without Luke ever moving his hands.

They made for a cattle grid that led out of the house yard and, for a heart-stopping moment, Taylor thought Luke meant for the horses to jump the metre-wide section, where dried weeds and thistles barely clinging to life poked from a ditch below the thick iron bars. But Luke swerved right. Standing in his stirrups, he leaned over Pferd's neck to unlatch a small gate almost hidden beneath a heavily flowering gum tree.

Taylor had noticed the blossoms on Gran's kitchen table, an explosion of delicate crimson filaments forming a starburst from the lime centre, each delicate strand tipped with a tiny yellow dot. The tree also had craggy, urn-like nuts that had featured heavily in the Christmas wreaths sold on the CWA trading table.

'Just watch out for the bees under here,' Luke said. 'They've got a hive in the hollow.'

She nodded, ducking warily as they passed beneath the tree's branches. 'Last time I came to South Australia, I thought the trees—the entire landscape in fact—was kind of grey. Or khaki, I guess, except for yellow bits.'

'You were here in spring, right? So the yellow bits would be canola, capeweed, acacia, soursobs.' Luke listed the plants without hesitation, obviously familiar with them all.

She lifted one shoulder, keeping a tight hold on the saddle. 'A couple of those, definitely. The thing is, now I realise how much colour there actually is out here. But it's hidden. I mean, there are obvious things—the show ponies, like the wattles and gums. But there are also minuscule flowers all through the scrub. You can't even see them unless you get down to ground level. They're tinier than . . . I don't know what. Tinier than a dewdrop. And in all the colours of the rainbow, like the most delicate confetti sprinkled among the moss and grass. I've ended up sitting under trees, staring at the ground for hours. It's as though I've discovered an entire miniature world now I have time to actually *look*.'

Goldie snorted derisively, but Luke remained silent.

Taylor sank into the saddle, wishing she could disappear. Why couldn't she just make normal 'it's a lovely, sunny day' type conversation, instead of rambling?

'Having time makes a lot of difference,' Luke said consideringly. 'I guess that's what I like about being on the land: my time is measured by the seasons and the sun, not by a watch. Or a phone,' he added with a grin, as her mobile chimed three times in quick succession.

'Sorry.' She didn't release the safety of the leather grip to pull the phone out of her pocket. 'Though at least now I know there's reception halfway across this paddock. There's not much in the house.'

Taylor winced, remembering that he owned the house, but Luke nodded. 'Yeah, signal's real patchy around here. Small price to pay for not having telco towers sprouting all over the land, I reckon. But I guess it makes it hard for you to stay in touch with everyone back home.'

'Not so many people to bother staying in touch with.' She groaned silently. Really? Why was she making it obvious she was single? 'Uni students all go their own way over summer. Dad works FIFO, so it's hard to get hold of him at the best of times. And these messages will be photos of the Seine, or the Eiffel Tower, or something like that, from my bestie, who's off exploring Europe.'

'Ah. Her Christmas is a bit different to yours in Settlers Bridge, then.' Luke rode in silence for a minute or so, his body seeming an extension of the horse. She watched him from the corner of her eye, trying to emulate the easy motion. 'Have you travelled much?'

Her legs clamped Goldie's warm sides as she struggled against the unsettling flash of déjà vu. She refused to slip into the conversations that seemed imprinted on her memory. 'Not really. Hawaii, Queensland. You?'

Luke shook his head, turning their horses to pick a path through the short, hollow stalks of grass, toward a thick stand of trees she hadn't ventured into. Every few metres a rectangular bale of hay, tied with two pink strands of twine, waited to be collected. 'Never really had any interest in leaving Settlers. Can't get my head around the idea of taking the time to travel somewhere to do nothing but gawk when there's always something to be done here. And plenty enough to look at.' He gave a self-deprecatory huff. 'Guess I'm just a small-town guy at heart. No grand designs or plans.'

'You've always lived here?'

'Born and bred.'

She nodded thoughtfully. 'I can't imagine what it would be like to know everyone in a place. I mean, in Sydney I know our neighbours, obviously, but only on a nod-hello basis. It blew my mind how everyone who came by the CWA trading table the other week was on first-name terms.'

Luke gave a rumble of laughter and Pferd's ears flicked back. 'Blessing and a curse. Everyone in Settlers not only knows everyone else, but knows their business, too.'

'Like your church attendance record?' she teased.

'Ha. Perfect example.'

On the trail ahead of them, half-a-dozen galahs strutted across the ground self-importantly, pausing every few steps to peck the beaten red-earth path.

'They eat dirt?'

'Scabbing around for the last few spilled grains from harvest. Though there's plenty of hopping mice out here, so the birds will be lucky to find any. When they give up on that, they'll dig for insects, larvae, the tiny tubers on the native plants.' Luke clicked his tongue and Pferd turned off the path, leading them around the birds. 'This lot are teenagers, so they don't have a brain between them. You want to watch out for them on the road, because they won't move out of your way.'

A couple of the birds cocked their heads to watch the horses' progress. But they didn't take fright, didn't fly away. Like everything out here, they seemed content. Life might move at a slower pace, but it had inherent meaning and purpose, instead of being a constant chase for fulfillment.

Taylor took a deep breath, her lungs expanding as though she could absorb the tranquillity. The tiniest breeze, scented with eucalyptus, smoothed like silk across her bare arms, and she turned her face up to the balmy sunshine. 'I guess the whole small-town thing makes for a nice place to bring up kids, though.'

'Kids? Yeah, I suppose.'

Luke sounded surprised by her observation but, living here all his life, he wouldn't be aware of the benefits his children had been born into.

'I mean, it's so quiet, so much less frenetic here.'

Luke screwed up his face, as though he didn't entirely agree. 'You've come right at the end of harvest, going into our slow season. But I wouldn't say we're not busy. Difference is, in the city you have thousands of people spending an hour sitting miserably on a train to get to an office to sit miserably at a desk, staring miserably at a screen, simply because that's where they've been told they're supposed to be five days a week. Most of them probably don't actually need to be in that office right that minute; they're not growing or harvesting or creating or even connecting.

They're there because we have entire industries created by our need to *appear* busy. Out here, you go somewhere to do something because it needs to be done. Seven days a week.'

'I think . . .' Taylor frowned as she ordered her thoughts. The stubble of the harvested crop created symmetrically spaced lines swooping around the scrub. The waves made it apparent that the machinery hadn't been mindlessly driven straight up and down the paddock; instead it had skirted the ragged edge of the grove, creating rows of crop that mirrored the soft curves and dips of the forest fringe, the pattern extending across the paddock in a serene ocean that hinted at thoughtfulness, an understanding of the land. 'I think, in the city, we're so intent on protecting our tiny allocation of personal space that we try to exist in a bubble. You know, pretend we can't see what's happening around us, don't risk acknowledging anything that might force us to interact with someone else.' Her mind flashed back to running from Zac, having no idea where to look for help, for shelter. She suppressed the shudder that rippled through her. 'And I guess that's why city life can seem miserable. Or, like you make it sound, vacuous.'

Luke grimaced. 'Sorry. Wasn't my intention. It's just, for me, out here—' he waved an arm to encompass the open paddocks '—this is more logical. This is where life makes sense. Though we might seem laid back, everything about farming is quite literally life and death; whether it's stock, crops or feeding a nation.' He shook his head, a wry smile creasing one cheek. 'But then, you're in the life-or-death business yourself.'

'Only studying.'

'But obviously you have passion, a plan. You're not letting life pass you by. Which proves I'm generalising like hell about city folk and should shut my mouth.'

A bird burst from the trees in front of them. Brown and cream rippled wings sped it into the soaring blue sky.

'Is that an eagle?' Taylor asked, keen to turn the conversation away from her aspirations—although she did appreciate that Luke saw her as having focus, a career path that actually mattered, rather than being . . . ordinary.

Luke tipped his head back, watching the bird's effortless ascent. 'Goshawk.' He shot her a considering glance, then looked back to the bird. 'Reckon I'll come back as a hawk. Spend my time spiralling lazily in the thermals, keeping an eye on my land, my family. I don't plan to ever leave what I love.' He rubbed at his chin, looking a little abashed. 'And I probably should have kept that thought to myself. Now that I say it out loud, it sounds like I'm tripping.'

'Not even. It must be cool to have such purpose and certainty—and love—that you even have your afterlife planned out. Honestly, I'm in enough trouble just trying to keep *this* one straight, never mind thinking that far into the future.' Clearly, the Lukes of both her imagination and her actuality were all-round good guys. That kind of planning must come with having a family to care for. 'Your wife's from here, too?' She tried to keep the flash of jealousy from her tone.

'Wife?'

'Yeah. You mentioned your kids . . . girls . . .?'

The track narrowed as they entered the heavily wooded scrub and Pferd moved closer to Goldie, picking his way around the metre-high clumps of silvery tussock grass and navigating the fallen branches that littered the dry earth like bones from a distant past. As the horses touched, Luke's leg brushed hers. Taylor instinctively jerked sideways and he reached to cover her hand on the pommel.

'Easy. Keep your core a little stiffer, your back straighter, and use your thighs to grip. Let your hips absorb the motion.' His gaze dropped, as though he was monitoring whether she took the direction. He nodded and released her hands. 'They're my sister's girls. Up from Adelaide for the holidays. Took me two weeks to get them off their devices and out onto the horses and bikes, so I guess that's why I'm dissing city life. Of course, now Lina can't keep them inside, so she's pretty ticked at me.' He sounded smug about the havoc he'd created.

He also sounded very single.

Suddenly the air in the scrub seemed heavy and unbreathable, thick with memory.

And promise.

26
Taylor

Still determined Taylor should master the art of jam making, Gran had collected kilos of apricots from the ancient walled orchard alongside the house.

It took forever to split and stone the fruit, but the repetitive action was therapeutic, and Taylor let her mind wander back to the morning with Luke. Or, more specifically, to the last few minutes of it. She'd made an excuse to end the ride, claiming that, despite the shade of the trees, she was burning. But the heat consuming her hadn't had anything to do with the sun, and she'd struggled to keep up the conversation on the way back to the farmhouse. She had to remember that being single didn't magically imbue this Luke with the impossible perfection of her dream man. She'd made that mistake with Zac, and wasn't in any hurry to repeat it. Fortunately, Luke had seemed comfortable riding in silence.

'The trick is,' Gran said, interrupting her thoughts, 'to never double a jam recipe. It simply doesn't work. So I cook three pots at a time to make it worth the mess.'

Taylor nodded, surveying that chaos. The kitchen table was covered with mounds of apricots: sweet, succulent fruit waiting to be cut, bowls of chopped flesh, and tureens of overripe and blemished pieces put aside for the chickens. Gran stood at the stovetop, banging pans and arranging ladles, and Mum, red-faced but looking happy, pulled trays of golden raw sugar from the oven.

'And always use warmed sugar,' Gran said, following Taylor's gaze. 'Okay, fruit into the pan and add the sugar. Then the lemon juice and a good handful of the whole kernels. They're supposedly poisonous, but your grandfather will have a fit if he doesn't get a kernel on every slice of toast. Silly old bugger.'

'It'd be the amygdalin,' Taylor said.

Gran looked interested, impressed and slightly wary all at once. 'You mean they are poisonous?' Her spoonful of kernels hovered above the pan.

'It's a plant toxin that converts to cyanide in the body. I think cooking might negate the effect, but maybe keep an eye on how many Gramps has. One or two a day should be fine.'

Gran shook her head in wonder. 'The things you learn.'

'Told you she's a smart cookie,' Mum said proudly. 'Though I don't know how you're going to stop Dad from eating them.'

Gran laughed. 'No one stops that man from doing anything.'

By mid-afternoon, a carnival of different-sized jars, each sealed with a rubber-banded cellophane disc that tightened as it dried, sparkled like jewels on the windowsill above the sink. Mum sloshed sudsy water around in the sink as Gran scraped jam off the countertops. Ladling hot syrup into equally hot jars was as delicate as any surgery.

Gramps bustled in. 'Rescue is at hand. C'mon, Peach, time to hit the road.'

Taylor snatched up her cap and banged out the back door behind him. A cloud of dust accompanied the protest of the springs as Gramps groaned into the driver's seat of the old ute.

Scraping sticky jam sweetness from beneath her nails with her teeth, Taylor slammed the car door. It bounced open and she slammed again. Bounce. 'Some kind of trick with this, Gramps?'

'Ah, yeah. Latch is a bit dicky. Hang on to the handle, that'll keep it closed.'

The jagged stub where the handle should be cut into her fingers and the door felt about as secure as a spider web blowing in the breeze. 'Promise me you won't take any hard corners.'

Gramps cranked the engine. 'Forgot the handle's dodgy, too. Wind your window down and stick your elbow over the edge, then. We're only going a bit up the track.'

The window squealed and she shifted her knees as a daddy long-legs evacuated the air vent.

His stomach shoved against the faded steering wheel, Gramps swiped dust from the windscreen with his forearm, not bothering to slow. 'You look 'bout as thoughtful as a Thursday, Peach. Cheer up. Magpie's teasing; it's not only oldies out at the hangars. Plenty of the young fellas round here have got wings. We even have a few crop dusters knock around with us.'

Judging by his awed tone, crop dusters were a rare breed.

'A couple of them have been asking after you. S'pose they're gonna be disappointed once they hear you've been out riding with Luke.'

Despite her stern lectures to herself, Taylor's chest tightened at his name. 'Hear?'

'Small town, Peach. They'll know before we even get there. Anyway, how did it go?'

'Not really my thing, Gramps.'

'The lad or the riding?'

'Either or.' It surprised her to discover she could lie so blatantly. Because Luke—single, childless, *available* Luke—seemed to be quite literally everything she had imagined. But she knew she was confusing the man she'd met with the man of her dreams.

Grey eyebrows crawled up to where Gramps' hair should be. 'Oh, one of that lot, are you? Wouldn't have picked it. Clearly, neither would Luke.' He chortled.

Good to know that Mum's lack of filter was hereditary. Gave her something to look forward to. 'No, it's not that.'

They swerved onto a rutted track and bounced across the paddock. 'Had your heart broken then?' Gramps said.

Taylor's bicep ached from holding the door closed with her elbow and her gaze was glued to the track that wound through the paddocks. It seemed like one of them should watch it. 'Something like that.'

Gramps observed her for an uncomfortably long moment. 'Only one cure for that, Peach.'

'Which is?'

'Find your true love. A full heart can't be broken.'

'I don't have time in my life for that kind of stuff.' She was irritated he'd think it so simple.

'Don't have time?' Gramps' attention was now fully on her. 'Peach, love is *all* that life is. Think about it. Everyone searches for love. Whether it's a man, woman, child or animal, we all love something. There is no life without love. Love is literally what we exist for.'

Taylor gestured futilely at the windscreen, trying to redirect his focus.

'Even axe murderers love,' Gramps proclaimed solemnly.

She snorted with sudden laughter. 'I don't think that was your finest analogy, Gramps, but point taken. The thing is, do you know how many millions of people there are in the world? If I have to find just one, statistically speaking, my chances are pretty darn slim.'

'Yet I found Magpie.'

'What is with that name, anyway? Gran's name isn't even Maggie.' She'd checked with Mum, who hadn't been able to explain the nickname.

'Nothing to do with her name. Magpies mate for life, you see. My one true love.'

'Ah.' Her grandparents were adorable. The realisation was bittersweet, because while life might be about love, it was also about loss. One of her grandparents would break the other's heart.

She flicked a finger toward the window as Gramps hurtled across a dirt intersection and onto another track. 'Speaking of names, are Frahns common around here? Seeing as there's a road named for them and all?' While stirring the jam, being careful not to let the sugar crystallise on the side of the pan, she had reassured herself the name must have appeared on the route she'd mapped from Sydney, not trusting to Mum's much touted 'natural sense of direction'. The explanation sat comfortably. There was nothing at all sinister in the coincidence of it appearing in her dreams.

Yet as she said the name aloud, her heart beat like she was walking into a final exam.

'Sure, sure.' Gramps cornered hard. Taylor squeaked, clutching the edge of the torn vinyl bench seat with her free hand. 'Frahns everywhere. Likely the most common name in the district. Darren—with the hangars up here—' he nodded toward the huge, steel-clad buildings they approached way too fast '—is a Frahn. And I guess about every fourth or fifth person round here is a Frahn. Or married to one.'

'The local equivalent of Smith, then.' The tightness in her chest eased. Logic and proof, that's what she liked. The evidence that her dreams had been fleshed out by subconscious absorption of everyday information. 'And Hartmann? That's another good German name. I guess the district's full of them, too?'

Gramps shook his head. 'Yeah, nah.' He pulled up alongside a grey ute, similar to the one in the churchyard.

The flecks of silver in the car's paintwork glittered like the mica in the rocks strewn across the dusty paddock. 'Look at that. The car's the same shade as your eyes, Peach.'

She didn't respond. No Hartmanns. That had to be good. Luke's name existed only in her imagination, proving there was nothing abnormal about her dreams—or about her. Yet disappointment cascaded through her like some ephemeral, unformed hope had been crushed.

The handbrake creaked as Gramps ratcheted it up. 'Hartmann's not common,' he continued, grabbing a green cap emblazoned with the purple word FLY from behind his seat. 'Only the one lot I know of around here. The homestead must go about five generations back, though. Explains the dodgy plumbing, right? The family traded up to a flash new house a few hundred hectares behind us. Well, not so new anymore, I suppose.'

'Your homestead, you mean? But you're renting from . . . Luke?'

'Yep. They kept the name going.'

'Name?' she murmured, her lips feeling disembodied.

Gramps tugged the cap low on his forehead. 'Like you said, Luke. The Hartmanns apparently name the first son of each generation the same. The lad would be only too glad to tell you why, I imagine.' Gramps clambered from the car.

Black spots crowded Taylor's vision. The shed in front of them receded, swirling down a long, dark tunnel like a movie fade-out. Unable to breathe, she thrust the door open, slamming her feet to the ground. *Shit, shit, shit.*

'Peach, you okay?'

'Sure.' She clutched at her necklace as she fought the dizziness.

The necklace from the Hartmann homestead.

Jesus. She dropped the crucifix as though the silver burned, her brain freewheeling inside her skull.

'Peach?'

She had to get a grip. Fake it while she worked out what the hell was going on.

Hands braced on her thighs, she shoved upright. 'Sugar rush. Must have licked too much jam out of the pot. Maybe I don't feel good enough for a party, though. I don't want to mess up your day, Gramps. How about I take the ute and I'll come back for you in a few hours?'

'Sure, sure. Take the car.' Gramps waved, already stomping in the direction of the hangar, trouser leg tucked into one of his socks. 'Just don't let your Gran know I'm on the loose. I'll get a lift home with one of the boys.'

Luke was real. No—*Luke Hartmann* was real.

And somehow she'd predicted—stolen, dreamed, imagined—both of his names?

Along with exactly how he looked.

And sounded.

Smelled.

Her breathing was too shallow and the oxygen depletion was making her nauseous. She needed to get out of there. Not that physical distance could separate her from the machinations of her brain.

Taylor slid across the bench seat and stared at the column shift. She'd only driven an automatic, but knew the basics. If Anna could handle an unfamiliar horse and trap, she could handle an unfamiliar vehicle.

No! She couldn't think like that. Wouldn't allow it.

Perched on the edge of the seat, she gingerly pushed in the clutch and twisted the ignition. The car was so old it slid into reverse easily and chuntered backward. First was smooth, but second gear was hard to find, the metal teeth grinding and clashing. The passenger door creaked open, inviting an unseen rider as the car bounced across the rutted ground. A rash of goosebumps raised the flesh on her arms.

Luke Hartmann was real.

But his history had to be purely in her imagination.

She couldn't go back to the farm yet.

Luke's farm.

She shook off the too-familiar voice in her head. Focused on the road. There was something she had to do first. Something she had to prove to herself; something that would calm the mad turmoil in her head, the shuddering, quivering apprehension that had her breaking out in a cold sweat.

Taylor sucked in to squeeze the vehicle between the white-painted posts framing the cattle grid. The church was straight down the road, it would take only minutes to get there in the old ute.

Far quicker than walking.

A hedge of red bottlebrush and yellow wattle screened the car park sheltered by the grove of gum trees, and until she pulled in Taylor couldn't be certain the church was deserted.

Though she'd turned the engine off, she sat with both hands wrapped around the steering wheel, not daring to move. Psychologically, there was nothing wrong with creating an alternative fantasy world. But doing so unintentionally was unchaining reality, allowing it to spiral beyond normal, acceptable parameters. And still there was no explanation for how she'd known Luke's name or exactly how he would look *before she had met him*. So was she creating or, impossibly, *re*creating a world in her head?

The answer lay here, behind the church, in details that no one could have provided to flesh out her dream. But she hesitated, unwilling to face what she might find. Or might not find.

Taylor's gaze crept to the church. If she focused only on the white-painted door, the red flare of potted geraniums on either side, everything was as it had been.

As it should be.

Her hands loosened on the wheel and she breathed deep, tranquillity easing through her.

Did she step from the car or did she dream that she drifted toward the hall? Long skirts swished across polished floorboards, the tinkling of china cups and saucers a haunting melody, like ghostly fingers playing a distant piano. The earthy smell of the stables wrapped around her, the slap of a leather harness accompanied by the soft snicker of a tethered horse and the creak of a buggy.

The fragrance, the sounds, the memories; they spoke to her. Calling her *back*.

No. Fists clenched, she furiously willed the figments of her imagination to retreat.

Now the only sound was the soughing of the wind in the grove of tall gums.

Behind the hall, a barely visible trail wound through a paddock filled with wild grasses. A dirt road also led to her destination, but Taylor's feet chose the forgotten path trod by sorrow. Heat bounced up at her, golden sun on golden wheat, and her eyes watered. Her hand closed around the pendant on her necklace. She didn't need to see to know where she was going.

An oasis of serenity, the graveyard pulled her closer. The post and rail fence had been replaced by wire mesh, and the entrance was now guarded by engraved pillars commemorating soldiers who'd died in three wars. Battles fought, lives lived and lost, since Anna and Luke were here.

Only a dozen trees remained of the thick forest opposite the entrance. Their skeleton leaves littered the barren ground. Long peels of bark flashed sunset hues of pink and apricot as they rolled and tumbled on a caressing breeze. The wrought-iron gate creaked at her touch and fluffy-tailed rabbits disappeared in a kick of dust into burrows beneath the cracked and toppling headstones. The broad path of white gravel, tied like a ribbon around the graveyard, sparkled beneath her feet. The wind dropped, the silence absolute. Weeds sprouted and died among fractured stone slabs, the sunken graves slowly reclaimed by the earth. Dusty jam jars lay empty against headstones, the owners' urge to bring flowers fading with the memories. Low fences of fancy-worked iron bled rust, and white crosses stood sentinel over tiny, forlorn mounds. Saints towered and angels wept.

And what should feel lonely felt like coming home.

There were many more graves now, but she didn't pause to read the faded inscriptions or choose a row to explore. Taylor knew where she needed to be. She turned right, the fourth row from the boundary—the row where too many of Anna's family had been laid before their time—and stopped exactly halfway down the path. Not counting, just knowing.

At the end of the row stood a single eucalypt, the trunk as wide as a small car, the bark glowing ethereal white. The tree where Luke had embraced Anna. Eyes closed, Taylor remembered.

Then she turned to the graves.

A black slab of gold-speckled granite covered the raw wound of her dreams. Two small graves encased in white marble nestled on each side, inscribed headstones replacing the wooden crosses that had been carved in times of sorrow and drought. The hard-baked earth around the plot lent a look of undisturbed permanence.

Tears trembled on her lashes. She knew what she would find.

There were no weeds in this plot, no dust on the granite. Roses filled a vase set into a raised block at the foot of the slab, their heavy heads drooping only slightly, the rich perfume thick in the still air.

Legs folded beneath her, Taylor laid a hand on the slab. Red geraniums bordered the plot, challenging the darkness of death. The refraction of light on the granite made it pulse with life. With love.

She slowly raised her eyes to the headstone.

Johanna Frahn (nee *Schmidt*) *1832–1877*
At rest with her children
Not dead, but gone before
&
Johann Frahn 1820–1877
Called to join his beloved wife
Sadly missed by Dieter, Anna, Emilie, Frederik, Frederika

The words engraved in stone proved her madness, but Taylor didn't care.

Because the truth of death had broken her heart.

27
Anna

September 1877

She was angry with Father.

For more than three months, he had tried to exist without Mother, but it was almost as though they had lost him when they had lost her; he had distanced himself from them, hiding his pain. Yet Anna could not forgive him. Too much of her life had been spent in the church and graveyard, burying her family.

'Do you wish me to stay away for the month of deep mourning?' Luke's voice was low, his hand lingering on her waist as they turned from the fresh earth on Father's grave.

'No.' Her hiss was fierce, but she was tired of losing all she loved. 'No, I do not want you to stay away. Not ever.'

His eyes soft with pity, Luke nodded. 'I shall be there tomorrow.'

He visited every day for a month, perhaps trying to lessen her pain. He could not, but maybe that was because she simply did not allow herself to hurt this time. She had to believe that Father was happier now, that he was where he wanted to be.

Guiltily knowing she had stolen Luke during a busy farming season, still her day revolved around his visit. His vitality sustained her. Each day dragged long, her heart beating sluggish until she heard the familiar clop of his horse. Eyes closed, she would visualise him tying the gelding to the hitching rail, crossing the yard, carefully wiping his feet on the hessian sack that lay outside the house. Only then would she pull open the door, her heart so full of love it swelled her chest. She could not imagine life without being able to see him every day. She would not want such a life.

Perhaps she did understand Father's choice.

At the end of the month, they attended Father's memorial service, then dined once again at the Schenschers'. It was sad that such things had become their tradition, yet even in the sombre occasion, they found a little joy; Caroline and Dieter, Emilie and Otto, Luke and Anna all stole moments together. And in those moments lay the promise of life.

The morning after the memorial dawned fine and crisp, with only a hint of the sunshine that would take a few more weeks to become intolerable. Everyone fed and dispatched to their duties for the day—although, as usual, Emilie's sole chore was to keep the twins entertained—Anna filled the copper in the yard. Stirring and pounding Dieter's spare set of clothes with the large paddle, trying to free some of the greasy lanolin that permeated the fabric during lambing season, she eyed the grey water. It must be carted to the vegetable garden, a bucketful at a time. After that, she would make her third trip to the well for water to mop the floors. But, despite her best efforts, the flagstones had not looked properly clean since Mother had died. Perhaps the laundry water could be used to mop the floor? She sighed heavily. No. Mother would never have countenanced such laziness.

The sound of a horse and trap alerted her to a visitor. She patted her hair into place. If it was Mrs Ernst come to visit, there was enough for her to find lacking in Anna's housekeeping without adding a slovenly appearance to her shortcomings and sins.

Luke's horse, harnessed to an unfamiliar vehicle, clopped into view. Anna frowned. He was hours early. Anxiety pounded through her veins. Routine might be boring, but it was safe.

Her skirts gathered, she ducked beneath the billowing washing and ran across the yard, straight into his arms.

'My love.' Luke's embrace erased her irrational fear. She would only ever need his arms to reassure and protect her. He glanced around the yard, then kissed her cheek. His lips lingered, hands sliding to her hips. 'I wish to take you somewhere today. I know it is a lot to ask you to accompany me unchaperoned—but will you?'

He did not need to ask. It seemed a long time since she had been truly concerned with any opinion of her but his.

At Anna's nod, he smiled, looking relieved. 'I have brought the trap as it is a little distance.'

She was unwilling to move from his arms, but lanolin had become her perfume and hair straggled across her face. 'Can you wait a few minutes?'

Luke seemed unusually solemn. 'Of course. Is Dieter in the home paddock? There is something I must ask him.'

'I believe you will find him there.'

She thrust her head through the bakehouse doorway. 'Emilie, I need your help.'

Emilie glanced up from the pieces of dough the littlies were gradually turning black with their mucky hands and lifted an eyebrow.

The tiny buttons on her bodice fought Anna's urgent hands. 'I need you to do my hair and help me choose a dress. I shall not wear black any longer.'

Emilie's appalled gasp followed her to the house, but Anna was determined—she would never wear black again. There had been enough mourning in her life.

❧

They took an early luncheon and it was mid-afternoon by the time they skirted Luke's family homestead. A billow of sweet almond blossom scented the air. Peach and apricot trees flowered in soft shades of pink in a walled orchard.

Stone outbuildings gave way to older pug-and-pine constructions as they left the farmyard, the trap bouncing and jolting deep into the scrub along a narrow, rutted path. Huge flowering eucalypts overhung them, the falling blossoms spiralling to earth like tiny ballerinas, the ground beneath the trees blanketed in red. The air was thick with the smell of wild honey and heavy with pollen.

With the horse tethered to a tree, Luke lifted her down and drew her close. He pulled her against the firmness of his chest, lips seeking hers, tongue sliding into her mouth.

She had no idea if other lovers kissed like this, but it did not matter: when Luke kissed her, she wanted to give all to him. A tremor ran through her at the knowledge of their absolute privacy, but it was a thrill of excitement, not of fear. She pressed against Luke, her skirts folding around them both in a slight breeze.

Luke drew back a little, restricting his attention to her lips. 'Not yet, not yet,' he murmured.

'Not yet what?' If he needed her permission, Anna would gladly give it.

His mouth lifted on one side, though he looked unsure. There was something unfamiliar about him, something she could not quite pinpoint. He seemed almost . . . nervous.

'Come. This way.' He led her along a winding trail. Tall tussocks of spinifex occasionally barred their path, the scrub thickening until it seemed impenetrable. He halted. 'Close your eyes. Don't worry, I shall lead you.'

Despite Luke's guidance, she immediately stumbled.

He chuckled and swept her from her feet. 'I shall carry you, then. But keep your eyes closed.'

She wound her arms around his neck. The sun caressed her skin, the light on her eyelids changing from red to gold. Luke's heart beat strong against her ear, reminding her of the first time he had carried her like this. She hoped he would walk slowly; she wanted him to never put her down.

Finches loudly challenged their intrusion and willy wagtails chattered with annoyance.

'Now, Anna, open your eyes.' Luke's voice rumbled through her.

She almost did not want to, longing for the moment to last forever.

He lowered her to her feet.

They stood in the centre of a glade so beautiful it seemed impossible it could exist anywhere but her imagination. Made private by wattle bushes, a slight rise gave way to a gentle slope, a lush carpet of grass studded with the bright yellow flowers of capeweed. Tiny white-and-purple butterflies, no larger than a baby's fingernail, spiralled together through the cream and pink spires of miniature orchids. Granite boulders bordered the meadow, smoothed by unseen forces into dappled hollows and enticing caves. Tall gums stood guard on the near side and a winding ribbon of long grass indicated the presence of a creek at the low point.

But all of this she took in with the quickest glance, because Luke was down on one knee before her.

His hand engulfed hers, fingers gripping tightly, as though he feared she would flee. 'I do not want to be apart from you. Not for a single minute of a single day.' His chest swelled as he took a deep breath. 'Anna, will you marry me?'

Uncaring of grass stains, she dropped to her knees to lessen the gap between them. Heart pounding, her throat constricted so she almost could not speak. She should demur with ladylike uncertainty, but Luke was her entire life, her every dream, both waking and sleeping.

'Yes, Luke. Yes, yes.'

'One yes will suffice, as I intend to hold you to that word.' He slid a plain band onto the third finger of her left hand and then kissed her palm and each of her finger-tips. His indigo eyes were dark as he looked into hers. 'I promise we shall be happy, Anna, for the rest of our lives.'

The intensity of her love for him swelled inside her in a wave, almost unbearable, and she wanted to both laugh and cry. Her eagerness was uncouth, but knowing he would one day be hers made the thought of separation harder to bear. She did not want to let him go, not even for one night. Mother was right—an entire lifetime with Luke would never be enough.

'But when can we m-marry?' She tripped on the word and blushed. For so long, she had thought she would never discuss marriage with any man, far less one she adored beyond all imagination. 'I should still be in mourning. Is this what you spoke with Dieter about earlier? And where will we live?'

Sitting in the sweet-smelling grass, Luke gently tugged her until she reclined against him. An unfelt breeze swayed the silvered branches of gum trees stretching into a blue sky a hundred feet above, but her gaze locked to his face. She would never be able to look her fill.

Luke loosened a tendril of hair from her braid and wound it around his finger. 'Ah, so many questions, my betrothed. Let me see if I can answer all. Firstly, I have asked Dieter's permission, which he gave with a number of stipulations about how I am to treat his little sister.' He smoothed the strand of hair across her shoulder, his fingertips brushing the bare skin of her neck. 'Fortunately, we are quite agreed on just how precious you are.

'Secondly, I plan to build a house at the far side of this glade, so the meadow remains. That is why I wished to propose to you here. Although, of course, had you refused me, I would have been forced to raze the land.' He bent to kiss her.

After long moments he pulled away, shaking his head in mock exasperation. 'Ah, you distract me. What was I saying? That's right, a home for us, so we can be wed. I am afraid building the house I want for you will take months.'

'Oh.' She snuggled closer to him, trying to hide the disappointment that tightened her chest. Months. Months until she could be Luke's wife, months until he was entirely hers. Her chin wobbled and she ducked her head to hide it from him.

Luke's fingertip drew the corner of her mouth up into a smile. 'Ah, I long to tease you, Anna, but I cannot bear to see you look sad. I am not prepared to wait for you to become my wife. In fact, if you are in agreement, I propose we should marry next month, while it is still spring. Dieter suggests, although your father's house is now his, we remain there until our home is ready.'

Joy brought tears to her eyes, her heart swelling so it actually hurt. Clearly, Dieter had known about this for some time, yet he'd never given her a clue. She had seen little of him lately as he spent whatever free time he had with Caroline. Like Anna, he ignored mourning in favour of life.

For the first time, she dared to trace her finger down the cleft in Luke's cheek. His warm skin was roughened by traces of blonde stubble and her fingertips throbbed with the thrill of touching him. 'I would marry you tomorrow and happily live in your barn.'

He pressed his cheek against her palm, closing his eyes momentarily. 'I do not think the barn will be necessary. And the cottage we cannot live in for long—I hear a rumour your brother plans to bring his own bride to live there by next winter.'

Even surprise wasn't enough to startle her from Luke, his thighs firm beneath her back. 'Dieter will ask Caroline?'

Stretching to pick tiny pink orchids, Luke threaded them through her hair. 'Well, it may be more that Dieter anticipates Caroline asking him, but it seems you will both be newlyweds within the span of a year.'

Anna sighed, finally daring to close her eyes, knowing this moment could not be stolen from her.

⁓

The four weeks of their betrothal passed quickly, as there was much to do.

At the sound of the gig's iron wheels, Anna set aside the nightdress she worked on for her trousseau. Fortunately, Emilie sewed most of her garments, as those Anna worked were clumsy and covered with dots of red from her needle-pricked fingers. Sudden sadness washed through her, a lament for something that had not yet disappeared; this was the last time Luke would visit, for tomorrow they would wed. Though she was happy beyond words, she mourned that the beauty of what they had was at an end.

The door handle in her grasp, she pressed a hand to her chest. Her heart beat fast, as it did every time she saw Luke. He was handsome beyond imagination, yet she could not find the words to tell him how she felt without seeming foolish.

Emilie hid the knickers she embroidered with blue French knots, folding her skirts over them and reclining Mother's chair on its rockers.

Luke tipped his hat toward her and embraced Anna with unusual reserve. Amusement danced in his eyes, his skin bronzed deeper by extra hours in the sun. Despite his polite demeanour, she knew exactly what he wished to do.

And tomorrow, he would have every right to do it.

Luke took her hand. 'Come, Anna, I have something to show you.'

Their engagement official, it was acceptable for them to spend daylight hours unchaperoned, but as building their house with the help of the other farmers had added to Luke's workload, the opportunity was rare. Anna snatched up a shawl and hurried to the trap.

She had not been to the glade since he proposed The long track to the house site was more obvious now, with wheel ruts scarring the dirt, the overhanging trees cut back.

'So, this is the last time you shall ride this way with an unmarried woman?' she teased as she laid her head against his shoulder.

He slid his arm around her. 'I'm afraid that is one promise I cannot make, Anna.'

She jerked upright. Lines of laughter played around Luke's eyes, though he kept them trained on the track. She tightened her lips.

He glanced down at her and laughed aloud. 'I cannot promise, as it will depend on how many children you intend to bear me. I am certain some will be girls, and perhaps almost as beautiful as their mother.'

She flushed at his words, the intimation of the togetherness that would give them children. 'I think I would prefer many boys, as strong and handsome as their father, to help you with the farm.' But not for a long time. She wanted Luke all to herself.

'I will be happy with whatever God sends us. Though, in truth—' Luke seemed suddenly serious '—I shall be content to spend my life with only you.'

Despite his animated daily reports, Anna was unprepared for her first sight of the foundations of their home. Magically appearing like mushrooms after rain, stone walls eighteen inches thick, some of them already three feet tall, outlined the skeleton of a square building. With four rooms opening from a central hallway and an outside bakehouse, wash house and storeroom, their house would truly be massive. It looked so . . . permanent.

Luke lifted Anna from the trap, and she closed her eyes to better feel the pressure of his grasp on her waist. Would there ever come a day that excitement failed to thrill through her at his touch?

His hair reflected the sun as he ran his fingers through it. 'Come, Anna. Let me show you our home.' Replacing his hat, Luke folded her hand into the crook of his arm, his biceps tense against her palm.

Her heart fluttered with sudden misgiving. She had done nothing to deserve this good fortune. Was it unfair, greedy, that her life should be filled with such love and happiness? A tremor of apprehension passed through her and she blew through pursed lips, shaking off the notion before Luke questioned her.

'See there, Anna?' He moved behind her, resting his chin on her head as he pointed across the meadow toward the creek line. 'I think I shall be able to sink a well. And I plan to grow an orchard alongside.' His hands slid to her hips, his breath hot in her ear, making her knees tremble. 'I have already put cuttings from Mother's fig trees in and fenced them off. Hopefully, some will survive the rabbits. Come see the rest of the house.'

They toured hand in hand as Luke shared his plans and dreams. In Anna's imagination, the walls grew around them, just as their love had grown. She could see life unfurling, the house becoming a home filled with years of their love and memories.

'I need you to do something with me.' Luke led her to the front doorway. A huge stone slab, four inches thick and bearing the marks of chisel and pick, leaned against a wall on her left.

He stood behind her, wrapping her in his arms and kissing her ear before he spoke. She closed her eyes, inhaling the perfume of sunshine and hay that always accompanied him. He smelled of spring, a promise of life and happiness. 'This is our threshold stone. We shall step on it every day for the rest of our lives. I want you to help me place it.'

Tears filled her eyes and she bit at her trembling lip, determined not to shed them. Their love would be forever embedded in the stone, outlasting their lives. Yet it made her sad to realise that one day *they* would be no more.

With an iron bar, Luke levered the slab into place. With only an inch to go, he restrained the massive weight, his fingers curled over the edge of the stone. 'Quick, lay your hand on the rock, Anna.' Despite the strain, he snorted with laughter as she complied, bending to put a hand under the rock. 'No, not there, on *top* of it. We must place it together.'

Her hand traced the cool surface, the gritty, ridged texture that would be worn smooth by years of their tread, and Luke lowered the slab. A dull thud resounded through the earth as it reached its final resting place.

Blowing out a heavy breath, Luke slid to the ground, tossing his hat aside and pulling Anna into his lap. He leaned back against the wall of their home, his long legs across the slab. She nestled into him, turning her face up to his kisses.

'Anna, I adore you.' He interlaced their fingers and leaned forward. His hand pressed hers onto the warm slab. 'This stone will be here forever. Still, it is not as enduring as my love for you.' His mouth, soft against hers now, sealed his promise.

'Luke, I love you so much.' She had told him before. So many times. But it would never be enough.

His lips curved into a wicked smile against her mouth. 'I could get quite accustomed to kissing a betrothed woman, you know.'

She slapped at his arm and her palm smarted, although she was quite certain he didn't feel a thing. 'Then that, Mr Hartmann, is the last kiss you shall ever have from a betrothed woman. I believe you need to take me home now, before we incur ill luck.'

'Never say that.' His face suddenly serious, Luke traced her cheek with a finger. 'I am already indebted to God. It can only be a matter of time before I must start paying.'

His words were too close to the premonition that haunted her and she replied quickly, 'But we marry on a Wednesday. That means we are favoured. However, I shall allow you one more kiss, if it makes you feel better.'

'Better is not the only thing it will make me feel,' he murmured against her mouth. His lips were firm, his mouth salty, and she would willingly drown in him.

She lost all sense of time and propriety in Luke's embrace, pressing herself brazenly against him. She need wait only one more day, but it seemed it might never come.

'Enough.' Luke gripped her arms above the elbows like he would push her away, yet he kept her cradled in his lap, holding her so close, so tight. His words were a groan. 'Ah, I cannot let you go.'

As he kissed her, she flicked her tongue across his lips. Blood rushed to her cheeks but she forced her gaze to his. The blue eyes were now a summer's midnight, his pupils huge. Perhaps they mirrored her own desire. Their breath mingled and she cautiously extended the tip of her tongue again and traced his lips. Never before had she been daring enough to initiate their embrace.

Luke inhaled sharply, then held his breath. She was unable to do the same, the air panting from her. She wanted more. Her hands twined around the back of his neck, she pulled him close, thrusting her tongue into his mouth. She wanted to touch him, taste him, completely lose herself in the essence of him. His hand moved from the small of her back to her breast, gently stroking. This time it was she who groaned.

He released her. 'I am sorry, I did not mean—'

Her words disjointed, she struggled to explain. 'No, Luke. I—I want you.' She did not know exactly what it was that she wanted, only that she needed to be closer to him.

Luke ran a hand through his hair, pushing it from his face. He shifted beneath her as though uncomfortable and slid her from his lap. 'Ah, Anna, you will never understand how much I want you. But I would do this thing right. I would that you were my wife before I go any further. Though, in truth, I do not know how I will survive the next twenty-four hours, thinking of what you have given me here.'

She knew he was right. They must do this correctly and be blessed before they created the memory of their first union.

It was hard to leave him, but she scrambled from his lap, laughingly offering her hand as though she could pull this massive man from the ground. 'Then, Mr Hartmann, you had best take me home. The quicker you do so, the quicker the morrow will arrive.'

He grinned up at her and waved away her assistance.

'Wait, I almost forgot.' She dashed across the meadow and sank to her knees among the soft green grasses. Skirt spread, she filled it with nodding plumes of miniature pink orchids, tiny yellow puffballs, the flat, papery stars of flannel flowers, and wild violets the colour of Luke's eyes.

Luke dropped to the ground beside her and she leaned against him, glancing up shyly from beneath her lashes. He would think her foolish. 'For my bouquet.'

He kissed the top of her head, then plucked wildflowers from the warm earth to add to her collection.

28
Anna

November 1877

Emilie's knee was hard in the small of Anna's back as she tightened her laces. Just once more, Anna would wear a corset, to do full justice to Mother's wedding dress. Emilie had preserved the basic shape of the beautiful milk-white silk Mother brought with her from Germany, but removed the bell-shaped cage of the crinoline underskirt and reworked the fabric into a more fashionable bustle.

Her sister's grunt as she tied the laces was decidedly unfeminine. 'Are you not at all nervous?'

'Too excited.' Anna swallowed the butterflies that battered for escape.

'But are you not concerned about ... *after?*' Emilie leaned forward to whisper the word in her ear, then arched to stretch her shoulders before starting to layer on Anna's petticoats.

Anna shook her head, then nodded, but only to assuage Emilie's sense of propriety. 'Maybe. A little.' Caught out, her neck flushed. She was not nervous. Luke's kisses inflamed her and she wanted more. Her only concern was hoping he knew what to do, as she most certainly did not.

Emilie dropped the heavy gown over Anna's head, threading two dozen tiny white pearl buttons through their embroidered holes at the back of the bodice. Then she stepped back to admire her handiwork. 'You look beautiful, Anna.' She grinned. 'I only hope Otto thinks all the Frahn women will make such perfect brides.'

'You believe he will declare, then?'

'I am quite certain he will.' Emilie had never been in doubt of her charms. 'But have you never noticed Karl Gogel?'

'Emilie!' If her sister believed herself in love with Otto, how could she look at another man? There would never be another for Anna. Luke was her everything.

Emilie grinned, unchastened. 'Shoes, and I proclaim you ready.' She slid the slippers onto Anna's feet, then pushed back upright. 'I will make certain Dieter has the Hartmanns' good trap drawn up.'

Anna knew full well he had—checking his suit and the time frequently, her brother was far more nervous than she.

Well, until this moment, at least. Suddenly, the fact that she was about to leave her childhood home to marry the man of her dreams seemed momentous. She glanced around the familiar room. It was not that she wouldn't return; they would be back here in a few hours. But, by then, everything in her life would have changed.

Her bouquet lay on the chair and she plucked two of the tiny wild orchids from it, one pink, one cream. Crossing to Mother's Aussteuerschrank, she placed them carefully between the pages of *Great Expectations.*

～

Dieter handed Anna from the borrowed carriage and escorted her to the base of the broad steps leading to the white-painted double doors of the church. Deep red geraniums brightened the entrance, the air filled with their peppery perfume. Hidden in the grove of tall gum trees bordering the graveyard and church, a magpie burst into song, the notes rich and wet.

Her brother's gaze was on the cross that adorned the top of the church, shining white against a blue sky so clear it seemed punctured by tiny black dots. On the journey he had broken his silence only occasionally, teasing her gently but seeming concerned he would distress her. 'So, Mauschën, who would have thought you would be the first of us to tread this way?'

Certainly not her. She had never even dared to have a dream this greedy and beautiful. Today had only one flaw. Her throat swelled and she tugged on Dieter's arm to halt him. The doors of the church loomed huge and blank before them.

'Anna? Are you all right?'

She nodded, forcing her tongue between dry lips. 'Yes. Just . . . I miss them, Dieter.' Her eyes welled and she dug her nails into her gloved palms, staring at the dust settling on her slippers. She must not cry now, or people would think she regretted her decision. And she didn't, not for a heartbeat. But she would have liked her parents to share her joy. It did not seem possible that she could be so sad and so happy at the same moment.

Dieter nodded, squeezing her shoulders then releasing her, as though he feared he would ruin her dress. 'Ah, Mauschën, that is what kept me quiet all the way here. I felt I stole Father's rightful place, as Emilie stole Mother's. But I have thought hard on it, and I know both Mother and Father watch over you, as they do all of us. You must believe they are together now, and happy. Come, enjoy your day.' He flashed a smile, relieving his solemnity before she began truly sobbing. 'Make the most of the occasion. Soon enough you shall be mired in the humdrum of being a farmer's wife.'

Much as she loved her brother, he was wrong. There would never be anything humdrum about being Luke's wife.

Caroline flitted behind them, arranging the lace over Anna's bustle. Both she and Emilie were bridesmaids, beautiful in white dresses Emilie had cleverly refurbished using the contents of Mother's Aussteuerschrank. As flower girl, Frederika also wore white, a dress Anna had never laid eyes on. She suspected Mrs Ernst had something to do with the miraculous appearance of the lace-layered confection. The twins and Emilie would stay with Mrs Ernst for the night, while Dieter had been invited to join Caroline's family, affording Luke and Anna some privacy for their wedding night. Thoughts of the reason for such arrangements sent a flush crawling into Anna's bodice and she released Dieter's arm to push away the veil that seemed to have wrapped about her neck. She fanned herself with one hand.

'Anna, what is wrong? Is it the heat? Are you faint?' Emilie snapped open her fan, energetically wafting the breeze over her sister. 'Oh no, wait, I have disturbed your hair.' She stepped in front of Dieter and Anna, critically surveying the braid it had taken her two hours to arrange and stud with tiny violets. Her full lips shrivelled in concentration as she adjusted a couple of tendrils. 'Better. Now, your veil.' She and Caroline lifted the cloud of silk tulle stitched to the coronet of flowers woven through Anna's hair, billowing it over her face. Although the fabric was quite sheer, Anna was relieved to be at least partially hidden from observation.

'You are beautiful.' Though she spoke to Anna, Caroline's eyes were on Dieter, and Anna's heart swelled with love for them. Dieter touched Caroline's forearm, his fingertips transferring unspoken words between them. It was fortunate Anna had found her own true love, or the sight of her brother and his beloved, the adoration in their eyes almost embarrassing to witness, would cause her much jealousy.

Organ music swelled through the closed door and Dieter settled her hand in the crook of his arm, squeezing it reassuringly. 'Come, sister.'

He nodded to the Elders and they swung the heavy wooden doors open as the group mounted the six steps into the vestibule. Walking daintily, Caroline and Emilie preceded Anna and Dieter. Frederika skipped before them, oblivious to Wilhelmina Ernst's admonishing glare as the orange blossoms symbolising Anna's purity showered from the basket she carried.

Not content to allow his twin all the attention, Frederik tugged from Mrs Ernst's grip. Seizing a handful of the tiny white flowers, he threw them into the air before the wedding party. Anna bit her lips together, waiting for the blonde-and-pink explosion of Frederika's tantrum. Instead, she offered the basket to her brother and, sharing the handle, they walked down the aisle together.

'Well, that was somewhat unexpected,' Dieter rumbled as he tried not to laugh at their siblings.

A rustle passed through the congregation as they entered. Sunday-best fabrics polished the wooden benches as everyone swivelled toward them, but this time Anna did not mind that they stared. The solid slab ends of each pew were decorated with a spray of golden wattle, the honeyed flowers competing with the heavy perfume of rose-scented wax.

High above the altar, recessed into the whitewashed wall, the stained-glass window pulsed with a ruby glow. Dust motes spiralled in the waterfall of light that cascaded to where Luke waited for her.

Her steps faltered. She wanted to rush to him, but fear tightened her chest; moments passed them by too quickly and she must draw every second out to its fullest extent.

Gaze fixed on Luke, she trod the polished boards slowly. Dressed in morning coat and dark trousers, his gloves and cravat were of the same uncommon shade as his eyes. His lips curved into that familiar one-sided smile and her knees weakened enough that she stumbled.

349

Dieter steadied her, placing his hand over hers, and she clutched onto his arm. Her fingertips and toes tingled as though she had escaped the snow Mother said blanketed Deutschland at this time of year and now approached a blazing fire that would forever keep her warm. She was not certain she could manage the last few steps—but Luke's eyes drew her onward and every part of her body yearned to be near him. Always handsome, today he was more beautiful than should be possible.

Dieter formally kissed her farewell, but she could not spare him a glance, could not tear her eyes from Luke as Pastor mumbled through prayers and readings. In minutes, she would be Luke's wife. Forever.

Pastor's tone lifted, as though proceedings were suddenly more interesting. 'Now, the vows.'

Caroline stepped forward and Anna unclenched her fingers from the ribbon-bound bouquet, relinquishing it so Emilie could remove her gloves, drawing them carefully over the scar that was a reminder of the day Luke and she had met. Together, Emilie and Caroline lifted Anna's veil. She stared at Luke's broad chest, focused on a tiny violet pin he wore in his tie. This moment could not be real. If she dared look at him, she would wake from the most beautiful dream.

Firm fingers wrapped around her hand, transferring strength, and she gazed up at the man who would be her husband, wishing she never need look away.

In a rush to repeat her name after Pastor, Anna stammered. Luke's eyes laughed at her and later he would tease, but his thumb caressed her hand.

Taking his vows, Luke's voice was deep and assured—yet he clenched Anna's hands so tightly it hurt. A good pain. Warm and reassuring; she knew he would never release her. She was sad she could not hear his words over the furious drumming of her heart, but she saw him slip the ring onto her finger, lift her hand to his lips.

And then he leaned forward to kiss her, sealing their union. The warmth of his lips against hers was a promise of eternity, yet there were tears in the twilight depths of his eyes.

The thin, cold whisper of premonition threatened to steal her joy.

But Luke smiled, taking her arm to lead her to the vestry to sign the registry. 'My wife,' he murmured in her ear as they walked down the aisle. 'Forever, my wife.'

Now her tears fell. Tears of longing for her parents. Tears of relief. Tears of inexplicable melancholy. But, mostly, tears of joy. She and Luke would have their own wedding portrait to hang on the wall of their home, a reminder of youth and passion, as they grew old and grey together.

❧

As custom dictated, the newlyweds slipped discreetly from the church hall as the celebratory luncheon continued. Although the beautifully decorated tables were laden with cold cuts and dainty sandwiches and slices of cake generously provided by the Lutheran Ladies Guild, neither she nor Luke had an appetite. It would be difficult to eat with one hand, and it seemed neither of them was prepared to release the other.

She sat close to her husband in the trap, the leather reins lying loosely across his palm. 'Can your horse go no faster?' she teased.

Luke cocked his head to one side and narrowed his eyes at her. 'I am considering hitching up under those trees . . .'

With folded gloves, Anna slapped at his knee, then rested her cheek against his shoulder, inhaling deeply the scent of sunshine and hay that would always be his. There were fewer rules of decorum to which she must now adhere; she could touch her husband, her love, without pretending a ladylike reticence. Timidly, she wrapped both hands around his bicep, drawing his arm close to her breast. Hopefully, he would not notice her trembling.

His arm pressed warm against her and her breath caught, a heady mixture of excitement and nerves leaving her a little dizzy. While Mother had made it clear that Emilie, Frederika and she should strive toward the ultimate goal of finding suitable husbands and becoming good wives, she had never shared details of the more intimate marital duties. However, the sounds Anna had heard from her parents' side of the curtain made it seem such obligations were likely far from unpleasant. And, if the yearning ache of her loins was to be trusted, she had no need for fear. Still, she could not quite fathom how Luke's body was made to fit with her own.

The ride home was both too fast and too slow.

'Wait.' Luke reined in the horse and tied it to the hitching rail before coming to her side of the trap. He lifted her down but kept her in his arms. 'I know this is not truly our home, but I would carry you over the threshold, wife, so you don't trip and invite ill fortune.'

'Do you accuse me of clumsiness, husband?' As the title slipped from her lips for the first time, love washed through her with such intensity, she needed to close her eyes.

Luke kissed the tip of her nose. 'I seek only to keep you in my arms for every moment I can.'

Ducking beneath the lintel, he carried her into the house, then paused. His chest rose and fell rapidly.

The walls of the room receded as Anna focused only on him. She could barely speak. 'The bedroom.' Both her pointing finger and her voice trembled.

'Now?' Husky voiced, he cleared his throat.

She nodded.

Her arm around his neck, Luke's heart pounded against her breast and he sounded uncertain. 'Are you sure? We can . . . eat first. It is early in the day.'

She blew out a breath, determined, though her voice quavered. 'Now, Luke. I have waited long enough.'

He needed no more encouragement. Crossing the room in three strides, he shouldered aside the curtain that concealed her parents' bedroom.

No—*their* bedroom.

Emilie had decorated the small space with bright geraniums in jars and a new bedspread covered the iron-framed bed.

The bed where her mother had died.

She bit her lip. She must not think of that.

'Anna?'

Still in his arms, she slid her palm up the back of her husband's neck and into his thick hair. Seizing a handful, she pulled his head to hers, kissed him full on the mouth and slid her tongue between his lips.

Luke groaned, lowering Anna to her feet but holding her close against his body. 'Would you have me leave while you . . .?' He gestured at her wedding finery.

She nodded nervously, then gasped. 'Wait—I cannot.'

Disappointment darkened his face, and Luke dropped his hands and nodded. 'I understand. We can wait.'

The nerves disappeared and laughter bubbled from her. 'No, Luke. I have no intention of waiting a moment longer. I only meant I cannot undress without assistance. I am laced in. I pray your fingers are adept, as Emilie ties very firm knots.'

'Mrs Hartmann, I intend to show you just how adept my fingers are.' Luke tugged her against his chest, his hands working on the tiny buttons on the back of her dress. He fumbled and groaned into her hair. 'Would you be terribly angry if I tore the buttons apart? The confounded things are too small for my fingers.'

Her face pressed against his chest, absorbing the wild beat of his heart, Anna smiled. 'You may do as you wish, but you shall have to sweet-talk Emilie to sew them back on. Perhaps I should have warned you of my lack of talent in that area.' Even as she spoke, a twinge of jealousy plucked at her heart at the thought of Luke sweet-talking anyone else. He was hers, now and forever.

The buttons showered the floor as he tugged the fabric apart. 'Ah, you think you captured me under false pretences,

Mrs Hartmann? Even if you were to tell me you are neither seamstress nor cook, I would wed you.' He slid the dress from her shoulders, a soft grunt escaping his lips as her petticoats were revealed. Seizing her about the waist, his tongue thrust intimately into her mouth, then his hands slid down, over her hips, tugging up the many layers of petticoat to cup her buttocks in his roughened palms.

She could not breathe, yet she pressed against him, pulling his shirt free of his breeches and sliding her hands beneath it, across the naked heat of his skin.

Luke released her mouth, his indrawn breath a hiss as her hands explored. She felt him smile against her hair. 'Wife, I can see I shall have to be very stern with you. I am quite certain I told you before how I feel about these infernal corsets. I believe my first rule as your husband shall be to banish the things.'

Her petticoats fell to the floor around her feet as he untied the strings at her waist.

She pulled back a little to look up at him, though not far enough that he would have to shift his warm hands, which had once again found her bottom. 'Indeed, I shall happily dispose of the corsets. In fact, I was thinking I will don trousers and help you in the fields.' She jested, of course. 'That way, I will not have to be apart from you.'

There was a long pause, Luke's lips busy on hers again, before he answered. He kissed a trail of fire down her neck and across the exposed top of her breasts. 'I would not be away from you for a single moment, were it possible, Anna. But I am not so very fond of the idea of you in trousers.'

'No?'

His hands were working on the laces of her corset. 'No. Because then my access would be even more inhibited.'

Her hands slid reluctantly from his chest and she took a half-step away. She had teased about needing him to unlace her corset—it was easily removed by unhooking the steel clasps at the front. Suddenly shy, her fingers trembled as she grasped the stiffened fabric, drawing the boned edges closer together to release the hooks.

Luke's eyes were dark, intent on her hands. His nostrils flared slightly, and his chest heaved.

She dropped the fabric shell to the floor.

His hands moved to her chemise, drawing it over her head. 'Mein Gott, Anna. You are so beautiful.' He pulled her nakedness to him.

Everywhere she was soft, he was hard against her. They fit together perfectly, her breasts crushed against his abdomen, his firm thighs pressed to the soft rounding of her belly, his hard arms caging her white shoulders.

He framed her face between his hands. 'Anna, my love. I would make you truly my wife, now.' All banter had disappeared from his tone.

Unable to speak, she could only silently adore him. Anna nodded, and Luke carried her to the bed. Their bed.

29
Taylor

Baked beans spread across the plate Taylor shoved into the microwave, the modern appliance incongruous in the homely, shabby farm kitchen. Her face reflected in the glass door as the plate spun, the image blurred and distorted.

Like a dream should be.

Except her dreams were never blurry. They were like going back to collect pieces of herself she had somehow lost along the way.

Concentrating as intently as she would on a surgical procedure, Taylor sliced Gran's crusty loaf. She needed to remain present and focused, not allow her imagination to wander forbidden pathways where every breath she took, heavy with the fragrance of sweet hay and summer sunshine, encouraged her to rebel against accepting that her dreams were nothing but a fantasy.

Battling the barely there satellite internet, she had spent two days trawling psychology and medical sites, looking for an explanation for what was going on in her head. Dusting breadcrumbs from her hands, she opened the notes she'd made on her phone.

One: Paracosm. Creating a detailed imaginary world. Usually originates in childhood.

So that was out. This was nothing like the imagined friends of her youth.

Two: Dissociative disorder, most likely deperson-alisation or derealisation, causes a sense of unreality or disconnectedness.

Three: Maladaptive daydreaming. A coping mecha-nism used in response to trauma, abuse or loneliness. The daydreamer conjures a complex imaginary world to escape into.

She drummed her fingers on the countertop, staring at the screen. The problem with the second diagnosis was that she wasn't so much disconnected from her real life, as she felt equally connected to another. Instead of a sense of unreal-ity, she had developed an enhanced sense of reality, creating a parallel existence. But if she added the second and third diagnoses together, she almost had it covered. Escaping the stress and disappointment of her reality, she had picked up snippets of information about people who'd lived around here and woven that knowledge into her dreams.

She chose to ignore the inexplicable fact that she knew not only scattered names but entire family trees. At least the minutiae of their lives, the fleshing out of their person-alities, their *love* all existed only in her head. While Luke

Hartmann was a real person, the perfect Luke Hartmann of her dreams was entirely her creation. An escapist fantasy stemming from her trauma, predicated on her need to believe such a man could exist.

And it was irrational to expect any real guy to compare favourably with her dream boyfriend.

Damned if she'd be irrational.

She tried to slide her gaze over the final possibility on her list, as though she didn't have it memorised.

Four. Déjà vécu. The hardcore big brother of déjà vu, a permanent and lingering sense of having lived before, complete with all the sensory attributes of that life.

The explanation sounded mild. The problem was in what she hadn't noted, choosing not to commit it to writing: her research indicated that documented cases of chronic déjà vécu had been linked to epilepsy and brain injuries.

Bile rose in her throat, the knife dropping from her nerveless hands. She swallowed repeatedly, fighting the nausea. She was too young to consider the possibility of a future filled with MRIs and CAT scans. She was supposed to be the doctor, not the patient.

But that diagnosis would explain everything.

Almost everything, she corrected, as the tragic serenity of the cemetery again filled her head.

She gave a ragged sigh. No amount of knowledge could relieve the pervasive melancholy, the sense of loss. Yet disconcertingly layered with that was an odd longing and excitement, as though a joyous surprise lay barely hidden and only just beyond her reach.

Gramps shuffled into the kitchen. 'Morning, Peach. You're up early. Wet the bed?'

'Ew, Gramps.' She pulled the plate from the micro-wave, wiped the splatter from the interior and handballed the paper towel into the bin. 'No. Things to do.'

He held his hands out from his body like a little kid pretending to be an aeroplane. 'Coming up?'

No matter what, she was a long way from crazy enough to let Gramps take her flying. 'Thanks, but no thanks. I noticed a wire on the bottom gate has snapped. I figured I'll fix it before the sheep push through.'

Gramps snaffled her plate of beans and toast. 'I'll get Luke to take a look. He'll be round the place today. Said he's moving sheep into next year's fallow paddocks to start on the stubble, so he can hold off on putting out feed for them.'

Luke. Heart pounding, face hidden by the cupboard door, Taylor took another can of beans from the pantry. Hearing the name stirred the yearning—when she saw the farmer again she would compare him and the Luke of her imagination, set her mind at rest with evidence of their differences. Prove to herself that it was the fantasy she was attracted to, not the man.

Although wouldn't it be far better to be falling for a flesh-and-blood man?

Even if it was a man it seemed she'd known before.

'That's okay, Gramps. He's got plenty on at the moment. So much for slow season. He said he has to get all the hay bales in this week, too.'

'And yet he made time for you,' Gramps said slyly.

⟡

The side cutters snipped through a length of galvanised wire from the roll looped over Taylor's shoulder. Though she'd finally relented and started doing yoga with Mum each morning, bending low enough to work on the strand had been impossible. So she sat in the dust, one leg thrust under the fence, her other knee bracing the gate as she used pliers to pull the wire taut.

A dry crackle in the scrub, barely a noise, but different from the regular patterns of life, made Taylor jerk her head up. Breath held, she traced each sound back to its source. Sheep in a back paddock, the lambs bleating in dismay as the ewes wandered. The distant rolling thunder of a tractor moving slowly, picking up the last of the baled hay. The high-pitched keen of a hawk. Wild bees working in the honeycomb near the shearing shed, cicadas down toward the creek.

But this noise was closer: the pile of dried-out branches near her left foot. She waited. More barely perceptible rustling, then a snake slithered through the camouflage, betrayed by the snapping of a dead leaf beneath his creamy yellow belly. Beautiful russet and umber scales shimmered in the bright sunlight. Tongue flickering toward her boot, it tasted the wind, smelling for danger. Satisfied she wasn't prey, or even vaguely interesting, the snake slid past, winding through the soft dirt along the fence line.

Remaining motionless until the creature was out of sight, Taylor bent back to her job, a ragged thumbnail pressing the loose end of the wire against the star dropper as she crimped the centre of the repair. A final squeeze of the pliers and she scrambled to her feet. Dust clouded her as she slapped her backside then rubbed her hands on her thighs.

The frayed edge of a rip in the denim shorts occupied her fingers as she surveyed the expanse of golden stubble, the paddocks stretching to meet the endless azure of the horizon. Though she'd already inspected the fences, Taylor was in no hurry to return to the homestead. A girl could only drink so much tea. And out here she didn't feel so guilty when her imagination ran free, didn't feel the same compulsion to rationalise what was going on in her head.

The scrub beckoned. She put the tools on the seat of her motorbike, then slipped through the gate, wiring it closed behind her.

Her footfalls were muffled on the rocky, undulating ground as she wound between the trees. Eucalyptus rose from gum leaves crushed underfoot. Heat blanketed the earth. She knew the somnolent silence in the wood was because the tiny finches, willy wagtails and sparrows nested for the hottest part of the day.

And she knew the knowledge came from her dreams.

From Anna.

Taylor halted, biting her lower lip as she stared into the scrub. It seemed that to tread deeper would infer acceptance; she would irrevocably cross some final threshold. Yet the pull of the past beckoned her and she was consumed by a hollow *wanting*, an unassuageable longing to return, to find the love that was lost. She took a deep breath, then let it ease from her. Willing it to take away the impossible weight of imagined grief.

The hell with trying to find rational explanations.

She *knew*. That was enough.

A magpie defied the silence, his warble flowing like water over rocks, drawing her further into the bushland. But it wasn't the bird she searched for. It was peace. Acceptance. Memories. Hidden deep in the scrub, away from all trace of modern life, nothing could intrude to insist her dreams weren't real. Perhaps there she could find Luke and Anna, steal a secret moment with them without waiting for night to fall.

Serenity enfolded her among the tranquil grey and olive shades of the scrub. Her back against the smooth trunk of a silver gum, she slid to the ground among the peels of bark. In air sweetly creamed with wattle and wild honey, bull ants widened a path as they tracked back and forth through the leaf litter. The endless rhythm of their march, the ageless sounds and scents of a world it seemed Taylor had always known, freed her mind.

Eyes closed, she embraced the deep sense of belonging.

Time slipped away.

∽

A chough's caw startled Taylor awake. The sun had dipped behind the ranges to the west and guilt lent her speed as she clambered to her feet and headed out of the scrub.

But it had worked. Though it was daytime, she had dreamed of Luke and Anna. Still her mind played dangerous games, twisting the dream, insisting that not only was it reality, but a memory of *her* and Luke together. It was as though Anna's feelings and emotions and experiences were her own, and Luke's embrace, the caress of his eyes, his words of promise, were meant for her.

As Taylor emerged from the trees, far further up the paddock than she'd anticipated, she noticed a brown cloud staining the sky. Smoke? Fear coiled in her stomach and she looked toward the distant homestead, as though help would be found there. Instead, a mob of sandy beige sheep bore down on her, their churning feet throwing a curtain of dirt into the air.

They weren't moving fast, stopping to snatch a mouthful of dry grass or wandering to investigate the odd tree, but there were dozens of them. A pair of dusty red dogs raced alongside the flock, dashing back and forth, keeping the animals in a loose, forward-moving circle.

And behind them, sitting high on his gelding, was Luke.

For just a heartbeat, Taylor wondered whether she was still asleep. Had she reached the point where she could truly no longer distinguish fact from fantasy?

The horse broke into an easy canter and Luke approached swiftly. 'Taylor.'

Definitely the real Luke.

'Your grandfather mentioned you might need a hand.' He nodded toward the gate, the best part of half a kilometre further along the fence line. 'But I had a look on the way up to fetch the sheep and you've aced it. Must've been country in a previous life.'

His words were throwaway, yet they sent a chill through her. Briskly rubbing her arms, Taylor forced a smile. 'Maybe I should give med school a miss, then?'

'Don't reckon so. Farmers are two a hectare, but we're short on doctors around here.'

She wasn't sure whether to be amused or offended by what seemed a district-wide assumption that she had nowhere better to be.

Although, did she? Luke's thoughts about the inherent purpose in country life had struck a chord—but she couldn't let what was clearly a growing infatuation with a farmer who barely knew she existed sway a decision that would affect the rest of her life. That was where she'd gone wrong with Zac. Well, that and not picking him as an absolute tosser.

'You've already put the fox in the chicken yard,' Luke said. 'Your mum and gran were in the IGA last week, telling Lynn that you're not too sure about going to uni in Adelaide.'

She groaned. 'Of course they were.'

Luke shot her a commiserating grin. 'I warned you how well the grapevine works here. Settlers being Settlers, anyone who missed out on the newsflash will have been brought up to speed by now. Me included. So I hope you were sitting in the scrub working out your escape plan.'

'Plan?' It was odd talking with him, feeling that she knew him so intimately, but forced to remind herself that she had no right to fall into an easy camaraderie. He was practically a stranger.

One she'd like to get to know a whole lot better.

'It looks like Settlers Bridge has decided we need a medical practice. And, equally informally but completely bindingly, you've been declared "it".'

Luke was laughing, but she got the impression that there was a measure of intent behind his words. Or was that her own wishful thinking? She swiped a hand across her forehead, trying to banish the ghosts of her imagination. Grit coated her fingers, and she hoped she hadn't smeared it across her face. 'Even if I go to Adelaide Uni, it'll be years before I'm fully qualified.'

'Lucky time is something we've got plenty of, then.'

A shiver rippled through Taylor despite the sunshine that forced her to adjust her cap to shade her eyes as she looked up at Luke. 'Well, just between us, I have enrolled at Adelaide.'

'But you've not told anyone?' He seemed surprised she'd kept it to herself. Or perhaps that she chose to share with him.

'The admissions process is a bit of a kick in the pants, with no guarantee of getting in, so I didn't want to count my chickens. You know, what with all the foxes around here. Besides, I couldn't risk disappointing everyone.' She gave a soft, reflective laugh. 'And by "everyone", I mean my family. Can't say I realised I had to consider the whole town.' And yet, what should feel like interference felt surprisingly like caring. Interest. Community.

Luke chuckled. 'Guess I should give you a heads-up. Autonomy falls in the same category as privacy in Settlers Bridge: non-existent. Pretty much everything that goes on around here is decided by completely unofficial vote.' He ran his fingers through Pferd's mane. 'But considering the whole town will get to be second nature if we can persuade you to hang around.'

Persuade? Did she imagine his inference?

'I see.' Flustered, she blew off his comment, reaching to pat Pferd's shoulder. The gelding's satiny coat radiated warmth, muscles rippling and twitching at her touch. 'Gramps said you didn't use the horse for mustering?'

'Honestly, a bike is easier. But I got all the hay in this morning so I'm in no rush—and the sheep are even slower. So two birds, one stone; this is as much relaxation as work. Don't tell my old man that, though. Wouldn't want him to think I'm slacking.'

'Relaxing, even though you're doing it bareback?' She cringed as she realised that her statement gave away the fact that she'd copped a decent look at his muscular thighs, the tanned legs clamped against the horse's silky sides. To be fair, they were close to eye level. 'Isn't that harder?'

'Only in that there are no stirrups.' He raised his feet, the thick socks rolled down above his boots covered in the fat burrs that seemed to be a hazard of country living. 'I noticed when we rode the other week that Pferd's getting a bit lazy about taking cues from my legs, so I figured he needed some close contact time.'

She'd never expected to be jealous of a horse.

'Want to give it a try?'

'What?' She jerked back. 'No! I had enough trouble staying on Goldie even with that Western saddle.'

'You did just fine.'

'In case you've forgotten, I could barely get up—even with a saddle.'

Luke hooked his sunglasses onto the pocket of his chambray shirt. 'Haven't forgotten a thing.'

Those eyes. 'Well, I kind of wish you would,' she muttered. Okay, she wasn't a complete idiot. He was flirting.

'Not how memories work though, is it?' His voice suddenly low, Luke's gaze searched her face. 'They're more random, don't turn up on demand.'

No. They couldn't have a conversation about memories. She didn't want to think about her brain's betrayal, didn't want to run her symptoms and possible prognosis again. 'How do you plan for me to get up there, then?' she said with far more bravado than she felt.

The unusual yet far too familiar cleft creased Luke's cheek. Urging Pferd closer to Taylor, he reached across the horse with his left hand. 'Grab on.'

His long fingers closed around her left wrist, then slid to her upper arm as he bent lower. His hand was strong, slightly callused. 'Hup.' Before she had a chance to think or protest, Luke tensed his arm, straightened his back and swung her up in front of him.

She gasped, clutching Pferd's mane. 'Oh God, sorry. I'm probably hurting him.' But she wasn't letting go.

'You're not,' Luke said, so close to her ear that ripples of desire shivered through her. 'But you don't need to hang on quite so desperately. I've got you.' He wrapped one arm loosely around her waist, gripping the reins with his other hand. 'And we'll take it as slow as you like.'

Why did she think—no, hope—that he was talking about more than riding?

Why? Because she was sliding into insanity. There was no doubt about it. Everything about this complete stranger felt *right*. His voice. His touch. Even his scent. Hay and sunshine. They should bottle that stuff.

They probably did, she thought with a slightly mad internal laugh. It was likely cologne that she was smelling. Because it was ridiculous to think a man could be so effortlessly attractive. Anywhere other than in her imagination, anyway.

Luke's thighs pressed against the naked length of hers and she could feel the flex of his muscles. The warmth of his skin. The tickle of the golden hairs on his legs, both thrillingly erotic and unbelievably intimate. He clicked his tongue and Pferd moved forward.

The sensation of movement beneath her, yet entirely out of her control, was disturbing. Almost like her dreams rushing toward her, unregulated. But she felt safe with Luke—the *real* Luke.

'Do you want to take the reins?' he asked.

She shook her head, leaning back against his chest. 'Nope. I'll only get it wrong.'

'Not much you can get wrong. Besides, I'm controlling Pferd with my knees, so at worst he's going to come to a complete stop while he waits for us to get our act together.'

Not waiting for her reply, he dropped the reins.

Taylor was about to protest, then she realised he was signalling with his free hand, either bending it to the right or left, occasionally holding it up, palm out. 'What are you doing?'

'The dogs.'

'They're controlled by hand signals? I thought you had to carry a special whistle or something.'

'Nothing special.' Luke chuckled. 'More like this.' He gave a short whistle, not overloud, and the dog on the left of the mob immediately stopped, cocking one ear as it looked back at him. Another whistle and a flick of his hand to the left, and the dog turned to the sheep, who had been contentedly munching the short, dry stalks of stubble, forcing them toward the fence.

'Oh, she went the wrong way,' Taylor said.

'How so?'

'You pointed left, she went right.'

'Which is correct. The hand signals are based on the way the dogs and sheep are facing, not the way I'm facing. It's kind of a confusing concept. But there are also different whistles and a half-dozen verbal commands. The dogs learn all of them, so what I use depends on how far away the dogs are, whether they can see me or if it's too windy and a whistle will carry easier than my voice.'

As he spoke, she noticed he continued to direct the dogs with the occasional flick of his wrist. It seemed the connection between him and the animals was effortless, subconscious.

'Your dad farms too, you said?'

She could feel his nod. 'Yep. Family business for generations. Guess that's partly what I like about it. The connection with the land that's formed such a big part of my family history. I mean, it's nothing compared to Aboriginal history, obviously, but we go as far back as it's possible for white fellas around here, which is pretty huge. I can look at any building, any fence, any paddock, and know that it was one of my ancestors who built it, created it, cleared it.'

One of his ancestors. Those who lay in the graveyard she'd discovered? 'I can't even imagine what it's like to have that sense of place.' She lied: she could imagine it all too perfectly. 'I feel like I've only just properly discovered my own grandparents.'

'See, that's weird for me,' Luke said, slowing the horse as they neared the gate where she'd left the motorbike. 'I can't imagine not being related to three-quarters of the district. Guess that's partly why we're all in each other's business. If we trace back far enough, we're mostly family. Wait, I'll lift you down.' As he spoke, he threw one leg over Pferd's backside and dropped to the ground. He reached up, gripping her waist. 'Swing your right leg over his head, I've got you.'

Her heart swooped as Luke lifted her from her precarious perch. Sandwiched between him and Pferd's warmth, Taylor breathed in the sweet smell of the horse. And the more seductive smell of the man.

She stared at the tanned V where Luke's unbuttoned shirt revealed his chest. Didn't dare raise her eyes, couldn't bring herself to look into his deep blue gaze.

Luke was real, and she suddenly knew that she would never again need to dream him. The realisation should be a relief, but a sense of loss clouded the thrill of his nearness.

'I really hope I haven't scared you off. Either from the town or . . . horses. You'll still ride with me again later in the week?' Hands still loosely on her waist, Luke's voice was low, yet intense, as though her response was important.

The words meant nothing. But the pause meant everything.

30
Anna

December 1877

In the six weeks that followed their wedding, married life in a small house with Anna's four siblings proved awkward. Dieter retained his quarters in the bakehouse, but the newlyweds had to wait for the rhythmic breathing that signalled Emilie and the twins slept before they furtively embraced beneath the scant privacy of the bedspread.

Labouring on his family property each day before turning his attention to building their home, Luke must kiss her farewell while it was still dark. As he made to rise, she pressed her lips to his neck. Tomorrow she would trim the golden hair that curled thick and low against it. The thought excited her, as did any opportunity to touch him. She tried to imagine his hair turning grey, years from now. Or perhaps he would lose it, as his father had? It didn't matter. He would still be her Luke.

'Must you leave already?'

He smiled at her pout. 'A few more days, Anna. The walls are almost complete, the roof ready to raise. Our house will be finished and I shall have you all to myself.'

Wearing only a thin nightdress, she knelt on the bed to reach for him. 'I know, but I don't want you to leave. Just a little longer, please. Listen, they are all asleep.'

Luke's flat stomach tensed beneath her hand, amusement rolling through his chest. 'Wife, you shall wear me out and I shall be unable to build your house.' His stomach growled. 'And I shall likely starve before that unhappy conclusion, anyway.'

Heat flared in her cheeks; already she neglected the first of her duties. The porridge should be made and the bread proving by now. With an entire bed to herself, there was little point waiting for Emilie to rise unbidden. 'I am sorry.' Anna's chastened gaze travelled across Luke's strong features. Then she shook her head. 'No, I am not. I *shall* starve you, husband. Just for a few more minutes. Please?' She was always desperate to steal a little more time with him.

Luke chuckled at her whispered entreaty and drew the loose gown over her head. He kissed her breast and she pulled him close. His voice muffled, he sighed in mock defeat. 'Very well, wife, just once more.'

Laying her on the bed, he covered her with his body.

She shook her head, palms up to hold him off. 'No, remove your nightshirt. I want you naked against me.'

Luke's nostrils flared as his muscular arms flexed, tugging the shirt over his head. He was so perfect. Bronzed and so strong, work-hardened ridges of muscle crossed his abdomen. Pinned by his knees on either side of her hips, Anna struggled to sit, leaning on her elbows so she could run her tongue up the indentation of his chest. He was salty and sweet, and she was uncertain whether it was love or desire that made her cling to him.

'Anna, my sweet Anna.' Luke's deep voice broke and he lowered his weight onto her. 'I shall never have enough of you.'

She arched to him, giving all that she had, greedy for all that he offered.

~

It seemed too few minutes later, although the faintest light haloed Luke, that he kissed her and pushed from the bed. 'I must go.'

She struggled upright. 'Wait, I shall make you breakfast.'

He grinned, leaning in for another kiss. 'I have no time. Somebody stole it all. But I happen to adore that thief.'

As he left, Anna snuggled under the covers, rolling into the Luke-shaped hollow of the feather-filled mattress, enjoying the smell of him trapped in the linen, the taste of his salt upon her lips.

It was only the first week of summer, yet already warm inside. Tendrils of sun crept around the edge of the curtain that separated their bedroom from the kitchen. Playing across her face, they stroked her awake; she had fallen back to sleep, dreaming of Luke. There was no sound in the house. Emilie must have taken the children outdoors. Dieter would already be shearing. Guilt stirred Anna's unusual apathy. She must rise.

A reluctant sigh puffed her cheeks. Flinging aside the bedclothes, she thrust her legs over the edge of the high bed. Dizzy, she gasped, clapping a hand across her mouth. Her knees hit the floor as she dragged the chamber-pot from beneath the bed just in time.

She was certain more came out of her mouth than had gone in over the last full day. She vomited again and again, her stomach cramping with the continual heaving.

Emilie's uncertain footfalls stopped near the curtain. 'Anna, are you all right?'

As Anna vomited again, Emilie swept aside the fabric. Anna snatched at the bed cover, dragging it down to hide her nakedness.

Emilie's eyes anxious, she clapped her hand to Anna's forehead. She had seen too much death. 'Anna?'

Anna pushed her hand away testily. 'I am not ill, Emilie.' She should know; she had also seen much life.

'Not ill? That certainly looks like ill.' Emilie pointed with distaste at the contents of the chamber-pot.

Anna's mouth prickled with saliva, but she swallowed it determinedly. 'I am not ill, Emilie,' she repeated. 'I am late.'

'Late?' Emilie frowned her incomprehension, her blue eyes puzzled.

Anna groaned, too sick to explain.

'You mean you are with child? Already? Is that possible?'

'Apparently so,' Anna replied dryly, shoving her fear down deep inside.

'But when? How far along are you?'

'Obviously, no more than six weeks.' Her reply was more acerbic than appropriate, but she was not ready for this. Though she had promised him children, she wanted Luke to herself. She did not want to share him—or her body—with anyone else. Not yet. She had seen what babies could do to women. The memory of Mother's lifeless body, stretched out on this very bed, drove an icicle of fear into her heart.

'I have the clothes and swaddling cloths we put away in the oak wardrobe. I will also stitch new ones. We have plenty of time.' Emilie's excitement would be infectious, were Anna not so terrified. 'And Anna, you must take the crib, set it up in your house.'

'No!' She would not carry death into her new home.

Emilie poured water from the pitcher on the nightstand into a mug. 'Luke is not aware?'

'No. But I must tell him.' Her flow late and nipples tender, she had suspected this for a week now, although she had told herself the effects were from over-zealous lovemaking.

Emilie dropped a cloth over the chamber-pot and smoothed the hair from Anna's perspiring face. 'You would tell him already? Is that proper?'

How would she know? She had no one to tell her what was proper. Anna sipped the water. Surely there was nothing that she and Luke should not share . . . perhaps even her fears? 'I shall use the small trap and take Luke some lunch. He plans to spend all afternoon working on our home.' The last two words made her feel better. Of course it would be all right; she was young and healthy. Her body wasn't worn out from carrying too many babies.

And they would have months together, just the two of them, before the baby came. *Luke's baby.* Anna passed a hand across her stomach, imagining a slight swell. A son with Luke's golden hair and indigo eyes. A child made of their love.

It would be all right.

It must be.

∽

Much of the scrub around the cottage was cleared, but the many planned outbuildings were nothing but fresh scars on the earth. As the trap drew closer, Anna could make out Luke balanced on a suspended beam, hammering nails into corrugated roof sheeting. Spying her, he dropped to the ground and quickly closed the distance between them. Lifting her from the trap, he pressed her against the vehicle, trying to lift her skirts as the horse snorted impatiently, snapping at flies.

Laughter swelled through her. 'You are not worn out, husband?'

'My tiredness flees when I see you.' He kissed the side of her neck, running his hands over her sensitive breasts. 'And, if my wife will travel to come to me in the middle of the afternoon, where no one can see us, what sort of man would I be to refuse her?'

Her breath already short, she nipped at his earlobe, whispering, 'I meant worn out from your work. You have the roof on?'

'One more day and I will be finished. My plan was to surprise you.'

She grinned as his knee shifted between her thighs. 'Oh, you do surprise me.'

Luke chuckled, making a renewed attempt to worm his hands beneath her skirts. 'Wife, I am pleased you listened to me and abandoned those horrible corsets, but truly, we must do something about all these petticoats. Oh—' His eyes grew darker, the blue-black of a summer thunderstorm. 'I had heard a rumour that ladies' drawers are not stitched at the centre seam. I cannot tell you how pleased I am to find the story true.'

Heat warmed her cheeks although the sun hid behind a passing cloud. Her eyes half-closed with pleasure at his touch.

'I must have you. Now.' Luke murmured. 'Here, where there is no reason to be quiet about my lovemaking, here where I can be open in my adoration. I wanted to wait until our house was finished, but, sweet Anna, let me have you now.'

Luke's deep voice sent her pulse racing. She stretched up to hold his face between her palms. 'Now, Luke. Now and always. I promise I shall never refuse you.'

The horse stamped, harness jingling as the gig inched forward. Anna gasped, moulding herself closer to Luke's strength, away from the huge iron-rimmed wheels.

He swept her from her feet, one arm reaching into the rear of the trap to snatch the blanket kept there. 'I recall the first time I carried you, Anna. I thought you quite the most beautiful thing I had ever seen. But you were nothing, then, compared to the woman now in my arms.'

'I remember the first time I opened my eyes to you,' she whispered shyly, nestling into him. 'I thought you too handsome to exist in this world.'

Luke bent his head, kissing her, then spoke against her lips. 'I would carry you over the threshold to our home now, my love, even though it is not complete.'

She nodded and he strode to the house, pausing on the stone they had laid in the doorway together. 'Welcome home, my Anna.'

Though the windows had yet to be glassed, the roof covered their bedroom, nailed to beams that their children would wake to each day, counting the whorls and knots as Anna had done all the years in her parents' home.

Our children.

A house full of their love. She secretly pressed a hand to her stomach, hiding a smile.

Still holding her, Luke dropped the blanket, kicking it into place among the piles of stone and rubble that littered the floor. He glanced around and twisted his mouth, shrugging broad shoulders. 'I planned to have a bed before I brought you here. But I can wait no longer.'

'Nor I.' She refused to release him as he lowered her to the blanket.

Luke lay on his left side, one leg thrown heavily across Anna's thighs, his chest heaving. He traced a finger through the moisture between her breasts, his eyes dancing as he grinned. 'I do not know why I trouble to sink a well. I know exactly how to find water—' He paused, his head cocked to one side, as though he listened to something.

Her fingers in his hair, Anna tugged his mouth to hers. She could never kiss him enough. It was as though their souls joined; they were only complete when they were together. Her fingers traced the shadowed depths of the cleft in his cheek that so fascinated her.

Luke turned his head, kissing her hand. 'I recall when your hand was all I dared kiss.'

She quivered at the memory. 'And I recall when you were the first man to kiss my hand . . . or anywhere else.'

'I plan on being the only man who will ever do so.'

'You need have no fear. I swear it shall be so. I adore you, Luke.' Had she read every book in the world, still she would not have the words to adequately express what he meant to her.

'And I love you, beyond all the realms of possibility—' Luke broke off with a sudden grunt. 'Mein Gott. Was zum Teufel?' He thrust himself up, hand clutched to the shoulder that had been pressed to the floor.

The brown snake slithering quickly back to hide in the rubble was small, no larger than the span of Luke's palm and relief sighed from Anna's lips. 'Lucky—' she began, but the fear in Luke's eyes halted her.

'No, Anna, you know—'

Yes, she knew.

She knew that a newly hatched snake was as venomous as a six-foot adult.

She knew that a single strike could kill a horse.

She knew that the worm-like creature had sunk its fangs into her husband's shoulder, near his heart.

She knew there was nothing she could do to stop the poison.

But she did not want to know any of this.

She surged to her knees, snatching at her clothes. 'I shall ride for help. You must stay still.' His parents were more than twenty minutes away. If she unharnessed the carriage, she could ride bareback. Yet it would take time to unstrap the leather, shift the poles.

Luke's hand shot out, locking around her wrist. His eyes were dark. Midnight, not twilight. 'No, Anna. Stay with me. There is no time.' He tried to smile, but it looked like he might cry. 'I always knew I would be robbed of you. But this. This is not so bad.'

Her lips trembled and she remained on her knees, torn between the urge to ride for help and the terror of losing moments with Luke. 'It is not?' He would be all right, then? Surely it must be so, no God could be so cruel.

His fingers stroked the side of her face and a soft, sad laugh huffed from his chest. 'Ah, see, I forgot to warn you how selfish I am. This is not so bad, because it means I will not have to live without you. I knew I did not deserve you, that I would have to pay for the blessing. I was almost afraid to love you, fearing you would one day be stolen from me. I knew if that happened, I could not go on.' Luke pulled her closer, his lips pressed to hers for the longest moment. 'The day I found you during the bushfire, I vowed I would spend my life protecting you. But I did not expect to be permitted so little time to do so.'

This was not possible; it could only be a nightmare. She wanted to wake. Her hands trembled across Luke's shoulder, as though she could undo what the snake had done. Hope flared; the beast may have already hunted, perhaps it had no poison left?

Poison! She knew what she must do. Luke's shoulder was discoloured, the light-purple bloom of a bruise spreading around two tiny punctures. She quickly pressed her lips to the wound.

Luke's voice was harsh with fear. 'Do not swallow, Anna.'

She sucked hard and turned from him, pretending to spit the poison aside. Pretending, because nothing had come out, his muscled shoulder hard and ungiving beneath her lips. Did that mean no poison went in? Yet already the evil bruise had spread, darker veins wriggling through it like serpents.

His lips rimmed in white, Luke's strong jaw locked in a spasm of pain. Teeth clenched, he slid a hand around the back of her neck. 'Anna. There is no time.' He drew her down, pillowing her against his firm torso. 'Come, lie with me one last time, sweet Anna.'

Her ear against his heart, she could hear his breath was already laboured. She balled her fists, wanting to beat them against his chest, force his heart to continue.

'No! Not the last time, Luke. I am cutting your hair tomorrow.' Ridiculous words, but she had to find something to make him stay. Her husband was so strong and beautiful and good, God had no right to steal him.

His arm tightened around her naked shoulders, crushing her to his chest. 'I never imagined this for us. We were supposed to grow old together, raise a family. I wanted a home filled with miniatures of you.' His voice vibrated with betrayal.

Children. She must tell him. He would never leave her then. Anna pushed herself up, leaning over him. 'Luke, I carry your child. Luke? Luke? Do you hear me? We are to have a baby.' Her heart thundered so loud, she feared she would miss his reply, his promise to stay. Because he had to stay.

A slow, sad smile lifted the corner of his mouth. His hand pressed to her stomach and a tear slid through the white lines creasing his tanned skin. 'Our baby.'

This could not be. She would not lose him. 'No, Luke, no. You swore to me. Remember? You swore that nothing would ever come between us.' Not even death.

'I am so sorry, Anna. But at least you will not be alone.' His words were breathless, the cleft in his cheek deepening in pain, and she had to look away.

But she could not. He was hers. Forever.

Now she could barely see his beauty through her tears. She pressed her lips to the wound that blossomed in livid shades of purple and blue, spreading a pattern of sorrow across his chest. She sucked hard. Swallowed. Sucked again. Swallowed. Prayed that she was ingesting the poison injected into him. For if Luke died, she would not live without him.

Life faded from his twilight eyes. They grew dim, as in an old man. The old man he should have become beside her.

'Luke. You cannot leave me. You cannot leave *us*.' The plea ached in her throat. Her fingers clawed against his chest as she tried to catch and hold the last beats of his heart.

His hand gripped hers, still strong, still firm, still Luke. But his eyes closed and his words were an echoing whisper. 'Sweet Anna. I love you beyond the end of time. I promise I shall always be with you.'

31
Taylor

Sobs woke Taylor, wrenching up from her stomach to tear through her swollen throat.

Mum rushed into the bedroom, her hair wild, kaftan tangling her legs. She dropped down onto the edge of the bed, her arm around Taylor's shaking shoulders as she struggled upright.

'Taylor, baby. What's wrong?'

'He's dead. Luke's dead.' Gulping for air, she could barely get the words out. Saying his name released a tidal wave of grief.

'Luke?' Mum's green eyes huge, her voice pitched high.

Taylor's hands burrowed into the linen, clutching at it as though she could hold onto the dream.

No, forget the dream. She didn't want it anymore. Her fingers dragged through her hair, dug into her scalp, trying to erase the memory.

Luke is gone.

Mum shook her. 'Taylor. Talk to me. What is it?'

Fear shone in her mother's eyes and Taylor searched for words to explain the inexplicable. 'Anna's husband. Luke.'

'Taylor.' Mum stood, backing slowly from the bed, hands repeatedly smoothing her patterned front. 'Taylor, I'm calling for an ambulance. You're not making any sense. Have you . . . taken something?'

She dragged in a breath, fighting down the hysteria. 'No, I'm fine. It was just a dream.'

Liar. On both counts.

'Oh, baby. A nightmare, you mean? You're okay? You're sure?'

Sure it was a dream? No. Sure she was okay? No.

If she went back to sleep, perhaps she could change the ending? Maybe, if she found her way back to the right place, the right time, she could make all this right. Anna and Luke would have a long, happy life, the houseful of babies they wanted. Because it was impossible that a love that had burned so brightly could simply vanish into the dust of time, as though it had never been.

Mum rubbed her back. 'You know, this relates to your birthday. You dreamed of an ending because you're making new beginnings.'

Was Mum right? Often she seemed to have a knack for understanding other people, one that Taylor dismissed too easily. 'Maybe,' she said uncertainly, desperately hoping Mum would channel the magic of her childhood, when any hurt or problem had been solved with a hug and soothing words.

'You've set aside all your stress and know where you're headed, now,' Mum continued, as though she heard Taylor's silent plea.

Taylor forced a bright birthday-girl smile as her heart broke. Maybe Mum didn't always have to be right, but at least she was there, providing strength and support, as Johanna had longed to do for Anna. 'Go on, put the kettle on, Mum. It has to be time for a cuppa.'

As her mother left, Taylor clutched the cover to her chest. How did she navigate the loss of something that had never been? How could she mourn someone she had never known? She should have confided in Mum, because there was no rational way to untangle her emotions, no medicine to banish her pain.

Yet it wasn't hers alone—Anna had wanted to die.

Taylor's hand clenched. Neither swallowing venom nor a broken heart would have killed Anna. She *knew* that. Yet she also knew that her own heart had fractured as Luke took his last breath. She had stayed close as Anna lay across him, both of them praying his strong chest would rise again, the indigo eyes would flicker open.

When Anna shifted to cradle Luke's head in her lap, Taylor sat beside them.

Night approached, and she remained, trying to warm Anna with her presence, willing Luke alive. Emptiness engulfed them as his body grew cold and darkness crept through the scrub, probing fingers into the tiny house and chilling their souls.

When all hope had fled and she couldn't face the pain any longer, Taylor woke.

Completely alone then, what had Anna done? With love stolen from her, had she, like her father, chosen death?

∽

Despite her misery, Taylor couldn't search for solitude. Instead, she accepted birthday hugs, drank cups of tea, made conversation and laughed off her nightmare, when all she wanted was to grieve. It was impossible that a love so pure and complete could be as brief as a summer morning mist. Such love should defy death and conquer time.

While Gramps regaled her with stories of his crash landings and then presented her with a handmade voucher for unlimited flights in his plane, Mum headed into the city to pick up Dad from the airport.

A couple of hours later, her parents barrelled into the house, laughing like old friends. Dad waggled his crooked pinkie finger at Taylor. 'I was just telling Mum, that chip in the wall cost us a thousand bucks. It was listed on the issues to remedy before handover, but I missed it. So then we had to get a tradie in after the fact, and I'm pretty darn sure they must've put up a whole new wall for what they charged.'

'Pays to read the fine print,' Taylor said, moving into his embrace. Her parents seemed less . . . prickly . . . now that they'd moved on.

'It's coming out of your inheritance,' Dad warned. 'My old-age medical care might be, too.'

'Lucky you're fit as an ox, then,' Mum said. 'As evidenced by your bull-headedness.'

Dad released Taylor and took a seat at the table alongside Mum. 'I'm going to play the old and ill card, just so I get to brag to the other dodderers about how my daughter's a brilliant doctor and dedicated to my care.'

'You'd best look at moving closer then,' Gramps said. 'Because no one in Settlers Bridge is about—'

'—to let Taylor go,' Gran finished.

Taylor choked back tears. Her family might not be perfect, but they were hers. And she knew she was lucky to have them. Yet, there was something missing. Something that could never be replaced.

Lunch was a feast, Gran making certain to feature every dish Taylor had enjoyed over the last few months—even fish fingers—and Gramps delightedly pointing out every item as though he'd orchestrated the menu. Taylor eventually stood to escape.

'Hang on a minute, Peach,' Gramps said. 'There's—'

'—more,' Gran finished.

The vinyl-covered chair let out a soft hiss as she reluctantly dropped onto the seat.

Gramps grinned. 'Don't worry, love. They'll think it was me.'

'You keep that up, old man,' Gran said, 'and we'll have to get—'

'—a Labrador,' Gramps finished.

'Are you serious?' Taylor gasped as Mum entered from the lounge, bearing a cake covered in sparklers.

'Well, it's either that or a German Shepherd,' Gramps said.

'Shh.' Gran patted his hand. 'Enough, now.'

A lump tightened Taylor's throat. Apparently, some things in her world remained constant. As always, her birthday included Mum, Dad, cake and sparklers. And now, a bonus, her grandparents. And Brrt, she thought, as the untidy cat jumped onto Gran's lap, shaking dirt from her shaggy black coat as she accepted a fingerful of cream from the Black Forest cake.

Taylor leaned across the table for one of the teacups that sat upside down on a towel. Pink stripes today, to match the bunch of pink daisies Gramps had brought in from the garden that morning. He had presented them with a flourish to Gran. Flicking a couple of lime-green aphids from the bouquet, Gran had kissed him, as delighted as if she'd received long-stemmed roses in a crystal vase.

Two slices of cake later, Taylor pushed back from the table. 'Great lunch, Gran. But if I'm going to fit in dinner, I'll need to work it off.' She turned to Gramps, who was plying Dad with stories of his near-misses, the details embellished from that morning's version. 'My gate fix was a bit dodgy, so I'm going to check on it.'

'Sure, Peach,' Gramps said. He turned to Dad. 'I tell you, this young lady is plenty useful around here.'

Dad gave her an appreciative nod. 'I'm sure she's plenty useful wherever she is.'

Useful and ordinary, I'm uncertain where this leaves me. Like Anna, Taylor wanted more than to be useful. And she knew exactly how she would be.

'And just imagine when she has her qualifications,' Gran said proudly, as though she'd heard Taylor's thought.

'Make sure you put long sleeves on. That sun has got a heck of a—'

'—bite today,' Gramps said above the clatter of the cake plates in the steel sink as he rinsed and stacked them in the draining rack.

Taylor slipped out the back door, careful not to let the flies in. Her ears strained to catch the usual singsong reminder, so she could pretend, for a brief moment, that everything was still as it should be.

The bike started easily, her foot and wrist well practised. She knew her work on the gate didn't need checking; after all, Luke had okayed it.

Luke.

Was there a chance she'd see him today? And would that be enough to chase away the lingering sorrow? Yet how could she be thinking of him, when she knew Anna's heart had broken?

She climbed through the wire, crossing the parched ground to the stretch of tumbledown stone fence she had forced herself to stay away from. Now, eyes closed, she pictured Luke from long ago, labouring in the unforgiving but beautiful land, determined to create an enduring legacy for his family, something that would withstand the ravages of time.

Time.

Anna had sensed time was fleeting, that she couldn't catch and hold it. But, without Luke, had time become heavy, a burden rather than a blessing?

I swear never to love another.

Taylor tore her hand from the solid warmth of the wall and shoved it through her hair, trying to order her thoughts. Anna had sworn she would never love another. Yet it was Taylor's own heart that ached at the memories, her own soul that wept at his loss. How could she bear the impossible weight of grief for the Luke she had never known?

Luke, my Luke.

She lifted her head, inhaling the heady eucalyptus scent released by the afternoon sun. A faint breeze stroked her and she turned to face it. South, toward die Kirche. The graveyard.

The call pulsed deep within her.

She knew it was time to listen.

She made her way back to the motorbike. An ancient path, worn by the heavy tread of grief and then buried by the sands of time, unfurled before her. Even on the motorbike, the faint track, winding through paddocks and scrubland and crisscrossing the creek, took longer to traverse than if she had used the road. Yet the journey had a comforting familiarity. Huge gums, stone fences, granite boulders she'd never before seen marked the way, each awakening a distant memory that never quite came into focus.

Twenty minutes later, Taylor hauled the motorbike onto its stand and climbed off. She paused, eyes closed, allowing the serenity to envelop her, to banish all measure of time and reality.

Then she made her way across the dusty earth and pushed open the wrought-iron gate. She turned left, bypassing the row that held Johann and Johanna's grave, flanked by the smaller markers of Anna's siblings. She should be lost now; her dreams had never led her to this point. Yet, like the tracks to get here, an innate knowledge guided her.

A gifted memory.

Although tears climbed her throat, Taylor swallowed them down, blinking her eyes clear. Because, before she could face another dream, she needed to know what would happen.

Had Anna survived the night? Had the baby lived?

Three rows down, rose bushes stood watch over a double plot where Luke and Anna lay together for eternity. She dropped to her knees in the gravel. Stroked the smooth white marble on the left side of the grave. Luke's side. She didn't read his headstone, couldn't bear to see the dates of a life cut too short. She turned her eyes to the inscription on the right.

Anna Hartmann nee *Frahn*
1859–1949
Finally laid to rest with her true love
Forever missed by son Luke and family

The sorrow welled up from deep inside, tearing apart Taylor's soul. Her biggest fear had been discovering that Anna had died with Luke, that she would never again see them in her dreams. Yet the reality was far worse: Anna had lived a long life. She had endured countless days and nights, years of loneliness, cheated of Luke's love.

Grief ripped through Taylor like wildfire.

She would never dare sleep again, for how could she bear to witness Anna's anguish, her longing to be reunited with Luke, while knowing how very long they must spend apart?

Sobs wracked her body and she hunched forward, head pressed to the stone, arms crossed over her chest.

Trying to hold together the pieces of her breaking heart.

32
Taylor

The gate creaked and footsteps crunched on gravel, the noises bringing Taylor back to reality.

Except everything was now her reality. There were no lines to cross, no boundaries. No dreams and no fantasies. There was only her life: then and now.

A shaft of light played across the marble headstone and she blinked in bemusement at the dying sun. It should be mid-afternoon, yet somehow time had cheated her again, and the fluffy clouds of soft pink, orange and yellow painted across the horizon hid the approaching darkness.

Legs stiff, she pushed upright. Pressed a hand against her aching chest. The crucifix imprinted on her palm and a spark flickered to life within her, as though a far-off candle lit the way.

Love lights my loneliest nights.

The words from an unheard voice weren't hers, but they provided hope.

Chin tucked down to avoid the other visitor to the secluded graveyard, Taylor skirted around the plots and made her way to the gate, slipping through as sunshine and hay curled past on a breeze that swirled then died.

She rushed past a grey ute, praying no one would see her, and started the bike.

Her vision blurred, she'd ridden for fifteen minutes along the hidden track before she realised she had missed a turn. Although she could make out the open expanse of paddocks in the distance, she was surrounded by thick bushland on either side and the path had become indistinguishable. She was lost. Panic fluttered in her stomach. Her sense of direction had never been great and with the sun sinking, she didn't have a hope of retracing her steps across the vast acreages in the dark.

But as she broke from the confines of the trees, allowing the motorbike to roll to a halt before she cut the engine, an impossible sense of familiarity eased her fear.

Ahead on her left, a low stone wall held the scrub back from the fields that spread to the horizon. A broad, shallow creek meandered across the paddock. On the bank, two huge fig trees, trunks gnarled with age, wove together in a tight embrace.

They survived the rabbits.

Birds flitted in and out of hidden green caverns, the air filled with their evening song. Taylor climbed the wall and sat atop it, looking out over the twilight paddocks. A cathartic, shuddering breath ached through her chest as she inhaled the forgotten scents, the smells that time could never change.

No more tears.

Hand closed around the crucifix, her knuckles pressed against the warmth within her, the flame burning brighter by the minute. The last of the sunlight bled across the land, kissing her face. The fragrance of red dirt and green trees filled her lungs and slowly the realisation came: she was not lost. For the first time in her life, she knew exactly where she was.

Luke. My Luke.

She turned to the tangled scrub. A rusted piece of metal dislodged from the wall and hit the ground with a dull chime as she jumped down. She retrieved the ploughshare and replaced it on the topmost stone, ready for use, then headed across the paddock, into the dappled softness of the bushland.

Tiny finches trilled as she threaded through the trees. Her breath quickened, her pulse surged. Anticipation tingled through her, urging her on until her pounding feet were unable to cover the ground fast enough. It was as though she had taken forever to get here, yet these last few seconds stretched longer than the previous century.

She broke from the trees and checked her step. Beaten by the decades into soft, cresting waves, a granite ridge flowed into the meadow. The dry grass bent beneath her tread, but in a few months the clearing would become lush and green, carpeted with wildflowers in shades of blue and purple.

She lifted her gaze to the horizon, knowing now what she would find.

Home.

The cottage stood proud above the meadow, each stone a permanent record of love. Polished windows splintered the dying sun into a shower of diamonds. Sure paces took Taylor to the rear of the house, which was flanked by outbuildings not yet weathered by the years. A cement mixer and rubble formed an untidy sculpture. The back door stood wide.

She stepped inside and the house enfolded her. Warm and comforting, drawing her in, deeper and deeper. Reawakening the memories.

Waiting for love.

The kitchen lay on her right, a broad fireplace opposite the window beside which Anna could sit in Johanna's rocking chair, sewing while watching the children at play in the meadow. The memory of Luke's laughter when she told him—no, when *Anna* told him—she would dispatch the sewing to Emelie and don trousers to assist him around the farm tugged at Taylor's lips.

The time for mourning is over.

The thought whispered across her ears, the voice not her own, but completely familiar, as she drifted toward the wooden mantel above the fireplace. Luke had intended to add to Anna's book collection, but only a single leather-bound, dog-eared edition lay upon the ledge. Taylor didn't need to turn it to read the title. She knew what it was: *Great Expectations*, by Charles Dickens.

The stone chimney breast was almost hidden by a glass case. The height of a man and twice as wide, but only a handspan deep, it held a circular rug. The centre of the grey-toned mat worn flat and thin, the outside circles told a story of increasing affluence in brighter colours and softer fabrics.

Mutti's rug.

Her fingers trembled toward the frame, aching to connect with the memories woven into the fabric, to fill in the years she had not yet dreamed. Luke's violet tie pin was hooked through the lower edge of the rug above two pressed flowers nestled in the corner of the case. Though a vibrant pink in the wedding bouquet, the wild orchid now held only the vaguest hint of colour and the cream flower had faded to soft ecru, the petals transparent and fragile. As fragile as life.

But still here.

Tears blurred Taylor's vision and she tore her gaze from the rug. Across the polished floorboards of the hall lay the children's room and, in front of that, a parlour where Anna had planned to entertain her sister and sister-in-law.

The second room on her right was the bedroom. The room where Luke took his final breath. The room where Anna's heart broke.

Luke, my Luke.

His name keened within her and the ache of longing blossomed. Her fingernails scarred the wooden doorframe—but she couldn't enter. She couldn't face the finality.

Boots loud on the boards, she bypassed the room, refusing to look at the bare expanse of wall Anna had declared perfect for displaying a wedding portrait. As she dragged open the front door, the air pulsed, and she glanced over her shoulder. A grey ute pulled up alongside the cement mixer at the rear of the house.

Taylor paused. She would be caught trespassing—yet there was one more thing she must do.

The threshold stone still bore the marks of chisel and pick, never worn smooth by the feet that should have stepped on it every day. Taylor dropped to her knees. She knew the exact spot where Luke had pressed Anna's hand to the rock, promising his love would last longer than the stone itself.

The mica-filled dust of centuries past clouded the air like glitter as her palm brushed the timeless surface. Energy surged through her hand, vibrating up her arm. Exploded in her mind in a wave of sweet, tingling darkness.

Her eyes could be open or closed—she could no longer tell as velvet softness swirled around her, swooping and spiralling like floor-length skirts dancing across her memory. Fresh-baked bread, rosewood polish and wood smoke filled her senses as tears of longing and remembrance ached in her chest. The voices of years long gone called; haunting memories of laughter and tears, pain and joy, longing and loss jumbled together and tore apart again, an ever-changing kaleidoscope of fragmented time.

Births and deaths, weddings and funerals, sorrow and happiness. Over and over, time moved faster with each generation, until the flashes were of the present: a tall form riding a horse along the distant creek bed; the necklace in the farmhouse swinging from a nail on the chimney breast. A grey ute appeared over and again: at the church; the graveyard; the airfield. And now, on the baked earth behind the cottage. A grey ute the exact shade of her eyes.

Of Anna's eyes.

Past and present crashed together, the dizziness building within Taylor until she could stand it no longer. As she slumped over the stone, the pictures in her mind faded and darkness fell, warm and soothing.

She imagined she lay in Luke's arms and relief washed through her; at least she could still dream. Handsome beyond fantasy, his blue eyes deeper than the twilight summer sky, he held her close. She had been terrified she'd lost him, but he was more real than ever before, as though she had only to reach up to touch his summer-wheat hair. Her fingers moved to his cheek.

Luke, my Luke.

His arm tightened around her back. 'Hey, there. Slow down,' he murmured. 'Take it easy for a minute.'

Taylor's stomach plummeted. His words were too modern. Even her dream had been stolen by time.

Immeasurable in its infinity, Time is fluid and endless, neither benefactor nor thief.

The familiar voice in her head calmed her mind, a waft of sunshine and hay chasing the fragrance of impossible memories. Boots scraped against the threshold stone as Luke pulled her closer. His heart beat strong against her shoulder.

Beat.

A living pulse. Proof of life.

She jerked back to look up at him properly. Her eyes were wide open, yet Luke was *there*. The timelines blurred in her mind, wraiths of the past dancing in the present, dreams and reality too tightly interwoven to separate.

'Are you okay?' he said, his brow furrowed.

She shook her head, scrambling for understanding. 'I wanted to see—' Taylor gestured at the house, as though she could somehow explain her trespass.

Reality crashed through and Luke's presence made sense, although she wasn't sure whether to be relieved or disappointed. This was the cottage that Marian had spoken about him renovating. But it was also Luke and Anna's house.

'I know. I've been searching for you.'

She had been missing that long?

Luke gave a sheepish grin. 'Though, given that you make an excuse to disappear every time I find you, I was about to call it quits and wait for you to come looking for me.'

'Searching?' she said cautiously.

He groaned. 'I managed to make that sound creepy as all hell, didn't I? I promise I'm not the local stalker. Besides, it's Settlers Bridge: if I was, someone would have clued you in pretty darn quick. But—' He paused, screwing up his face. 'Hell. Okay, I'm going out on a limb here, Taylor. Perhaps *longing* would be a better choice of word. Yearning for something intangible that always seems—no, *seemed*—to be just out of my grasp. It feels like I've waited for you longer than I've been alive.' He shrugged, as though trying to dismiss his own words. 'And, yeah, I know how whack that sounds, but I swear I'm not on anything.' He gave a short laugh, though it rang with frustration rather than amusement. 'I wish I was. Then I wouldn't have to stay awake nights, worrying about what the heck is going on in my head.'

Taylor's heart faltered and she barely dared breathe. 'In your head?'

Luke shifted uncomfortably. 'I get weird dreams some-times.'

'About?'

He rifled a hand through his hair. 'You know, stuff. Well, mostly those long-gone ancestors I was telling you about the other day, I guess. Though the dreams aren't because I mentioned them,' he added hastily, as though she'd try to rationalise away his experience. 'They started before then. A couple of years ago. That's what motivated me to do up this place.' He tilted his head toward the passageway behind them. 'There was a bit of family drama attached to the cottage and it's never been lived in. Well, not by anything other than feral cats and colonies of spoggies and ravens. But it seemed like it was always on my mind, so I figured the best way to deal with that was to get to work, clean it up. That somehow snowballed into a full reno. Then a year or so back the dreams changed—probably because I had this place in hand, so didn't need to sweat on it so much. Or at least, more in hand,' he added with an eyeroll. 'Seems like these renovations never end. But I began to feel like there was something missing. Not to do with the house—in my life.' He tapped his chest. 'No joke, I even wondered if I was depressed. But the thing is, I never felt down, just . . . I don't know. Incomplete, I guess.' He blew out a long breath, slightly unsteady, and Taylor suspected he hadn't shared his thoughts before. 'Yet now I think that perhaps there's a chance I'm not losing my marbles. Because for some reason, you're here. Lying on my floor. That has to mean something.' He frowned, his tone almost imploring her to agree. 'Like, maybe you also . . . felt it?'

'It's not a feeling.'

Luke's face tightened in disappointment, his jaw twitching as though he clenched his teeth.

'It's more than a feeling.' Understanding bloomed within her like a flower unfurling to the sun. 'It's . . . knowing.'

The tension in Luke's arms eased and she could feel the deep breath sigh through his chest. 'You're right. *Knowing.*'

'And I also know that we can't both have brain injuries,' she said, giddy with sudden relief. 'It's statistically improbable, if not impossible.'

Luke chuckled. 'Way to embrace the moment. But I am happy to hear that.' He stood, offering his hand.

'And even if we both had déjà vécu, we wouldn't share the same mental illusion, the same feelings,' she continued, clambering to her feet.

'Unless you mean déjà vu, I've really no idea what you're talking about.' Luke gave an apologetic grimace. 'I was hanging my hat more on the "I'm going nuts" scenario, than on anything scientific.'

'We're not nuts,' she said with relieved certainty. 'Déjà vécu is when déjà vu becomes reality. But that isn't the explanation, there has to be something else.'

'All I know is that, somehow, we've ended up in the same place at the same time.' Luke's arm was warm and strong in the small of her back. 'And that seems right.'

'Time,' she said pensively. 'You're right. The same time. And if time isn't linear . . .'

'Told you, not a clue what you're talking about.' Luke drew her into the cottage.

A feeling of *rightness* wrapped her as the walls blocked the outside world. 'Neither do I,' she admitted. 'But I'm trying to make sense of what's going on here.'

'Got me beat.' Now Luke sounded remarkably unfazed, and she envied his easy adaptation. 'All I know is how I feel, and that maybe we have to accept that not everything needs a rational explanation.'

Taylor snorted. 'You don't know me well if you think that's going to happen.'

'You're right,' Luke said softly. 'I don't.' His blue eyes embraced her and the cleft in his cheek deepened. 'But I look forward to taking our time to remedy that.'

Epilogue
Taylor

November 2012

Taylor eyed her reflection in the long, oak-framed cheval mirror Gran had directed Gramps wheel into what was still known as her bedroom, though she'd had few occasions to use the room over the last three years since she'd moved into Luke's cottage.

Not that their home could really be considered a cottage, now. Tracing the family tree with the help of Luke's parents, she'd learned that Anna, Luke's great-grandmother from five generations back, had moved in with her in-laws, raising her baby with their help ... in the house where Gran and Pops now lived. Anna had never been able to bring herself to return to the cottage, the scene of such love and tragedy.

Luke had kept intact the heart of the stone cottage, but extended its footprint, creating a seamless blend of the old and the new. She liked to tease that perhaps he should have been an architect rather than a farmer, but Luke's firm retort was always that he would only ever have two loves: her and the land.

'Oh, the energy this gives off is just perfect,' Mum breathed, flitting around Taylor and adjusting the dress in a whisper of silk.

'Careful, Mum.' The fabric was more than one-hundred-and-sixty years old. Lovingly stored by Luke's family, the dress hadn't been worn for one-hundred-and-thirty-five years. To the day.

The day Luke and Anna had married.

With the bustle and heavy petticoats removed, Taylor had arranged for the skirt to be altered to a more slim-line fitting. But the beautiful, hand-stitched bodice with dozens of tiny pearl buttons running down the spine was completely original. She assumed that Emilie must have reattached the buttons after Luke had torn them free on Anna's wedding night, but she didn't know for sure; after meeting her Luke at the cottage she'd never dreamed of Luke and Anna's life again. But that was okay, because *her Luke* was both her dream and her reality. Her life.

Mum wiped her eyes on her kaftan sleeve. After only a few months at the farm, she had realised that not only was Settlers Bridge not quite ready for her yoga studio and counselling business, but that she and Gran were always going to argue about how to cut carrots. As her parents neither needed nor wanted round-the-clock care, the solution was in Michelle moving to a cottage in Stirling, in the heart of the Adelaide Hills, less than an hour from the farm. She used the front room as an office for her clients and the rear sunroom as a yoga studio for her growing band of devotees.

Mum sniffed, then stroked a hand down Taylor's arm. 'Oh, love, you look radiant. Blessed be.'

With her back turned to Michelle, Cassie rolled her eyes. 'Even if you wouldn't let me bring you something from France to wear. Who'd have thought you'd be the first of us to get here, Tay?'

The words stirred a memory, as so many did, but Taylor tipped her head toward her friend's daughter. 'I don't know about first, Cass.'

Cassie stroked Lyon's golden hair as her daughter sifted pudgy fingers through the basket of sweet-scented orange blossoms. 'Well, yeah, but you're doing it in the right order. Me and Anton, we get everything arse-up. You guys have been together for so long now, I'm surprised you didn't beat me to the baby-making bit, too.'

'We're not in any rush.' None at all. Taylor wanted Luke to herself for a long time first. Lifetimes would not be enough to make up for the time it felt they had been apart. Yet, despite finding Luke, Taylor had realised that she also needed to be certain she had found herself. She had finished her degree and an internship before the time was finally right, and when Luke once again proposed, she had accepted.

Dad appeared in the doorway. 'Ready, girls?' They saw far more of him since he'd relocated to the Kanmantoo mines only a few kilometres away. He and Mum got on well, sharing laughter and memories, but seemed to have no inclination to rekindle their romance. Which was fine. Endless love wasn't for everyone. Only the lucky few.

Taylor shook her hands, her fingertips tingling. She shouldn't be nervous. It wasn't like this was a rash decision. She loved Luke. Had loved him forever. A secretive smile curved her lips. No one else would understand that their forever extended far beyond the four years since they'd first met. Even Luke didn't discuss it much, the strong, silent farmer in him preferring to simply accept the fact of their love. His memories of before weren't the same as hers, either in detail or quantity. But, as he said, he adored her: always had, always would. And only the two of them understood how long *always* was.

Unable to completely embrace blind acceptance, Taylor had researched the phenomenon of ancestral memories. Eventually, she concluded that if the likes of Carl Jung and a score of other scientists theorised genetics played a role in recollections that spanned generations, she could accept the concept. However, while kissing cousins might be fine with the tree-hugging, yoga-hippie group Mum and Gran ran from Mum's new home, they were definitely not okay with her. Numerous European royal families had proved the danger of a non-diversified bloodline. So, along with a slew of genetic tests, she'd had her genealogy traced back for generations.

She hadn't felt able to breathe properly until she held the results in her hand: she wasn't related to Luke, nor to Anna or any of her siblings, whose descendants were numerous in the district under a multitude of surnames thanks to Dieter, Emelie and the twins.

Which meant that, although genetic memory could credibly account for Luke's attachment to the property, Taylor's dreams seemed to have formed from Anna's memories, in turn creating her reality. Acceptance of that implausible fact was the only time Taylor allowed her beliefs to stray from the medicine and science that provided safe boundaries to her existence. As Luke often reminded her, perhaps she didn't need to understand their miracle to appreciate it.

It only took minutes for Dad to drive them the few kilometres from Gran and Gramps' place to the church. Luke and Anna's church, the place that held so many of their memories of both love and loss.

Despite the cars crowding the parking lot and lining both sides of the road beyond the eucalypt grove—most of the Settlers Bridge community had turned out for the wedding of the popular farmer and the GP recently appointed to the practice that had opened two years earlier—the church looked as it had for almost a century and a half.

Mum and Cassie fussed with her veil, then Taylor took Dad's arm, mounting the six stone steps to where the Elders waited to swing open the heavy wooden doors into the vestibule.

As she had requested, the end of each pew was decorated with a spray of golden wattle, the honeyed scent heavy in the spring air. She breathed out a tremulous memory, her heart full with the joy and melancholy of times past.

Lyon toddled ahead, casting generous handfuls of the orange blossoms on the polished boards. As she reached the front pew, Gran scooped her up. Dressed in an unusually sombre black skirt and jacket with a ruffled white blouse, Gran's silver hair was threaded with tiny pink and purple wildflowers. Gramps had managed to acquire a white suit, complete with white boots, reminiscent of Colonel Sanders. Laughter bubbled within Taylor as she noticed the front of his black t-shirt, emblazoned with a giant peach, the top indented so it resembled a heart. Gran reached to pull off his black cap, leaving his hair sticking out at crazy angles, and Gramps caught her hand, kissed the arthritic knuckles, then smiled at Taylor.

Her heart swelled. Her grandparents were truly magpies, mated for life.

High above the altar, recessed into the whitewashed wall, the stained-glass window pulsed with a ruby glow. Dust motes danced in the waterfall of light that cascaded to where Luke waited.

The silver warm beneath her palm, Taylor pressed the crucifix against her chest, acknowledging that, as always, Anna was with her. But while Anna had walked the aisle slowly, careful to draw every second out to its fullest extent, Taylor intended to greedily seize each moment, to treat it with intention, to enjoy it to full measure.

Luke's dove-grey suit matched her eyes. As his lips curved into that familiar one-sided smile, the crevasse in his cheek deepened and it seemed her legs could barely carry her to his arms fast enough.

They had chosen a short service, and the pastor obligingly sped through it as Luke held both of her hands, his gaze steadfastly on hers.

The pastor's tone lifted. 'Now, the vows.'

Though their oaths were based on traditional Lutheran vows, they had chosen to remove the standard 'til death do us part' or 'as long as we both shall live' conclusion: neither would ever apply to them.

Taylor gazed up at Luke. Mutti had spoken the truth: a lifetime of loving the right man could never be enough.

His voice deep and assured, Luke spoke without hesitation. 'I take you, Taylor, my love, to be my wife from this day forward, to join with you and share all that has been and all that will be.' Sunshine and hay enveloped her as his fingertips caressed her cheek, his twilight eyes filled with the love he had sworn would never be lost. 'I promise this to you always and forever.'

'Luke, I enter into this marriage with you knowing the true magic of love.' Though tears filled her eyes, they were tears of joy. More powerful than time itself, Luke and Anna's love had echoed across the centuries until they found one another again. 'I will share my life with you, through the best and the worst of what is to come. Our souls forever bound, our love is more enduring than stone, more infinite than the skies.'

She laid her palm against Luke's sun-bronzed cheek. 'I promise you all this, my husband. Far beyond the end of time.'

Author's note

The book of my heart, this story has been a labour of love.

It was conceived in 2016, when Taylor (aka The Kid) and I were camping on the family farm in the South Australian Murraylands, an area of incredible hidden beauty. At about twelve years old, Taylor wasn't much of a fiction reader (she's still—inexplicably—only into law and politics!) so I was trying to engage her by recounting a book that had enthralled me at her age. I couldn't remember much of the story, except that it had a dual timeline and something of an *Outlander* vibe, though set in World War II.

After I'd banged on about it for some time, Taylor got frustrated. 'If you liked it so much, why don't you just write a book like that?' she asked.

As I'm passionate about South Australian history, the idea of writing a dual timeline set in different centuries took hold; so Taylor and I sat by the campfire brainstorming.

The family property has a deep, peaceful sense of ancestral belonging for us, having only been lived on by two families—mine and the Hartmanns—since European settlement. The Hartmanns have a tragic history, and the surroundings are deeply evocative of the labour, love and sacrifice that went into clearing the land by hand and building, stone by stone, the cottage, homestead, fences and sheds.

Taylor and I returned to camp frequently, each time exploring the acres of scrub that border a deep, usually-dry creek bed. On one occasion, we discovered the remnants of a stone fence, only about forty centimetres high and a metre long. Deciding it was a shame for this history be lost to the encroaching bushland, we set about clearing the stonework.

As we worked—or sat at the campfire swatting mozzies and eating indistinguishable charred morsels—we'd talk about how the story could play out. Within a month I had written the book, based on the farm where I grew up.

With the months turning to seasons, we chopped down boxthorns and shovelled literally tons of soil and rocks from our 'archaeological dig' site. Eventually, the fragment of stone fence we'd set out to expose was revealed to be a deep, twelve-foot square, stone-walled kiln (the photos are on my socials). We also discovered and excavated the remnants of a blacksmith's workshop and the beautiful rock-slab flooring of the original two-roomed Hartmann cottage.

And the story of my heart, which at that time was a Young Adult (YA) book with a teen protagonist, had won me a New York agent.

Now, the path to publication is rarely smooth. Although this was the first book I set in the fictional Settlers Bridge district, it would not be published until four years after *The Farm at Peppertree Crossing*. By this time it had evolved, with the help of my team at Allen & Unwin, from a YA story to a heartbreaking adult love story. Readers of the Settlers Bridge linked books will have already met the local doctor, Taylor Hartmann (yes, I stole my own kid's name . . . after all, this is her story)—and this is the origin story of how Taylor came to be in Settlers Bridge.

But it's also another story, one of love found and lost much longer ago.

When it came to investing the historical perspective with factual believability and compelling research, I am fortunate to have a background working for the History Trust of South Australia. More importantly, though, I had the invaluable assistance of a copy of *George Hartmann of the Prince George* by Reg Butler, gifted to me by Glen Hartmann.

Glen's father, Ben, was tragically killed while establishing the property. He would have had a hand in much of the stonework Taylor and I worked to restore, and our thoughts were frequently with him: had he touched this stone, placed that rock? Would he approve of what we were doing? Ben left behind his own heartbreaking love story, one that was never far from our minds, and it is so rich and beautiful, it deserves its own book . . . one day.

So, fair warning: if you come along to any of my author talks, be prepared for a long evening, as I'll happily chat for hours about this story, the characters that are so very real to me and the land that I love. And photos. There'll be photos, too.

My thanks to my publisher Annette Barlow for allowing me licence to take a risk in straying from the normal conventions of the genre. And my love to my editor Courtney Lick, who tolerates all my idiosyncrasies and minor tantrums.

My enduring gratitude to fellow writers Marty Mayberry and Sandie Docker, who have been unswerving in their love for the tale.

And to Taylor: I know you don't want to share our story, baby. But, like the early farmers, sometimes we have to bear the pain to reap the reward. It's another step along the path to keeping our forever home.

Fiction *with* heart

Craving more heartwarming tales from the countryside? Join our online rural fiction community, **FICTION** *with* **HEART**, where you'll discover a treasure trove of similar books that will capture your imagination and warm your soul.

Visit **fictionwithheart.com.au** or scan the QR code below to access exclusive content from our authors, stay updated on upcoming events, participate in exciting competitions and much more.

See you there!

A&U